Dead Friends Walking

Natalie Carlisle

Dead Friends Walking

By Natalie Carlisle
© 2016 Natalie Carlisle

Tell-Tale Publishing Group, LLC
Swartz Creek, MI 48473
Cover design by Clarissa Yeo

Tell-Tale Publishing Group, LLC
5714 Peri St
Swartz Creek, MI 48737

For Frickle: For always being there for me, for the great memories, and most of all for inspiring the story. You are the reason I even wrote this book. Love ya bestie!

1

We have to get Spencer.

We have to hurry.

We have to save him.

I jammed my sneaker down on the accelerator. The car couldn't get there fast enough. *To hell with the speed limit signs,* I thought. *Holy crap, Spencer called. He called. He's alive. He wants to come home.*

But then reason overcame panic.

The actual *limit* my car had was undetermined, but once it got near seventy, it did start shaking and making some not so promising sounds. We had to arrive in one piece to do anything at all to help Spencer. And that's why we were traveling through Pennsylvania right now. *To get Spencer.*

Finally.

Spencer ran away from home six months ago, without a word to anyone. Not even us, his best friends. Cops were looking for him. His face is probably on one of those milk cartons—though I never actually saw it on one.

I was a little scared because we didn't tell anyone he called us. I didn't know if that was considered *breaking the law,* but I did know it was just wrong to do to his mother and father.

We probably should have told Mr. and Mrs. Reign, but Spencer begged us not to tell anyone, so we didn't. We sure didn't want the cops to get to him first. His parents thought we were a bad influence, so if they had anything to say about it we wouldn't see him at all after he got back home. And we wanted to see Spencer. God, we spent months ourselves looking for him, every day after school.

"Can't this heap go any faster?" Missy complained.

"Not if we want it to keep going," I reminded her.

"He was in trouble. He needs help!" she said for the tenth time.

I checked the rear-view mirror a few times. I was aware I was just being paranoid, but I couldn't help it. Trees, cows and deteriorating barns flashed by with more frequency the further we headed west. We hadn't passed a car, cop or otherwise, in miles.

We had an address—not a street number, just the street— entered into the GPS that was suction-cupped to my windshield. The connection last night when Spencer called absolutely sucked.

The B, which is the name my best friend gave my GPS, told me to make a right in two miles. My fingers fidgeted on the steering wheel. We were getting closer. According to *her,* we had another fifteen miles to go.

After turning on the blinker, I eased onto the narrow road that was actually the base of a pretty steep mountain. *And I was worried about my car before.* The road wound up…and up…and up. One side was all rocks and trees, but the other side was a sheer drop off. *Yup.* The higher we drove, the further the drop was and my car was only a white line away from it.

I was humming along to a song playing through the speakers to calm my nerves when suddenly Missy cursed, jolting forward in the passenger seat.

"What? What's wrong?" From the corner of my eye I saw her reaching outward, her long blond hair concealing her face.

"*The B* just crapped out," she groaned, hitting the sides of it anxiously.

"Seriously?" A knot twisted in my stomach. This was the last place I wanted to be lost. "Try holding it next to the window or something. Or shut it off, maybe it over-heated."

"Doubtful," she sighed, yanking it off the windshield and dropping back against the car seat. "We are in the middle of a freaking mountain. It's probably blocking the satellite." She held the device desperately to the window anyway.

Making a face, I kept my eyes focused on the road. I studied the narrow stretch of black pavement, curving, turning, and twisting, currently in a descent before us. The whole 'one wrong swerve and it was a free fall off the side of the road' was really making my heart pound.

A string of curses broke the edgy silence in less than a minute. Missy had a mouth on her that probably could make my dead grandmother roll over in her grave. I was used to it. Nothing she said ever shocked me, but hearing that the GPS still wasn't working did.

We were so screwed.

"Can't you use your cell phone?" I urged, worriedly. I was pretty sure there was an app for that.

The sun was beginning to set in the horizon and we still had to make it down the rest of this mountain and into town before night fall. That was the thing I hated about country roads, they didn't have street lamps. So once the sun set you were pretty much in the dark unless you had high beams. And the last thing I wanted to be doing was driving around in the dark, in a place I didn't know, looking for a house for which I didn't have an address. Luckily I still remembered the street name.

Melissa dropped the GPS onto her lap, and dug her cell phone out of her pocket. Almost immediately she started shaking her head. "Damn it. I can't."

"Let me guess," I groaned. "No service." *Stupid technology.*

"That," she sighed, "but mostly low battery." She started looking around the car, opening the center console and the glove compartment. "Where's your car charger? I have about fifteen percent of juice left in this thing."

I bit the inside of my cheek. I could picture where it was clearly, lying beside the door, next to my pur*se, in my bedroom.* "Shit. Shit. Shit." I slapped my hands against the steering wheel in frustration. So, so, screwed. I didn't even have a license on me. Hell with the charger.

"Don't tell me." Missy held up her hand, stopping me. "I can't believe this is happening. Where's *your* stupid phone?"

I resisted the urge to bang my head against the steering wheel. It was a three hour drive back. I couldn't believe in three hours I hadn't realized once that I left my bag at the house. I pinched the bridge of my nose. "At home…*with everything else.*"

"Terrific." She exhaled sharply. "Freaking terrific. *Now what,* Dee? What the hell do we do now? What if *The B* doesn't work once we get off this mountain? What if my cell dies and Spencer tries to call us again? Huh? *Huh?*" She kicked the dashboard. "What are we supposed to do *then*?"

Do not panic. Do not flip out. Breathe. I glanced at her again, trying to think of something. "Missy, we are going to find him. I know you miss him. I do too, but he's okay. We have to believe he's okay. He—"

Her blue eyes suddenly widened. "Dee! *Watch out!*"

I flashed my attention back to the road, instantly jerking the wheel. Tires screeching, I tried to stop. Too late. A loud *thud* echoed in my ears as a body rolled across the hood of the Toyota.

I screamed.

Missy screamed.

And then we were falling. Well, more like driving uncontrollably down the side of the mountain. *The man* was falling. Tumbling. Flipping. Rolling. My throat hurt from the shouting.

We were about to crash and I just hit a person. And we were all probably going to die. If not us, definitely the man would. And, I didn't even have my license.

Forget it. It was definitely time to panic.

This was worse than a roller coaster—even the really scary one we went on last summer that had a forty-five story drop. I was at least mentally prepared for that one. I chose to go on it. No one *chooses* to drive off a mountain unless they have some severely deep mental issues.

We were bouncing up and down in our seats, the movement range constricted only by our seatbelts. My arms were up, my fingers spread wide across the roof, trying to hold myself in place. I had given up trying to steer. There was no point anymore. The tops of my knees met the steering wheel more than once and my head wobbled back and forth like one of those ridiculous dashboard accessories.

I continued to scream.

Missy was screaming even louder.

The side of my car ground against a tree—the impact instantly jarred me to the right as metal scraped against bark, obnoxiously loud.

The vehicle shifted direction, tilting sideways. I cringed, waiting to flip. Instead we slammed into another tree on the passenger side. The impact almost stopped the car completely. The battered car rolled over a fallen limb and the bumper crashed into a freakishly large uprooted oak. My head whipped forward, then back. Most of my brown shoulder-length hair had slipped out of my ponytail and was currently in my face, poking me in the eyes, sticking to my lips…

I didn't swipe the strands away until my heart *un*-lodged itself from the back of my throat and I made sure I still had feeling in all my limbs.

"Are you all right?" I asked Missy, in a panic, uselessly clinging to the steering wheel now that the car had stopped. I could hear her breathing beside me. When she didn't answer, I turned my head, cringing slightly in deference to the stiffness in my neck. She seemed to be going through the whole 'moving the fingers and toes' process I just did. Just as she nodded an affirmation, I spotted the man I hit laying on the ground twenty yards away. Not moving. And just like that, everything came back to me.

Shit. "Call 911," I urged, jumping out of the front seat in a flash. I forgot I still had the seatbelt on so I was whipped back against the seat roughly. I cursed again, unbuckled, and scrambled out of the car.

Please be alive. Please be alive. I sprinted around the back bumper. The man was face-first on the ground. His clothes were torn, dirt-stained and blood was seeping out of open flesh wounds on his arms. Dead leaves stuck to his black hair and flannel-clad back.

"Sir! *Sir!* Can you hear me?"

I stopped, freezing in my tracks when I saw him move, when I heard him groan. *Thank God, he was alive.* "Sir! Don't move. Stay where you are. Help is coming."

A car door slammed behind me, followed by the sound of Missy's frantic voice. My heart continued to race.

"I'm so sorry sir, but it's going to be okay. You are going to be okay. She's calling someone now."

The man continued to hunch up onto his knees, blood dripping to the ground slowly. It was painful to watch him move. "It's better if you don't try to stand, sir. You could have broken something."

Another sound came from him, something almost feral, or ravenous, reminding me of a starving animal. It was then I noticed the way his clothes hung on him. *Was he a homeless man? Did I just hit a homeless guy? Oh God!*

"Sir? Can you hear me? Can you tell me your name? What's your name?"

I heard Missy getting angry. "I don't know where the hell we are. Some freaking mountain in the middle of Pa. No I wasn't paying attention. No there are no damn signs. Did you miss the part where I said we just crashed off a freaking mountain?"

I spared her a glance, frowning at her attitude—that's how Missy got when she was really worked up—then turned back toward the guy. He was still panting, grunting…no higher off his hands and knees then before. It was like he didn't hear a word I said to him. Or

maybe it was just too painful for him to talk. Cringing, I hunched down at little, trying to see his face.

"Sir? If it's too painful to talk you really should lie back down."

The man hunched even taller, pulling his feet forward to straighten out. I heard barking.

Raising my eyebrow, I stood up too. It wasn't the man. He was still moaning and panting. But there was definitely a dog. Close.

Or maybe a coyote? *Did coyotes bark?*

"Sir," I said, panic rising. "Maybe you…"

His head snapped up, his black, sunken eyes glaring at me. Large purple circles below them shadowed most of his cheeks. A dark, short beard covered the rest. Perspiration dripped down the sides of his face catching in the coarse hair. Labored breathing wheezed out of his mouth, out of his chapped, peeling, blood-stained lips.

I stepped backward on reflex. This man wasn't just hurt. He was sick. *Very* sick.

He stepped forward.

I stepped back again, feeling my stomach twist in fear. From the corner of my eye I spotted a dog running toward me. *Not a coyote.* A pit bull.

I gulped.

The man in front of me lunged. *At me.*

I stumbled backward, tripping as a sick, crazy—possibly homeless—guy that I just hit with my car attacked me.

3

The loud, startling sound of a gunshot exploded through the woods. I froze, horror-struck. The man staggered back, blood gushing from his chest.

What the—

He teetered unsteadily only a moment, just long enough for me to process that he was shot, then he *pounced* at me *again*. My heart leapt back into my throat.

Another shot fired, and another. The *popping* sound was still ringing in my ears when I felt Missy's hand grab mine. She pulled, trying to tug me away, but I didn't move. I couldn't move. She gave another yank, only to fall to the ground beside me.

After the fourth shot, he finally hit the ground with a heavy *thump*. It wasn't silent or graceful like in the movies.

I almost lost my lunch.

Hot, fishy breath panting near my ear didn't help the matter. The pit bull was right beside me, no doubt hearing the unhealthy pounding of my heart with his super sensitive canine ears. Missy was on the other side of me, squeezing my hand so tight it was now starting to hurt.

Two mud-coated boots stepped forward, into my peripheral vision, then walked past us toward the lifeless body. My eyes hesitantly swept up a pair of camouflaged pants, resting finally on the gun still aimed at the fallen man.

"Duke, come!" a deep voice demanded as he turned. I flinched when he pointed the gun toward us. The dog didn't move. He just stayed there. Still staring. Still panting. His damn breath *still* blowing across my face. My nose crinkled. *Geez, what the hell did he just eat?*

"*Come,*" the guy commanded, this time louder. I didn't think it was possible but Missy squeezed my hand even more.

The dog trotted off this time. No tail wagging but not between his legs either, just sort of there. He sat right beside him, his nose tilting up, reminding me of a soldier standing at attention, waiting on his next command. I followed his gaze, anxious. A black t-shirt clung to a flat stomach and two thick backpack straps wrapped around his shoulders, tucking under his arm pits. Muscles popped in his forearms as he leveled the gun and a sweat-stained collar circled a sun-kissed neck.

"What's your name?" he shouted. My eyes watched his full lips move with each word. A five o'clock shadow dirtied up the lower half of his face. Light freckles crossed his cheeks. But it was his eyes—wide, hazel eyes that were more green than brown—that gave away his fear and his age. He couldn't be much older than Missy and I, and he was definitely rattled though his stance and his voice gave away nothing. "What's your damn name? Answer me." He flicked his wrist to emphasize the fact he had a gun. Trust me he didn't have to do that. I already knew he had a gun. That wasn't something someone was likely to forget. Even if he was kind of hot.

"Why are you the one yelling?" Missy blurted, her voice hitching up. "You are the one who just popped four bullets into some dude's chest. We should be the ones freaking yelling."

The boy ignored her. "Answer the question." Again with the flick of the gun.

"Geez. Dude. What the hell? You gonna kill us next and chop us up into little pieces and feed us to all your redneck friends? Is this how you spend your Friday nights?"

"Missy, *shut up*," I snapped, glaring at her. *Was she crazy?* Did she *want* to get us killed? My friend's face was the color of chalk. She was pale normally, probably the whitest girl I ever met but right now her ashen complexion made her look sickly instead of beautiful. I wasn't exactly winning any sunbathing competitions myself but the fact I was quarter Native American Indian, I always had a more olive skin tone. Great for tans, unlike her skin that burnt within fifteen minutes of direct sun exposure. I doubted that mattered right now though, I was pretty certain at the moment my face was as white as hers.

"I'm Dee," I said, turning back toward the teenage guy; trying to show him at least one of us had manners. "And her name's Melissa." I gestured to Missy with my thumb. I figured it was better to be nice to the guy with the gun.

He stared at me, contemplatively, his harsh expression calming. "Dee what?"

I wasn't sure why that mattered. "Forrester."

His green-brown eyes gave me a sort of nerve-wrecking once-over before he glanced at Missy. "And yours?"

I nervously shot my best friend a look, pleading for her cooperation.

"Frink," she grumbled, biting down on her lip seconds later. Guess she was afraid she'd run her mouth again. *I* was afraid she'd run her mouth again.

"Did you know him?" He waved the gun casually toward the dead guy. The guy he killed. His voice held no sense of remorse, and my stomach rolled again at the thought of it and at glancing at the lifeless body.

"No." I tore my eyes away from the body, looking back at the him. "I just hit him with my car."

The corner of his lip curled up faintly, but instantly faded, as his eyes trailed the full-length of my body again, this time in a very scrutinizing way. His expression grew serious. "Did that man touch you? Or cough on you? …Get any blood on you?"

The intense way he was staring at me, had me fidgeting. "No," I answered as confidently as I could.

"Are you *sure*?" he pressed, his eyes catching mine.

I gulped, my voice squeaking. "Yes, I'm sure." I couldn't sound more opposite.

"And what about you, Mouth?" He sent Missy a sidelong glance. "Did he make contact with you in any way?"

"It's Melissa," she hissed, her eyes narrowing.

"I know," he nodded, unfazed, "that's what she said, but I'll call you whatever I want. Just answer the question."

"No." Her voice rose. "You'll call me by my name." A quick peek showed me color was returning to my friend's cheeks. *Of course it was.*

"Yeah, probably not." A muscle popped in his jaw. "So, get over it. Now tell me," he urged, impatience written all over him. "*Yes* or *no*?"

I was afraid my best friend was going to flip out, so I answered, hoping to stop the flood of insulting curse words I knew were at the tip of her tongue. Because once you got her started it was hard to get her to stop. "No, he didn't go near her. She was on the phone with 911." I fidgeted on the ground again— I think a pine cone was stabbing me in the butt—and peered over at her. "Speaking of which what happened? What did they say? Are they coming?"

Missy exhaled sharply, no doubt thinking I was as bad as him now. "I accidentally hung up, *alright*...and I didn't bother calling back because...*well*, I'm sorry, some psychopath started shooting and all I thought about was running to you." Her blue eyes looked at me anxiously, seeking my understanding. And it was quite clear how worked up she was.

I squeezed her hand, to let her know it was okay, but I really wished the cops were here because I was freaking out. I just didn't want her to know I was.

Surprisingly the guy lowered the gun to his side, pointing it toward the ground. He didn't put it away, but it was better than before. Safer. I felt like I could breathe again. "If you called the police," he prompted, his expression changing, "then we need to leave. Now. Before they come."

"I'm sorry, what?" That was a horrible idea. We wanted the police to come. We *needed* the police to come.

"I don't know about you," he said matter-of-factly, looking me in the eye, "but I don't want to be thrown in jail for murder."

Missy laughed dryly, snagging his attention. "You should have thought about that *before* you killed someone. Just saying." I almost elbowed her in the side.

"And what?" he pressed in almost a snicker. "Let him kill her...than you... because that's what was about to happen."

I swallowed, trying to clear the lump lodged in my throat. "He was sick," I mumbled. "He was probably just delusional. And I did hit him with my car." I wasn't exactly sure why I was making excuses for someone who almost assaulted me, but I guess guilt had something to do it. And fear.

"Yeah. He *was* sick and he *was* delusional. That was the problem. He would have eaten your damn face off."

Missy muttered under her breath. "Okay don't be so melodramatic."

"I'm not," he sighed in frustration, his hazel eyes darkening. "You aren't from around here, are you? I can tell by the way you're dressed and by your car."

I peered down at my long sleeve teal shirt and my faded jean shorts. Missy was wearing dark denim and a black tank top. *What was so weird about how we were dressed? And what about my car?*

"I'm not following," Missy said (Exactly what I was thinking).

"Look, something twisted is going on around here. People are getting sick. Nobody knows why and it's not everybody. But it seems to happen in stages. This guy was in the final stage. I've seen it before. A woman bit right into a man's arm as if she was starving. It took like six shots before she died. I've never seen anything like it. Until just now. *With him.*"

The urge to puke was back as strong as ever. "Zombies? Awesome. We *would* stumble into a town full of flesh-eaters." I hugged my stomach, groaning.

"They aren't zombies. They are just sick. And the further the stage gets the worst they get. I was just saving you and putting him out of his misery." *Wasn't that what people did to their sick dogs? Did that somehow make murdering a man right?*

"If you were saving us, why was a gun pointed at our faces?" Missy accused. "*Huh?*" Leave it to her to always call people out. I stared up at him, wanting to know the answer to that too.

"I had to make sure you weren't infected. I didn't think you were. That's what he is for." His left hand rubbed the dog between the ears. The pit bull was short, stocky, and had a big head. All black with a white patch around his neck and one on his right paw.

"I think he senses the difference between us and the others. He wasn't barking at you, only at him. It was my first giveaway, but I still had to be certain." He paused, glancing down at the dog, then back at us. "This is Duke."

"Yeah, we've already met." I stood up, pulling Missy with me. "What did you feed him? Tuna fish?"

He laughed and seemed almost normal. "Actually, yeah. We split a can about two hours ago but I didn't think I should give a dog a piece of gum too."

"Hmm…" I started brushing off my backside. *Maybe he should have anyway.*

Missy was eyeing the dog admiringly. She was a big animal lover. "He's a really cute dog. Does he bite?" For a second Missy actually sounded like herself.

"Only if I want him too." He peered back down at Duke, practically ignoring her.

"And are you going to tell it to?" Bitterness instantly returned to her voice. It was safe to assume she had taken an instant dislike to the guy. The dog was probably his only saving grace.

"Have I yet?" His lips curved into a sneer, as he shifted his gaze to her. "Don't piss me off." *Perhaps he didn't like her either.*

"Funny…" I looked back and forth between him and the dog. "I don't know what's worse. Your gun or him?"

His expression fell. "Don't tell me you're one of those people that think pit bulls are horrible dogs."

"I'm not," I admitted, staring at Duke with uneasiness. "I'm just scared of big dogs."

"Really?" His voice changed to something suspiciously like disappointment. "Why?"

I shrugged. "I was bit when I was a kid by a German Sheppard. I guess I haven't really gotten over it."

"Was it your dog?" His green-brown eyes were watching me tentatively.

I shook my head. "No. It was the neighbor's dog."

"Oh." He rubbed at his scruff. "Have you ever owned a dog before?"

I thought about my parent's dog. It was close enough to owning my own dog. "Yeah, a Jack Russell."

He started laughing, dropping his hand away from his face. "That's not a dog." Confused, my brows scrunched together. "Yes, it is." *Last I checked it had four legs, fur, and yapped a lot.*

"No," he disagreed again, still chuckling. "A real dog weighs over fifty pounds. Small dogs are just stupid, ankle biters with personality disorders."

Missy snorted. "Yeah. Well you are a stupid, zombie killer with a personality disorder. *So there.*" That was my best friend, always defending the animals.

He rolled his eyes. "For the second time, he wasn't a zombie."

"Fine, whatever. You're *still* stupid, *still* a killer, and *still* have a personality disorder." She seemed utterly pleased with herself.

"Okay wow, I am so glad I ran into you two." He sounded bored and completely unoffended.

Now Missy rolled *her* eyes. "Yeah, well, I can't say the same." I mentally face-planted my palm, Missy was asking for trouble. *Didn't she know when to just shut her mouth... hello, he still had a gun.*

For a moment he stared at her like he never heard someone talk back to him before. Then he just shook his head. "Okay, enough chit chat. Do you know if that still runs?" He gestured toward my crashed car, turning all serious again, thankfully brushing off Missy's snippiness.

Sighing in relief, I blew a strand of hair out of my face and glanced at my Toyota. "It still runs. I don't know if it still drives, and at least the front tire is flat." Not to mention, the entire front end smashed in and the sides dented, and paint scrapped off. I was going to be in so much trouble when I got home.

"I don't care if it has a flat," he said, tucking his gun into his waistband. "I just want to drive it away from here unless you *want* the cops to run your license plate and put a warrant out for your arrest for murder?" The knot in my stomach was back instantly. I hadn't thought of that. "This isn't fair. We didn't kill him," I whined, panicking.

"No you just hit him with your car. That totally makes you innocent." His tone was sarcastic. I stood there, staring at him. *Shit.* He had a point.

4

The car wasn't budging. We needed a tow-truck to get it off the side of the mountain, just like I expected all along. But of course, I wasn't going to say that.

"Okay, Plan B," he said, digging into his backpack and pulling out a pair of gloves. "We have to carry the body out of here. Any chance you have gloves somewhere in this piece of junk of yours?" He banged on the hood of the engine as he walked around the bumper. He had been trying to push the Toyota, but it was pointless. "I don't want any of us actually touching him. Until we know what exactly he had, we treat him like he had leprosy."

I was sitting in the driver's seat with the car door propped open. My job was to first try and reverse the car then it was just to put it in neutral. Neither of which had worked. Mostly I just sat there staring at him. My eyes barely veered from the handle of the gun sticking out the side of his pants unless he was talking to me—like now—then I couldn't pull my eyes away from his face.

"No. I don't have any gloves." I drummed my fingers on the steering wheel thinking. I wasn't entirely sure I was okay with *Plan B*. "But there's a blanket in the trunk. Would that work?" I kept the navy blue fleece blanket back there in case of emergencies. I guess this counted as one.

"Actually, yeah." He paused mid-step. "I can wrap it around his legs and then you girls can hold onto that." He was already putting on his gloves as if this wasn't a big deal.

"I can hardly wait." Missy leaned back against the car, crossing her arms. Popping the trunk, I lifted myself out of the driver's seat, ignoring her. I knew she wasn't happy about this, but what other choice did we have?

I purposely stared at my sneakers as I walked by her so I wouldn't have to see "the look" I knew she was shooting me. And also, so I wouldn't inappropriately stare any longer at *him*, whoever *he* was.

I crumbled the soft material in my hands anxiously before tossing it his way. I wanted to ask him his name, but since he didn't offer it, I assumed he didn't want us to know. *Made sense. Less information to give the police if they caught us.* But still, I really wished I knew his name. The material fell short, landing about seven feet in front of him. Duke padded up to it, sniffing at it excitedly, tail wagging. *Maybe he thought I was trying to play fetch?*

"Sorry boy, I need this." Bending down, he picked up the blanket, giving the dog a quick pat to the head in apology before straightening out. "Get whatever you need out of the car," he said, turning his attention back to me. "This should only take a minute."

I nodded, shutting the trunk. The only thing I had to carry was my set of car keys, so I just made sure I locked everything up then I handed Missy her purse with my keys inside it. Guess technically that meant I didn't have to carry anything. I braced myself against the car door beside her, and we stood there waiting uncomfortably until he beckoned us over. When he did, I headed slowly toward him because I couldn't believe this was really happening. We were *really* about to carry a dead dude through the woods.

The moment I saw the bullet wounds up close, I felt sick all over again. *Doing this made me and Missy just as guilty of murder, didn't it?*

"Are you okay?" The boy with those alluring hazel eyes was staring at me funny as I placed my palm against my queasy stomach. *Was I?*

"She's fine," Missy responded, pulling her hair back into a ponytail. "She just has a weak stomach. Blood and guts aren't her thing." Missy was an avid horror fan, but that didn't mean *this* was cool with her. On the contrary, real life scares she couldn't handle. Right now, she was just *acting* like she could, but that's what my best friend did. She acted that way so she wouldn't cry.

"I didn't realize they were anyone's *thing*." He bent down behind the head of the man, still staring at me. "Come on. This doesn't sit well with me either, if it makes you feel better."

"It doesn't." I purposely averted my eyes from the blood-stained wounds. "But it has to be done, right?"

Swallowing, I repeated *I can do this, I can do this* a few quick times in my head then I forced myself to hunch down too, placing my hands around the man's covered ankles.

Missy squatted hesitantly down next to me. "So where are the cops? Shouldn't they have come checking on us by now even though I hung up?"

"Well the way I see it," he declared, putting his gloved hands under the guy's armpits, "if you didn't give them a location then they have to use the cell towers and satellite to try and *find* your location. It all depends on where they are placed. You could have one within a five-mile radius or one within a hundred-mile radius and they go from there. Given we are in the middle of nowhere, it's safe to assume we have some time. Service never is good in these parts."

"Oh." There was a beat of silence as Missy placed her hands beside mine, careful not to touch anything but the blanket. I couldn't tell if she was happy with his response or upset. I no longer knew if I wanted the cops here either. At this point, I think we were just too deep in the shit water any way we looked at it.

"You two ready?" he asked, impatiently waiting on us no doubt. I spared Missy a sidelong glance and she nodded though there was no mistaking how *un*ready she really was. I slowly nodded too. I guess I was as ready as I would ever be.

"Okay, on the count of three…"

I grunted when we finally lifted him. He was heavier than I was expecting.

My arms strained while we quickly kicked dirt about with our shoes until the ground no longer looked like a murder scene.

"I'm Jason Ollie, by the way." His hazel eyes shot us a quick glance before he peered over his shoulder to watch where he was going. "I forgot to introduce myself."

Missy snickered beside me. "Oh, my mom is going to be so happy when I tell her I met a super cute boy while helping him dispose of a dead body. I just can't wait to share the news with her."

I mentally sighed, shaking my head at my best friend's acerbity. More strands fell out of my lopsided ponytail and annoyingly I couldn't do anything about it. "It's nice to meet you, Jason." I tried sounding as benevolent as I could to make up for her sarcasm. It was nice putting a name to his face finally. "I think what my best friend is trying to say though is perhaps it would have been better if we met under other circumstances. That's all."

Jason surprised me by chuckling. "Hey, at least the first impression will be memorable, eh?" He turned his face back to us briefly, his light brown hair windblown and slightly damp from sweat across his forehead. "So, Mouth…" His lips curved up. "You really think I'm *super cute*?"

My best friend narrowed her eyes, her blonde eyebrows pulling together to empathize the scowl. "Maybe I'll just drop the body here…" She slowed down, forcing us to too.

Jason's smirk instantly faded. "Wow. You need to learn to take a joke." He was completely incredulous.

"You are the only one who thinks this is funny," she snapped at him.

He half-shrugged, not really showing emotion. "What can I say? I guess I try and stay positive, even in shitty situations."

Missy snorted again almost in laughter. "Terrific," she mumbled, turning her face fully toward me. "We got a walking, talking real-life *Hallmark* card in front of us. Aren't we lucky?" Bitter sharp sarcasm filled her voice.

Jason made an inaudible sound, turning his head back over his shoulder and I was starting to get a headache. "How about we just concentrate on walking," I suggested changing the subject. The last thing I needed right now was to be playing referee.

They agreed to a truce, though it seemed like a struggle for both of them, and we continued on. Silently. Duke panted beside us, his ears flicking back and forth as if he was always listening for something. *Or them.* And my stress level was rising by the second. *So much for thinking the silence would make things better.*

Ten minutes later the phone in Missy's purse started ringing.

"Ignore it," Jason said, keeping his eyes on the rocky terrain coming up.

"But what if—"

"Just ignore it." He whirled his head around this time to glare at her like she was an idiot for even considering answering it right now while we had our hands full.

"*Dee*," she whined, her voice desperate, clearly ignoring him. The phone continued ringing.

I bit my bottom lip, unsure what to do. I knew what she was trying to say, *What if it was Spencer?* But I also understood what Jason meant. We *were* kind of in the middle of something.

"You can call whoever it is back later." Impatience sounded in his voice. "Just keep walking."

But I couldn't do it. Each step, my heart started pounding faster. I couldn't ignore the fact it *could be* Spencer. He *was* the reason we were even in this situation after all. Just as I was about to tell them to drop the body and answer the phone the ringing stopped. I cursed.

Jason looked at me differently. "If it's important, they will leave a message." Suddenly his voice was a lot less condescending. *Had he picked up on our anxiety finally?* The three of us hesitated, my arms struggling to hold the body, as we waited to see if we heard the familiar beeps that followed a message. Sure enough, about twenty seconds later there they were.

Crap.

Those beeps echoed in my mind. Since we missed the call, we didn't even bother at that moment checking who it was. We just kept walking. But I couldn't ignore the twisting of my gut as we moved. I just had a feeling something was wrong and it had nothing to do with the dead guy. And I was worried sick over it.

Not to mention, my muscles were starting to scream in protest, my neck was hurting even more from the crash, I was thirsty, hungry and I had to pee. This was definitely turning into a rotten day, possibly even the worst day of my life.

Missy was beside me, her shoulder bumping into mine every time we took a step, her panting almost as loud as the dog's but she was saying nothing. More like sulking or just extremely pissed. I couldn't help but wonder if she was picturing us carrying Jason's dead body instead. Also, I was beginning to wonder where the heck we were carrying this man to anyway. *Was there a special spot to hide dead people and if so, how come Jason knew about it?*

The ground was uneven and my ankle twisted now and again as we stepped down the decline. A soft wind was rustling through the treetops. Minus what we were doing, the scenery was actually kind of pretty. Spring in the Pennsylvania Mountains was definitely something to see, but I am sure autumn would have been better. Either way, I couldn't really admire it much right now anyway, I was too on edge. And the fact the sun was starting to set, darkening the sky above us, didn't help. Then Duke started barking. Loudly. His hair rising on his back as he glared off toward the right and I almost had a heart attack right there.

"Shit." Jason slowed his steps. We all did. "Duke. Quiet. Quiet boy." Duke barked one more time, proceeding to an anxious whimpering. Turning his head, Jason glanced in the direction Duke was focused on, his attention darting through the woods, searching. "He senses something," Jason urged, his stance growing rigid.

"No shit, *Sherlock Holmes*," Missy grumbled, her voice winded. Her face was turned toward the same direction. "What do we do?" Fear mixed with sarcasm in her voice.

I stared at Jason as if he had all the answers. A muscle popped in his jaw again as if he didn't like that I expected him to have them. Exhaling, he glanced at us. "Well, I can't get to my gun unless we put him down. Maybe it's better…" All of a sudden Duke spun around, running behind Jason, full blown barking. He no sooner said the dog's name when a woman came charging out of nowhere. I stifled a scream, my heart now pounding in my ears.

The woman was crazed. Tangled red hair, dirt-stained face, dark eyes, skin pulled tight over her cheekbones. And she was coming right for us, with that same hungry, desperate look the dead guy had given me before *well, he was dead.*

"Throw the body," Jason quickly yelled. "*At her.*"

We didn't hesitate. We chucked the dude right into her, knocking her down like a bowling pin. Then we took off like bats out of hell. Jason was yelling at Duke to follow, his hand already grabbing the gun out of his waistband. Missy suddenly screamed and I stupidly stopped, looking over. Another man came running out of the woods. This man had scars on his face, chest-length blonde stringy hair, same cold eyes, but he didn't look as sick as the redhead. Jason aimed his gun, coming up beside me, pushing me backward with his other arm. Duke was barking again. But this man didn't come for us. This man ran straight toward the woman.

My heart was pounding so fast that I had to hunch over to catch my breath. I knew we should still be running, but I just couldn't bring myself to. I was quickly scanning every direction to make sure a whole swarm of sick people weren't coming. I didn't want us to be ambushed. I was trying of think of what we'd do if we *were* ambushed, when I heard a sound. A god-awful sound. Turning my head, I gagged. The sound was the redhead screaming as the man sunk his teeth into her and began eating away her flesh. By the red ring around her mouth, I realized she had been doing the same thing to the dead guy just moments before.

My eyes drifted to the now stomach*less* man on the ground.

I finally puked.

"Here," Missy said, after we ran for a good ten minutes straight. I was out of breath and had the worst taste in my mouth. She handed me her water bottle from her purse.

"Thanks." I swished the warm water around my mouth for about thirty seconds, then spit it out. Next I took a swig of it.

"Why didn't you shoot them?" Missy asked Jason, who was sipping his own water out of a tube connected to his backpack. He had tossed his gloves somewhere along the way. I didn't approve of littering, but he didn't want to put the contaminated gloves back in his bag. *Couldn't really blame him there.*

He clicked the tube back on his strap. "I would have if they came after us, but they didn't. I figured it was smarter to save the bullets. We still have about ten more miles to walk before we get back to town. And it's going to be night soon."

I handed Missy back her water bottle and instead of drinking from it, she tilted the rest of it into Duke's mouth.

"Thanks," Jason said with a slight smile.

Missy nodded, but she didn't smile back. "We have to walk ten more miles?"

"Yeah."

"Terrific." She tossed the empty plastic bottle back into her purse and took out her tin of breath mints. Popping two in her mouth, she offered them to me. I took two as well, grateful. I didn't want to talk with puke breath. "Well let's get going. I don't want to be out here all night." Shoving the tin back into her bag, she took off past us with Duke following behind.

I hesitated again, looking behind me for a brief second, my eyes carefully watching the way from which we just came.

"Are you sure you're okay?" Jason stepped up next to me.

I turned to face him, biting my lip. "Yeah. It was just..." I struggled for a fitting word but couldn't find one. There were no words for what I just saw.

"I know," he said, his eyes sympathetic. "It's hard to digest. I wish you didn't have to see it."

Me too. A shiver went down my spine when I realized Jason hadn't been lying. That's exactly what the man was going to do to me if Jason hadn't shot him. And I hadn't even thanked him for helping me. *Good job, Dee.* "For what it's worth..." I looked up at him both grateful and scared. "Thank you for saving me today."

"You're welcome..." We started to walk again, his eyes drifting toward our left momentarily. "But keep in mind the day isn't over yet."

And as we walked side by side, I knew what he meant. He couldn't promise we'd stay alive.

5

We finally stopped to pee because I was starting to do the "ants in my pants" dance. It was moments like this that I was happy I wasn't one of those girly girls—you know the ones that are too scared or too dainty to actually *go* in the woods. I could care less. I *should* have cared though when I noticed my fingers starting to shake, especially since it was a bitch trying to button up my shorts. But I ignored it.

I couldn't see Missy or Jason due to the tree I squatted behind, but I heard her voice and footsteps as she moved away from *her* tree. "Yo, *Hallmark*…. I meant to ask you, why didn't Duke hear the redhead first? She was obviously closer."

We made it to the clearing about the same time. Jason was leaning up against a tree, arms crossed waiting for us. Duke was chewing on a stick, lying on the ground by his feet.

Jason appeared impassive. "He can't hear too well in his left ear," he replied, unmoving. "That's why." By the looks of him, you would have never known he just killed a man or that he just ran from two flesh-eating sickos not too long ago.

Missy, on the other hand, was a little more obvious. Her cheeks were flushed but the rest of her face was still chalky white. Her hair was windblown and frizzy due to the run, and when she spoke, she still sounded slightly frazzled.

My best friend picked up her yellow purse that she left sitting on a rotting tree stump and stared at him in disbelief. "That's something you probably should have mentioned a little earlier. Don't you think?"

Yea, seriously.

"Eh. It didn't cross my mind." He kicked away from the maple tree, dropping his arms to his sides. "I don't doubt my dog. Duke always gives enough warning to protect me." He bent some to pet Duke's head. "Ain't that right, boy?" He gave the pit bull a short, strained smile.

Missy's entire demeanor changed as she looked at them. "But why can't he hear well? Isn't he too young to have hearing issues?"

"Duke is a rescue dog." He motioned for us to start walking again. "I got him from the pound two years ago. Apparently he was in a really bad situation and barely survived. I didn't ask what happened. I didn't want to know what happened. I just wanted to bring him home with me and offer him a better life."

"Ohmigod, that's awful." Missy trailed a few steps behind them. "Not the part where you rescued him but that someone hurt him." She was staring solely at Duke, no doubt on the verge of crying or beating someone up. "Like what the hell is wrong with people, why do they have to be such assholes?"

"I don't know." He peered down at Duke too. The dog was trotting beside him, tail wagging, as if he didn't care we were talking about his previous abuse, but just happy to be next to his new owner. "But I do know," he added a smile instantly forming on his face when Duke looked up and licked his hand, "is he was the best decision I ever made. And I will make sure he always knows he's a good boy." Pausing, he hunched down in front of his dog, giving him a quick kiss on the snout. "Yes, that's right. You are a *good* boy." Duke's tail wagged even faster and the dog gave him a slobbery kiss back on his cheek. Jason's smile instantly spread and one tugged at my own lips as I watched the exchange.

It was evident under the entire "no emotion, nothing you say will ever bother me, I can kill someone and not even cringe," exterior, Jason was a big-hearted sap with an odd sense of humor. The nickname *Hallmark* fit better than Missy realized. And it was because of this moment—that smile at his rescued pit bull—that I suddenly felt calmer than I had since we all met. If I was certain of anything tonight, it was that Jason would never hurt us intentionally. And that's all I needed to know to assure me that sticking with him was the right decision, even if I hadn't a clue *what* we were up to now. I mean, the body was gone. *Now what? Were we just moving along to get away from the scene of the crime? We were running from more sickos? Were we on our path to finding Spencer?* I didn't know, but something told me to just trust Jason for the time being.

I continued to watch his profile as we walked, wondering what nationality he was. Irish? German? English? His skin was sun-kissed and freckly, darker than Missy's skin but paler than mine. I didn't really have freckles, only a few across my nose that the sun brought out in the summer. His freckles spread lightly down his neck and arms too. I think the freckles added to his "cute" factor but the scruff, the definition in his arms, the flat stomach, and the confidence in his step— oh and the camouflaged pants— added to his "hot" factor. As for the eyes and the smile… *well, that was a category all of its own.*

The last thing I needed was a crush on a boy I'll probably never see again, and I knew I should have had more self-restraint against inconspicuously shooting him the "googly eyes," but I still did it. At least until everything started getting fuzzy.

We had probably gone another mile or two tops, but maybe less because of the uneven terrain, when I started to notice it. I should have said something then, but instead I kept walking, slowing down with each step, until I couldn't walk anymore. The woods started spinning, I stumbled, and everything went black.

The first thing I heard was panting in my ear, and then I felt hot fish-breath blowing across my face again.

"Are you sure the guy didn't cough on her or touch her?" Jason's voice sounded a little funny, but I didn't miss the panicked edge to it.

"Oh, shut up. No one got her sick. She just has low blood sugar, you ass." Missy's voice was a lot closer and clearer. "Not all of us can walk a freaking marathon without any food." She put her warm hands on my face. "*Dee? Dee...* are you okay?"

"If you slap me across the face," I grumbled, struggling to open my eyes, "I *will* hit you back." *I wouldn't put it past her to do that.*

She laughed in relief, moving her hands away. "She's gonna be fine."

Sure I was. Lifting one eyelid, cautiously, I refrained from saying something sarcastic or negative back.

"Duke, come," Jason said, when I flinched at the sight of Duke's big mouth near mine. His tail barely missed my head as Missy helped me sit up. I blinked a couple times regaining focus. I was still light-headed and weak, but at least it wasn't fuzzy anymore.

Jason was looking at me, worry surprisingly written all over his face. "You have low blood sugar?"

"Yeah." I pushed my bangs out of my eyes, feeling for any leaves that might be stuck in my hair.

His entire expression changed in an instant. "Then why didn't you say something?" His tone sharpened. "You should have said you had a condition."

For some reason the way he said it bothered me. "Because I was ignoring my *condition*," I replied bitterly, dropping my hands to my lap. I flashed my dark eyes up at him. "I figured it would be better to get out of the woods before nightfall."

"Well that was kind of stupid, wasn't it?" He was standing there in his camouflaged *I'm hot and awesome* outfit and staring at me like I was the idiot now instead of Missy.

I rolled my eyes. "Whatever." *At the moment I hated how tight that shirt fit him. And that he was right.*

Missy put her bag on the ground and started digging through it. "Okay here…I have five *Tootsie Rolls* left and a small bag of *Swedish Fish*." She dumped them onto my lap. "That should help pick up your sugar."

"Yeah, but it won't stabilize it." Jason shook his head. "She needs protein or something more nutritional. Not just pure sugar." Removing one strap of his backpack off his shoulder, he spun it in front of him. "I should have something."

"The candy is fine," I grumbled, still annoyed at him. I shoved a few red fishes in my mouth, but handed Missy back the chocolate. They may have been her favorite, but they definitely weren't mine.

"Don't be ridiculous." He started rummaging through his bag without looking up. "You obviously need it. Now where is…*aha* thought I still had one." Pulling his head up, he tossed his hazel assessment my way. "You don't have a peanut allergy, do you?" The sharp edge to his voice was gone just like that.

I furrowed my brow. "No."

"Okay, just checking." He took something out of his pack, tossing it at me. A granola bar. "It has peanut butter in it. That's good for low blood sugar."

I stared down at the packaged bar in my hand for a brief second confused. "Uh, thanks?"

He nodded. "My little sister is diabetic. It's all kind of the same thing. Well at least the same concept."

"You have a sister?" Okay, dumb question. He just said he did.

His lips twitched. "Actually I have a brother and a sister, they are twins." He turned his attention to Missy. "Are you hungry too?"

From the corner of my eye, I saw her shrug. "I'm good with the candy for now."

"Okay, well I'm hungry but I don't have much left." He zippered up his backpack and repositioned it on his shoulders. "So why don't we take a mini break here and I'll go see if I can find something we can eat for dinner before it gets completely dark out."

"Oh yum, pine bark," Missy mumbled sarcastically through her mouthful of chocolate.

Jason just shook his head again. "Stay here. I'll leave Duke with you. You'll be safe." He started to walk away and I panicked.

"*Wait*. What about you?" *Who was going to keep him safe?* He might have frustrated me but I wasn't about to let him just walk off alone with *those* people out there, he didn't piss me off *that* bad. Plus, he gave me a granola bar that cancelled everything out in my book anyway.

Jason's eyes met mine for a brief second with an odd expression. "Duke isn't barking and I have this." He patted the handle of his gun as he pulled his gaze away. "I'm not scared. Be right back. Don't go anywhere."

Missy was teasing Duke playfully with a stick while I finished off the granola bar and ate some more candy. I was feeling better every second, but I felt restless waiting for Jason to get back. My eyes kept veering off in the direction he went, anxiously darting around looking for him. *He said he'd be right back, so where was he?*

"Dee," Missy said, grabbing my attention. She was hunched down, resting the stick on her knee, looking at me. "What are we doing?" Her pale blue eyes were outlined with now smeared black eyeliner. It was a perfect example why I didn't wear makeup. It ran off too easily.

I scrunched my forehead in confusion. "What do you mean? I don't understand." *We were waiting for Jason.*

"I'm talking about with Jason. What are we doing *with* him?"

Oh. "He saved our life today, Missy." It was the only response I could think of.

"I know," she sighed. "But we don't know anything about him. It's kind of scary how he can so easily shoot people, don't you think?"

I undid my ponytail and redid it just to do something with my hands. I was trying to see from her point of view, trying to acknowledge the facts, but all I could think was *he saved our lives*. I didn't care how he did it, I was just thankful he did.

"It was like a self-defense type thing and you know that. If he wanted to hurt us, he could have done so already or just let the guy do it." I paused, forcing my lips into a smile. "You need to lay off the horror movies, they are making you paranoid."

"Ya think?" She bit her bottom lip obviously not agreeing with me.

"Yes." I thought about the best way to explain why I wasn't worried. "For starters, you might not have noticed but when Jason was aiming the gun at us, I could see in his eyes that he was freaking out. I think shooting that man wasn't easy for him. I think he just puts up this front. And I think it's pretty awesome of him that he didn't leave us to deal with the cops and put the blame on us. He could have easily run off and left us with a dead body, but he didn't. And that probably just saved us from a long time in the slammer." I cringed, just the thought of being arrested for murder made my heart jump.

She was silent for a moment. When Duke nudged her side with his nose, she absently gave him the stick but kept her eyes toward me. "Do you think they will find out? The cops, I mean." The fear was clear in her voice.

I considered that. "I don't know. I think they will be looking for us because you said we crashed off a mountain, but I hope they don't put two and two together. I mean we did kick dirt over the blood, you can't even tell it's there. But say they do spot it. I am hoping they think it's just one of us who got injured."

"But what if while they are looking for us they find the body?" She was definitely anxious.

I thought back to the redhead and the blonde-haired guy, and my stomach did its queasy thing again. "I have a feeling they are just going to assume he was eaten by coyotes or a bear, something like that."

She made a face. No doubt remembering the dead guy no longer had a stomach too. "What do you think is going on around here? I'm scared."

So was I. "I don't know." I pulled my knees up to my chest, kind of hugging myself.

"Do you think…do you think all of this is the reason Spencer called us?"

When we stopped to pee, Missy had checked her voicemail. Turns out it was from her mother, not Spencer. *Thankfully.* Mrs. Frink was just complaining about how Melissa didn't call her when we left school and that she tried my cell but I wasn't answering either. Missy didn't call her back though. She said she didn't want to waste the battery because if that call wasn't from Spencer, sooner or later there would be one.

As I looked at my best friend, both of us shivering a little with the turn of the temperature and the knowledge of what was going on around us, I wished I could say something different. But the truth was I didn't doubt for a second this illness was the reason Spencer had called.

"Yes Missy, and I think he's in trouble. Otherwise, he wouldn't have called. He ran away six months ago. We never heard from him. No one has. Then, suddenly, he calls us? You know there is a reason, just as much as I do. Spencer didn't want to be found and now he does, it's too coincidental."

There was a long pause that followed.

"You think he's one of them, don't you?" Her question was both of accusation and worry.

I didn't want to answer her because I wasn't sure what I thought and I didn't want to think about it. "Let's just stay positive."

She laughed in disbelief. "You and I are the most negative people in the world."

A forced chuckle left me as I tried to change the subject. "And that's why we get along so well. Misery likes company…" I turned my eyes back to the trees anxiously. "So… how long do you think Jason has been gone?"

Missy immediately sighed. "I don't know, not that long. Five minutes, seven tops." *Oh that's all?* "But who cares."

I turned my face back toward her after mentally telling myself to relax. "You really dislike Jason *that* much?"

She didn't respond for about forty seconds. She just sat there, squatting down, petting Duke between the ears as he gnawed on the stick. Then she exhaled as if she was truly annoyed. "I guess Jason isn't too bad, I mean he did rescue this handsome fella and you know how I feel about helping animals."

"Yeah," I said my lips curving when Duke stopped chewing on the stick and peered up at Missy with his light brown dog eyes, wagging his tail. "And he must know it because Duke seems to have taken a liking to you, that's for sure."

She chuckled when Duke put his head on her thigh. "Yeah, seems that way, just like his master has taken a liking to you and vise versa."

"What?" My eyes widened. "*Please.* Where did you ever come up with an idea like that?" My face felt hot.

Her smirk spread and she shook her head. "You know, it's not completely dark yet. So I can see the blush on your face."

"You're seeing things." I turned my head. "I'm just flushed from walking."

"You've been sitting for at least ten minutes," she laughed. "So?"

"*So*… just admit you think he's sexy and you want him."

"Shut up." I stood up.

She laughed louder. "Come on, just admit it. Even I think he's cute. And you and I have totally different tastes in guys."

"Then it's possible I *don't* think he's cute if you do." I started brushing off my backside. I didn't know why I was denying it.

"He's got *your* type written all over him. You might as well fess up, because you know I'm always right."

"I know you *think* you're always right, there's a big difference."

"Whatever, you ass."

We both were laughing, but I was trying not to, which just made me laugh even more. "Okay. Okay. Fine. You win. Yes. I think he's hot." *Definitely hot.*

"I love being right," Missy said, all smug. That was probably why I was denying it, just for principle. But it did make me wonder, *was she right about him?* I was about to say something else, when the sound of a gunshot suddenly echoed through the woods.

6

"What the hell is that?" Missy's eyes widened as Jason came stomping back through the brush.

Jason walked right past us, expression indifferent. "A chipmunk." He placed its tiny body onto a large rock and tucked his gun back into the side of his pants.

"Are you kidding me?" She jumped up, storming right up to him as he took off his backpack.

"What?" He unzipped the side compartment of his pack, pulling out a pocket knife and flipping it open. "Would you rather I roasted my dog for dinner?"

She gasped, stepping backward. "Ohmigod, what is wrong with you?"

His green-brown eyes peered up at her, unbothered. "We need to eat something with protein. It's the only thing I spotted."

She started waving her hands around. "I'm not eating that. You son of a—"

He shrugged, placing the knife down beside the dead animal. "Suit yourself."

"*Dee!*" She cried in exasperation, turning toward me, her eyes tearing up.

I was standing there with my arms crossed over my chest, flinching because I knew how much this was hurting my best friend and because it was a chipmunk. "I hate to say it, but I might be with her on this one. That's like a rodent."

"That's like a freaking animal, you jerk. I don't eat animals." Now she was really crying.

Duke made his way over to her, I guess sensing her distress.

"I'm sorry," Jason said, crawling around picking up sticks now. "I didn't mean to make you upset. I didn't know you were a vegetarian, and you'll just have to get over it. Most of America eats animals. It's no different from chicken or cow."

"Yes it is," she snapped.

"How?"

"It just is, damn it. I mean who the hell eats a freaking chipmunk?" She gave Duke a short pat to the head as he nuzzled her hand, sensing her distress. But her attention and tears were entirely on Jason.

He appeared unfazed as he reached down to pick up another branch. "People eat squirrel all the time around here."

"A squirrel is not a chipmunk." Missy swiped the back of her hand roughly across her cheeks. "You're just being cruel."

"I know it's not," he sighed as if he thought she was getting a little ridiculous, "and no I'm not. People eat whatever they can in this neck of the woods."

"Yeah, I know," she shot back, her anger clearer than the sky above us. "Apparently, even cannibalism is the new thing here."

With that said, Jason stopped talking.

Awkward silence stretched between the three of us as Jason went about making a fire and skinning the chipmunk. I didn't offer to help him because I didn't want to upset Missy anymore and I didn't bother talking to Missy—who was sniffling and focusing all her attention now on Duke—because I knew when to leave well enough alone. So instead I just sat in front of the flames and kept myself warm.

As soon as Jason put the chipmunk over the fire, Missy and Duke walked away. She sat down with her back toward us a little way up, and since we still had view of her and she had Duke, I wasn't freaking out about her absence. In fact I think it was for the best.

Jason fidgeted beside me, turning the stick in his hand. "I really didn't mean to upset her so bad. I guess I'm just so used to the ways around here. I forget it might be different from where you're from."

I turned my face toward him. "She'll get over it. You just startled her. That's all. Missy even cries over road-kill because she feels bad for them."

He shot a shamefaced glance toward her in the distance. "She's really great with Duke. That should have been my clue that she was so sensitive toward animals."

"Don't worry about it, Jason, seriously. She'll get over it." I think he was mostly upset that he made her cry. Guys hated doing that. "I eat hamburgers in front of her all the time."

His posture seemed to relax. "Oh, so you're not a vegetarian too?" His green-brown eyes peered over at me for the first time since he sat beside me.

I laughed. "Hardly. I need the protein. Otherwise I get too shaky."

"Ah, that's right." He nodded, turning his attention to the stick again. I didn't really enjoy seeing the skinned chipmunk roasting over the fire either, but it didn't bother me.

"Have you ever had that before? Like do you know how to cook it without getting sick?"

"Yeah. My buddies and I have had it a few times. It tastes just like jerky, at least when you roast it like this. I'm sure there are other ways to eat it."

I thought about that. *Chipmunk stew. Chipmunk pot pie.* Yeah. It didn't really have the same ring as Beef stew or Chicken pot pie.

"It's just weird."

He turned his face toward me again. "Why?"

I shrugged. "I don't know. I just never pictured someone actually eating one I guess. Like I can't picture my mom saying, *tonight we are having chipmunk for dinner.*"

He chuckled, his expression amused. "Guess it takes some getting used to." He was silent for a moment. "So where are you from, if you don't mind me asking?" He seemed suddenly introverted despite his question.

A small smile started at the corner of my lips. *Was he trying to get to know me? Was I making him nervous?* "Jersey, actually."

"Really?" He looked shocked. "What are you doing out *here*?" He made it sound like it was two different worlds.

I bit my bottom lip, thinking of Spencer. "A friend of ours called last night in a panic. He asked us to pick him up after school today."

"Your friend lives here?" Skepticism crept into his voice.

"I guess." I started fiddling with a thread on my sleeve. "I mean he ran away six months ago and everyone's been looking for him. All of a sudden he wants to come home."

"Oh." That response said it all. He completely understood where I was going with that. *These sick people…*

I inhaled the scent of the smoke and it brought back many memories of camping when I was a kid. I suddenly had a strong urge for marshmallows.

"What's his name?"

"Hmm?"

"Your friend? What's his name?"

I snapped out of it. "Oh, uh Spencer. Spencer Reign."

Jason cocked his head, thinking. "Hey I think I know him. I think he's the new roommate my buddy got a few months ago. He lives on the outskirts of town."

My heart skipped instantly. "Seriously?" I turned to face him fully. My excitement barely contained.

"Yeah. I know most people in this town. I've been here my whole life and we aren't that big a town. Tall kid, blonde hair, dresses skater-like?"

"Ohmigod, yes that's him." I wanted to jump up and down. I was so happy.

Jason frowned.

"What?" I was unable to control my smile. We weren't lost after all. Jason could lead us *directly* to Spencer's place, that's even better than the *GPS* would have done if it hadn't crapped out and we hadn't hit someone. This was awesome. We could still find Spencer. And now I knew why my instinct was telling me to trust Jason, we were meant to run into him. My smile spread.

"Are you and he—I mean were you two an item or something?"

"*What?* No." The question caught me off guard and my smile faltered.

Jason seemed unsure. "You just seem really happy right now to find some guy."

"Not some guy," I mumbled, in his defense. "It's hard to explain. But he's like a brother to me."

"Oh…" He spun the stick in his hands again. "That didn't sound too hard to explain."

I raised my eyebrow at him and he turned his attention back to the fire. He didn't say anything for about a minute. It was a long minute. I listened to the fire crackling. "So… is there… *a guy?*"

I fidgeted beside him, grateful I could use the fire as an excuse to why my face suddenly felt hot. "No. My ex and I broke up a few months ago. It wasn't anything serious."

A pause. "Yeah...I'm not involved with anyone either. Been too much going on lately."

Ohmigod, what was he implying? Was he trying to hint at something? Was Missy right?

"Do you mind me asking how old you are?" He sent me a sidelong glance.

Nope. "Eighteen. You?"

"Nineteen."

I nodded. *I mean what else was I supposed to do?* Turning my attention back to the fire, I watched the flames dance and flicker in front of us. Deep rich orange. Dark red. Electric blue. The smoke rose into the air in swirls of charcoal. Over top of it, I could still see Missy and Duke sitting there, her back toward us, her arm around the dog, his head rested against her side. It was too cute.

After God knows how long, I finally looked away to sneak a peek at Jason. He was staring *right* at me. And instead of pulling his eyes away when I caught him, he just smiled.

I smiled nervously back. Then the thread on my shirt sleeve seemed really interesting again. I went back to pulling at it. I wasn't good at any of this. Cute boys made me feel awkward when they stared at me like that, especially this cute boy.

"You know; you might have the darkest eyes I ever saw. When I first looked at you, I almost thought they were black. I'm not gonna lie, they still kinda look that way."

A nervous laugh escaped my lips as I wrapped a string around my finger. "I've heard that before. It's my Indian blood. I get it from my grandmother's side."

"Oh, you're Indian? But you're so pale?"

I laughed again, peering over at him in another short burst. "I'm mostly Irish."

"Oh so I can't call you *Pocahontas* then?" He flashed me a teasing smile. An adorable teasing smile and my gut tightened.

"I've heard that before too." It was all I could think to say.

"Eh, you look more like her friend in the movie than her, anyway. You have the shorter hair and bangs like that girl did."

I let go of the string and self-consciously—and way too obviously—finger fluffed my bangs at the mention of it. God only knew what I looked like.

Then I remembered I puked in front of him earlier, almost on his shoes. *Oh yeah. I was just abounding with class.*

"I've heard that as well, actually," I mumbled. My cheeks instantly grew hot and I wanted to smack myself in the forehead. *Geez, I was so glad I had such a wide vocabulary. Hell, I almost said the same damn thing three times now. Yup. I am that lame.*

"Damn, is there anything you *haven't* heard?" he chuckled, his tone still playful.

"From anyone?" I asked, forcing myself to say something different. "Or just from guys?" I gulped down the stupid knot in my throat, trying to sound teasing too. "Because that's two completely opposite categories." I spared him another glance.

He was still smiling. I'm not sure if he was amused by me, trying to help ease my nerves, or just—I don't know—smiling. "From guys."

This time I laughed, only slightly forced. "The list is *way* too long. We'd be here all night."

"Either that's not true," he said, his smile fading. "Or the guys in Jersey are idiots."

Something about the way he said it, made my heart skip another beat.

After Jason ate the chipmunk—I tried some because I was hungry but I wasn't admitting that *ever* to Missy—and put out the fire, he took his headlamp out of his back pack. It was almost completely dark now.

"Okay, first," he said, taking out a bottle of bug spray and holding it out, "Now that the fire is out, spray yourselves with some of this because the bugs around here get pretty bad at night. Lucky for us, it's spring and not summer."

We willingly sprayed ourselves from head to toe and then I sprayed Jason's back for him. "Second," he said after he put away the bottle. "Would either of you like a drink before we start walking again?" He swung the pack back over his shoulder and unclipped the drinking tube from the little latch. "I promise I don't have anything contagious and the water is clean."

I agreed, reluctantly. Call me crazy, but I was just really thirsty. And I knew if I drank some, Missy would too. As I stepped up to him though, I felt my heart and stomach get all funky again and almost decided against it. But I was pretty certain a boy crush was a stupid reason to get dehydration so I caved, drinking quickly. I avoided looking him in the eyes as best I could, but he seemed so intent on staring at me it made it almost impossible not to.

Missy drank less than I did, stepping back even faster.

Jason took one last sip of water then started clicking the tube back in place.

"Wait—what about Duke?" Melissa asked.

"There's a stream about a mile from here. He can drink something there." Jason was turning back into that commander mode, the *whatever I say, goes* mode again.

"You mean you actually know where you are going?" She sounded surprised. For the most part she had let the whole chipmunk issue go now that it was no longer visible.

"Yes. In about two more miles we are going to hit a dirt road."

"Wait, we are going to be out of the woods?" I couldn't keep the relief out of my voice.

"Yeah. The dirt road leads to a friend of mine. I figure we can stop there until morning. It's too dangerous for us to be walking out here now."

"But I thought you said it was a ten mile walk to town?" Missy was confused.

"Yeah, well I decided we've risked our lives enough for one night and I don't know about you but I'm pretty beat."

"Hell yeah. I feel like a Mack truck hit me, and my feet are starting to get blisters. I'd love to sleep."

"Oh crap," he said as if suddenly realizing something. His head lamp was shining us in the eyes as he looked us. "I'm sorry. I'm such an insensitive jerk."

"Huh? Why?" Sometimes I found it hard to follow him.

"I never asked you guys if you were okay from your crash. I've just been pushing you to keep moving. You probably *are* hurting." He seriously looked bothered by this.

"Don't beat yourself up over it *Hallmark*, girls are tougher than you think." Missy adjusted the strap of her purse on her shoulder, impatient to move.

"Actually I'm surprised neither of you are whining. When my sister gets hurt she complains every chance she gets."

Missy started laughing. "I think if it were different circumstances we both *would be* whining. But now that you mention it."

He chuckled. "Can you two make it two more miles?" There was honest concern there.

Missy and I both looked at each other. I nodded. "Yeah."

"*Without* the whining?" he teased.

That, I couldn't promise him.

Lucky for him, though, we were too focused on seeing where we were walking to do much talking.

I got the feeling Jason could have moved a lot faster without us, but he even kept checking to make sure we were keeping up without any problems.

"Look," he said, after we'd been walking for about ten minutes. "I think I know who you're looking for. His name is Spencer, right?"

"You know him?" Missy exclaimed.

"Yeah. As a matter of fact, I can take you right to him, first thing in the morning."

"Why are you just telling us this?" I asked, feeling annoyed that he hadn't alleviated our concern as soon as we'd told him about Spencer.

"I had to decide whether you were who you said you were, and whether Spencer wanted you to find him," he said without apology in his tone.

"Well, who cares, we know now! He's okay and we're gonna see him tomorrow!" Missy said, grabbing me up in a big hug. I hugged her back, wondering why Jason hadn't asked Missy what her relationship with Spencer was, the way he had me, if as he said he was just being cautious.

For some reason I was more anxious than ever to see Spencer.

7

The house wasn't really a *house*. It was a trailer. Well, a double wide. And one in poor shape from what I could tell in the distance. Half the shingles were missing off the roof, there was a boarded up window. A ripped awning stretched out from above it. Christmas lights sparkled across it, some bulbs not working. There was a man sitting out front, a shadow of something rested on his lap. And from the little orange flicker of light ever so often, it was obvious he was smoking something, though I wasn't one-hundred-percent certain it was a cigarette.

"Hey, Buck!" Jason suddenly hollered, snagging his attention. The unexpected sound of his voice made me jump, making me feel completely ridiculous especially since the three of us were standing there holding hands. The *holding hands* part was actually Jason's idea. Since the headlamp he had didn't provide as much light as he would have liked, Jason wanted to make sure we stuck together. So he held his gun in his right hand, *my* hand in his left hand, I held onto Missy with my other hand and Missy was responsible to hold Duke's leash. And in a single line, we made it through the woods together. I wasn't complaining about the method.

Jason squeezed my hand no doubt in apology for startling me, but he didn't look at me or let go. I knew my palms were sweating and that I should have pulled my hand away, but I didn't. Because? *Well,* he hadn't. And I didn't want to be the first one to do it. It may have meant nothing to him, after all he was just trying to lead us to safety, but I was starting to think it had potential to mean something more to me and I couldn't help but wonder what it meant that he still hadn't let go even though our destination was in clear sight. But just to be on the safe side, I continued to hold Missy's hand too, so it didn't look like I *wanted* to hold on to just his because that would be embarrassing.

The guy Jason shouted to must have been Buck because he stood up and I realized with a growing uneasiness that the thing in his lap —now in his hand— was a really big gun. Like *really* big.

"Ollie? Is that you? You're back already?"

Back?

"Yeah," Jason shouted. "And I have two people with me that need a place to crash for the night, if that's okay?"

"Depends. Are they sick?"

"No."

The guy took another drag of whatever it was he was smoking. "Are you sure? Did you ask them their names?"

Geez, what was with the way they demanded names around here?

"Yes and we don't have to worry, they aren't from around here."

A pause.

"Oh, where are they from?"

"Jersey," Jason called, tucking his gun in the waistband of his pants. "They came to get Jacob's roommate."

"Spencer? No shit! Well, what are you three waiting for, come on in?!" Turning, Buck walked to the front door, swinging it open. "Yo, Kyle!" he yelled, heading inside. The door slammed behind him.

Exhaling, Jason turned his face toward us, his headlamp blinding us again. "Ready?"

Missy let go of my hand to shield her face. "Ugh, stop doing that. You're gonna fry my eyeballs or something." Even I was cringing at the light.

Thankfully, he shut it off quickly. "Sorry. I keep forgetting."

She spread her fingers open a little to peek out, and once she realized the light was gone, she dropped her hand. "Thank you."

Jason nodded, looking silly with the black and orange band around his head. "I must warn you, they are pretty extreme."

"They?" Missy pressed, skeptical.

"Him and his cousin."

"Why?"

He just laughed. "You'll see. Come on." He started to walk toward the manufactured house, pulling me along, and I became achingly aware that now we were the *only* ones still holding hands.

The moment I walked into the trailer, I gasped. If Jason heard me, he didn't acknowledge it. Instead he just silently pulled me a few feet to the left so Missy and Duke could come in too, then he let go of my hand. I was almost tempted to grasp it back or run out the door. Either one.

I stared at my best friend, watching her reaction. Missy stood there as wide-eyed as I, taking in the place. She blinked, blinked again, and I could tell she was trying to think of something to say, but like me her words left her.

After about a minute of just the sound of breathing, she turned toward the two guys standing in the sitting room and gestured to the walls. "Seriously? *What* the hell? Can you be any more hillbilly?"

The walls were lined with guns. All sorts of guns. I recognized a few. Pistol. Rifle. Shot gun. That's about as extensive as my gun knowledge was. Then there were bows and arrows. Not just one, a few. Different sizes and different kinds of arrows. On one wall was this gigantic deer head. Its beady black eyes stared at me, as if telling us to run or we'd get our heads mounted on the wall next. There was a coffee table next to a really scratched up leather couch. On the slanted table there was a littering of empty beer cans. The beer cans seemed to spread into the kitchen, trashing the counter top. The sink was filled with ice and more beer cans. Unopened ones.

The place reeked of booze, cigarette smoke, probably something a little more illegal than tobacco smoke, and the outdoors. It quickly occurred to me that I may have had better chances sleeping outside with the cannibals then sleeping in the same place as these drunken rednecks.

One of the guys smiled, and surprisingly he had all his teeth. He looked about mid-twenties, dark brown hair, blue eyes, and a grizzly beard. He was tall, too, at least three inches taller than Jason, who I'd figured from standing next to him for around five-foot-ten. This guy, however, was standing without obvious concern in his underwear. Well, plaid boxers.

"Geez, Kyle, will you go put some pants on?" Jason said, rolling his eyes. "You are going to scare the girls."

Kyle scratched his stomach. Again I was surprised to see he didn't have a beer gut, but I still didn't want to see his underwear.

Buck was stocky, shorter than Kyle and Jason. He had a buzzed haircut, and wore thin-framed glasses. He was clean-shaven and thankfully, dressed. All in redneck attire, of course. He started pushing his cousin toward the back of the trailer.

"Seriously dude, none of us want to see your junk. How many times do I have to tell you? Put some clothes on."

Kyle laughed, snatching a beer out of the sink, before disappearing into his bedroom. When the door shut behind him, Buck glanced back at us. "I'm sorry about that. My cousin is a little drunk right now."

"No shit. I wonder why," Missy said, sarcastically, still standing in front of the doorway as if she didn't want to come any further into the place either. I, myself, had unconsciously stepped closer to Jason. I only know this because I accidently bumped into him. My cheeks were burning in embarrassment, but Jason didn't seem to mind.

Buck's eyes scanned the room. "Eh, we didn't drink all these tonight. Though I'm sure my brain-dead cousin had a good amount. I'm Buck, by the way." He focused on Missy. "What's your name?"

After she answered him, I introduced myself too.

"Nice to meet you guys. Welcome to my casa. Guess it wasn't what you were expecting."

"You can say that again," Missy mumbled.

He started to laugh, then he suddenly smacked his arm, cursing. "Son of a—" Looking down at his palm, he made a face. "Damn mosquitoes." He walked over to a shirt tossed precariously over a chair and wiped his palm across it. "Yo, Melissa, shut the door before more of these bastards come in, will ya?"

"What? Oh right. Sorry." She turned, pulling the door shut behind her.

"You can unleash him now too," Jason said, pointing to Duke. "But just keep an eye on him. He has an obsession with beer."

"Does he come here a lot?" Hunching down, she unsnapped the buckle from his collar.

"Yeah, at least once or twice a week, why?"

"Explains his addiction."

Jason laughed, but I didn't. I couldn't. I wasn't exactly comfortable with all this weaponry out in the open and I was worried Missy's fresh mouth was going to get us in trouble, or offend them or something.

But Buck surprised me by laughing too. "You're spunky, I like it." He turned toward me, giving me the whole once-over assessment. "What about you though? What are you like? You haven't said anything yet?"

I didn't like the way he looked at me. "Not true," I gulped, trying to level my voice. "I said my name."

A comforting arm went around my shoulder and before I knew it, Jason was squeezing me lightly against his side. "I like that she's more reserved. It doesn't give me a headache. Mouth, on the other hand, never stops." He looked behind me, no doubt making a face or winking at Missy.

"Shut up, *Hallmark*," she retorted, and from the corner of my eye I saw her give him the finger.

"See," he chuckled. "It's never ending."

Buck laughed again, peering over his shoulder. "What the hell is taking Kyle so long to put on a pair of pants?"

"I bet you twenty," Jason said, dropping his arm from my shoulder. "That he's face first on the bed passed out."

Buck's head instantly turned. "Oh you're on."

A smirk spread on Jason's face as he removed his backpack, dropping it to the floor by my feet. "Be right back," he prompted, eagerly following Buck down the hallway without another word.

Raising my eyebrow, I looked over at my best friend. She was shaking her head, still staring at the walls.

"This place looks like it coughed up *Budweiser* and shit out ammo. Seriously, where the hell are we?"

"Right smack in the middle of my worst nightmare." My eyes took in the room again. "I can't believe we were sleeping here. Do you think they have bed bugs?"

"Oh God, stop. I don't even want to think about what's crawling inside this place. When was the last time they cleaned this trailer, *never*?"

The bedroom door down the hall creaked open, followed by the boys' laughter and footsteps. Sparing my best friend one more glance, I mumbled, "Last chance, stay in here or stay out there?" I pointed toward the door behind her. "Your call." I already knew what I wanted.

She considered it. "Well, at least here if someone comes to bite our faces off, we get our choice of whatever weapon we want to blow theirs off first, right?" Sadly, she was completely serious.

I sighed, looking at the sink with apprehension. *We were staying.* "I think I might need one of those beers."

My best friend exhaled sharply beside me. "I want a lot more than one."

8

We were sitting in the small room with all the guns, drinking and talking. Kyle wasn't with us. Jason was right, Kyle was passed out on the bed, but since he wasn't passed out *face-first* on the bed, Buck wouldn't cough up the twenty bucks. I probably wouldn't have either. That's what happens when you make specifics. *A bet is a bet.* Jason mucked that one up.

I finished drinking my can of beer and placed it on the coffee table, feeling slightly buzzed. I wasn't sure what everyone was talking about because my thoughts were jumbled and all over the place so my attention span was pretty pathetic. It was like my brain was a load of laundry, spinning round and round just getting more tangled up by the second. Plus, there was the deer head directly in front of me on the wall, and for some reason I couldn't ignore it. I was almost convinced it was staring specifically at me. And after two minutes of staring back at it, I couldn't handle it anymore.

"Okay, that thing is starting to really freak me out," I said out loud, to no one in particular. When I realized I called it a *thing*, I erupted into a giggling fit. I'm not sure why.

"Oh boy," Missy sighed, taking a sip of her beer. "Dee's had one too many."

No I haven't, I thought stubbornly, my giggles instantly stopping.

"I thought you only had one?" Buck stared at me confused.

"I did. Missy doesn't know what she's talking about."

Missy started to laugh. "She never drinks. One is all it takes. Trust me, I know from experience."

I rolled my eyes. *Whatever.*

"Nice, a cheap date." Buck picked up his beer, chugged it and crushed the can. "I can dig that."

Uh, wait…what?

"You ain't diggin' anything," Jason suddenly said, scooting the kitchen chair he was sitting on closer to me, placing his hand on my back. I gulped. He was so close. *Too* close. "So don't get any ideas."

"Yeah," I mumbled, uncomfortably. It took everything in me to *not* move the chair away and to *not* move even closer to him. I went to reach for a new beer.

"No. I think you've had enough for one night." Jason pushed the can out of my reach.

"Excuse me?"

"Look you hardly ate anything, you're tired, you're buzzed, and it's probably best if you call it a night."

Was he kidding me? Who did he think he was? My father?

"Wow. Party pooper," Buck said, cracking up. "You got it bad for this chick, huh?"

I didn't miss the way Jason rolled his eyes. It was that obvious. *Fine, I thought. Whatever. He could get his hand off my back then.*

I jumped up, pissed, with every intention to storm off, but once I started walking, I realized I had nowhere to go.

A chair scrapped across the floor, followed by footsteps. "You and Melissa are sleeping in Buck's bed," Jason said, coming up behind me. "I'll show you where." His breath blew across my neck and my stomach did this strange little cartwheel. It aggravated me more.

"Look—" I spun around with every intention of telling him off, but once our eyes met, I instantly forgot what I wanted to say. His eyes looked amazing. I mean absolutely amazing, more now than ever. It must have been the light above our heads, because his eyes were shining more like an emerald now than topaz, my birth stone, and it took my breath away. I hadn't realized there was so much green in them before. Light green. Dark green. Bright green. They were beautiful. And I couldn't look away. *Damn it.*

But he did. *Of course. He could.* "Buck is crashing with Kyle and I'm going to take the couch." His tone was casual, unaffected, as if I hadn't just gotten completely tongue-tied looking at him, or he was ignoring that I did. His breath smelt like beer.

I exhaled in annoyance, realizing too late I probably just blew *my* beer breath all over *his* face. "Is there a lock on the door?" I didn't want any of these boys, including him, near me and Missy. I avoided his eyes when I spoke this time, but I still looked at him. I couldn't help it.

His lips twitched and I realized staring at his mouth didn't help either. "Yeah but if you lock it, Missy won't be able to get in." A smirk formed on his annoyingly handsome face.

Oh yeah. Duh. Nice one, Dee. You idiot. I pulled my eyes away from him all together. "What about bed bugs?" I hissed. "Clean sheets? Pillows?" I was starting to ramble. Insecurity, frustration and beer. Bad combination.

Jason just shook his head, amused. "Only thing I can promise you is there are pillows."

"Oh that makes me want to climb into bed."

He leaned forward, his breath tickling my skin and whispered in my ear, "I'd lie on top of the covers if I were you, just saying."

I suddenly got the heebie-jeebies just thinking about the bed. Or maybe it was from the near proximity of Jason? "On second thought, maybe I'll just take the couch." I tried to move past him to sit back down.

He chuckled, catching my arm. "Come on. It's fine. I'm just teasing." I wasn't so sure about that. *I just wasn't sure what I wasn't sure about, the bed or him?*

He pushed me lightly down the hall, into his friend's bedroom, and instantly I felt awkward. There I was standing in a bedroom with a guy I only met this afternoon, in a double-wide, with real guns as wallpaper, under the influence. *Yeah. I never saw this coming.* This was like those scenes you wanted to avoid at all costs because it was a recipe for disaster.

He put his hands on my shoulders and I tensed. "Hey, relax. You don't have to worry Dee. I'm not going to try anything and I won't let them either."

I snorted. *Of course he wouldn't because he didn't like me.* "Yeah…" I scooted his hand off my shoulder, so he wasn't touching me anymore. "I got that much already." The whole *rolling his eyes at Buck* thing came back to me very vividly.

I heard him take a step back, shutting the door behind him. "What are you talking about?" He actually sounded at a complete loss.

"Never mind." I walked toward the bed, blowing off his question. The last thing I wanted was to have this conversation so I would be offended out loud.

He caught up to me, spinning me around. "No. You can't say something like that and expect me to just let it go." His hazel eyes blazed greener yet.

"Forget it," I sighed, trying to think rationally for a moment. "Forget everything I say and do tonight. Okay. I'm just drunk."

"You aren't drunk." His tone accused me of just using it as an excuse to avoid answering him. *Which I kind of was.* "You just have a buzz... I have one too."

And then it hit me. *Wow. I couldn't even get a buzzed Jason to want me.*

I shook my head, trying to walk away from him again. His hand caught mine and there went that stomach cartwheel again.

He didn't say anything to me. I don't remember moving. I don't remember him moving. But suddenly he was *right* there. *Again.* His hand still holding mine.

"Tell me," he said, his warm breath hitting my face again.

I shook my head for the second time.

Letting go of my hand, he brushed a strand of hair out of my face, his fingertips lingering behind my ear. He was staring at me so intensely I thought I was going to have a heart attack. Slowly, *very slowly,* his fingertips trailed down my neck, burning a path across my skin. I couldn't breathe.

A line formed between his brows, as if he was trying to figure something out. On an exhale, as if he had been holding his breath too, he dropped his hand away. "Listen, I don't know what's going on in that head of yours but if it has anything to do with me not finding you attractive, you can toss that crap in the trash. You're not only beautiful..." He stepped backward, his eyes not leaving my face. "You're the most beautiful girl I ever met."

I stared at him, unblinking. My heart was beating so loudly in my chest I was certain he had to have heard it. I was certain everyone in the other room could hear it. "Why did you just tell me that?" Completely startled, I no longer knew what to think. Butterflies were rapidly filling my stomach.

He kept stepping slowly backward until his hand clasped the door knob, but his eyes never left mine. "Because I like it better when you stare at me like you like me instead of when you stare at me like you don't. Makes me think I have a chance. And with everything going on right now, I want something positive to look forward to." His cheeks flushed slightly as he turned the door knob and in that second, I realized he meant it. Every word of it. He did find me attractive. We did have a connection. *And he was leaving? What?*

I suddenly didn't want him to go. "I don't understand. If you like me, why didn't you just kiss me? You had the chance." *You still do.* Of course, I wasn't saying that out loud.

He hesitated in the doorway his eyes giving me a onceover that made me go weak in the knees. "I don't kiss a girl unless I am a hundred percent certain I'm the only guy she wants to kiss." His eyes settled back on my face. I could see his restraint in them. He *wanted* to kiss me. "When we kiss it will because we both want it and we are sober. Tonight isn't that night. Good night, Dee."

And just like that, he stepped out into the hallway, the door clicking softly back in place putting distance between us. I stood there, conflicted, trying to wrap my head around what he just said. I didn't understand. Did he think I didn't want to kiss him? Wait. Did I want to kiss him or was it just the beer talking? Or was that what he meant? I stood that way for a few more minutes, replaying everything over. His words came back to me, repeating in my mind like lines from poetry.

When we kiss.

Not if.

When.

I climbed on top of the comforter, shutting my eyes. My heart beat was still unsettled, butterflies still crazy wild in my stomach. *I was the most beautiful girl he'd ever met?* Now *that* was something I'd never heard from a guy before.

***

A phone was ringing. I groaned, turning on my side. Then it dawned on me. Shit. *A phone was ringing*. I jumped up, shoving Missy to wake her. She almost fell off the bed.

"Yo. What the hell, Dee?" she bitched, sounding entirely too pissed for this early in the morning. Then again if she woke me up that way, I'd be pissed too.

"Your phone is ringing," I said in a panic, and as if to prove the point, it rang again at that moment.

Her eyes widened and she immediately dove for her purse that was on the night stand, knocking over a picture frame in the process. Snatching it, she quickly flipped it over, dumping the contents of the purse onto the bed and started digging through everything to find her cell. She picked it up, staring down at the number. She didn't waste a beat. "Hello? Spencer?" Her voice no longer sounded groggy.

I was wide awake too, my heart already pounding, as she put the call on speaker.

"Where *are* you guys?" Spencer urged through the phone. Once again, it wasn't the best connection. There was a lot of background noise. I lowered my ear closer to the phone to try and hear better.

"We had a situation," Missy replied in apology. "But we are here. We are in town. We are coming to get you."

"Well hurry up, *please*, I need—" Suddenly Spencer was cursing. His voice somewhat mashed by the sound of something banging. Someone screaming.

"*Spencer?*" Missy cried, frantic. "What was that? Are you okay?"

Heavy breathing created more static. Then there was coughing. More screaming. Another loud bang. Some more cursing. Spencer started to say something then there was just abrupt silence.

The two of us stared at the phone in shock. Her battery just died.

"You've *got* to be kidding me?!"

That's exactly what I was thinking. Missy was trying to turn her phone back on anyway. "Come on. *Come on,* turn on you stupid piece of—"

"Missy—" I reached out, putting my hand on her arm. "Forget it. It's dead."

"But, *Dee.*" Her blue eyes were wide, almost in tears. "It was Spencer."

"I know. I know." I thought for a quick second, panicking. "Go wake the guys. Maybe one of them has a phone. We can call him back and—"

"And what? *Huh?*" She started shaking her head, her knotted blonde hair falling across her cheeks. "I don't remember the number; do you remember it?"

I made a face. Crap.

"Exactly. So even if they have a phone, how are we supposed to call him *back*?!" She tucked the strands behind her ears in frustration.

She had a point. I considered again, trying to think of something. Anything. "Well they know Spencer, right? So maybe they know the number to his roommate?"

She didn't say anything. She just rolled off the bed and hurried to the bedroom door, swinging it open. Someone fell back against her legs. She screamed. I jolted readying myself to run, but it was only Jason. He woke up instantly, Duke's head peeking up over the top of his shoeless feet.

"What are you doing?" Missy hissed, giving him a shove to get him to move off her faster.

I leaned forward on the bed, looking down the hallway past them. No one was sleeping on the couch. Furrowing my brow, I glanced at them. I didn't understand.

"I *was* sleeping." He stood up, stretching his back. His five o'clock shadow was even darker on his face and he had bags under his eyes.

Duke stood up too and padded over to Missy. She petted him but kept her face turned toward Jason in question.

"Why are you two up so early?" he yawned, staring down at his watch.

I self-consciously ran my fingers through my bedhead when he wasn't looking. "Why were you sleeping on the floor?"

"I asked first." His voice was still deep and groggy, thickened with sleepiness.

Missy tossed her hair up into a ponytail and stormed past him into the hall, frantic. "Spencer just called and my phone died in the middle of it." She flashed her eyes at him as if saying, *can you believe it?* "Something is going on over there. We *need* to call him back. Please tell me you have his roommate's number?"

Jason yawned again. "Jacob doesn't have a phone."

"What?" I was off the bed now, standing in my socks on the stained carpet, still wearing the same clothes from yesterday. "Then how did he just call us?" *Oh man, Jason looked so cute with bed hair.*

"I don't know," he mumbled. He sounded so damn tired. That was super sexy too for whatever reason.

Missy exhaled sharply and started pacing up and down the hallway. Leaning back against the wall, Jason raked a hand through his light brown, messy locks. "Actually there's an old pay phone in the campground near Jacob's place. Perhaps he used that?"

"A payphone? Really?" He had to be joking.

"No, serious. I'm not lying. It's ancient as shit but it still works."

"You don't think someone had a cell phone he could have used?" Missy stopped in her tracks, incredulous. She was obviously having a hard time believing a payphone still existed, let alone still worked. Like me.

He shrugged. "Anything's possible, I guess. But most people out this way don't have cell phones."

Missy grumbled beneath her breath. "Yeah because you are all hillbillies."

"No because reception sucks out here. We are in the middle of nowhere. I told you that yesterday."

Bewilderment and shock flashed across her face. "So you seriously don't own a phone?"

"No. I really don't own a phone. I don't even have a landline anymore."

She threw her hands out in frustration. "How do you guys communicate out here? Paper cups and strings? What do you do, just *play* telephone?"

He shook his head. "Look. I am not a morning person. Please hold off the hostility until later."

"I just want to go find our friend. That's all I want," she sighed. Her look was desperate. "You said you will help us find him. *How* are we going to do that?"

He spared a glance at me then back at Missy, the grogginess of sleep still fighting him. "Did he sound like he was in trouble?"

I walked closer, straightening out my shirt, hoping I didn't have pillow lines on my face. "It sounded like there was a lot of commotion going on. There was coughing and screaming…"

Jason nodded but made a face. "Okay. Let me wake up the guys. They can help us."

"Thank you," I mumbled. Really, Jason didn't have to help us out at all. It wasn't like Spencer was his friend. He only knew of him.

I bit the inside of my cheek as I stood there, really considering his help. Including Jason in our search for Spencer put him in danger, just as much as it put us in danger. It was wrong to ask him to do that, to risk his life for *our* friend. But even though I recognized this, I didn't think it mattered much because my mind kept saying, *this is Spencer* and I couldn't ignore the fact Missy and I were so close to finding him. His mom and dad would be so happy.

And maybe it was selfish of us, but we didn't get this far and dealt with all we had, to go home empty-handed. We *were* going to find Spencer and finally bring him home, no matter what. I just might need some psychological help afterward.

As Jason started to bang on the door of the room Kyle and Buck were in, I asked him again why he was sleeping on the floor.

He peered back at me, half-shrugging. "I decided it was safer for you two if I kept guard. Drunk guys who don't see that many hot girls don't really think straight. I just wanted to be sure you two were safe."

Missy and I just stared at him, shocked.

"You could have just let Duke lay there," my friend finally said, a very grateful tone in her voice.

He shook his head. "Duke only sleeps where I sleep. He protects me. I'll protect you."

9

Kyle and Buck were taking guns off the wall and shoving them into a duffel bag as if it was the end of the world. And by their conversation, they truly thought it was.

"I always knew this was going to happen," Kyle said, not showing an ounce of a hangover. That didn't give me high hopes for his liver. If he was that drunk last night and was fine today, that just meant he usually drank more.

"No you didn't," Buck countered, looking slightly rough this morning. His liver must have a better chance at surviving. "You always said it would end with the alien attack. I was the one that predicted the zombie attack."

Crossing my arms over my chest, I glanced over at Jason for the umpteenth time. He was sitting on the couch, lacing up his boots, shaking his head. No doubt, he was tempted to say they weren't zombies. Heck, so was I. But I didn't feel like opening that "can of worms" with those two.

Jason was oblivious to me staring at him. I was getting good at that—looking like I'm not looking. Plus it wasn't hard to do. Jason barely looked at me since we woke him up. I tried not to take it personal. It was obvious he was still half-asleep. I'd admit I felt a little disappointed he didn't mention anything about our "moment" last night, but then again, I'm not sure I was ready to dissect that "moment" either. Right now, this was about finding Spencer not finding out what's going on between us.

"So all these guns…" Missy pointed out, snagging my attention. "It's not just because you are sick, twisted deer hunters?"

"We hunt," Buck agreed, adjusting his glasses on his nose. "A man's gotta eat. But these babies…" He turned, picking up two crazy big guns off the rack. "We purchased for just *this* reason." He showed them to us, as if he was proud of them.

"And I worried that *he* was crazy." She pointed to Jason. "He at least shot someone to save us. I think you would shoot someone just for fun."

Buck laughed and started to shove the guns in the bag. "I haven't yet but I've been tempted a few times. I've been looking forward to this. We've been preparing."

It was definitely obvious.

"Wow, you really *are* crazy." Missy flashed me a look that clearly stated *what the hell? Who are these people?*

Kyle smiled as he held up a few boxes of ammo. "Being prepared does not make you crazy."

Missy just stared him. "Okay. Whatever you say."

My eyes drifted back to Jason inconspicuously. He was now digging through his backpack. Duke was lying on the cushion next to him, watching him intently like I was. "I think you two are getting carried away." He peered upward at them over the top of his bag. "All we need is to borrow your four-wheelers to get to town as quickly as possible. You don't need to come."

"When I bust a cap in some psycho bitch to save your ass, you'll be glad we came." Buck pretended to cock the gun in his hand.

"*Please*," Kyle urged, turning to Jason. "I'll probably be the one to save you. I'm a better shot then he is."

"Bull shit," Buck snapped. "Maybe in your dreams."

"Oh don't even go there." Kyle rounded on his cousin. "You know damn well—"

"Actually…" Jason cut in, shutting them up. "If you two came along *I'll* probably be the one to save *you* and I already have enough people to protect. I've changed my mind. I want you two to stay here."

Kyle's smile fell instantly. "You're joking, right?"

Jason shook his head.

"You're serious?" His eyes widened. "You actually expect us to stay here?"

Jason didn't cave. "Yes. I'd like you to. Someone needs to stay and guard this place anyway. I'm going to have to crash here again since I never got to where I was going. All we need is the four-wheelers. Please. It would help me out big time."

Buck let go of the gun he was about to pull off the wall and turned back to face us. "Buzz kill, Bro. Damn." He tucked his hands into the front pocket of his sweatshirt, shaking his head in disbelief. "So you really haven't gotten there yet?"

Jason stood up. "Does it *look* like I have a truck battery?" Frustration tightened his voice. "Crap came up. I'll get to it."

I gulped. I didn't know what they were talking about but I knew by *crap*, he meant Missy and me. We totally took over his life, all to find our friend. Suddenly I felt guilty. Maybe it all *did* matter.

"Okay, it's just that time is—"

"I'll get to it," Jason said again with more bite to his words, letting him know the conversation was over.

"Fine," Buck shrugged, sparing Missy and me a quick glance. "But if you are going to do this first for them, at least give the girls a gun each. I'd feel better. You have too much to risk."

"If Mouth had a gun, my life would be in more danger." A smirk spread on Jason's face this time. He was obviously trying to change the atmosphere inside the suddenly smaller trailer, but it didn't make me feel better.

"Ha. Ha. Very funny." Missy rolled her eyes. "But don't worry, I don't even know how to shoot a gun."

"Phew, that's good news." He was clearly teasing, but his green-brown eyes looked slightly relieved.

"What about you?" Kyle asked, peering down at me. He was finally coming back into the conversation, but he wasn't pleased.

I cracked my knuckles. "I've shot a few times. My grandmother's side is big into hunting and target practice." Missy made a face, but I've never killed an animal before. I only shot paper bodies and moving targets.

"What did you shoot?" Buck looked at me impressed and curious from behind his glasses.

I bit the inside of my cheek before answering. "A rifle and a pistol."

Nodding, he pulled a rifle out of his extra-large canvas bag. "Here, how about this one?"

"Uh…" I didn't know what to say. I didn't want to touch it, let alone take it.

He must have sensed my hesitation. "Jason can't protect you all the time and that dog of his can't hear shit on his left side." He wiggled the gun a little in his hand. "You should take this."

"Don't bash my dog," Jason glared at him. "And I'm sorry but she's not carrying that gun around. She has nowhere to put it."

"Alright, fine." He turned, putting it back on the wall. "But she should still have one." Facing us again, he reached back into the bag pulling out a pistol. He showed it to me. "How about this small fella? You can tuck this in the back of your shorts."

I spared Jason a glance to see his reaction. He wasn't saying *no*. So slowly I nodded, gingerly taking the gun. "Don't I need a permit to carry this though?

Buck laughed. "No one's supposed to be carrying anything, but this is the country. If you don't have a gun on you, then well you're just stupid."

"Then I'm stupid," Missy retorted, unbothered. "Because you are not going to change my mind, I'm not carrying one. I hate guns. They freak me out…. She can carry all she wants, but not me."

Kyle considered her. "Fine. What about bow and arrows. Or do you have an aversion to all weaponry?"

Missy blew out a breath. "I'm not lugging anything else besides my purse. My back is killing me from yesterday. That man was freaking heavy."

"Oh your back hurts? You should have told me," Buck quickly began, "I have something that's really good for—"

"No!" Jason and I blurted at the same time, with the same rash tone. Last thing we needed was my best friend to be high as a kite.

Buck started to laugh and Missy rolled her eyes, no doubt at us.

"Two guns are enough," Jason added, back to his "super-composed, let's get our shit together and go" stance. *How could he just flip the switch like that?* "But I will take some more ammo if you have it. I'm running low."

"Of course." Kyle headed toward the drawer because he was closer, but he was sulking.

"It's always better to be safe than sorry." Buck looked at his cousin. "Give them extra for both just in case."

"Thanks, man," Jason replied when Kyle handed him the ammo. He didn't waste any time storing it into the side compartment of his pack. After everything was zipped back up, Jason peered over at us, no expression on his face. "I'm ready when you two are."

I peered down at the gun in my hand, unsure. It took a lot of mental persuasion, but I finally tucked it into my waistband. Like Buck said, *better safe than sorry...* Taking a deep breath, I tried to appear confident. "Okay, I'm ready."

We both looked at Missy. She nodded. "Yup, me too."

"Alright," Jason said, placing his hands on the straps of his pack. "Let's get going then." He whistled and Duke instantly jumped off the couch, coming up beside him. "Thanks again guys for letting us crash here, and for the ammo and the quads. I appreciate it."

"You're welcome, Bro. Anytime," Buck replied.

"Yeah," Kyle sighed. "Though we should be going with you."

Jason clapped a hand between Kyle's shoulder blades, lips twitching. "I promise you dude when the end of the world *actually* comes, you can have my back. Alright?"

"I better," he groaned.

"Yeah you better," Jason agreed, holding back a smirk. "Because we all know you are a better shot than Buck."

We followed Jason outside and it was *cold*. Not like there is snow on the ground, your nose turns pink, and you can see your breath, cold, but that too-early-morning-thought-it-was-supposed-to-be-spring air that makes you realize winter isn't over and summer is way too far away cold. I crossed my arms and stomped through the weeds behind Missy. The partially frozen grass tickled my shins and I silently wished I had on pants instead of yesterday's shorts. But the sky was clear, so hopefully that meant the day would warm up soon.

Jason stopped and faced us once he reached the first quad. "Here…" He handed Missy and I something small. The material rubbed against my palm. "I made you both one. Wear them."

"You made us bracelets?" Missy stared down at her hand incredulously.

I was looking at my own palm. The bracelet was a braided, string bracelet about an inch thick. The weaving was very intricate.

"They aren't for fashion," Jason continued. "They are survival bracelets, made from the toughest *Paracord* I have. There's about five feet of it wrapped up like that. It's good to have in case of emergencies."

"What the heck would we do with five feet of string?" Missy's tone didn't change.

"Not string, *Paracord*," he corrected. "And a lot. You can lash together a shelter, make a bow, start a fire, fish, mark your trail, make a tourniquet, or even floss your teeth. And just so you know it can hold your body weight plus some before snapping."

Wow. Impressive. "That's insane. And you made these? For us?"

His green-brown eyes peered over at me and he shrugged. "I had a lot of time on my hands to waste last night."

I thought of him sitting outside the bedroom and felt guilty all over again.

"How didn't you pass out?" Missy pressed. "I drank as much as you and I passed right out."

He didn't seem fazed. "I have more body weight than you. You two are string beans."

"Well she's definitely a string bean," she instantly agreed. "But I'm rounder. I'm not sure what vegetable that makes me."

He rolled his eyes at her and pointed at me. "Okay. We need to get some food in your stomach," he said, not humoring her, "Before your blood sugar drops again."

I ran my tongue over my teeth. They felt icky. "Personally I'd rather have a toothbrush and toothpaste. Or mouthwash."

The mints Missy gave me still didn't give me minty fresh breath confidence. That's one of the reasons I wasn't talking much and one of the reasons I was keeping my distance from Jason. There was nothing sexy about bad breath.

"There's a convenience store just on the edge of town. We can stop at it, use the bathroom, grab some food and get your toothbrush. You two can save money and use my toothpaste, if you want."

"Wait. You have toothpaste?" I stared at him like *Are you kidding me?*

"Yeah. Of course." He furrowed his brow at me not understanding.

So I said it in plain English. "Why didn't you say something sooner? Give it to me."

He laughed, catching on. "I doubted you wanted to use my toothbrush."

"I can still use my finger. It's better than nothing. Duke has better breath than I do right now."

Jason laughed louder. "Okay. Okay. Sorry." He dropped his pack on the seat of the four-wheeler and dug through it again while Missy and I held our index fingers out to him. He untwisted the cap and squeezed some blue gel onto our fingertips.

As we scrubbed our teeth with our fingers, he pulled something else out of his bag and unrolled it. A long sleeve shirt. I was so jealous.

"Here…"he said, when I dropped my hand away from my mouth and spit on the grass. "You are shivering. This should help."

"Ohmigod, really? Thank you." I took the shirt from him and he offered me a small smile.

"It might smell a little. I wore it for like an hour the other day but it's the cleanest thing I have."

"That's fine." *What did I care? I was freezing.* I pulled the material over my head—gratefully—and realized it didn't smell bad. It smelt like campfire smoke and bug spray. And for some stupid reason it made my stomach flip again.

Before we left, we sprayed each other with bug spray again since it wouldn't be early-morning-freezing cold forever, then we waved goodbye to the boys who were smoking cigarettes on their fold-up chairs and jumped onto the four-wheelers. There were three of them: a black, a camouflaged, and a red and black one. Duke sat on the back of Jason's, strapped in behind him.

I was thankful mine was an automatic. I was never good at driving stick, even on the quads. Taking a big breath for courage, I turned on the engine and a few seconds later we were starting day two of our Spencer rescue mission. But this time we were aware that at any second a stranger might want to bite our faces off.

As I drove, the gun rested cold against my back as reminder.

10

The convenience store was small. One single gas pump was out front with three different nozzles. The premium nozzle had a black bag tied around it, obviously not working. The left side of the store was spray-painted with obscenities that I knew would impress Missy.

I was starting to think Spencer picked this place to live because it was the last place anyone would look for him. It was secluded, small, and hours away from his family. But how could he live out here?

Then I thought about it. Spencer didn't grow up with much, so he didn't need much. A town like this probably didn't bother him. But it bothered me and Missy that after all these years of friendship he could just get up and leave without even saying goodbye.

And worse, leave us—*for this*.

More than once I thought about why he ran away in the first place. I never expected him to be *that* teenager. But the moment he turned sixteen he was gone. Maybe there were signs and we ignored them. Had things been going on in Spencer's life that we never paid attention to? Bad things that would make him run and leave all his family and friends behind? Or did he just have enough of it—of us—and decided to take a break from reality for a while until he was scared enough to come back home?

I wish I knew the answers, or at least some of them.

"Cute place," Missy said, examining the storefront. "Like the art work."

"That's new." Jason raised an eyebrow, his tone weary. "It wasn't there last time I stopped here."

"Guess the owner pissed someone off?"

"Huh." Concern was written all over his face. "Graffiti isn't a big thing around here."

"Well someone always enjoys breaking the rules," Missy replied sarcastically, still staring at the spray paint.

Shaking his head at her, and probably the vivid curse words, Jason opened the door. A bell chimed lightly.

"Stay," he told Duke before he disappeared inside. Missy followed.

I hesitated for a moment, still thinking too much. Duke stared at me, whimpering quietly. I told him it was going to be okay as I started to walk through the doorway.

Then Missy screamed.

I ran the rest of the way inside, immediately freezing next to the candy section.

A gun was leveled at Jason.

Jason had his gun leveled too.

I didn't freak out. I immediately reached around my back, pulled the gun out of my waistband and leveled it at the man's face. Well, maybe that *was* me freaking out. Who knows?

All I knew was I was standing there, a cold pistol in my hand, while Missy stood clutching a bag of *Tootsie Rolls* to her chest and Duke barked anxiously outside, his paws slamming against the glass door, trying to get in.

"Drop the gun or I will shoot," I demanded. I was surprised and grateful to hear my voice wasn't quivering. Most likely it was because I had the upper hand—I was pointing the gun at him, not vice versa. Vice versa I'd probably be peeing myself or having a panic attack. I didn't look at Jason even though I had a strong urge to peek at him, to see what his reaction was. Instead I kept my eyes level on the Spanish guy in front of me so he knew I meant business.

He glanced over at me with just his eyes—brown, surprised eyes—then he stared back at Jason. "Name," he commanded, "And I'll lower it."

Again with the freaking name thing. I thought country folk were supposed to have manners?

"Jason. *Damn it,* Nunez. You know I'm not sick."

"I don't know anything anymore." Nunez lowered his gun though, sighing. "Lower your pieces, I'm not gonna shoot."

"You sure?" Jason said dryly. "I'm starting to see why people are spray-painting obscenities on your store. This how you greet all of them anymore?"

A short pause. "As of late…yeah."

An awkward moment followed. Duke's continuous barking was the only sound. Finally, Jason exhaled, tucking his gun back on his side. "I'll be right back. I'm going to go let Duke know we are okay." As he walked past me he whispered, "Don't lower your gun just yet."

I gulped, refocusing my attention to Nunez. He was around five feet, seven inches but what he lacked in height he made up for in weight. He was muscular and thick. His olive-skinned biceps stuck out of his convenience-store polo. He had his hair gelled down so it looked black, and portrayed a very pronounced, square jaw. I couldn't help but think if he got sick and bit someone, it probably would hurt like hell. He had a build like the pit bull outside.

"He just told you not to lower your gun, didn't he?" Nunez chuckled. "Very well, I'm going to go finish sweeping the floor though."

I kept my gun aimed on him. "How about you don't move instead and tell me why you asked his name like that when you already knew it?"

"Come on, you know why."

When I didn't say anything, he raised a dark, wide eyebrow. "You do know why, right?"

He glanced at Missy, who was still holding her candy but not in the death grip she originally had. She was staring at me, probably wondering who this girl with the gun was and what happened to her best friend. He gave Missy the same look of disbelief.

"Neither of you know. Wow." He furrowed his brow. "You're not from around here, are you? I never seen you two before, and trust me I'd remember two girls like you, especially *that senorita* over there."

"No," I said in a tone that warned him he better not be getting any ideas about my best friend. "So tell us, does it have to do with what's happening out there?"

Exhaling, he leaned his gun up against the end of the food rack. "You two picked a hell of a time to come visit." *Wasn't that the truth?* "Yes. This sickness is affecting people mentally. It makes them forget who they are, where they live, and so on. It's one of the first clear signs."

"Like Alzheimer's?" Missy asked timidly. "I hear that's how people with Alzheimer's get."

He shook his head. "This is worse. And it spreads so fast." The door chime went off again. Footsteps followed, but my attention stayed on him. "If anything I'd say it's more as how a rabid animal gets."

"Rabies," Jason said coming up beside me, touching my arm. I was glad I didn't have my finger on the trigger. "…is most commonly transferred through a bite." He nodded toward the gun and I knew it was okay to put the gun away now. His hazel eyes said *thank you* before turning his face toward Nunez. "And this illness affecting people is spreading without saliva contact, but it is spreading quickly like rabies does, faster even."

It was only when I put the gun back in my waistband that I realized my fingers were trembling. This all might be just a little bit too much for me to handle.

"Airborne, maybe?" *That would make it spread fast.*

"No or we'd all be sick, especially him," Nunez said, pointing at Jason. Jason's face gave away nothing, but his body tensed.

"Why him?" I couldn't help ask as I eyed the sudden change in Jason's stance.

More awkward silence. Nunez stared at Jason, and Jason stared back at him. Finally, Jason sighed. "I've just been exposed to more of the infected than I wanted." His expression gave nothing away, but his voice hinted at something more, something emotional. My gut twisted. He must have known someone that died of this illness. Or maybe he's just had to shoot more than one person and his guilt was weighing on him. Maybe he killed that girl that he spoke of, the one it took six shots to bring down, too?

I wasn't sure how I felt about that if he did.

"Maybe it's a cold?" Missy posed. "You get coughed on, sneezed on…you catch it."

"A cold that whacks out your brain function. That's a pretty messed up cold," Nunez replied.

"Well tick bites have been known to cause meningitis and Lyme's and stuff like that. Maybe it's from a tick bite or a poisonous spider bite. I mean this is the country," I retorted.

Jason rubbed at the back of his neck. "Tick bites don't progress this fast and poisonous spider bites would have swelling and an infected site. It's not that either."

"How did the plague start?" Missy asked, ripping her candy bag open.

"Very funny," Nunez said. "And I hope you plan to pay for those."

"No, I planned to eat them right in front of you then walk out of the store without paying, because I'm a rebel like that." Her words were sharp and sarcastic. "And furthermore nanez...ninez...nonez, *whatever* your name is, I was asking a serious question. I didn't pay attention in history. Maybe it's like the plague?"

"Well it's definitely killing people as fast as *the black death* did," Jason agreed. "Whatever it is."

Spencer's phone call instantly flashed in my head, my eyes widened. "Then we can't stand here procrastinating any longer," I said, bugging out, recalling the desperation in his voice. "We have to go, Jason. We have to get to Spencer."

A few more seconds of silence passed.

"Have you two considered it might be too late for your friend already?" Jason said, very slowly. "What happens if he's infected?"

"Shut up." Missy threw a handful of candies at him. "Don't jinx him. Spencer is going to be fine."

"But what happens if he is—"

"Spencer. Is. Fine," she hissed back. "He's fine."

"Okay." It didn't look like Jason believed her. And I know Missy and I wanted him to be fine, but what if he wasn't?

Jason started to walk past Nunez. "We will have to leave the quads here since we aren't allowed to ride them on the main road. It's about a three mile walk to Jacob's. Make sure you eat something before we go. I'm gonna hit the bathroom then we can go rescue your friend." He didn't sound too thrilled.

Rescuing Spencer gave me heart palpitations now. I couldn't ignore the look on Jason's face. Maybe the whole reason Spencer was calling us was because he knew he was sick. I mean if Spencer just wanted to leave this town, he could have just left. *Right?*

"And, Dee, *you* especially," Jason said, peering over his shoulder before opening the bathroom door. "Eat something."

Than it dawned on me. I didn't have any money.

I guess I'd just have to start a running tab with Missy or steal something for the first time in my life, but I doubt that would go over well with Nunez.

Thank goodness for best friends.

11

We were walking down the road, the sun rising above our heads, the cornfields to our right with stalks swaying in the wind. The stores we passed were rundown and mostly closed. Duke's tail was wagging back and forth as he glanced up at the birds that were flying around.

The day was warming up but still the temperature placed a chill down my spine. Or it could have been just the entire town in general. It gave me the creeps.

We were heading to Jacob's place at a steady pace. I was a bit winded, but I wasn't slowing down. Being in the wide open like this kind of made me feel vulnerable, but Duke wasn't barking so I wasn't too worried.

After what felt like forever we came to a fork in the road.

"About another mile straight and we are at Jacob's place," Jason said, slowing slightly as we neared the split. "Otherwise the campground is *that* way." He pointed toward the right. "Which way do you guys want to go?"

Jason hasn't said much the whole walk. In fact, none of us have. I wasn't talking because I didn't know what to say which for me isn't normal. I can always think of something to say. But since I met Jason I've been kind of lacking in that department.

I had no clue why Missy wasn't talking. Probably because she was realizing Jason might be right. Spencer might be one of them.

Or she was still pissed about him saying something might be wrong with Spencer. And Jason, well, I just couldn't figure out.

"He told us the address he was at, even if he called from the pay phone he probably went back to the house to wait for us or he would have told us to go to the campground," I said. "It's smarter to check there first."

"Okay." Jason picked his pace back up again. His backpack was bouncing against his back. I could see the outline of the gun under his shirt on his side, and a few strands of his light brown hair stood up in the breeze as he walked. His hand was clasping Duke's leash tightly—and though he was near us, it was like we weren't even there.

After about two minutes of silence, I suddenly couldn't take it anymore.

"Alright, what is the matter with you? Ever since we left the convenience store you've been all moody."

"*Thank you*, I thought it was just me," Missy huffed. "He's Mr. Grouchy all of a sudden. I prefer the sappy stay-positive-even-in-the-shitty-situations guy than this uptight negative ass."

"Gee, don't hold back how you truly feel," Jason said, sparing us a glance.

"Come on, what's your deal?" Missy pressed.

He shook his head, looking away. "I told you. I'm not a morning person."

"Don't give a cop-out answer."

He kept his eyes focused on the road. "I'm serious. And, I'm tired. Don't feel bad. It was my choice to stay up ninety-nine percent of the night, but it is starting to catch up to me."

I bit my lip, studying his profile. That wasn't all of it. "I know you are tired, but you look as if something is bothering you."

He sighed. "Yes. Okay. I have some crap on my mind. But no, I don't want to talk about it."

"Maybe we can help you?" I offered, curious to know what he was thinking about.

He shook his head again. He did that a lot. "I appreciate the concern, but you can't."

For some reason, I felt offended. *So he could help us, but we couldn't help him?*

I wasn't a damsel in distress. I've managed eighteen years of my life without his help. I could walk away now and it would be as if we never met. I could easily forget him. Well, maybe not forget him, but I could live without him.

I glanced at the woods to my left briefly then my eyes trailed down to Jason's waistline, and onto the outline of the gun again against his side. I became even more aware of the pistol shoved in my waistband.

Damn it, Missy and I could survive a whole town full of sick, flesh-eaters, couldn't we?

How come I didn't feel too confident in that?

"You know, you don't need to help us," Missy said matter-of-factly. "We never really asked you to. You just offered. From the beginning."

"I know," he agreed, absently staring at the woods. I was back to watching his profile.

"If you had plans, why did you help us?" I asked, crossing my arms over my chest. "You could have left us in the woods and you could have just told us where Jacob's house was. We would have found it eventually and you could have followed on with your own agenda."

Sighing, he turned his face toward us. "Look, I was heading on a trail up the mountain to get to the other town. I heard brakes screeching so I went toward the sound of it. That's when Duke started barking. I didn't really think. I just reacted. Then we were all just in it together." He paused, pulling his eyes back to the road. "I panicked thinking about the cops coming. I was saving my own ass, as much as yours. And honestly, I'm fine with that. I want to help you guys find your friend. I get it. I'd want to save someone I care about too."

I scrunched my brow in disbelief. "You know the other town is like thirty miles away, right?" *He seriously was going to walk that far for a car battery? Then what, lug it back another thirty miles, then trek back up a mountain, and down a mountain, and then walk another ten miles to this town? Was he crazy? Couldn't he just borrow someone's car or get a ride?*

He brought his eyes back to me. "Yeah? So?" I realized the idea wasn't ludicrous to him.

"*So?*" Missy replied, stunned. "That's a hell of a lot of walking. What are you, *Forest Gump?*"

"Gump ran, not walked." Jason shrugged again, his eyes drawn to the pavement. "Is this whole mile just going to be focused on me?"

"Is that a problem?" snapped Missy.

"Well I'd rather not talk about me."

"Yeah well, we don't always get what we want."

Jason made a sound somewhere between a laugh and groan. "Yeah. That's the story of my life lately."

Jacob's place was a small ranch, which had to be built over a hundred years ago by the sight of it. It was covered in green, asbestos siding, with brown, cracked shutters. The whole place was weather-stained with a filmy, mossy look. The roof probably leaked when it rained.

The front yard landscaping seemed trendy for this town. Trash cans, ripped lawn chairs, rusted bicycles with missing tires, snapped baseball bats, old bird cages, bags of hardened cement, and rotting fence posts.

Mostly, it resembled a junk yard.

It wasn't any of the crap that had me stopping immediately though. It was the fact that Duke was barking, hair sticking up, his entire being focused on the front door.

"Spencer!" Missy screamed, taking off toward the front steps. Jason instantly dropped Duke's leash and ran after her, grabbing her arm to yank her back. I was just steps behind him, my heart to my throat.

"Are you crazy?" He spun her around. "You know someone is sick in there."

"I know—" She glanced over her shoulder at the house, trying to pull away from him. "That's why I have to—that's why—" She kept fighting his grip. "Let me go!"

Duke ran past us to the door, his leash dragging behind him through the dirt, his bark loud.

Jason tightened his grip on her. "When are you going to get it into your head that he might be sick? You can't save someone who's sick with whatever this is, no matter how much you want to."

"I refuse to believe it," she snapped back, her blue eyes glowering at him.

"You can refuse all you want, but that won't change anything."

"I'm still going in! You won't stop me." Her pale face began to flush with anger.

He exhaled sharply. "I'm not trying to stop you."

"Yes you are," she whined in frustration as she tried to break free again.

"No, I'm not. I'm just trying to stop you from running in there blindly. You don't even have a weapon. For all you know the moment you open that door someone could attack you. Maybe Jacob. Maybe Spencer. Maybe someone else. I'm *just* trying to protect you. I don't want you to become infected too."

She stopped fighting him, startled. "Oh." Jason spared me a glance, an expression I didn't yet know him well enough to decipher, and started to loosen his grip on Missy's arm.

"Let Duke and me go in first at least." Jason stared at her, pleadingly. "That's all I want."

"Fine," she sighed, defeated, her eyes still drawn toward the house.

A vivid image of both of them getting attacked and getting infected suddenly crossed my mind and before I realized it I was reaching behind me, snatching the gun out of my waistband. *That was not happening when I had some way of stopping it.* I showed them my gun. "Let's not forget I have a gun too. I can go in first."

"Don't be ridiculous," Jason said, furrowing his brow at me. "Duke can smell and hear things we'd never pick up. We are safer if he goes in first."

I stared at him, unwavering. I could do this. "Then give me Duke."

A chuckle escaped his lips and he didn't even try to cover it up either. "You haven't even petted Duke yet and you want to walk in with him?"

"Yeah." *He was well trained, what was the big deal? I could get over my stupid fear of big dogs.*

Jason laughed louder. "Not gonna happen. I need to know whoever is holding on to him, has a strong handle on him. You are still too scared of him."

"I can do this," I said in my most confident voice I could find.

He walked up to me and put his hands on my shoulder. The barrel of the pistol was hitting him in the chest and my heart started thumping even faster. I was afraid if I dropped my hand away now, I'd accidentally fire and shoot our toes off or something. I gulped, paying close attention to my finger placement on the handle as Jason's eyes bore into mine. "And what if it's Spencer? Are you going to shoot him? Shoot him to protect my dog? And protect us?" I felt my confidence falter. "That's what I thought."

Missy suddenly grabbed his arm. "Please, whatever you do, don't kill Spencer."

He stared at her for about thirty seconds. The end of my gun still pressed against his shirt, not even bothering him in the slightest. He either had way too much trust in me or he knew I was too scared to ever pull the trigger. "Fine, I won't kill him… but if he comes after us I *will* pop one in his leg to slow him down then the three of us run like hell, deal?"

Missy and I exchanged a look, mentally communicating what we weren't saying. There was no way he was even shooting Spencer in the leg because a bleeding Spencer would give us less time to figure out a way to cure him. After we came to that conclusion, we both turned to Jason. "Deal."

We just didn't communicate how we would stop him.

12

Jason nudged the door open slowly with his shoulder, the mouth of his gun entering first as he held onto Duke's leash tightly. Duke was whimpering and Jason seemed to cock his head to the side listening intently before proceeding. Missy stood on the top step, anxiously, gripping her purse with both hands. I waited, my right foot on the first step, my left foot still on the ground. My hands were trembling on the handle of a pistol for the second time that day.

"Jacob? Spencer?" Jason called tentatively, waiting for a response. Nothing. "It's Jay. I'm coming in." A few more beats of silence then the door swung wider and he started to disappear inside, his backpack still visible from where I stood. Duke wasn't barking anymore because Jason had commanded him to be quiet. I had to hand it to the dog. For an animal he listened a lot better than I expected. Heck, a lot better than Missy and I did.

I couldn't deny though that there was just something about Jason that made you follow him. It must have been the confidence he displayed. A confidence that made you feel safe, even when you knew you weren't. And right now, I was thankful he appeared to have it all together, because somehow it was keeping *me* together, instead of me breaking down.

Missy walked in next and I hurried in behind them, closing the door. I almost opened it back up in fear it might become a hinder if we needed to leave quickly, but in the end I left it shut because I didn't want anything or anyone else coming in. I stepped further inside, cautiously looking around.

The place was in disorder. A lamp was lying on the ground, the light bulb shattered, blood stains on the cracked base, with a shade crumpled and misshapen. A coffee table was overturned. A couch was on its side some stuffing sticking out of the cushions. The beige carpet had a trail of dark stains leading to the hallway. A half-eaten pizza was upside down on the floor, cheese hardened into the carpet threads.

And the house was silent. *Too quiet.*

"I don't think anyone is in here." Disappointment and relief was clear in Missy's voice. "I don't think there has been anyone here in a while. And it smells in here. Like stinky trash."

Jason nodded. "It does stink in here, but not like a rotting body, so no one is dead in here."

"Should I even ask how you know what a rotting body smells like?" Her blue eyes stared at him accusingly.

He rolled his eyes at her but I found myself wondering as well. I mean, after all, we really didn't know anything about the guy.

"How *do* you know what one smells like?" Maybe I should have been pointing *my* gun at *him*.

"Oh geez. I don't really. I just know when you find an animal that's been dead awhile it has a bad smell. A distinct, god awful smell you can't ignore. This place just stinks like the trash hasn't been taken out in a few days."

Missy narrowed her eyes. "Okay, so if no one is dead or alive in here, why is Duke still whimpering?"

Jason had the leash wrapped so tightly around his hand that Duke was right up against his legs. He couldn't wander off if he wanted to.

"I never said no one is in here, you did." Jason started to pad further into the family room chaos. "Don't touch anything."

"No way in hell," Missy agreed.

Jason's eyes swept around the room. "Well obviously someone was attacked in the midst of dinner. Shame really. Tonios makes a bangin' pizza." He yanked on the leash, correcting Duke. "No, boy. I don't think so." Duke tilted his nose up at him and I swear he looked mad he was missing out on the spoiled pizza.

"Come on, let's check the bedrooms. If anyone is here, they would be in there. Although I'm starting to think Duke is just whining because of the blood and the food. Keep your eyes and ears open anyway. Don't want to just make assumptions now."

"Yea," Missy said, sidestepping around the lamp. She was staring at the floor with concern. "Looks like someone hit somebody pretty hard."

"Remember what Jason said…" I mumbled, stepping forward. "Don't make assumptions."

Missy nodded, her blonde hair falling forward but I could tell she was just doing it for me.

We trekked across the room, following Jason into the hallway, stopping abruptly. It didn't take a rocket scientist to figure out what room someone might be in. A book shelf was barricading one of the doorways and in front of it was a small side table. Whoever put it there was making sure the person in the bedroom wasn't getting out that's for sure. The blood trailed up the hardwood floor to the door. It was the second giveaway. *Duh!*

"Well, I doubt an infected person would drag a body to a bedroom. Ten bucks that the infected is behind *that* door."

"You and your bets," Missy mumbled, shaking her head.

"Just trying to keep it interesting." Jason paused, looking at us. "Would your friend be smart enough to think of this in a moment of panic?"

Missy shrugged, but a flicker of hope crossed her face.

"He's a smart kid," I urged, choosing my words carefully as I peered up at him. "But Spencer never has been a brave person. Him and her," I pointed at Missy, "Always crack under pressure in scary situations."

"Standing right here," Missy grumbled.

"I know that's why I pointed at you." I turned to face her. "What I am getting at is that you and Spencer usually hide behind me or come to me for answers, not the other way around. I want to believe he could think of this but he's always been the freak out and run type. I just wouldn't believe he would hit someone over the head, drag him down a hallway, lock him in a bedroom, and *then* barricade the door. I *would* believe he'd scream, maybe knock someone out, and then run like hell out *that* front door." I gestured toward it for more effect.

"Yeah..." Missy started picking at her chipping black nail polish nervously. "I can picture that. He *has* always been the first to run. Anything supernatural freaks him out."

"Right," I said in agreement, "and as much as you love the horror stuff, you only like it on TV."

She dropped her hand back to her side. "True."

"So wait—does that mean you're taking the bet or not taking the bet?" Jason asked, standing there staring at us with an expression that I took as, *Gee. Just take your time. You have all the time in the world. Nothing else matters.*

I sighed and tugged on Missy's arm. "Come on, let's go move some furniture."

"No bet then?" Jason snickered.

I ignored him.

"Personally I'd like to see you two try and move a book shelf. Should be interesting."

"Can I borrow your gun?" Missy looked at me expectantly, holding her hand out. "I'll give it right back."

I chuckled, shaking my head. "You hate guns and you don't know how to shoot it."

"Aim and pull the trigger?" Her blue eyes hinted at sarcasm.

Jason started laughing. "Yeah, something like that...okay, enough talking. Missy take Duke and Dee keep watch as I move everything away from the door."

"I'd make a rude comment back in regards to you ordering me around and all, but since it gets me out of moving furniture and gives me a cute pup to watch, I'll let it slide." Missy took the leash from him. "This time."

"Oh so the comment about shooting me was...what exactly? A promise? A joke? Didn't you say this morning I didn't have to worry about you?" He smirked at her over his shoulder.

"Oh shut up, *Hallmark*, and go move shit."

"Easier said than done," he mumbled, walking away. "Just hold onto my dog."

"You know I will."

As he started to take off his backpack, I kept my eyes alert on the hallway, just in case. That redhead in the woods did sneak up on us after all. The sound of furniture scrapping against the hardwood floor and different patterns of breathing—including my own—were the only noises I heard for a bit. I felt foolish standing guard while Jason moved everything alone. But, I guess it wouldn't be foolish if someone actually *did* attack. Then it would be foolish that none of us were watching guard.

As I stood there though, I couldn't help but wonder if I could truly pull the trigger if someone was coming toward us? I know I said I could, and I know I thought I could, but the way my heart was beating right now as I held the gun pointed toward the way we came in, with my index finger lingering over the trigger, I wasn't so sure. I didn't want to go to jail for murder. And even if it was self-defense, how does a person really move on from the image of shooting someone?

"Okay, the shit's moved," Jason said, slightly winded. The sound of his voice made me jolt. Checking one more time to make sure the coast was clear, I turned around to see him bending down to pick up his backpack. He pulled his arms through the straps and took the gun back out of his waistband. "Time to find out what's behind door number one." He placed his hand on the doorknob, pausing, to look back at Missy. "Are you sure you got a handle on Duke? Maybe I should take him?"

Missy tightened her grip. "I got him, he isn't going anywhere."

"Are you sure?"

"Yes," she grumbled.

"All right then. Get ready Dee." Jason started to turn the knob slowly with his left hand, his right hand aiming the gun at the door. "And don't accidentally shoot my dog if someone jumps out, okay?"

"Or me," Missy said.

"What the hell, me either."

I rolled my eyes. "I'm not going to shoot any of you," I mumbled impatiently, but my voice didn't sound too confident and that worried me. "Just open the damn door."

"Maybe we should just call his name first," Missy said, suddenly sounding like she was against the idea of finding out what's behind the door.

"If he's sick, he's not going to know it," Jason reminded her, his voice level. "And if he's unconscious, he's not going to answer. If you're worried, stay back. I'm opening the door."

Missy stepped back. "At least knock."

"Seriously?" He stared at her in disbelief. She nodded. "Fine." Taking his gun, Jason quickly tapped three times against the door with it, peering over his shoulder afterwards. "There. Happy?" Before she could respond, he opened the door and stepped inside.

A beat of silence passed as we waited for something. A scream. A gun shot. Jason running back out of the room. Duke barking. Something.

"Shit," Jason finally said his voice a little far away.

"What?" I hurried past Missy into the room, stopping short, staring. And kept staring, past the dresser, and the bed, toward the window and then out of it. The glass was shattered. A few bloody pieces stuck out at the edges, the rest was on the floor. There was something on the ground outside, but I couldn't tell what. Jason was staring out the window. I took a few steps closer.

He heard me and spun around. "I don't think you want to look out there."

"Why?" My tone got skeptical.

"Trust me I just don't think you do." *That* made me want to look. I took three steps forward. "Dee—you don't want to look out there." He took two steps toward me, grabbing my arm gently. "Trust me," he repeated.

I was closer to the window now. I was able to make out more. I was able to make out a…

Suddenly Jason was spinning me around. "*Don't* look, Dee."

"What's going on?" Missy paused in the doorway. I could see Duke sniffing the air and heard a small whine starting from him again. He started to pull at the leash. "What does he smell? What is that?"

"Probably just the blood," Jason said, pulling me with him as he started to walk toward her. "Whoever was in here is gone. He made a prison break."

I yanked my arm away from Jason as I processed it. *A shoe*. It was a shoe. I saw a shoe. And a leg… *Oh crap.*

Before Jason could catch me I lunged back toward the window. I heard him call my name but I ignored it, peering outside once I was at the windowsill.

Breakfast instantly came back up, burning the back of my throat. I put my hand over my mouth to try and hold it down. A body was lying on the ground under the window, or a half-mangled body. The shins were still intact but the thighs were ripped apart, clear down to the bone. The stomach was split open, intestines pulled out, maggots crawling around in it. Rib bones were sticking out, cracked and pulled apart. The shirt was torn open, lying away from the chest like an open vest, the shorts barely longer than a pair of briefs. Material littered the blood-stained ground around the legs. The neck was still there but the face… the face was completely eaten off. All I saw was blonde hair. Then it dawned on me.

Blonde hair. Ohmigod. It was Spencer.

I bent over and immediately started vomiting.

13

"Damn it, Dee. I told you not to look," Jason said, taking my gun from me, rubbing circles on my back as I remained hunched, now dry-heaving with tears in my eyes. Missy had run forward, halting just far enough away that Duke wouldn't get glass in his paws and she wouldn't get vomit on her shoes. She hadn't said anything.

She wasn't crying, screaming, or puking. Maybe she was in shock. Hell, I was in shock.

"I'm sorry," Jason mumbled, his voice sounding choked up. "Really guys, I'm sorry. I know how it feels to lose someone you care about from this. My—"

"It's not him," Missy suddenly blurted, cutting him off.

"W-what?" I croaked, peering up at her, ignoring whatever Jason was about to say. Her face was white but she was smiling. *Smiling?*

"It's not Spencer." She whirled around to fully face us, her smile even more noticeable now.

Jason exhaled, his hand hesitating on my back. "Look, I know you want it to be—"

She started shaking her head. "No. No, seriously. It's not him." She looked directly at me. "Dee, really… check it out! His shin! There's no scar."

"Huh?" *What was she talking about?* I stretched out making a face against the taste in my mouth and the smell the breeze just blew in through the broken window.

"Remember two years ago Spencer wiped out on his bike and busted open his shin on the curb," she prompted. "He has that big scar now. There's no scar here." She pointed again. "Look!"

I didn't want to look. *Now*, I didn't. Go figure. "I'll take your word for it. I didn't know Spencer had a scar."

"Yeah. He did." But her expression fell, as she seemed to really consider it. "I think…*no*, I am almost positive he got a scar or at least he should have. That was a nasty gash." Now it seemed to finally be hitting her it could be him.

Jason stepped away from me, glancing back out the window. "Spencer called you two this morning, right?"

"Yeah," I managed, still hugging my stomach.

"Well, it's not Spencer then. She's right." He faced us. "That body has maggots. I should have noticed that first. Spencer's body wouldn't have maggots yet. The eggs wouldn't have hatched yet. Those buggers have been feeding for a bit too, telling from their size."

"Ugh, please." The thought made me want to vomit again. "I don't want to hear it. Seeing was bad enough."

"Don't you get it," Missy said, smiling again. "This is good news. Spencer is still alive."

"Yeah, but someone else is dead," I countered, anxiously, still nauseated. "That's not exactly good and whoever was in this room is out there and we still don't know if it's Spencer or Jacob."

"It wasn't your friend," Jason said somberly, almost right away, no questions asked. "If he called you today, he's alert. That means he's not in *this* stage yet," he pointed toward the window as Missy had. "Once they are like this, once they are doing stuff like that, they can't process logical thoughts anymore. They only want to feed. Which means, that it must have been Jacob who did this. Jacob must be the one who is sick." His voice lowered and I instantly felt bad for him. Jacob was his friend.

"But before you do the happy dance," he prompted, staring directly at Missy, who's smile was even bigger now. "Consider this, if Spencer was staying with Jacob and Jacob got sick, then it's quite possible Spencer is infected. Maybe he is not at the final stages just yet. So when we do find him, take caution. Pay attention, and *don't* let him get close to you until we know for sure if he is infected."

"*When, not if* …you say that a lot. You really are always positive, huh?" I was feeling slightly better but also in need of major oral hygiene refresher again. I also felt bad for Jason's loss. Spencer might not be dead, but we all knew Jacob was as good as *gone*.

He shrugged. "This town isn't big. Eventually we will find him. We know he's not here, so let's go…" He reached out, handing my gun back. "To the campground. Let's not waste daylight." He took Duke from Missy, wrapping the leash around his hand as he started toward the bedroom door.

"Wait, *Hallmark*," Missy said, making him stop. "I'm guessing Jacob doesn't have blonde hair, eh? Is that how you knew it wasn't your friend right away lying out there?"

Jason peered over his shoulder at us, petting Duke. "Well that…and the fact the dude out there is pale. Jacob is Spanish. He's even darker than Nunez is."

"Jacob is Spanish?" A crease formed between her blonde eyebrows. "But his name is Jacob."

"Jacobo, actually," he prompted. "Jacobo Miquel Romero, we just shortened it to Jacob because it pissed him off." The corner of his lips curved up, but his eyes remained sad. "Jacob was a cool dude. In fact, you two would have hit it off. You both had that same damn big mouth." He paused, sighing. "Well, *anyway*, seriously can we go?"

All I could think as we followed him out of the bedroom, was if the dead guy lying outside wasn't Jacob or Spencer, then *who* was he?

We were heading back down the road toward the campground. Before we left I brushed my teeth for the third time that morning but my stomach was still all twisty and turny from the image still in my head. I don't know what was worse. Seeing someone actually eating someone's flesh or seeing the remains of what one of these sick people could do to someone.

Missy was beside us, playing with her earring anxiously. She had been doing it for two minutes. I know. I counted. "Jason…" she finally said, her voice worried.

He scrunched his forehead, looking at her. "Yeah?"

"About what you said back there at the house, about Spencer. There still is a possibility he's okay, right? Just because he was around him doesn't mean he has something, does it? I know the odds aren't good, but please tell me there's a chance. I need to know there is still a chance."

Her voice hitched up at the end and I wanted to put my arm around her, but I didn't because I knew she wasn't into hugs. Missy wasn't big on showing emotion, she had the biggest heart, but she didn't like to make a huge deal about it. But I knew if something happened to Spencer, she would be devastated, and right now she was really freaking out. You'd never tell by how she appeared on the outside. She and Jason were kind of alike that way.

Jason slowed down the pace. "I think that's the first time you called me by my first name. I'm not sure how I feel about that. I was kind of getting used to the nickname."

My best friend's lips twitched, but she still fiddled with her jewelry, her blue eyes staring at him for an answer.

"Yes," he continued evenly. "There is the possibility your friend is fine."

Her hand stopped fidgeting. "You aren't just saying that to make me feel better, are you?"

"No," he said, shaking his head, his voice changing, saddening. "I know from experience." Suddenly I had the urge to hug *him* now.

"Oh, you lived with someone who got sick? Is that what the convenience store guy was talking about?" She stared at him, her voice concerned. "He said you would have had it or something if it were airborne, didn't he? So that's what he was referring to?"

Jason didn't answer right away, but just walked slowly, quietly. I could tell he wasn't ignoring her, but merely trying to find the words to answer. His eyes were drawn to the ground, his grip tightening on Duke's leash, and I got one of those uneasy feelings in the pit of my stomach. Like when you see a guy crying—that whole, you don't know what to do or say thing because it's not something you see every day. Well Jason wasn't crying, but there was just something about him at that moment that made me think of someone crying.

"Yeah," he finally answered, his voice choked up. "I did. Remember that woman I told you it took six shots to take down…"

"Yeah?"

Jason cleared his throat. "She was my mother."

Missy stopped walking. "Holy freaking shit. You shot your Mom?"

"Miss—" I warned in a voice that told her to shut up, stopping short because Jason did. My heart beat picked up.

"I didn't shoot my mom," he sighed in exasperation, the pain so clear in his eyes. "I was just there when someone did."

"Ohmigod, that's horrible." My best friend's eyes were wide and owl-like. "Who did?"

Mentally, I shook my head. Sure, I wanted to know just as much as her, but I didn't have the guts to ask. We shouldn't ask. It was kind of *super* personal shit, if you asked me. And men as a rule weren't big on sharing emotional crap and usually didn't like women prying.

Surprisingly, Jason answered. "My father."

My jaw instantly dropped. From the corner of my eye, I saw Missy's did too. *His father? Holy smokes.*

"Your dad shot your mom?" Missy regained her composure faster than me. "What the hell? *Why?* Who was she biting?"

Jason's posture tensed again, and it was clear he was not comfortable at all talking about this, which made me wonder why he was even answering her. Was it just to make her feel better? To give us reassurance about Spencer? Or did he want to talk about it, he just didn't know how?

He finally spared us a glance, his green-brown eyes sad and haunted. "She was biting him..."

"So he shot her?" Missy was incredulous, her voice hitched up. "Couldn't he have just pushed her off him? I'm sure he was stronger than her."

"He did...but once he did, she came after me. He had no choice."

"Ohmigod, what did you do? What happened? How is your dad?"

Jason hesitated too long.

"Holy crap, you killed your dad?" Missy's eyes were practically bugging out of her head now. I got that creepy crawly sensation under my skin.

"No. I didn't. He shot himself."

"In front of you?" Missy sounded horrified. "That *has* to screw a kid up."

Jason fidgeted with the leash again, loosening it and tightening it in his grip. His eyes drifted back to the road, then back to us, back to the road. He took a deep breath, and exhaled. "My dad thought it was the only way to prevent him from attacking me and my brother and sister. I couldn't do it. And he didn't want me to have to do it. And he didn't want us to experience him getting sick like our mom."

My stomach knotted tighter. "Were your brother and sister there with you? Did they see it happen too?" I was cautious, sympathetic. I couldn't even imagine what he must have gone through.

He shook his head. "No. They were at the neighbors. That's where we were staying. I had come by to check on my mom, to see if she was getting any better. She was the first case we knew of." He sighed, starting to walk again. "I wish I hadn't visited that day."

A beat of silence as we followed him.

"What happened afterward?" Missy pressed, about thirty seconds later. "People didn't try to kill you, thinking you had it too?"

"No one tried to kill us," he replied. "We were kids. I mean my brother and sister are kids. They are only thirteen." He peered over his shoulder. "My neighbors quarantined us in a bedroom for a couple days, but when we never got sick, people began to realize it wasn't airborne, but someone did burn down our house and my parents' bodies. That's all I know. Like I said, we were locked in a bedroom for a couple days so I don't know what exactly happened after. Only bits and pieces from what I've heard from others."

I stared at him, feeling sympathetic for him and all he's been through. "I'm *so* sorry." I didn't know what else to say.

He shrugged, brushing it off like usual. "Eh. Shit happens."

"No. Shit like that does *not* just happen," Missy said in disbelief. "I'm sorry too. And about being such an ass to you too."

Jason stopped walking, spinning around immediately, his eyes fierce. "Enough. I don't want sympathy. You asked a question. I answered it. *That* is how I know there is a chance Spencer may be okay. I was in that room with my mom many times and *I* am fine. But if you want to save your friend we need to hurry. Whatever is going on around here is spreading fast, and I am not sure how it is spreading. But it *is* spreading and I don't want any of us to catch it."

A pause.

"Okay?" He stared at us, his tone a little less intense now than seconds before.

I stared back. *No. It wasn't okay. None of this was okay.* Something occurred to me and I couldn't ignore it. My heart was jumping inside my chest. I eyed Jason carefully, so he wouldn't think I pitied him but I had to know. I had to know why he helped us. *Why in the world would he ever help us?*

I swallowed, trying to find my voice. "Jason, why were you going for a car battery?" I knew it may have seemed like a random question, but it was really bugging me. And I think I already knew after everything he just said about his folks, but I wanted to hear it from him anyway. I needed to hear I was wrong, but I don't think I was. My dark eyes met his.

His brow rose. "What?" My question seemed to throw him off after all.

"*Why* were you going for a car battery?" I repeated, not looking away, being even more forward about it, like Missy usually was.

He stared back at me, sort of startled, and yet said completely straightforward, "Why else?" A pause. "I want to get out of here. I want to take my brother and sister and get as far away from this town as we possibly can get. I want to keep them safe. Start over somewhere…somewhere where we aren't reminded of our mom and dad every day. You know?"

I cringed. Oh I got it all right. I got that we were screwing everything up for him. No. Spencer was screwing everything up for all of us. Jason should have never stopped to help us. He should have kept going. He should have gotten the battery and gotten out of here. He *needed* to get out of here. And Spencer…Spencer should have never run away from home and we wouldn't be here. Messing. Everything. Up. For. *Them.*

"Why would you ever help us?" I mumbled, my eyes instantly tearing up. No wonder Buck was being so hard on him back at the trailer for going with us instead of getting the battery. He saw it to. That we were just a bunch of strangers he was putting above his family. "Why did you do it? You didn't even know us."

I couldn't fathom it. I couldn't understand why he would put his and his brother and sister's lives at stake for us. We shouldn't have mattered. We *still* shouldn't matter.

"Dee," he began, no doubt making an excuse.

I started shaking my head. "Don't. There's nothing to say. You shouldn't be here. *Go.* Get out of here. Save your brother and sister.   Save yourself. You showed us the direction of the campground. We will find it. We will find Spencer. Please. Just go. I don't want to be responsible if something happens to you. Please." I wiped a tear off my cheek, feeling completely guilty. "You've been through too much already. Just leave."

Jason listened. He started walking. But, he started walking toward me instead. His green-brown eyes never leaving mine. He must have handed the leash to Missy at some point because suddenly he was taking me in his arms and hugging me.

I wanted to pull away and push him. He must have sensed that because he hugged me tighter. "Listen. I like you two. Okay? I like that you care so much for your friend and want to save him even now that you know what is at stake for you. It's exactly how I feel for my brother and my sister. And why I wouldn't let Kyle and Buck come with us. I want to help you guys. Don't you get that? My truck is almost fixed. I've been working on it for a couple weeks. I just need the battery. Once I have it, we can leave and I can tow your car out of the woods so you can leave too."

"But I don't get it—" I started, mumbling into his chest.

He cut me off.

"My brother and sister are fine. They are safe. My neighbors aren't leaving them and they aren't leaving the house until I get back. That's been the plan all along. You two *aren't* safe. You never were. That's why I helped you. You didn't have anywhere to stay. You didn't know anyone. You didn't even know what was going on around here. And you just crashed your car. I'm not an asshole. I'd never leave you two out here alone."

Suddenly my arms wrapped around his sides, pulling me even closer into his embrace. Jason was a better person than I think I ever could be. And it was the only way I could think to say *thank you.* All this time and we didn't even realize what he was doing, and even when we did, I could tell he still wanted to help us.

"*Hallmark,* I, uh, I don't know what to say." The sound of my best friend's voice had me turning my head. She was standing there, holding Duke, looking very uncomfortable. Jason's heartbeat, slightly raised, echoed in my ear as I stood in his grasp looking at her.

He forced a short chuckle. "Mouth, ya know, I find that hard to believe." Peering up, I didn't miss the way the corner of his lips curved. But he still held me. I had a feeling he needed that hug, just as much as I did.

Finally, he pulled away, taking Duke's leash back from Missy, offering us a smile. "Come on you two. You won't make me change my mind now." And in that instant I knew we were all in this together.

No matter what happened next.

Even if I thought it was completely wrong.

14

The road descended before us, at a pretty steep decline. My calf muscles were already burning from all of yesterday's walking. So, needless to say this sucked. I cringed every so often when no one was looking at me, but I didn't complain. I had a feeling we had a lot more walking to do before the day was over and if I started complaining now it was going to be a *long* day.

I put my hand to the back of my neck and started to rub. It was still stiff from the crash yesterday. "So Jason," I said, out of curiosity, "What's your brother and sister's names?"

Jason peered over at me, a soft smile forming on his face. I could see how much he cared about them just by the way he looked at me right now. Like he was pleased I wanted to know. Honestly I don't know why I hadn't asked sooner. "Brandon and Frankie."

"Frankie?" I furrowed my brow in confusion.

He chuckled with sincerity this time. "Well my sister's real name is Francine, but since she's always been more of a tomboy growing up, we started calling her Frankie and it just kinda stuck."

Frankie. Hmm. I sort of liked it. "That's cool, different for a girl." I paused, considering him. His light brown messy hair, his thickening scruff, his hazel eyes, his freckled skin… "Does either of them look like you?"

"Eh, not really. Frankie has my eyes and Brandon has my hair color, but that's about it."

I nodded and looked over at Missy. She was making a face. "What's wrong with that?"

"Huh?" Her blue eyes stared at me blankly.

"You have no idea what we are talking about, do you?"

She shook her head. "Sorry. I wasn't paying attention. I was thinking about something."

I looked at my best friend, frowning. She was gimping slightly, I guess from the blisters on her feet. She was still in yesterday's clothes. Her hair was still frizzy and pulled back into a knotted ponytail. Her face and arms were already getting sunburnt. I couldn't help but wonder how bad she really hurt from the accident yesterday. I knew she'd never tell me because she wouldn't want to make me feel bad.

"What are you thinking about?" I said, feeling bad regardless. It was my fault we crashed the Toyota.

"Oh you know, just that you and I are probably grounded for life when we get home."

I started to laugh. I couldn't help it. "*That's* what you were thinking about right now?" *I mean out of everything…*

 "Well…yeah," she mumbled.

"Why?" Jason sounded as humored as me.

"Well, you said there's a payphone at this campground, possibly the one Spencer called us from, and I'm having a debate in my head right now about it. I'm trying to decide whether I should call my mom to let her know we are okay when we get to it or no…" She looked at me for an answer.

Crap. I don't know. "Um…"

On one hand, we definitely *should* call our parents. Knowing how paranoid my parents got, they were probably freaking out because I didn't come home last night. Then again, they probably figured I just stayed at Missy's since my purse and cell were still at the house. I'm sure they knew I wouldn't run off without any of that. I wasn't sure if they would call Missy's mom though. And if they did, and realized I wasn't with Missy, than they might have already called every hospital and cop in the entire Jersey State.

But on the other hand, if we didn't call, it might be better. If we told them we were in Pennsylvania they'd want to know why. Then we'd have to tell them Spencer called us and I crashed the car and I wasn't sure that would go over well.

Yeah. The more I thought of it, the more I didn't want to tell them. I just didn't want to have that conversation. I was chickening out. "Maybe we should wait…"

"No, actually I think it's a good idea," Jason said, looking at us.

"You do?"

He nodded.

I resisted the urge to groan. "Why?"

"Eh. I just do. I think it's the smarter option." He thought for a moment. "I think you should call your folks and tell them you ran into a ditch and now you have to wait for a tow truck on Monday to come tow the car. And that you are staying at a friend's house from school that lives right up the road and not to worry, you are fine, you just left your cell at home." A pause. "Then when you are done, I think you should call the police and let them know you two are fine. That you left your car because it was getting dark out, and you walked back to town and had a friend come pick you up. And that on Monday you will have the car towed away and that you already reported everything to the insurance company."

I just stared at him. "We didn't report anything to the insurance company."

"Then scratch that part, but I still think you should call before cops start swarming the town looking for you. It's better to keep people *out* of this town."

"You don't think the cops came yet?" Missy sounded surprised. "It's been almost twenty-fours since I called."

"Honestly I don't know. You said you hung up on them. For all I know, they may have just thought it was a prank call. From what you told me you didn't tell them your whereabouts, you didn't tell them you hit someone, you just said you were in an accident, and you did a lot of cursing. Is that right?"

"Yeah." She made another face.

"Even if they took the call seriously, it's better to end the missing person search *now* don't you think? Especially since a lot of sick people are roaming around that mountain."

He was right, when he put it that way.

"Why is that?" I asked, brushing my bangs out of my eyes. "About them being on the mountain, I mean."

"Simple. It's the woods. There are all kinds of animals in the woods. There's a lot of stuff they can feed on. I don't think they are just eating people."

Missy's face paled. "I didn't want to hear that."

"Sorry, but it's true."

"Yeah, still didn't want to hear that though."

We all walked a few more steps before Jason spoke up again. "Okay, so is it settled then, you two are making the calls when we get to the booth?"

We both nodded. *If I had to.*

"Okay. Good. At least we have a plan. In the meantime," he said, slowing to a stop. "I think you should eat something, Dee.

We've been doing a lot of walking and you did throw up your breakfast."

"I probably could use a snack, but I'm not sure I can stomach it."

"At least try," he prompted, turning, so his back pack was in front of me. "I bought some trail mix in the store, it's in the front pocket, help yourself."

"Thanks," I mumbled, before I started to unzip the pack. "Do you need anything else out of here while I'm in it?"

"I'm good." He looked over his shoulder. "Unless Mouth wants something?"

"Nope, I'm fine, I have my candy."

He chuckled, shaking his head. "Do you ever eat anything else?"

"Yes."

"Rarely." I took the trail mix out. "Trust me."

"Whatever," she grumbled. "And what about Duke? Maybe he wants something. You have a treat or anything to give him? Maybe he's hungry."

My hand hesitated in zippering up the pack. She cared more about the dog's health than her own apparently.

"He's good on food," Jason said, slightly humored. "He only eats twice a day, but he probably could use some water." He peered over his shoulder at me again. "There's a small collapsible bowl in there for him. It's the second compartment, take that out for me, will ya?"

"Of course." I held the trail mix bag with my teeth while I unzipped the second zipper taking out the bowl. I handed it to him over his shoulder then took the trail mix bag out of my mouth, opening it as Jason turned to Missy.

"Can I have the water you bought this morning? If you get thirsty you can drink from my pack—it's just if I try to drain the water out of this tube, we might be here a while."

Missy was already digging in her purse. "Sure." *Anything for the animals...* She pulled out the bottle and handed it to him, the top already popped up. He held the bowl in his left hand, squeezing the water into it with his right. Duke waited patiently, his tail wagging, until Jason lowered it to his snout. Then he started drinking immediately, lapping water up noisily, as Jason reached over his head to hand Missy back the rest of the bottle.

"Thank you."

She nodded, stuffing it back in her bag. "It's the least I can do."

I was munching on the trail mix, my hand in the bag, staring off toward the bottom of the road. There was a sharp gravel bend coming up. "Hey, is that the entrance to the campground down there?"

Jason didn't even look, he just looked at me. "Yeah. It's two miles down that gravel road then it opens up into the parking area. Straight from there is about another half-mile path that leads to the phone and recreation area. You know refreshments, bathrooms, yada, yada, yada."

Missy groaned.

"What?" He asked, turning his attention to her.

"All I heard was walk here, then walk there, and once you get there, walk some more... yada, yada, yada."

Jason laughed. "Yup. That's pretty much what I just said. We *do* have a lot of walking to do still."

Missy made another inaudible sound. "How big is this campground?" She was eyeing the gravel road with an expression I knew too well. She was *so* done with walking.

"Not too big. No worries." He folded up the now empty drinking cup, glancing back at me. "Do you mind putting this away?"

"Not at all," I mumbled through a mouth full of trail mix. I took the cup from him as he turned his back toward me again. Missy tapped her foot restlessly on the ground beside us.

"Not too big to who, *you* or *us*?" she pressed, speaking entirely to Jason. "Because your idea of walking is a lot different than mine."

"Good question. Not sure. Probably somewhere in the middle." When I assured him everything was zipped up on the backpack, he faced both of us again. "Would you two like to take a break for a bit? We can."

"No," I said quickly before Missy could answer. "We are fine. Missy is just getting comfortable with you so she's starting to whine."

Jason stared at me, blank expression. "Oh."

I started to laugh. "Trust me. It's a compliment, as much as it is annoying. She only complains to those she's close with."

He considered that. "Shit. So does this mean we are becoming friends?" He stared at Missy in fake horror.

"Oh shut up, *Hallmark*. I'm just cranky and my feet hurt. It has nothing to do with you." Her lips curved into a smile though, as the three of us started forward again.

The gravel *crunched* beneath our feet as we walked. Somewhere nearby a bird or two sang. We stuck to the right edge of the road because of Duke's ear. We figured if someone jumped out at us it would be better to have a chance to react. We knew Duke would warn us if anyone was coming up on our right. I was just happy Duke wasn't barking yet. That meant things weren't as bad as we thought.

The late morning air was warming up, but even though I was sweating, I didn't take off Jason's shirt. Instead I wrapped my arms across my chest and kind of hugged myself. Despite Duke's lack of barking, the closer we were getting the more nervous I was feeling because honestly I was scared to find out about Spencer.

Was he or was he not sick?

"May I ask you guys something?" Jason said, his eyes scanning back and forth vigilantly. There was something in his voice that set off warning bells in my head. When we agreed, he seemed to hesitate, perturbing me more. He avoided looking at us. "If the tables were turned, would your friend be doing this for you?"

"What do you mean?" Missy asked, her tone becoming defensive.

"I mean, if one of you ran away and never said goodbye, and out of the blue you called him for help, would he come rescue you? And would he stick it out, if he knew his life were in danger too?"

We were both quiet as we considered it. *Would he?* I didn't know how to answer that without feeling offended. I didn't think he would. How awful is that?

"He wouldn't, would he?" Jason said sadly, after a minute of silence. I could tell he felt uncomfortable asking us this, just as much as it bothered us hearing it. "And yet you two do this anyway?" He paused, finally looking at us. "Why?"

Missy started fussing with the bracelet Jason made her. "Because that's just how we are. He's our friend. And when we are friends with someone we don't bail on them, no matter what happens."

"But doesn't it bother you?" His green-brown eyes were full of disbelief.

"That he wouldn't return the favor? No not really. It's not about that. The fact is out of everyone he knows, Jason, he called *us*."

"I know," he agreed, "But what if that was because he knew you'd come—that he knew you would drop everything to help him, even though he hadn't spoken to you in so long."

"That *is* why he called." Missy's voice didn't waver. "Because he knew he could rely on us. His life is in danger here, and he needed help. Just the fact he wanted *us* to help him, proves to me that we mean something to him. Even after all this time. And to me it's worth it."

"Do you feel that way too?" Jason asked, turning to face me. His hazel eyes searched mine for answers.

Was it entirely crazy what we were doing right now? *Yes*. Am I hurt that Spencer just up and left us without so much as saying anything to us? *Of course*. But would I have still come to his rescue if I had known what we would be stumbling into…*probably*. Like Missy said, it's just how we are. I could never live with myself if I had a chance to save Spencer and didn't. No matter how hurt I was by him. I knew I wouldn't forgive myself for letting emotions get in the way of helping him.

I nodded. "Spencer needs us. That's all there is to it. Even if we can't save him, we can at least know we tried."

"Exactly," Missy said, offering me a tight smile. "But you know as well as I know, we are going to try our damnedest to bring him home."

"Yes. Yes we are."

Jason stared at me for a few more seconds, before pulling his eyes back to the road. "He's lucky to have you two. I hope he realizes that." A pause. "And I truly hope for your sake, he had a good reason for running away."

"Yeah, me too," I mumbled, thinking of everything we've been through so far and the town in which he was living. "Because he traded us for *this*."

"Yeah," Missy added, her own voice hinting at her disappointment. "Plus he's missing out on our morning cappuccino runs, and skipping class with us. *Oh*…and don't forget double gulp slurpees. I doubt they have them here." She glanced at Jason, as if to prove her wrong.

Jason shook his head. "Nope."

"See, Jersey is so much better."

"Now I don't know about that. Pennsylvania has some things we don't," I said, in the state's defense.

"Zombie wannabes?" She snickered.

I rolled my eyes. "I was thinking more of the scenery." Jason was staring off at the woods to our left and I furrowed my brow. "Something wrong?"

He shrugged. "Just thought I heard something. Think I'm just being paranoid." He turned his face to us. "So, what exactly is a double gulp slurpee?"

We started to laugh. "You don't get out of this town much do you?"

He readjusted his grip on Duke's leash as he looked at my best friend. "I've never left PA if that's what you mean."

"Have you at least been to Philly?"

"No."

"Not even for school?" I said, shocked.

"Nope. I was homeschooled. So are my brother and sister."

Huh. I wasn't expecting that.

"Wow, lame. That means you could never cut class." Missy glanced at me like, *ohmigod what planet are these people from?* "A double gulp by the way," she said, turning her attention back to him, "is this extra, extra large frozen slushie. So good. You are missing out."

"Yeah it's a real shame I am missing fancy coffee and frozen drinks," he said sarcastically. "And that I couldn't skip out on my education."

"Trust me, it is," she sighed. "Man what I would do for either one of those drinks right now." She turned her head toward me, smiling. "Hey, remember that time we were walking down the road drinking the slurpee and a car came by, hit a puddle and you got drenched."

"Yeah." I thought back to that day for a moment, shaking my head. "That completely sucked by the way."

She started laughing. "You really had to see your face."

I resisted the urge to roll my eyes again. "You know if I remember correctly—"

Duke started barking.

Suddenly I heard yelling. Getting louder. Getting closer. To my left.

15

"Help! Somebody help *me*!"

A boy, no older than eight, came running toward us. He was skinny, knobby-kneed, and breathing heavily. Sweat drenched his hair and his shirt. He was sprinting at full-speed through the woods. "My brother is trying to eat me!" he cried, panic sharp in his voice. "Help!"

He glanced up at us, tripped, and stumbled forward. That's when we saw him, his brother running behind him about thirty yards away. He was a few inches taller. Same sandy blonde hair, except his hair was to his chin instead of his ears, and was greasier-looking. He had sweat rings all over his shirt. His dark, cold eyes were locked onto his younger brother. His lips parted, his chest heaving up and down as he breathed.

He was definitely sick—there was no mistaking it—but I was pretty certain the younger boy was too, he just wasn't at *that* stage yet. By now the boy had picked himself up, regaining his speed. "*Please,*" he cried in desperation, "Help me." The fall had closed the gap between them. His brother was getting closer to him, and the two of them were getting closer to us, and I wasn't sure what we were going to do about either of them.

Jason had whipped his gun out, aiming it with one hand while his other hand tried controlling Duke, who was now barking wildly and pulling. I yanked the pistol out of my waistband, mimicking Jason's stance—it was the only thing I could think of to do—except I had both hands wrapped around the handle. And even then, the gun still shook in my grip as I pointed it forward.

Jason stood next to me, his finger resting against the trigger, but not shooting. I wasn't sure what he was waiting for. The boy was nearing us. I could hear his panting now as he gasped for air.

We had about thirty seconds before he reached us, thirty seconds to shoot or thirty seconds to run. We weren't doing either. My heart was pounding against my chest so fast *I* was having trouble breathing.

Jason started to pull the trigger. *This was it*. He was going to shoot and I knew I had to be ready just in case. I repositioned my stance, trying to steady the gun and waited. Nothing happened. My eyes flashed back to Jason, and I realized he had let go of the trigger. His finger was just lingering in front of it. I flashed my eyes back to the boy. *Too freaking close.*

My eyes darted back to his gun. His finger was on the trigger again but once again he released it.

"What the hell, Jason?" I snapped, my voice cracking as my eyes went back to the boy.

Suddenly he cursed beside me and from the corner of my eye I saw him lower the gun. "I'm sorry. I can't do it. I can't shoot a freaking kid." He looked around, bugging out, as if trying to come up with a better solution. Missy tugged on my arm, pulling me backward.

"Help!" The boy cried louder, raspier, his arms pumping forcefully through the air. He was so close now that I could see the beads of sweat dripping down his face. I could see the freckles on his nose. Jason was right. We couldn't do this. It was wrong. I dropped my gun-clad hand toward the ground and let Missy drag me away.

Jason inched backward, yanking on Duke's leash.

"Well what are we doing?" Missy shouted above his barking. She stepped back further. This time I stepped in front of her protectively, tempted to raise my gun again because the screaming boy was *right* there. Duke jumped at him, incisors exposed, and Jason immediately jerked the leash, causing Duke to yelp.

He glanced over his shoulder, jaw clenched, struggling to hold Duke and a gun. *"Run!"* he shouted. "Get away from them."

Jason started to move toward us, Missy reattached herself to my arm and we ran, sprinting up the gravel road toward the campground. She let go of me once she was certain I was coming with her. But too soon I became aware I didn't hear any footsteps behind me, and I slowed down, turning my head in time to see the kid reach out for Jason, missing his arm by a hand's length. Jason cursed, yanking firmly on Duke's leash, trying so hard to control him, but the dog wasn't listening. Duke was trying to protect him. Barking, jumping, trying to attack, and Jason couldn't run because of it.

And I knew he wouldn't leave his dog.

"Get away from me, Kid," Jason grunted loudly, barely keeping out of reach of the boy. The boy kept pressing forward, reaching, pleading, crying. His older brother was steps away now, gaining on him, gaining on Jason.

I turned fully around and started running back. Missy must have seen me. "What are you doing?" She yelled.

"Helping Jason," I said without hesitation, trying to catch my breath.

"Dee—"

"Shut up and run," I demanded, coming to a stop. I lifted my hand.

"*No.* Don't shoot Duke," she cried, freaking out. I could hear her running toward me. I didn't have a choice. I had to do this. Jason was as good as dead otherwise.

I flinched when the shot fired. *What if I missed?* The boy went to reach out to Jason again and that's when I heard the yowl. I almost shut my eyes. Missy was hunched next to me, gasping for breath, eyes wide.

The boy stopped and spun around, staring in disbelief. I had a clear shot of his older brother from this angle, so I took it. I had to. For Jason. For Duke. My bullet lodged into his chest perfectly. Proving my target practices paid off. I fired again when the kid kept running. This one hit him right between the eyes. He paused, swayed, and finally dropped to the ground.

"Randy!" The knobby-kneed boy suddenly cried, running away from Jason toward him, as if he hadn't just been running *from* him. Then it dawned on me what I just did and the gun slipped from my hands hitting the ground. My legs immediately turned to jelly and I could barely hold my weight.

"Holy shit," Missy gasped beside me.

Yeah. Holy shit was right. *Holy freaking shit.* I just killed someone. I immediately started to hyperventilate.

"Crap. *Jason!*" Missy hollered before awkwardly putting her arm around me. "Dee? Dee it's okay. You saved his life. He's okay. Breathe. Deep, calm breathes. *Jason—*"

I could hear her clearly but I couldn't see her clearly. Everything was blurring together as tears burned in my eyes. I knew I had to get it together. I knew I couldn't break down here. We were still in danger. The other boy was still here. I panicked. Did he touch Jason? *Ohmigod, what if he made contact with Jason?* He was so close to him, too damn close.

What if Jason got sick now?

I couldn't calm down. No matter how many times Missy told me to take a slow, deep breath. I never realized it was so hard to breathe before. In a world full of oxygen, I couldn't get any.

Everything started getting weirder. Sounds were becoming distorted. Missy sounded miles away even though her arm was wrapped around me. Duke's bark was just a loud, unclear monotonous sound fading into the background. My cheeks felt wet, and my lips tasted of salt. But still, I felt like I couldn't get any air.

I started to feel weaker.

It made me anxious.

I saw Jason. He was right in front of me now. His lips were moving, but his voice didn't match the movements. It was like bad audio timing in a movie. My brain was fuzzy as I tried to listen. But all I could focus on was him. *Was he okay?* I wanted to ask him but I couldn't. I couldn't really do anything.

And I couldn't get any air.

"Purse your lips," I *think* he said, as he inched closer to me. "Like this." I was pretty certain he was making a duck face but I wasn't positive. I continued to gasp for breath.

"Dee, you have to purse your lips and breathe, you are getting too much oxygen."

Too much oxygen? I must have heard him wrong. I couldn't get any oxygen. That was the problem.

"It feels like you can't breathe, but you are breathing," he pressed. "You are breathing too much. Trust me." That can't be right. That didn't make sense. He must have said, *I'm not breathing enough.* I tried gasping for more air. Jason cursed.

I saw him doing something. There was some sort of blurred movement. Sounds that weren't recognizable or comprehendible. My ears were ringing.

Jason was fading away from me.

That's when something went around my mouth.

It deflated and inflated every time I took a breath. Slowly but steadily I was breathing normally again. My hearing wasn't like a warping video tape, and my vision wasn't splotchy and swaying. Tears still lingered in my eyes and still dried on my cheeks, but I wasn't sobbing.

Jason remained hunched in front of me as I held the bag over my nose and lips. His green-brown eyes locked on my face, staring at me intently. There was no mistaking the worry in them. I scared him. But I was only scared *for* him. I still didn't know if the boy made contact with him.

After a few more even breaths, I pulled the bag away staring at it in confusion. *What the heck was it?* It was bright neon orange and a thin, smooth material. It wasn't plastic. *Maybe nylon*?

"Are you sure you're okay?" Jason asked, eyeing me with concern as I held the bag out to him. I took a breath to make sure I wasn't going to go back into freak-out mode again. It was still calm and even. I nodded.

Sighing loudly, he dropped his face to his palm. Missy pushed me. "Damn it, Dee," she said, her voice clipped. "You scared the crap out of me. I thought you were going to shoot Duke."

"Sorry." I fidgeted. The gravel was digging into my bare legs and it was starting to hurt. I didn't remember sitting, but there I was sitting on the road, Missy beside me holding Duke, Jason in front of me—face to palm—looking like I *did* shoot his dog. I didn't understand. Contents of his backpack were dumped by his feet.

I flashed my eyes toward the wooded area where I shot the kid. The knobby-kneed boy was gone, but the body was still there, lying motionless, forever, because of me. My heart started to pound again, I forced myself to look away. I couldn't undo what I did, and I knew I'd do it again, to save Jason.

But *did I* save Jason?

"Dee…I…" Jason began, speaking into his hand, at the same moment I asked if he was okay. He dropped his fingers away from his face instantly and stared at me like I was being absurd. "Am *I* okay? You are kidding me, right?"

I shook my head. "No. The boy. Did he—"

Jason seemed to catch on. "No. He never made contact with me."

I exhaled in relief.

"But Dee—"

"What?" I said in a panic. *Did something worse happen?*

"He was about to before you fired the gun. If you didn't do what you did, if you—" I didn't let him finish. Reaching over, I placed my finger over Jason's mouth to shut him up.

"I don't want to talk about it. I don't want to hear about it. Understood?" I practically pleaded with him. As our eyes connected, I became aware of how soft his lips felt against my fingertip and how rough his scruff was against the rest of my skin. I pulled my hand away only when he nodded, but his eyes clearly protested.

Jason busied himself with cleaning up his belongings on the ground, picking up the neon bag he started shoving things into it.

"What is that?" I asked, curious.

He didn't look over at me, but continued filling it back up. "It's called a *stuff sack*. It makes hiking and camping so much easier." When I didn't respond, he sent me a sideways glance. "I didn't have any paper bags and you needed something to decrease your oxygen levels. I improvised."

Oh. "Thank y—" Suddenly *his* finger was on *my* mouth. My eyes widened.

"If I can't say thank you, neither can you." He dropped his hand, shoved the full neon sack into his pack again, and picked up *my* gun. "Come on. I want to get out of this area before the blood attracts something." Standing up, he took the gun with him. The outline of his gun showed through his shirt again. My stomach twisted.

"Jason, I don't need a thank you." *I didn't want a "thank you."*

He kept his eyes averted, staring down at his backpack in his left hand. His light brown hair fell across his forehead. "Neither do I," he said sharply, dropping *my* pistol into the center compartment.

I immediately jumped up, brushing off my backside. *"Hey wait*—I need that."

"Not anymore, you don't."

"What the hell is that supposed to mean?"

He zippered up his pack and pulled both arms through the straps, positioning it properly on his back before answering. "The last thing I am giving you is that gun."

"Excuse me," I felt my cheeks starting to burn. *He had a lot of nerve.* "That freaking gun just saved your life."

He laughed dryly. "Oh, *now* you want to acknowledge it. A second ago you didn't want to talk about it."

He started to walk past me. Reaching out I grabbed his arm. "Jason, give *me* the damn gun."

"No." He yanked his arm away.

"Jason, *come on.*"

He stopped, turned, and glared down at me. "You just hyperventilated and *dropped* a loaded weapon. I don't care how excellent a shot you are, you *can't* do that. And I can't be worrying about if you are going to do that again. I'm sorry. The gun stays with me."

I wanted to argue. I wanted to reach in his pack and grab the stupid gun. But I couldn't. I couldn't because he was right. I *did* drop a loaded weapon. It could have gone off and killed him, or me, or even Missy. I backed up, feeling embarrassed.

"I'm sorry, Dee," he sighed. "We just can't take the chances." He walked up to Missy, taking the leash from her hand. Duke was still whimpering, but he wasn't barking. And why would he be? The threat was gone. *I* eliminated him. With the gun I was apparently too immature to handle now.

Whether Jason realized it or not that was one hell of a *thank you.*

16

I was mumbling to myself as we headed toward the parking lot. Just loud enough that I know they heard but just quiet enough they couldn't *hear* me. Pretty much I was just being whiny and irrational. And at this point I didn't care anymore. Even if Jason was right, I was still pissed. I was really hurt by him taking the gun from me.

So I had a total freak-out moment. Truthfully I'd be a little concerned with myself if I *didn't* have one after killing someone. But I guess I answered my own question. *Yes, if I had to, I could shoot someone.* At least all my "protectiveness" wasn't just talk. I really did want to protect people I care about. I'm just not sure when Jason became one of those people. But somehow he did. *Somehow his windblown oily brown hair, lazy scruff, sunburnt neck, freckly face, and shorter-than-any-guy-I've-ever-liked height somehow made him super damn sexy and I couldn't keep my eyes off him.* Even now.

It just irked me more.

I had no business liking *this* guy. I just wanted to grab Spencer and get the hell out of here before Missy or I ended up dead. The problem was the more time we spent looking for Spencer, the more time I was spending with Jason. And that meant there were more times he looked at me with those green-brown eyes that made my stomach feel funny, smiled at me in a completely different way than he did toward Missy, and more time for me to remember what he said last night about kissing me. *He said when. Not if. When.*

I was caring too much for a stranger that I just met yesterday. But in that one day, this stranger had selflessly saved my life before he even knew me and had been protecting me ever since. He was protecting me, and not whining or complaining about it either, as I was doing now.

Great, I couldn't even have a decent self-pitying moment. Shaking my head, I followed Jason, Duke, and Missy into the clearing. I figured I probably should apologize or something just to break our silence though I wasn't really sure if I was apologizing for killing a kid, for dropping the gun, for carrying on, or for having a crush on Jason. Perhaps all of it. "Guys, I just want to say sor—" Missy suddenly stopped and I bumped into her, cutting off my words. She cursed.

But she wasn't cursing at me.

I stepped around her and stared out at the parking lot, my jaw dropped.

I was the least of our problems.

Duke was barking again.

A rusted old pickup was rear-ended into a station wagon. More accurately, into a person. The person was smashed up against the bumper, half-folded on to the hood. His face was turned toward us. His eyes were sunken, and were surrounded by dark circles. They stared—blankly— back at us.

My heart immediately started to pound. *That* look, that cold, vacant stare, was the same I saw on all the infected people. And that's when it hit me why they bothered me so much—I mean despite the whole flesh-eating part. Because even though these people were very much alive when they came after you, you could see in their eyes they were already *gone.*

What the hell was going on around here? What was causing this? How could a person appear dead before they actually died?

Stomach acid rose to the back of my throat as I briefly glanced at the rest of him. He had salt-and-pepper hair, tanned skin and broad shoulders. I would guess he was somewhere around the age of thirty-five to forty. And from the look of his attire, it was apparent he'd spent some time out here in the woods. I couldn't help but wonder if he was a camper, or just passing through for *dinner.* The thought made me taste the bile more.

I shifted my eyes toward the station wagon. The driver's door was open and a woman hung out on a slant, her left arm completely torn open dangling to the ground. A puddle of blood discolored the dirt below it. Her lavender shirt was stained, indicating the wound most likely occurred *before* the crash. From the amount of blood on the ground, and on her clothes, it made me believe she died from loss of blood, not from anything else. A second person was in the passenger seat beside her, his head up against the cracked windshield. Not moving. He mostly likely died *from* the crash which meant the truck had to be going pretty damn fast. Kind of hard to process considering the parking lot wasn't that big.

I crinkled my nose against the smell the breeze sent toward us. I watched in disgust as flies circled around the bodies, flying in and out of the vehicle and around the older man's head. A few even buzzed near our ears, but I hardly heard them over Duke. I hadn't seen anyone else in the car—the back seat looked empty just like the pickup. There were, however, a set of footprints leading toward the back tires of the Chevy, so whoever was driving the truck had taken off. I didn't see any blood in his trail and it made me curious if he was even injured. As I was following the prints with my eyes, I caught glimpse of the sneakers sticking out under the truck. *Four dead and counting…*

I continued to survey the scene, covering my mouth to stop me from puking when I saw the bodies—yes, more than one—about fifteen yards to my right. I couldn't believe I hadn't noticed them until now. But now that I had, I wished immediately I could *un*-notice them.

A body was lying on the ground, face half-gone. She was young, no older than me. Her brown hair (close to the color of mine) was lying in a knot ripped from her head. There was a body crumpled over her legs, the back of the head caved in, the neck kind of bent in an awful position. Someone else was lying on the ground beside them, but from where I stood I could not see who clearly. I was glad for that.

"They are all dead," Missy said, aghast. Yanking my attention away, I looked over at her. She was squeezing the strap of her purse again so tight her knuckles were turning white.

Jason was staring at the truck, his expression enigmatic. Something about it made me think something was wrong, and given the situation that shouldn't have surprised me but it did. "Yes," he replied, not facing us. His tone gave away nothing. "They are."

How could he do that? How could he just turn off emotion? I'd heard of poker faces, but seriously, *come on*. There were seven people dead in front of us. Even Duke was bugging out. But not Jason, not this Jason, not the guy who couldn't bring himself to kill a child.

"Come on," he started to move forward, toward the truck, and I almost pulled him back, momentarily ignoring *why* we were here. All I wanted to do was turn around. I wanted to go home.

But either way I was screwed. If I turned around, I'd see the dead guy *I* shot, and if I walked further toward the campground, I'd be closer to the dead people in front of me. There was really no avoiding any of this. This was all really happening and we were right smack in the middle of this freaking shit.

Jason inched closer to the truck, keeping careful hold of Duke. Missy and I peered at each other with uncertainty before taking a step. She gave me a half-nod to signal me that she was ready. I pretended to just be waiting for her, although I am sure I wasn't fooling anybody.

Covering my mouth again, I moved toward the path, hoping there were no bodies on the other side of the cars. Jason paused, hunching down to a half-standing, half-sitting position and peeked below the under carriage. I couldn't believe he was actually looking at the person. I didn't want to see any more dead people. He stood back up, tightening his grip on Duke's leash and stared back at the truck. He stared at it for a few more moments and then walked toward the back bumper. As we passed by him, he finally looked at us. "I know this truck. It's Jacob's." We both halted, terrified and confused. "Your friend must have taken it."

I stared at the hitch of the pickup, trying to keep my focus on something other than the feet sticking out. "Are you sure?" I was having trouble believing that Spencer could have done this to all these people. "Maybe it just looks like his truck. Chevy's are probably common around here, right?"

"Yeah," Jason agreed, still looking down at the bumper. "But it *is* his. I wasn't positive at first. I mean it has the same rust spot above the front wheel, but rust is common in old vehicles. But then, *look*...there's a Spanish flag sticker on the bumper." He shifted his eyes from Missy to me. "I was there the day he put that on."

Damn. I was really hoping it wasn't Jacob's. But it was just further proof our friend was here at the campground. A horrifying thought suddenly hit me. "Ohmigod, who's under the truck?"

"Not Spencer," Jason answered immediately. "Someone I don't know." There was a very faint sound of relief in his voice.

I blew out my breath. *Thank God.*

"Geez, I'm gonna have a heart attack," Missy groaned, placing her hand over her chest, "if this shit keeps up."

"Don't worry, I know CPR," Jason said wryly, bending to pet Duke. I think he was trying to calm him down.

Missy shook her head. "Of course you do, you know everything."

He chuckled dryly. "Hardly." He straightened back out. "If I knew everything, I'd know what the heck was going on around here and how to stop it." He tilted his head to gesture toward the path and started moving again. "I think we really have to call the state troopers now."

I picked up my pace, scrunching my brow in confusion. "I thought you didn't want them coming here." *Did he change the plan?*

"I don't," he said, peering over his shoulder. "But there are only two cars in this parking lot. If people were infected and left, that means it's now spreading elsewhere."

Oh Crap. My stomach knotted. That *wouldn't* be good. "Maybe there's a Registry or something at the front desk," I urged, trying to think of something. "Maybe we could ask how many campers were staying here? Maybe there was only the family in the station wagon? It's possible." *Please be only that family.*

"Maybe," he muttered, sounding doubtful. "We'll ask." A beat of silence. "But still, we *should* call." He said it as if he was leaving the decision up to us.

At that second, I hadn't a clue what the right choice should be.

17

I stopped the moment we got to the recreation area, the color draining from my face instantly. After everything that had been happening, it was hard to believe I could still be surprised, but I was. My stomach was starting to get used to it though. Or, at this point, my brain just gave up processing everything so thoroughly. If I got sick over every horrible thing, I was going to be sick a lot.

This camp area was even more horrific than the parking lot, in my opinion. There were tents all across the ground. Flattened, torn, rummaged. Some bodies were still lying inside on their sleeping bags. I may have thought they were just sleeping, if it weren't for the fact their faces were bitten off.

Other people were lying beside still-smoking campfires, devoured as well.

Some people that were obviously *"the infected"* were shot… stabbed… impaled against trees with cars. *Yes, there were at least three cars back here, which made me feel slightly better. Maybe not everyone left the campground after all.*

One person was tossed into a fire, charred and burnt, as if they were trying to cremate him alive. I only assumed it was a man of course because the body was kind of stocky and thick. Whoever it was had flat, wide feet. The foot was the only part that wasn't fried. It was still flesh toned, but dirt stained.

Besides bodies, dirt, tents, and campfires, the ground was covered in broken fishing poles, ripped clothing, a littering of trash, and a lot of blood.

I think there was even an oil leak trailing behind the SUV.

I counted a total of ten tents, over twenty people— not the infected—dead, at least four still steaming fires, the cars, and one very ancient looking phone booth—a phone booth that had an RV backed into it. *Son of a*—one look at the smashed and broken remains and I knew it was completely useless to us. We couldn't call even if we wanted to, even if we had to. *Now* my stomach twisted.

We needed an entirely new plan.

Duke was sniffing the area, whimpering in that low-pitch cry that I was getting accustomed to. Every time he started to bark, Jason corrected him with a yank on his leash. He said it was "safer" that way because whoever killed these campers was somewhere still out there.

Missy's hand was squeezing my bicep, as we followed Jason and Duke around the remains. We peeked at the phone booth as we passed, though we knew it was a lost cause. I guess we were still trying to keep a smidgeon of hope.

Jason peered back over his shoulder at us, pointing to his right. "The front desk is just up that hill. Maybe there is a phone in there." The question and doubt was so clear in his voice it gave me no reassurance.

I nodded, but said nothing. Missy, who was carefully stepping over the dirt as if she was afraid her sneakers would melt or something, sighed loudly. "Either that *isn't* the phone Spencer called us from or it is, and this mayhem happened since this morning and Spencer is now..." Her voice trailed off, as she slowly looked around, upset. "Dead."

"Hey, try and stay positive," Jason said, moving ahead of us a few more paces. "Don't kill Spencer off yet. He could still have a chance."

Missy stopped walking, dropping her hand from my arm. "Are you kidding me? How are we supposed to stay positive?" Her tone was incredulous. "How does anyone stay positive in the middle of *this*?"

I flinched, because I wasn't feeling too positive either.

"You just do," Jason shrugged.

"Yeah? And how exactly do you do it, *Hallmark*?" Missy pressed, "I mean, you are the one that's been saying from the beginning that Spencer is probably sick. Now all of a sudden you think he's fine, *after* seeing all of this?"

Sighing, Jason glanced toward the small cabin at the top of the hill again. "You just do what I do," he answered quietly, not looking at us. "You fake it."

"Fake it?" Missy's eyes rounded. "That's what you've been doing?"

"That's all I've been doing." He adjusted his grip on Duke's leash. "It's the only way to get through each day. Now come on," he urged, his green-brown eyes looking at her, then me, "this isn't the time to talk about this. I promise, until we find Spencer, or his body," he added, cautiously, "We will keep searching, but first let's try and locate a phone or this Registry. I want to know how many people left this camp."

We quickly hurried up the hill, as if getting there faster would make our problems go away sooner. I tried not to dwell on the fact that I wanted to know how Jason really felt, not just what he was pretending to feel. But, now was not the time to be caring.

The office was a small white building. When we walked inside, we noticed it was actually a tiny store. The cash register and paperwork were toward our right, a bathroom door toward our left, and straight ahead of us was a refrigerator with drinks. The walls were lined with camping gear and tools, the same kind of fishing poles I noticed broken outside, and a rack of flyers. The aisle I had eye access to from where I was standing was filled with snacks and bread. There seemed to be two other aisles behind it, but I didn't care about any of that. I turned my attention back toward the right, and peered over the counter like Missy.

"Hello?" Jason called tentatively. "Anyone in here?"

The lights were on above our heads, and nothing *smelt* dead. The place was quiet, except for the *buzzing* hum of the refrigerator.

Jason was walking around, pulling Duke with him. He stopped at the other end of the store. "I don't think anyone is here. Is there a phone?"

My eyes did another quick scan and I shook my head, disappointed. "No. I don't see one."

"Me either," Missy mumbled, leaning back.

Jason made an inaudible sound, or at least from here it was inaudible. "I do see a binder on the second shelf back here," I prompted, "maybe it's the Registry?" I was tempted to just reach over and grab it, but I waited for Jason's decision. Not sure why, I just did.

"Check it out," he said, and I didn't waste a beat. Leaning further over the counter, until my feet were barely touching the ground, I snatched the folder, bringing it back toward me and Missy. Flipping it open, I began to read the contents. I could hear Missy breathing over my shoulder as she tried to see too.

Names started to fill the pages, and for a second my heart jumped. That is until I realized the dates were wrong. These were previous campers from last month. I rustled page after page until I came to this month's latest entries.

Missy cursed beside me. "There were *that* many."

"How many?" Jason suddenly panicked, rushing over to us.

My finger traced the first line across all the columns on the page, until I got to the last one. "No," I said, before answering Jason. "Those pages were last month. This column here—I tapped my finger on it for Missy and now Jason to see—is the list of the past two weeks. There weren't too many. And this column," I moved my finger, "shows most of them checked out over a week ago. The rest of these people," I started counting the lines, "either didn't check out or are dead."

Jason exhaled sharply. "Thirty people."

"Yeah." I turned my face so I was looking over at him. "But there were twenty-four people dead so far, not including the obvious sick ones. Maybe they were all of them."

Jason's green-brown eyes glanced at me. "And their cars are where exactly?"

I bit my lip, backing away from the counter. "I don't know. There are three down there, maybe they are just scattered throughout the campsite."

"Right."

"Hey mister, didn't you just tell me to *try and stay positive*," Missy said dryly, pointing a finger.

"I also said to *fake it.*" Turning, he leaned against the counter with his backside. Duke was trying to pull away from him, but he kept correcting his leash. "But okay, let's say you're right. Say there were four people per car. We've seen four cars so far excluding Jacob's truck. So that would mean we'd need to find at least four more cars. Figure seven cars with four people accounts for twenty-eight people and one more car with just a couple.

That's thirty people…that's implying that there were four people per car though…I doubt…"

"Hush now, stay positive remember," I mumbled. I *didn't* sound that way.

"What is Duke trying to do?" Missy suddenly said, drawing our attention to the dog. He was trying to inch his way across the floor. "It's like he's trying to get to something."

We all stared at the closed bathroom door in front of us. "You don't think—"

"Well that might make missing person number twenty-five," I groaned. I did not want to see who was behind that door, but Jason was already stepping away from the counter, aiming his gun.

He cautiously stepped across the wooden floor to the bathroom door and knocked. No response. Duke was definitely getting worked up. Something or someone was behind that door.

Jason peeked back at us then started to turn the door knob, opening the door slowly. A man was lying on the floor beside the toilet, his head back against the wall, with blood coming from his nose. There were no bullet wounds, stab wounds, bite wounds. His eyes were closed and it took me staring at him for a good thirty seconds before I noticed the slight movement of his chest. He was still alive.

Duke barked and the man opened his eyes. Dark blue eyes.

"Stay away from me," he moaned, his voice tired. "I'm not well."

We didn't move any closer, but I had to strain my ears to hear him.

"Who are you?" Jason asked making sure he had full control of Duke.

"Ralph Loral. I run this place." He didn't make any effort to move either.

"What's happening out there?" Missy blurted.

"Illness, and it's spreading." He paused, lifting his finger to his nose and smearing the blood away.

"Do you know how?" Jason studied him very carefully, his body tense. "Were you attacked?"

"No."

"Did someone cough on you? Get blood on you?"

"No."

"Did they touch you?"

"Yes. I helped someone carry a case of water. She said she was feeling too weak to carry it."

A muscle popped in Jason's jaw. "When was this?"

"A week and a half ago." Ralph was taking shallow, slow breaths.

"That can't be right," Jason mumbled quietly, almost to himself. I could just barely hear him. "Has anyone else touched you?"

"No. Why?"

Jason ignored his question. "When did you start feeling sick?"

"Two days ago."

"Are you getting worse?"

The guy shrugged. He had brown curly hair, tan skin, and bags under his eyes. He was dressed in these stained jeans and a green camp logo sweatshirt. "I don't know. I'm really hungry though. I haven't eaten much since yesterday. Can one of you toss me a bag of chips or something?"

Jason flashed his eyes to me and I bit my lip. "This is what my mom was saying before she snapped," he urged, talking only loud enough for me and Missy to hear. "She was complaining about being hungry and not feeling well. And she had the nosebleeds."

"We need to leave then," I sighed, trying to avoid looking at the dying man.

"Hungry," the guy pressed, this time louder. "Please."

"Hold on," Missy snapped, as she started to walk off.

Jason turned his attention back to Ralph, who was now trying to stand up by gripping the handicap bar to assist him. "What's the matter with you? You say you're sick, what's wrong?"

"Besides the nosebleed," he groaned, straightening out his legs. "I'm weak. My body hurts. And my head is pounding."

"What was the first symptom?" Jason held out his gun hand to stop Missy when she went to walk past him with the snacks. She paused, immediately backing away from the gun.

Ralph's legs were shaking slightly as he stood there. "I felt like I was getting the flu and my head was pounding. Medicine wasn't helping."

Jason nodded, tucking the gun into his pants again. "Has anyone else said how they got sick? Or think they got sick? Were any of them complaining about being sick when they left?"

Ralph must have gotten tired of standing because he was now lowering himself onto the closed toilet lid. "I don't know. They said they just felt sick. I said the flu must be going around. I sold out on all my over the counter medicines."

"It's not the flu," Jason pressed.

"I know that now." Ralph rubbed at his temples, his back rising slightly as he took strained breathes. Without looking up from the floor, he asked, "So really, how about those chips?"

Jason took the bag from Missy, crinkling it slightly in his hands. "Hold up, are you sure no one touched you since last week?"

No answer.

"Ralph?"

Duke started to whimper again.

"Ralph?" Jason repeated, louder.

Ten seconds later, Ralph dropped his hands away from his face and I sighed in relief. For a dreadful moment I thought the worse.

Then Duke started barking.

Ralph turned his head deliberately and I realized right away I hadn't been wrong. My gut was right. Two black eyes stared back at us. Vacant. Cold. Lifeless. And just like that, I knew Ralph was *gone*. We barely had time to process it. Ralph launched himself off the toilet right for us, as if he never had trouble standing before, as if he just hadn't been telling us to stay away from him because he was sick. Jason cursed, bolted *forward*, and I screamed in disbelief. A bag of chips hit the ground. Missy grabbed my arm.

Just as Ralph lunged, Jason clasped the bathroom door handle, swinging it shut again. Two fingers squished and *crunched* in the jam, followed by a muffled howl. Jason backed away, slightly winded, yanking a barking Duke with him, and once again, we were on the run *after* he barricaded the door.

"W-what, w-what the hell was that?" Missy gasped, clutching her stomach. "It happens *that* fast? I don't understand. *How*?"

Jason shook his head, leaning over to calm Duke down. "I don't know. That's how quick my mom turned too." His breath was only slightly winded, and I hated him for his endurance.

Inhaling and exhaling out in big breaths, I felt the burn still in my chest from running. As my breathing slowed, I really started to think about it. "Should we have just left him like that?" I asked thinking of Ralph locked in the bathroom. I know it was crazy given the situation, but Ralph was a person.

They both turned toward me, disbelief on their faces.

"You're joking, right?" Missy urged her blue eyes round. "Please tell me you're joking."

"I…uh…"

"Ohmigod, you're not! Dee! What's the matter with you?!"

"I don't know, okay?" I started waving my hands around. "It just feels wrong. This all feels wrong. These are people, and we are killing them like it's nothing." My voice quivered.

"We didn't kill him," Jason said, trying to sound more understanding than Missy.

"No we just locked him in a room to starve to death," I groaned. "That's even worse."

"At this point—" he began.

But I cut him off instantly. "Don't even say 'at this point it doesn't matter' because it does matter. To me, it matters." I thought of the boy I killed earlier, and my heart started pounding again. "Sick or not, they still matter to me. I'm *not* this person. I didn't sign up for this."

"No one signed up for this," Jason retaliated. "It just happened. You think I wanted my mom and dad to die? Or Jacob?" His hazel eyes stared at me sharply. "Because trust me, I didn't, but I will be damned if I let myself die too. I have a brother and sister to protect. So if that means I have to knock off a few people to do it, I will."

Cringing, I realized I was probably sounding like the bad guy. There I was feeling sympathetic for the sick people, and these sick people were out killing innocent people. Possibly even Spencer.

Okay, something was definitely wrong with me. Maybe I was getting sick.

"No, you are right, sorry. I must have just sounded like a terrible person."

Jason's eyes didn't leave my face. "No, you didn't. A terrible person wouldn't care so much, but a naïve person would. You just have to accept this is reality and its survival of the fittest right now."

"Yeah," Missy urged. "And if I ever hear you feel sorry for these sickos again, I'll make you regret it. Zombies in movies are dangerous for a reason, and that's why the characters are always kicking their asses because if they didn't they'd get their asses bit."

Jason rolled his eyes. "Okay, for the last time they aren't zombies."

"Well they sure the heck act like it," she huffed, pushing hair out of her eyes. "And I was just using them as a metaphor really."

"Whatever, how about *you*—" All of a sudden, Duke took off, pulling Jason forward so fast he fell to his knees, dropping the leash, his words cutting off with a groan.

He recovered quickly. "Duke!" he shouted, panicking instantly. "Stay. *Stay*!" I only just became aware that someone was yelling in the distance.

Jumping up, Jason cursed and sprinted off after his dog when Duke *didn't* stay. I was sort of surprised he didn't, considering yesterday the pit bull seemed so obedient. Today, not so much. I guess this was what Jason meant by not letting me handle Duke at Jacob's house, I wouldn't have been able to handle him.

Missy and I started running after them, trying to keep up. Jason's backpack was flapping up and down as he ran and he was hollering, his voice cracking. There was no mistaking the emotion and fear in his voice now. He sounded and looked like a completely different person than he was a moment ago. My chest was burning again, as air wheezed in and out of my lungs. Missy was falling behind me, huffing and puffing, her footsteps heavily pounding over the asphalt path. She was screaming Duke's name too.

This could all end very badly.

18

Jason caught up with Duke, grabbing his collar instantly to stop him. He gave it a correctional yank, but Duke continued barking vociferously.

I bent over, hands on knees, trying to catch my breath as I stared forward trying to figure out what we do *now*.

Three people—three sick people—were hovering in on one guy. He was standing with his back toward us, swinging an aluminum baseball bat wildly. He was dressed in blue jeans, a sweaty white (well it probably used to be white) t-shirt and an orange ball cap. He was sweating so much that the cotton was now see-through and sticking to his back, portraying a spine-length quote tattoo. *Fuerza*. Whatever that meant.

He took down two like it was nothing, then swung, smashing the bat right into the gut of the third person, who keeled over, dropping to the ground. The guy with the tattoo didn't waste a beat. He readied his stance again, fixing the placement of his hands on the bat like he was stepping up to home plate and taunted them. "Come on you stupid zombie fuckers," he shouted, inching his hands up the aluminum, "that's all you got?"

I stared, my jaw dropping. *Was this dude serious? Why didn't he just run?*

The first person he whacked came forward again, and he quickly swung the bat into his face, snapping his nose immediately. The guy stumbled back—nose bent at an awful angle—while the girl picked herself up, running back at him from his right. He turned almost on cue, swinging low and fast, taking out her legs. She flipped backward again, head hitting the ground with a *crack*. The dude with the busted face rushed toward him again, and I understood now why the guy was sweating. It was like a nonstop video game, except the dude with the bat only had one lifeline to start with and he was fighting to keep that life alive.

And all this was happening in the span of two minutes tops. About the time it took us to catch our breath.

The shirtless dude he struck in the gut found his footing and sauntered forward, *toward us*, eyes blacker than coal. Bruises covered his entire torso and his gimp was no doubt caused by the swollen knee the size of a softball on his left leg.

Jason corrected Duke one more time then quickly snatched the leash off the ground, straightening out, his right hand immediately going to the gun on his side. Without even hesitating, he lifted the gun, aimed, and fired three times into the dude's bare chest. The guy with the bat glanced over his shoulder in shock—as if he just realized we were standing there and surprisingly hadn't heard Duke barking—and he almost dropped the bat.

The guy wasn't much older than Jason, maybe twenty, twenty-one. He was good-looking in a tough, intimidating way. Bronzed skin, brown startled eyes, black—slanted in confusion—eyebrows, and a busted lip.

Jason cursed.

I watched in horror as the girl took that second to lunge at the guy who was still staring over his shoulder at us. I didn't know what to do, so I just screamed. *"Watch out!"*

He turned his head fast, but she was too close for him to swing the bat again. He only had enough time to raise it horizontally between both hands and use it to block her from eating his face off. The broken nose guy came back at him, seizing the moment no doubt too. I was about to yell at Jason to do something to help him when suddenly the guy shouted through gritted teeth, "Yo, Jay, a little help here!"

Jason shook his head, the way someone might in disbelief, but he didn't rush forward or fire the gun or anything else. He just stood there and it dawned on me that maybe he was shaking his head *no. Was Jason that cold-hearted after all?*

The guy that knew Jason was grunting, struggling to fend off the girl, and sidestepping, to get out of the way of the other guy. "You do know your name, don't you?" He shouted, bugging out a little. If Jason didn't know his name, the guy obviously knew what that meant, *a lot more people to fight.*

Narrowing his eyes, Jason shouted back instantly, his tone sharp. "You know *yours?*"

The guy didn't look at Jason again, but continued to fight the two people, seeming to struggle more and more each second that passed. "You want my real name, or the American shit you guys call me?" he hissed.

Jason made a sound that was a half-chuckle, half-snort, half-curse, and unexpectedly shoved Duke's leash into Missy's grasp. Her eyes widened. "Do. Not. Let. Go," he said sternly, looking at her in desperation, then he spun back around, raising his gun again, trying to figure out no doubt how to kill two people without killing the guy he obviously knew and without the sick people killing him first. My stomach knotted anxiously as I stood there helpless.

"Move out of the way or I can't shoot," Jason urged, moments later, as he jogged back and forth trying to find a new angle but remaining unsuccessful.

"I'm working on it," the guy groaned. He stepped on the girl's foot, then pushed his arms up so the bat slammed into her chin, whipping her head back. He followed with a swift kick to her legs and turned, nailing the guy coming back up on his left in the groin with the end of the bat. It was awesome survival skills, I'll give him that, but when neither fell, and instantly began swarming in on him again, I realized he was seriously in trouble and my heart was pounding *for* him. *What the heck was he going to do?*

"Jacob!" Jason yelled, aiming the gun again. "Just run. I'll shoot when they run after you, stop trying to knock them down!"

Jacob? Suddenly everything came crashing in around me. That was Jacob? *The* Jacob? As in the Jacob who was supposed to be dead? My heart pounded faster. If Jacob was here and he was healthy then that meant Spencer was—I jolted at the loud, startling sound of gunfire—*not*?

My eyes flashed forward in panic. Right away I realized Jason missed.

He started cursing, but immediately fired again. The bullet whizzed through the air, successfully hitting the guy in the back of the head this time. He dropped, gracelessly to the ground, smearing blood on the asphalt when he fell. At the same moment, the girl lunged for Jacob and Jason wasted no time readying himself for another shot. She reached, arms out, then suddenly collapsed to the ground, face-planting it an inch from Jacob's feet.

"What the—" Jacob lowered his bat, darting a look at Jason, confused and slightly winded. I stared at the lifeless body by his feet, just as startled. I didn't know what the heck just happened, but Jason hadn't shot her.

Jacob peered down at the body, head slightly tilted in question. After he caught his breath, he lifted the bat, poking the girl at his feet with the end of it. We waited, my breath catching in my throat, knowing this would be the part that she would jump up and bite him, but she never stirred. Shrugging, he jabbed the bat harder into her side as if unconvinced too, but still there was no movement. No sound.

"She's dead dude," he said, stunned, talking to Jason as if Missy and I weren't standing there too. His brown eyes were still drawn to the body, but there was no mistaking the question and shock in his voice.

"Too many blows to the head maybe," Jason suggested, lowering his gun, but even he had his doubts.

"Who knows," Jacob replied. And all I could think in that moment as I stared at him was who cares *why* she died, she's dead, who really gave a damn. Jason was right. I shouldn't feel sorry for these people. It was all about survival. And if Jacob *survived*, and was *alive*, then what the hell happened at his house? Who was in the room? Who escaped? *Was* it Spencer after all?

Dread and uncertainty held me captive. I couldn't seem to move my feet.

Turning around, Jacob took everything in slowly. The dead people. Jason. Duke. Us. He did this for about a minute then finally he seemed to relax. It was about the same time I felt even more on edge.

"*Mierda*." He exhaled, wiping his brow with his arm. "That was close. Thanks, dude."

From the corner of my eye I saw Jason nod as he tucked the gun back in his waistband. Something about his expression had me turning my head. He was staring at Jacob with narrowed eyes, a muscle popping in his jaw. Just as I got the impression he was about to say something, Missy blurted beside me, her voice hitching, "Yo asshole, if you're still alive than where the hell is Spencer?"

Obviously she and I were thinking the same thing.

19

Jacob stepped over the bodies and walked toward us, the bat propped up against his shoulder like one of those baseball card poses. He didn't seem offended by Missy's mouth, and he didn't snap anything fresh back to her. But his eyes did assess her from head to toe—twice—before he answered.

"I don't know. He bugged out two nights ago, and I haven't seen him since."

Missy looked like she was about to throw a hissy fit. "That *doesn't* help us," she whined repositioning her grip on Duke's leash. Duke's whimpering had quieted but it was obvious he was still worked up. His tail was still lowered between his legs, ears flat, hair sticking up. And I wasn't sure if he was focused on Jacob like that or at the three dead people behind him.

"And who the heck are you?" Jacob said, his eyes traveling the whole length of Missy's body again with a look of unsuppressed interest. "I never seen you around here before and trust me, I'd remember you. How do you know Spencer?"

"He's our friend," she snapped back, her face flushing with anger, "and if you check me out again I'm going to take that bat of yours and whack you in the freaking nuts. Ok, *pendejo*?"

Jacob's lips turned up into a smirk, no doubt tempted to say something colorful back but Jason cut in, stopping him.

"Alright, you two, enough! Let's just focus on what matters right now, otherwise we'll be here all day. I swear," he said, shaking his head, "you're both cut from the same cloth."

Jason's eyes bounced back and forth between Missy and Jacob until they seemed to agree, then his narrowed gaze lowered toward Duke. He stared at his dog for a long moment, his brow pulling forward even more, before turning his head back toward Jacob...back to Duke....back to Jacob again. It dawned on me in that second why Jason's expression was bothering me so much. I understood why he was glaring like that at someone who was supposed to be his friend. Jason didn't trust Jacob to be entirely healthy. That is why he had been staring at him and watching Duke so carefully. Suddenly, I found myself looking at Jacob differently too.

Jacob *was* sweating, and sweating and dark eyes were immediate signs from what I've learned. Suddenly it hit me. *Dark eyes…crap, I had dark eyes*. No wonder Jason stared at me like that when he first met me…no wonder he brought that up in front of the fire last night. He had been skeptical of me too, just like he was of Jacob now. But I *wasn't* sick, and as I looked at Jacob, I honestly—would even put money down on it—didn't think Jacob was either. It was just a gut feeling I had.

Jacob raised an eyebrow. "No, *wait*, seriously, who are you?" His cocky attitude dropped from his voice. "At least tell me that."

Missy exhaled in annoyance, rolling her eyes. "I'm Missy and she's Dee. I'm sure you've heard of us." Jacob turned his face toward her, slowly shaking his head. Missy's expression fell. "*What?* He seriously never mentioned us?"

"Sorry, but no, and I'd remember if he did. I've been trying to get him to open up since we met. He's not much of a talker."

Spencer not a talker? That was news there. "How did you meet him?" I asked, trying not to appear as offended as I felt. We were risking our lives to save him and he hadn't even mentioned us? *God, what were we, stupid?*

"I was on my way home from dropping *mi madre* off at the airport. See she lives in Spain but comes and stays with me three months out of the year. *Anyway*, there I was on my way back when I spotted Spencer hitchhiking on the highway. Now I don't make it a habit to stop for hitchhikers, but he looked pretty pathetic. And young. I thought maybe he was lost or something. He didn't tell me anything about where he was going, I got the impression he didn't have a clue where he was heading. He said he had a little money, but I knew that wouldn't get him far. So I offered him a place to stay in exchange for his help with my landscaping business."

He paused, lowering the baseball bat off his shoulder so that it just kind of hung lightly from his grip now. "I didn't know his story but I figured it was safer for him to come live with me then it was for him to continue to hitchhike. Either one, he'd be arrested, two, hit by a car, or three, become the victim of a homicide. I didn't want him to be a part of any of it. I've been hoping one day he'd just wake up and say like, *Jacobo, will you take me home*. And I would have."

Missy and I didn't say anything right away. I watched her face very carefully, but she was masking her emotions well now. Even *I* couldn't really tell if she was pissed off or hurt. All I knew was that I was both.

"Do you know he called them Thursday night to come get him?" Jason said moments later as he took the leash from Missy's hand again. His green-brown eyes flashed to me before shifting back to Jacob. "What happened at your house that night, man?

We went there today, the place is destroyed and someone was obviously in the bedroom. Who was it? Was it Spencer?"

Jacob exhaled, wiping his brow again. "No, it wasn't Spencer. I don't know if you knew or not, but Dean Tanning's been staying with us since his wife kicked him out of the house three weeks ago after he had a one-night stand with that blonde-haired waitress at the diner. I don't normally condone that shit. I mean when you are with a girl you best be staying with that girl. Women should be respected, loved, treasured." He was staring at Missy now as if saying it directly to her. She rolled her eyes again.

"Oh please. Just get to the point."

I couldn't help but notice Jacob appeared a little disappointed.

"Well, anyway, since he had nowhere to go I gave him *mi madre's* room to crash in for a couple weeks. On Tuesday he said he thought he was coming down with something, so he was calling out of work and sleeping in. I didn't really see or hear from him Wednesday and then Thursday he came out of the bedroom saying he was hungry. I told him Spencer and I were ordering a pie and to pitch in, and he did. We were all sitting down about to eat and suddenly he just bugged out and lunged at us. His eyes were all black and creepy, just like theirs." He pointed to the dead people behind him. "How that is possible I don't know, but Spencer immediately jumped over the couch and sprinted out the front door while I knocked Dean out with a lamp and dragged him to a bedroom and barricaded the door."

I stood there silent, thinking. *So I was right about Spencer after all. He did run.*

"Did you use gloves?" Jason asked moments later.

Jacob turned his face back toward us. "No."

"Seriously?"

He sort of shrugged, unconcerned. "Well it wasn't like I had a lot of time to think about my options."

"You know that means you could be infected, right?"

Jacob brought his finger to his fat lip. "I honestly don't think I am. Besides my busted mouth, I feel great."

"It could still be early." Jason wrapped Duke's leash one more time around his palm, only proving more he didn't trust Jacob.

Jacob seemed unbothered though. "Nah, if I base it on Dean's symptoms, I would have been feeling it by now. I'm only feeling the swollen lip…and maybe a backache." He arched his back, stretching it. "It's been a while since I swung a bat."

His lip really did look painful. "How did you get that?" I asked, realizing I had taken a couple steps back. I hope I hadn't offended him.

His brown eyes peered over at me casually. "When I crashed the truck, my face smacked the steering wheel. It sucked."

I cringed, remembering the scene in the parking lot. "You had to be going pretty fast, huh?"

"I don't even know. I jumped in my truck and hit pedal to the metal. When I crashed, I jumped back out."

"And all this time," Jason prompted, doubtfully, chiming in again, "you never touched one of them besides Dean?"

Jacob shifted his eyes back to him. "Surprisingly no. This bat has been a life-saver." He fixed his grip on it. "Literally."

"Well that's awesome," Missy interjected coolly, sparing no hesitation. It didn't sound like she meant it at all either, "and I'm glad we are starting to fit pieces together and that you are okay." She paused, narrowing her eyes at Jacob. "But if you don't know where Spencer is, then either shut up or go home because we are going to go find him and that means we got to stop standing around talking and get moving. You all can swap stories later, *after* we find him."

I stared at my best friend shocked. "Really?"

She stared back at me. "What? I don't give a crap if I was rude. We are just wasting time here."

I started to shake my head. "No that's not what I meant." I couldn't believe her. "You seriously still want to find him?"

Her brow rose in confusion and her blue eyes looked at me oddly. "Yeah, of course."

"You heard Jacob, right?" I blurted in disbelief, to clarify she did. "Spencer hasn't even talked about us. We are risking our lives for *what* reason?"

"Because it's Spencer," she snapped back, her blue eyes narrowing. "And that's all there is to it. If you don't want to help me find him, then *you* can go home *too,* but I'm not. I promised him I'd help him and I don't break promises." Adjusting the strap of her purse on her shoulder Missy started walking without waiting for me to respond.

I watched her leaving, but didn't follow. "You don't even have a weapon," I hissed, my frustrations spiking. "You'll just get yourself killed."

"At this point," she grumbled, not stopping. "Death seems inevitable anyway."

Was she serious? "You're being ridiculous," I shouted, completely in shock.

She paused, swinging swiftly around to face me in the distance. "No!" she shouted back stubbornly. "I'm being a friend. *You* are being a coward."

"*A coward?*" *Wow.* I was not being a coward. She was being an idiot. "If that's how you truly feel, then just shut up and go Miss."

"I'm already leaving," she yelled, her blonde hair whipping around with the turn of her head. "Spencer and I don't need friends like you, anyway."

"I don't even know him anymore," I screamed. "Neither do you!"

"Last time, I DON'T CARE!" She kept walking.

"You're just going to let her go off alone?" Jacob said, surprised, staring at me like I was the person in the wrong.

I didn't answer. Pursing my lips, I just stood there and watched her go, ignoring him.

"Well, I'm not. It's not right." Lifting his bat, so that he was holding it with two hands, Jacob jogged off, leaving us. "*Chica, hold up!*"

A few seconds later I turned to Jason, fuming. "You going to go too?" I snapped.

ason just stood there, his eyes on me, another expression I couldn't decipher on his face. "No. I'll stay with you."

20

The wind blew my bangs in my eyes and I swiped them away, cursing. I had been standing there with Jason for about thirty minutes already, feeling like I was the rope in a game of tug-a-war. A part of me, the rational, wise part of me, was yelling at me to get the hell out of the campground—heck, out of town—fast, but the other part of me, obviously the less intelligent, you-care-too-much-for-your-own-good-part was shouting at me for letting Missy leave. I was constantly telling myself *she had Jacob,* to try and make myself feel better about it. But, the other side of my brain just kept reminding me that she didn't know Jacob. It was quite possible even he was sick, but just not showing signs yet.

Needless to say I had a pounding headache and guilt the size of Alaska. Jason hadn't said anything. He just petted Duke and listened to me rant and rave.

"Damn it, why is this so difficult?" I whined, crossing my arms. This had nothing to do with Spencer. "I *want* to leave. So why can't I?" Jason's green-brown eyes just continued to look at me, his expression the same. "Because you'll hate yourself forever if something happens to her. You know that." His hand continued to pat Duke on the side casually.

"But it's not my fault," I groaned, staring at his hands instead of his face. "She's a big girl. She can make her own decisions."

"Yeah, but that won't matter. If something happens to her, you'll never forgive yourself." He sounded so certain.

I cursed again.

"And there won't be a day that goes by you don't remind yourself of today," he pressed, being the Mr. Know-It-All he was. "Just saying."

I glared at him, wanting to throw a hissy fit, but I knew he was right. "She's my best friend."

His lips stretched into a tight smile. "I know."

"And you're right," I sighed, staring at him. "I have to go after her."

"I know," he nodded. "And you should."

I locked eyes with him momentarily, and everything about what *he* should be doing popped back into my head, and I knew what needed to happen. *He* needed to leave. And I needed to find Missy. "But you need to get to your brother and sister. You can't keep risking your life like this to save us."

"I know." But this time when he said it, he sounded uncertain.

I exhaled slowly, feeling my eyes starting to burn but grateful for the fact there were no tears. "So I guess this is goodbye?"

A long beat of silence followed.

I saw his own game of tug-a-war in his eyes.

"You have to save your brother and sister," I insisted, to make the decision easier for him. "They already lost their parents. Don't make them lose anyone else."

He didn't say anything.

"Jason, you *have* to. Every second out here, you are just risking it." I paused, biting the inside of my cheek. "I know you didn't stay behind for me. You wanted to go back. I'm telling you to go back."

Nodding, Jason stepped backward, lowering a strap from his shoulder and swung his backpack around to the front of him. "If I go," he said hesitantly, "You have to take the gun."

"Jason."

"No objections. You might need it, *take it*."

I swallowed, holding out my hand. "Okay."

He placed the cold pistol in my palm, his fingers brushing against my skin. "Please use it if you have to. I know you don't like killing people. I know you are hating yourself for what you did earlier. You have to get over that. It's about saving you and Mouth. There isn't time for second-guessing and guilt, or hyperventilating." His hazel eyes searched my face for reassurance and understanding.

This time I nodded. "Don't worry. I already figured that out. You were right, these people are already gone. It doesn't matter. I can't save them. We *are* just putting them out of their misery…And no, I won't drop the gun again. I promise." I tucked the gun into the back of my shorts again, but this time I wasn't scared of it. "And I don't regret saving you. I'd do it again. Just so you know."

Jason sighed, looking away. "I'm sorry, I know you told me not to but I have to say thank you for that…I can't walk away without you knowing I'm grateful."

I rocked back on my heels. "Then I have to say it too… for everything, including saving my life, thanks."

His lips smirked, but I could tell it was forced. "You've already thanked me for saving your life."

"Yeah, well, just want to be certain you know I meant it." I looked down at my feet, awkwardly, and only then did I remember I was wearing his shirt. "Oh…duh... here…" I grabbed the end of it. "Sorry. I forgot."

"Keep it," he replied without hesitation. "I have plenty others."

My hands paused and I smiled up at him. "I appreciate it."

"No prob."

We stood staring at each other again for a few silent minutes.

"So I guess this is it then," I mumbled, not wanting to pull my gaze away from his. *I couldn't believe it.*

"Yeah."

Another beat of silence. "Will I ever see you again?" I'm not sure why I asked, I already knew the odds of that.

Jason sighed again. "You have no idea how bad I wish we met under different circumstances." A frown was forming around his mouth. "I'd ask for your number, but I don't have a pen." He sounded very disappointed.

I knew I was. "I'd give it too, if I had one." I forced a smirk. "Guess trying to memorize it is a lost cause, right?" The look in his eyes changed and my stomach did a crazy flip-flop. "Oh well," I mumbled quickly, nervously, before he could respond, "I'm glad I got to meet you at least." I pulled my attention away and glanced at Duke, who was staring at me too. "And you too, buddy."

I reached out and gave him a quick pat to the head, his tail immediately wagging. "You take care of him, okay Duke? You get them out of this town safely."

Duke whined back.

I held out my hand. "You promise?"

He pawed my hand and I chuckled.

"Smart dog," I said, peering back at Jason.

"Huh, you actually petted him, never thought I'd see the day." The tone of his voice was a mixture of shocked and pleased.

"Yeah, well, I'm not so scared of him after all," I smiled. "He's been a good boy."

Jason leaned down, patting Duke's side again, smiling. "That he has…" His hand paused, his smile fading. "Well Dee, this is it. We can't keep prolonging this. The longer you wait, the further she gets."

My eyes immediately started to sting more. He was right. Again. "Okay," I mumbled, not moving. "Good bye Jason."

He straightened back out. "Bye, Dee." I could tell he didn't want me to leave just as much as I didn't want him to go. Readjusting his grip on Duke's leash, he looked at me one last time and then, slowly turned away. I almost lost it right there. I was kind of shocked about it too. *Hold it together. You only knew the guy a little over a day,* I reminded myself.

Just as I was about to take a step in the opposite direction, I heard him call my name again.

"Dee."

I turned my face toward him, probably a little too eager. "Yeah?"

"I almost forgot…" He took two steps forward, lightly placed his free hand on the back of my head and brought his lips to mine.

At first I was startled, but then my body seemed to respond earnestly. I kissed him back, letting my lips tell him exactly how much I thought saying goodbye sucked.

When our lips pulled apart, and I was still breathless, he murmured, "I promised I would kiss you."

And now I knew it was really goodbye.

***

"Missy!" I shouted for what felt like the thousandth time as I walked through the campground. It was probably not smart to be drawing attention to myself. I had been looking for her and Jacob for over an hour, and still haven't found them. Somehow I ended up walking in a circle—twice. Both times I ended up back in the area where Jason and I parted ways.

Yes, I was that much of an idiot.

"Missy!"

I wrapped my arms across my chest, feeling slightly freaked out. What if I couldn't find her? What if she was already dead?

"Jacob!" I yelled this time, for a change of pace.

The afternoon was drumming on as I dragged my tired, sore, blistering feet across the ground. I hadn't heard a sound from anyone, which wasn't too comforting. *Maybe everyone was dead?* The fact I never ran into Jason or Duke just further proved the point that they were really gone. I just hope they made it out alive. It's all I could hope for. No matter how hard I tried not to cry, I still wiped away a few tears. There was just something about him that I was going to miss terribly. And of course, it would figure I had the best kiss of my life today and then I had to say goodbye.

Up ahead, I saw a clearing between the trees and I couldn't help but wonder if it would bring me to another camp area or perhaps town. I wasn't sure which I was wishing for at this point more. I just wanted something other than nothing.

Low-hanging trees brushed across my shoulders. The sun was shining dimly between the leaves, kissing the tops of my sneakers as I walked. My shoelace was clicking against the dirt, almost completely untied. Clearing my voice, I shouted my best friend's name again, losing any ounce of faith I had left.

That's when I heard a guy's voice behind me, yelling something, and I realized I wasn't alone after all.

It took ten seconds before I realized he was calling for *me*. My heart skipped. Jason came *back*.

"Over here!" I hollered, moving toward his voice anxiously and excitedly.

It wasn't until I got closer that I saw it wasn't Jason. I was instantly flooded with a multitude of emotions, mostly disappointment and relief. But at least it was Jacob and Missy and *at least* they were *okay*. I jogged up to them.

"You asshole," Missy said, punching me in the arm, her voice hoarse. "I can't believe you just left me."

"Technically you left me," I winched, rubbing my bicep. "But I've been looking for you for the last hour." *If that somehow made up for it.*

"Just you? Where's Jason?" Jacob asked, looking over my shoulder, worry clear on his face.

"He left," I mumbled, feeling an ache in my chest. "He went back to his brother and sister, and I went looking for you two. I told him to," I added quickly just so he wouldn't think anything bad of Jason leaving me. "You guys okay?"

"Ugh, I've been crying the whole time, damn it. I thought they got you." Only then did I realize my best friend's eyes were bloodshot.

"Sorry." I made a face. "I'm fine, really. I didn't even see one person."

"Yeah. We didn't either." Jacob was skeptical. "Which I got to be honest, makes me a little on edge."

"Yeah, well," I followed his gaze around the campground. "Let's just be grateful for that."

"Oh, I *am* grateful, trust me." I looked over at him and he sent me a sidelong glance, while twirling the end of the bat in his hands, repeatedly. "What can I say? It's been a long few days."

"Tell me about it," I grumbled, taking in the puffy lavender circles under his brown eyes, his still swollen, cracked lip and a faint splotchy five o'clock shadow on his face. I then turned toward Missy. Dark shadows lined her blue eyes too. Day old makeup mixed with exhaustion, no doubt.

"Look," I said carefully, trying not to rile her up again. "I know you want to find Spencer. I get that. I know that's the whole reason we came here, why we've gone through all this. But Miss, at some point, we have to draw the line. Fighting over this is ridiculous. Risking our lives is ridiculous. Enough is enough already. Do you realize how lucky we've been? We could be dead right now."

"I know," she groaned, fiddling with her survival bracelet again, avoiding eye contact. "I'm being stupid." *Well, at least she admits it.* "And before you say anything else save your breath, Jacob already gave me this whole third-degree thing and told me I was out of line."

Furrowing my brow, I snuck a quick glance at him. Here I thought he thought *I* was out of line. Funny.

"But, *Dee*," Missy whined, snagging my attention, her baby blues peering up at me finally. "I know everything you say is right. I know everything Jacob said is right, but I *still* want to find him. I can't help it. It's Spencer. *Spencer*," she repeated, in a way that had me instantly feeling guilty and remembering how much I cared about him. "And he needs us. I'm sorry I said all those things about you. I didn't mean them, okay. I was just hurt and angry. See, you've always been there for us. You are the one we always turn to for help. Because let's face it you are the strong one. You said it yourself at Jacob's house today. Spencer and I can't handle this shit alone. And it bothered me that when we needed you the most, when I needed you to come with me, you bailed. I couldn't believe it."

"Bailed? Seriously?" I shook my head in disbelief. "Come on, Missy. I was trying to protect us. And I was angry too. It just seems stupid to risk our lives for someone who *literally* bailed on us, on our friendship. He didn't even say goodbye. He's never mentioned us. Does that sound like a *real* friend? Someone to die over?"

"But what about me, Dee? You just let me go? Are you crazy? You know I'd die the first second one of these zombies came after me. I don't even have a weapon."

"Like I said before, *you* left."

"Yeah, but I'm always dramatic. I always say dumb crap. You are the rational one. You were supposed to come after me and drag me back or come with me. You didn't do either."

Why was I feeling so guilty? "Okay, you're right. However, pointing fingers does nothing now. We need to make a decision, some sort of compromise. I know where you stand; you know where I stand."

She bit her lip and half-nodded, her hair falling across her face.

I didn't wait for her to say anything. "I'll give you, him, whatever, the rest of today. If we don't find Spencer by nightfall, we are out of here. Even if I have to steal a car to make that happen. Deal?"

She didn't answer right away. I saw her look at Jacob, and from the corner of my eye I saw him lip, *say yes.* I found it odd, in general, but I didn't comment. What did I care? He was siding with me.

"Make it tomorrow morning and I'll go," she insisted, glancing back at me, determined. "No arguments, whether we find him or not. Just give us *all* of tonight to find him, that's all I'm asking."

"You girls are not staying out here at night. Not happening," Jacob cut in, incredulous. "That's even more suicidal."

I wanted to object. Jacob was right. But as I stood there, staring at my best friend, I realized I just couldn't say no. Don't get me wrong. I wanted to go home. I really did. But in that moment, I saw how much Spencer meant to her, in the silent plead of her eyes, and I had to say yes. And I couldn't picture giving up now and having her regret it or hate me for it forever. And I had the gun anyway. I'd make sure we'd last the night.

"Okay, tomorrow," I sighed, giving in.

An unsure smile stretched across her face. "Really? You don't mind?" I could hear the torn emotions in her voice, the doubt and the happiness.

"No…*hello*…you listening to me?" Jacob leaned around her. "Don't be stupid. Tell her *no*, Dee."

I exhaled, ignoring him. "Well, Spencer isn't just going to drop from the sky, so standing here is doing nothing." I straightened my shoulders, picking my chin up as confidently as I could. "If we are going to find him, we better make a plan and start looking. The clock is ticking."

Missy's smile spread and Jacob started grumbling, shaking his head. "I don't understand women." He propped the bat on his shoulder and stepped backward, gesturing forward with his free hand, dramatically. "After you, ladies."

I raised an eyebrow, staring at him. "Huh?"

"You didn't think I was just going to leave, did you? I've been looking for the kid, too. Remember? And I'll be damned if I let you stay out here at night, alone."

"You'll be damned?" Missy mocked clearly amused. "How?"

"Shut up," he said, pushing at us. "Just start walking."

"Oh, so *that's* our wonderful plan?"

He rolled his eyes at her. "It's not *my* plan, *chica*. I'm just the poor bastard stuck here, with *you*."

"No one asked you to be," she said crossly.

He laughed. "Like you said before, you'd die the first second one of these zombies came after you. You need me here."

"I'd rather take my chances," she grumbled, coming up beside me, wrapping her arm around mine and dragging me away. "Come on, let's go this way."

"*Chica*, you'd be lost without me," He blurted, smugly. "Literally." After snagging our attention, he pointed toward the left, to the path we were heading toward. "You go that way, and you'll just end up back here again. It's a giant loop."

Missy made an inaudible sound. "I knew that," she hissed, dragging me by the arm the other way now, like I was her ragdoll.

"Of course you did," he smirked, amused.

He waited until we passed him before he started following, and suddenly I realized it wasn't Jason protecting us now, it was Jacob. And I had mixed feelings about that.

21

I slowed down to tie my shoelace, because it was finally completely undone."Maybe Spencer isn't even in the campground," I prompted, peering up at them, after double-knotting the lace. They both stared down at me, brows scrunched in confusion. I stood up. "What? You haven't thought about that?"

"No, he's definitely here or at least was," Jacob pressed, reaching in his pocket, pulling out something silver. "I found this today. It's Spencer's lighter." He held it out for us to see. My stomach knotted instantly when I saw it.

We gave him that lighter. His roommate really *was* Spencer. I guess a part of me thought maybe it was possible it was a different Spencer. Maybe I was hoping it was someone else. Or maybe I was just hoping Spencer wasn't at the campground. But there was no mistaking it now, because that *was* Spencer's lighter. It was the same small, silver lighter with his initials engraved on one side and a skateboard on the other that we gave to him for a *just because* gift—just because we saw it at the mall and instantly thought of him.

"You mean he never even told you where he got this lighter from?" Missy said, incredulous. "Not like, hey my two friends bought me this. Or there were these two girls…"

"No, but I never asked either," Jacob said, apologetically, tucking the lighter back into his pocket. "He was always flipping it open and flipping it closed. It was annoying, but he obviously loved it."

There was something about the way Jacob made a point to say that, that had me thinking. "You don't think he just dropped it, do you? Do you think he purposely left it there?"

Jacob tapped the bat on the ground, deliberating. "At first yeah, I thought he was leaving a trail but I never found anything else. I never found him. Now I think he might have just dropped it."

"If you loved something as much as you say he did, you wouldn't be so careless with it, right?" I considered. "Where did you find it? Maybe that's a clue."

"On the path leading toward the edge of the third campsite, but I already looked around there."

"Well maybe you missed something," Missy countered, "ever think about that?"

"I guess I could have, but seriously, I checked the area like three times."

"Well, doesn't hurt to check it out, anyway." She looked around, her blue eyes eager. "Which way do we go, navigator?"

"Well, if that's where you want to go, we have to head back the other way. That campsite is on the complete opposite side of the campground."

Missy groaned, her eager expression fading. "Of course it is."

The three of us turned around and started heading back the way we just came, my mind still trying to piece together facts.

"Spencer called us this morning and we thought it was from the payphone here but that seems highly unlikely now." I glanced over at Jacob. "Any idea where else he could have gotten a phone? That could be another clue."

He furrowed his brow. "Depends. What time did he call you?"

"Early. Like really early," Missy chimed in.

"The sun was up," I added, "not that early but definitely not after eight."

"Oh, then it's still possible he called from the pay phone. I mean, I didn't back the RV into it until around ten."

"*Wait*, what?" I halted mid-step, stumbling a little. A vivid memory of the first campsite came back to me. The dead bodies, the blood stained ground, the ripped tents, the campfires... *campfires?* "Ohmigod," I gasped, horrified. "It was you." It suddenly just dawned on me. Jacob had the lighter. He lit the fires. He lit the people *on* fire.

He killed *all* those people.

I grabbed Missy's arm, pulling her away from him.

Jacob stared at me, like I was over reacting. "Yeah, I just admitted I drove the RV. I don't see what—" Suddenly, his brown eyes widened. "Wait, you think I killed those people?"

"You have the lighter," I mumbled, almost incoherently. Missy was just staring at him, speechless, as if she couldn't comprehend it.

"*Listen* to me, I did *not* do that. I didn't find the lighter until later. I didn't start any fires. I didn't stab anyone. That's how I found them this morning, I swear. I swear on my *abuelo* and *abuela's* grave." He crossed his heart and brought his hand to his lips, kissing his fingers and raising them to the sky.

"I won't lie. I did beat the crap out of a number of people with my bat. I did kill some people with my truck. But, I *never* set anyone on fire. And the RV thing was an accident. I peered inside to see if Spencer was in it and when I turned around, a few people came out of nowhere and charged me. I barely had enough time to jump in the RV and shut the door. I saw the keys on the table, jumped into the front seat and tried to drive it out of there. Except

I am a moron, and I punched it in reverse instead of drive and took out the phone booth. Then the damn thing wouldn't start."

He exhaled, rubbing the back of his neck. "I had to climb out the driver's window and then I was chased for about fifteen minutes straight. And it's been an on and off "cat and mouse" ever since. You saw with your own eyes. If Jason didn't shoot them, I'd be dead right now."

I loosened my grip on Missy's arm, realizing I was starting to believe him.

"I don't know how far you got in this campground," he added, "but the other campsites are just as bad. Okay not *that* bad but still pretty messed up."

"I didn't see any other camp areas," I said, feeling slightly sick if that was true. "But then again, I walked in a circle most of the time looking for you two."

"Well, whatever happened seemed to mostly happen last night. Hence why I think being out here tonight is suicidal. Maybe night makes it worse or something. I don't know. But if we are going to be out here, we *have* to be careful. And you *have* to trust me…and we have to find a weapon, other than a bat, just in case".

I thought of how Jason wanted us to get out of the woods last night as soon as it was getting dark out and couldn't help but wonder if he knew more about this virus than he was letting on. And if anyone did, it would be Jason. His mom had it. Maybe night did make them worse. *No,* I quickly realized, correcting myself. Jason would never leave us out here alone if he knew how bad it got at night. He was just offering us a place to sleep because he knew we didn't have anywhere to go. If Jason was that cold-hearted he wouldn't have given me the gun to protect myself.

"Well we don't have to worry about that." I reached behind me, retrieving the pistol. "I have one."

Jacob's eyes widened. "Where did you get a gun?"

"From Jason," Missy said, shaking her head, a look of confusion on her face. "I thought he confiscated that."

"Um, actually the gun belongs to Kyle and Buck." I turned the gun over in my hands. "It's just a loner."

"You know Kyle and Buck?" Jacob looked real lost now.

"We slept at their place last night. Jason brought us there."

"That's the last place I'd bring girls," Jacob mumbled.

"What?" Missy said.

"Nothing." He eyed me skeptically. "Do you even know how to use it?"

"Yes," I grumbled, instantly annoyed. I was tired of men thinking I couldn't handle a gun just because I was a petite girl. I bet I had better aim than most of them.

"She saved Jason's life today with it," Missy prompted, in my defense.

He looked at her briefly before turning his face back to me. "Good to know. Do you want me to carry it?"

"Nope, I can handle it," I said, tucking it back into my waistband.

"Oh yeah? Why he confiscate it then?"

I glared up at him. "Doesn't really matter. I have it now, don't I?" I undid my ponytail and redid it, to pull my hair out of my face. "Let's just hope I don't have to use it."

"I'm just hoping," he said, as we started walking again. "That you have enough bullets when you do."

And just like that, I no longer felt confident.

"Hey, how about we don't talk like that?" Missy urged, her voice hitching up. "My nerves are already shot as it is."

"Sorry," Jacob said, swinging the bat back and forth. "I'm just a realist."

"And I'm just a damn high school student who can't even pass gym, but I can still kick a guy in the nuts," she warned.

He turned his head, a muscle popping in his jaw. "Point taken. I'll keep my mouth shut."

"Thank you," she grumbled.

And as I followed them, I realized I was starting to mentally count how many bullets were left in the chamber anyway. Just in case.

"Wait, what is *that*?" Missy suddenly blurted, snapping me out of zoning.

"What is what?" I said, my heart racing, eyes frantically looking around.

"Is that a car horn?"

I heard it, at the exact moment Jacob said, "Yup."

Missy glanced at us, eyebrow raised. "Someone's beeping? In a campground? Why?"

"I don't know." Jacob shrugged. "Maybe someone is trying to get someone to hurry up or get someone's attention. You know, like a cry for help?"

Missy stopped walking. "You don't think…"

Jacob and I halted too.

"Spencer?" I instantly started worrying, but shook my head. "No, where would he get a car?"

"There's cars all over the campground," Jacob pointed out. "He could have stolen one."

"Or worse," Missy freaked, her eyes widening. "What if he's locked inside one and he's surrounded and he doesn't have keys and they are breaking the windows and he's scared and trapped and…"

"Whoa, take a breath, *chica*." Jacob placed his hand on her shoulder. "We got the point."

"No I don't think you *do.*" She immediately brushed his hand off. "Otherwise you'd be bugging too."

A very clear picture was in my head now and I couldn't shake it. What if she was right?

"But what if it isn't him, Miss? What if it's someone else?"

"Then we should help them anyway. If you were trapped in a car, wouldn't you want help?"

"She does have a point. Of course, if it was me, I'd just hot wire the car."

She rolled her eyes. "Yeah, well, not everyone knows how to do that."

The horn echoed through the campground again, louder this time. I guess now it was all I could focus on.

"I was kidding," Jacob sighed. "Personally I think you have a death wish, but if that's what you want to do."

"It is," she insisted, without hesitating.

"Well, if it isn't Spencer," I warned, making myself very clear, before taking another step. "That's time wasted and we aren't here to save others."

"At least one of you uses common sense," Jacob grumbled, rocking back on his heels.

Missy rounded on him, eyes narrowing, no doubt on the verge of cursing him off when the horn blasted again. *Even* louder.

I spun to my left. "Is it just me or does it sound like it's getting closer?"

From the corner of my eye, I saw Jacob turn too.

"If it's getting closer, that throws Missy's theory out the window."

"Shut up," she hissed.

We stood there, listening.

Beep, beep, beep.

Definitely closer.

"Either Spencer is driving right to us or someone else is. And I doubt we'd be so lucky."

I gulped. Jacob was right. "Maybe it's a rescue vehicle."

"*Chica,* if anyone's coming to this town it's to condemn it, not evacuate it. This is the kind of shit the government *doesn't* want spreading worldwide. Plus there are no sirens."

"There's not always sirens."

He peered down at Missy. "In this situation, there'd be sirens. Hell, there probably be a freaking helicopter. Maybe even a goddamn tank. And if they catch us, we'd be quarantined, or worse, just straight up shot."

"So what are you saying?" I pressed, growing more on edge each second. He wasn't helping.

"I'm saying," he paused, considering. "Hide."

"Hide?" I raised an eyebrow instantly. "What? Why?"

He laughed, without humor. "Because whoever it is, is coming this way fast and I for sure, don't want to be road kill. If they come flying over that hill, we won't have enough time to get out of the way."

He reached out, pushing Missy along, not waiting for a response. "Don't worry, if by some luck of faith it's Spencer driving, you can just shoot the tire out and problem solved. We'll jump out of hiding, I'll change the tire, and you three can drive home and live happily ever after. Just drop me off at the airport first."

Missy made an inaudible sound and pushed him off her again. "Stop touching me damn it, I know how to walk."

"Yeah but that snail pace you do, doesn't fly right now."

She flipped him off and purposely walked slower.

"Is she always this hostile?" He shook his head.

"She just doesn't like you very much." I picked up my pace. "Come on, Miss. Don't be an idiot."

"But he's purposely being annoying," she whined.

"Still a pretty dumb reason to be run over," I countered, sending him a sidelong glance. "Don't make Spencer jokes," I muttered under my breath.

"But I thought it was a nice fairy-tale end—" The sound of the horn blasting again cut him off. And this time we heard the actual car coming too. He spun around. "Okay, fun's over." He dropped the bat, grabbed Missy's arm and swung her over his shoulder, hurrying past me. "*Move*."

I hesitated just long enough to pick up the bat then ran after them, across the rest of the field, as Missy kicked and punched Jacob repeatedly in the back, her curses mixing in with the sound of the nearing engine.

He let her down gently, peering over his shoulder to check on me no doubt and she immediately smacked him in the nuts with her purse. Hard. He bent over, cursing in Spanish, his knees dropping to the ground.

"I told you not to touch me," she grumbled, readjusting her purse on her shoulder, her hair disheveled.

I stumbled to a stop next to Jacob, making a face in apology, and yanked Missy behind a tree, just as the front of the car flew over the top of the hill.

When I heard the car passing us, I peeked around the bark, cautiously, curiously, my heart pounding.

My eyes instantly widened.

It wasn't a car.

It was a truck.

And not just any truck.

It was Jacob's truck.

And I was just standing there, watching the Spanish flag bumper sticker getting further and further away.

22

"Hey!" I started screaming, bolting out from behind the tree and sprinting out into the field.

Even Jacob was picking himself off the ground, running awkwardly with his hand between his pants toward me, hollering after *his* truck.

Missy was screaming too.

But the truck wasn't slowing down.

I tossed the bat and started jumping up and down, waving my hands wildly, yelling even louder. I could feel the gun slipping out of my waist band. I stopped, grabbing it before it fell to the ground again, but continued shouting just as Missy and Jacob hurried up next to me. Both out of breath, and Jacob slightly hunched over.

Popping the safety on the gun, I readied myself to shoot out the tire as a last resort. We shouted, I aimed, and the truck skidded to a stop, dirt kicking up behind it. I could no longer see the wheels; hell, I couldn't see any part of the truck. Cursing, I waited but it wasn't long before the truck slowly began reversing through the dust toward us.

I never had to shoot.

Missy squealed, circling in front of me. "Is it Spencer? Ohmigod, is it really him? Is it? *Is it*? Did you see?"

I exhaled, tucking the gun back into my waistband. "I don't know. I couldn't tell." I peered over her shoulder, watching the truck getting closer. "But who else could it be…" I'd admit it was a little ironic for Spencer to just be driving by, looking for us at that exact moment. It seemed a little too easy for us, after everything that is, but maybe the tables were finally turning for us.

How come I doubted that?

"What about you? Did you see?" Missy urged, speaking directly to Jacob. I shifted my eyes to him, reflexively. He was still slightly bent, face flushed and grimacing, his hand still cupping his *parts*.

"No," he groaned. "I just wanted my truck back to get away from *you*." A pause and a curse in Spanish. "Damn, *Chica*, I think you might have broken my *cojones*…what the hell do you have in that bag, lead?

"If you are expecting an apology, you're not getting one."

"That doesn't surprise me." He straightened back out, lifting his hat off his forehead to wipe his brow across his sleeve. "I feel sick."

"Sick?" I rounded on him, immediately bugging out, thinking the worse. "You think you're infected?"

"No, I think I'm going to hurl. Elementary school was the last time I got hit this hard."

Missy started laughing, but I didn't. And as I turned around to face the truck, I sent him one last glance, observing him. He was still sweating. A lot. I wasn't sure I believed him entirely.

The truck rolled to a stop, on an angle, about forty feet away from us. I fidgeted, nervously, having a brief second of panic. Maybe it wasn't anyone we knew. I never thought about that. And now Missy and I could be surrounded by *two* infected people. Then I thought of how Jacob just carried her. *Shit, I hope touch isn't how it spreads.*

A dog barking, snapped me out of freaking out. On the passenger side, Duke suddenly popped his head out of the window, eager to see us. And I've never been so happy to see a dog in my life. It was someone we could trust. *Thank god.*

But then it really seemed to dawn on me what that meant. Jason was back. *He was back and he wasn't supposed to be.*

I jogged forward, rounding the bumper, to head to the driver's side, anxiously. *What the hell was he doing here?*

He was rolling down the window just as I got there and before I could even say anything, he leaned out the window and said, "I found a pen."

I stopped and stared up at him, confused. "What?"

"A pen. You know, one of these." He half-turned in his seat and three seconds later turned back around sure enough holding one in his hand.

"I know what a pen is," I said, incredulous. "What is your point?"

"You told me you'd give me your number if I had one. Did you change your mind?" He gave me an exaggerated pouty face.

My mouth just dropped. "Please tell me you're joking. *Please.*"

He laughed and tossed the pen into the backseat. "I am. That's not why I'm back."

I took in his scruffy face, his green-brown eyes, cute smile and started getting all jittery again. A part of me wished that *was* why he came back. "Why *are* you?" I urged, demanding an answer.

He paused, staring out the windshield for a moment, tapping his fingers on the steering wheel before answering. "I just couldn't do it."

"Do what?"

Jason didn't turn his head. "I couldn't leave. I couldn't go without knowing if you found Mouth. And then I remembered you needed a truck to tow your car out of the mountain and that's why I was with you two for so long in the first place. I promised I'd help you, so I couldn't just go."

Sometimes this guy was too damn good of a person, but he was still a dumb idiot. "What about your brother and sister? They should be more important than us. Don't you understand that?"

He finally looked at me. "I told you Brandon and Frankie are fine right now where they are. They are safe. You two aren't. Plus I want to know if there are more cars somewhere in this campground. I have to find out how serious this situation is, how far the virus is spreading. Or how it is spreading, if I ever want to truly protect them anyway."

I didn't say anything right away, even if he had a point, because I still didn't think he should be here. Duke's barking took up the silence, and I saw his tail wagging back and forth as Missy came up to pet him through the window on the other side.

"Hey, *Hallmark*," she grumbled, snagging Jason's attention. "What took you so long to stop? I practically lost my voice yelling."

"Mouth, I could never be that lucky," he said, patting Duke on the butt to get him to stop barking and sit. "And I had my windows up."

"Well that was stupid."

"Whatever. I'm here, aren't I?"

"You know the funny thing is I don't remember asking you to be." But she smiled at him anyway.

He shook his head. "I'm glad to see you are still in one piece too...but you know, the break from the constant hatred was kind of nice, I won't lie."

"I wish I could say the same." She pointed behind her. "You're actually better than him, he's—"

"Like you?" Jason said sarcastically, cutting her off.

She narrowed her eyes. "Shut up."

Chuckling, he shifted forward in his seat a little to look around her. I couldn't see Missy anymore. "Yo, Jacob, what's wrong with you? I steal your truck and no comment? Not like you."

"She hit me in the *cojones*, dude," I heard him holler. "Not in the mood, right now."

Jason just laughed and leaned back into his seat, turning toward me, smiling. He looked at me for a beat, just a single look that sent a flutter of nerves throughout my whole body, before he leaned forward on his arms out the window and whispered, "Come on, aren't you at least a little happy to see me?"

His face was right next to mine. His breath warm on my cheeks. All I had to do was move an inch and I could kiss him. I wanted to kiss him. I saw the way his eyes lowered to my mouth. I could tell he wanted to kiss me too. I thought of how soft his lips were, of the slight tickle his scruff would give my skin, of how I thought I'd never see him again and suddenly I was leaning forward, half an inch, one inch. He lowered his head, I arched my weight onto my toes just slightly and brought my lips to his.

"Open the freaking door," Jacob suddenly yelled, pounding on the truck. Jason jolted back, smacking his head on the window frame, just as Duke started growling. Panic spread through me instantly, quickly engulfing those seconds of sweet anxiousness. Our lips barely touched before they were forced apart.

"Jacob, dude, what the hell?" Jason brought his palm to his head, grimacing. Jacob was at the door, jiggling the handle.

Duke's growling turned into barking, his fur rising on his back, his tail lowering between his legs. From where I stood, I saw him staring at Jacob. And my fears were instantly confirmed.

"Come on, damn it. Open. The. Freaking. Door." He was bugging out.

It must have been the intensity of his voice that had me suddenly standing all the way up on my tippy-toes to look across the bed of the truck. And that's when I saw him. Not Jacob. But a man. He was running forward, face white, eyes black even from here, and salt and pepper hair with a receding hair line. There was blood on his hands, around his mouth, grass-stains on the knees of his pants, tears in his shirt sleeves, scratch marks down his arms, and sweat soaking the cotton on his chest. And he was gaining ground fast, heading right toward Jacob and Missy with that hungry, dead look in his eyes. No wonder Duke was barking.

Jason instantly popped the locks on the door, urging Duke in the back. But Duke wouldn't stop barking and wouldn't move. Cursing, Jason reached forward, grabbing Duke's collar. "Hurry, before he jumps out."

Jacob nodded, pulled open the door and started shoving Missy inside, but the man was getting too close. So I grabbed the edge of the truck, put my foot on the wheel to help, and hurled myself into the bed, landing on my hands and knees.

Missy started screaming at me as she crawled into the back seat.

I didn't waste a second. I reached behind me, grabbing the gun, and fired, barely grazing the man in the shoulder. Jacob was just standing there, looking at me, obviously unsure what to do. So I yelled at him. "Get in you idiot. *Now!*" I fired again, hitting only the man's side this time. I cursed. It was hard to get a good shot in because he was running too damn fast.

Jacob didn't hesitate any longer. He jumped inside, slamming the door shut. I leaned forward smacking the back window and Missy immediately unlocked it. I fired one more shot, no clue where it went, and dove through the tiny space, tossing my gun on the seat. Duke continued to bark out the window, Missy and Jacob helped pulled me in, and Jason put the truck in drive, speeding off, running the man over in the process.

And as we drove and Duke sat between Jason and Jacob, his barking calming to a whimper, his whimper to a quiet panting, I realized, I was wrong. There was no way Jacob could be infected or Duke would know. I sighed in relief. For now we were *all* okay.

"What's the plan?" Jason asked, as he drove, cutting his own path through the campground. "Do we have one?"

"Yeah, keep going straight," Jacob answered, "and when you get to that sign up there, go right. They want to check out the third camp area."

"Why? What's there?"

"Hopefully Spencer," Missy said. "Or at least some damn clue as to where he is."

Jason looked back in the rearview mirror, eyebrow raised. "What am I missing?"

"I found Spencer's lighter there this morning, they think he purposely left it there." Jacob shook his head. "They are still determined to find this kid."

"Of course we are, damn it. That *is* why we are here," Missy prompted.

Jason sighed, bringing his eyes back to the road. "Well, at least we have the truck now. We are safer in here."

I stared out the back window, watching trees and bodies pass by. There weren't a lot of bodies, just a few, but all dead on the ground. Some faceless. Some not. And all I could think was this shouldn't be real. But it was. And I started really thinking about what could possibly be causing it because if it wasn't stopped, humanity was pretty much doomed. Maybe not today, or not tomorrow, but if it kept spreading it was only a matter of time. And it didn't matter if we were in this truck or a freaking bomb shelter, we were never going to be truly safe again. Right now, we were just avoiding the inevitable and this was all just a wasted effort, there was no saving Spencer. Not really.

"Hey, you okay?" Missy said, touching my arm.

I turned my face, snapping out of it. "What? Oh yeah, I'm fine." *Just having a moment.*

I looked down at the gun I had resting across my lap. There weren't enough bullets in the world to stop this. *Okay, maybe the start of a breakdown.*

I mentally smacked myself in the face. Get it together, Dee. *Damn it. Don't be that girl that curls up in a ball and cries. That will never help the situation. Use your brain. You have one, don't you? Think. And NOT about dying.*

I glanced back out the window, just as we were passing another dead body. One that still had a face, matted hair, and blood rings around the mouth, lying on her side. And just like that, it hit me.

"Stop the truck," I shouted loudly.

Jason slammed on the brakes, and Missy and I flew into the back of the front seats. Missy started cursing. I ignored her.

"What? What is it?" Jason blurted.

I half-turned in my seat trying to see the body again. "Back up. Just back up. Please."

Jason slowly put the truck in reverse, easing up to the dead body. When he stopped, I had perfect view of her. I studied her from head to toe. Looking for any sign she was killed. There were no bruises, no bites, nothing.

My heart started racing. I had my face practically pinned to the window.

The three of them were asking me what I was looking at, what was wrong, what were we doing. I just turned around in my seat completely, staring out across the bed of the truck to the other bodies we passed, trying to remember if the ones that had faces were the same as her. *Untouched.*

I could only vaguely remember one guy but I needed to know for sure and the only way I could do that was if I saw him again. "Hey Jason, see that pine tree back there," I said, keeping my eyes focused on the guy, "the one with the body next to it. Can you back up to there, please?"

"Will you tell me what's going on?" He urged, slightly frustrated at that.

"*Just back up* and I will."

I didn't say anything right away. I waited until he rolled to a stop next to the body and I was able to assess the guy first, just to be certain. When I verified that he was untouched too, I almost jumped up and down. It might not be the end of the world after all.

"I have a theory." My voice was oddly excited considering everything. "Remember that girl Jacob was fighting that just dropped dead?" I waited for them to acknowledge me. "I don't think it was from a blow to the head or anything like that. I think it was this virus." They started scrunching their brows, confused. I quickly thought of a different way to say it.

"Jason, remember when you first met us you told us that this virus happened in stages and that the *hunger* stage was the final stage? Well, what if it isn't? What if death is?"

I paused, peering at all of them. "I found it odd that the girl that was attacking Jacob just up and died, but considering she had injuries I brushed it off, thinking nothing of it, but this guy out there," I pointed to the window, "he doesn't have any injuries. There's no blood on the ground around him. He's just dead. And the woman up there is exactly the same way. You can tell they were infected. He has those eyes and she had the ring of blood around her mouth obviously from feeding." I took a breath and exhaled.

"Don't you get it? I honestly think the virus is killing them off without any of us having to shoot them. Maybe they are starving to death or just stroking out or having a heart attack or something. *I don't know*, but whatever the virus is doing to them, it's got a deadline. They are *actually* dying. They aren't just staying infected. So even if somebody infected drove out of town, they may die before it even spreads."

A beat of silence spread around me.

Jacob was stretching over Duke to look out the window, contemplating. "Any theories how it started? Where it started? How it's spreading? Or how to cure it before they die?"

He sent me a sidelong glance. My little ounce of relief was quickly diminishing. "No? Then it doesn't help much." He sank back in his seat, sighing.

"But at least it's something," Missy said, "and more than any of us thought of, *Jacobo*." She purposely over enunciated his real name, for whatever reason. "If she's right, it's a good fact to know."

"Any fact right now is good to know." Jason was tapping his hands on the steering wheel again. "And I agree with her theory, it's the only thing that makes sense."

"I wasn't saying I didn't agree," Jacob grumbled. "I was just making a point we still don't know shit about any of this."

"Well you chose a hell of a way to say it," Missy snapped.

"Miss, it's okay, really," I interjected, before she went off on him some more. "What I said *doesn't* help much, at least not right now. We still have to figure all the rest out or figure out, at least, how to prevent us from getting it. That's the most important."

"Yeah," Jason agreed, "We already know it's not airborne. And I'm starting to think it's not spread through physical contact either, but I'm not one-hundred-percent on that theory yet."

"Well I'm fine," Jacob said, "and I carried Dean. So that's kind of proof right there."

Jason just looked at him.

"What? I'd think I'd be feeling something by now, don't you?"

"Yeah," Jason sighed, looking away. "Plus Duke would be barking at you."

"You act like that's a bad thing that I'm okay." Jacob was incredulous.

"No, I'm glad you are." He didn't sound glad. "So okay, we can rule out touch then."

I was trying to lean around the seat inconspicuously to see Jason's facial expression, to understand what his problem was, when Missy suddenly blurted, "Maybe it's the water?" I paused, mid-lean, to stare at her. "That could infect people in mass quantities and would have fast results. People have to drink," she urged.

She had a point there.

"No," Jason replied, sounding confident. "That wouldn't make sense. Everyone has wells out here, and each house has a separate one."

"Okay, but that doesn't mean one person's well couldn't have a bacteria in it that started all this."

"No." He turned in his seat. "My mom was the first one anyone knew of. If we had bacteria in the well, the twins and I would have been infected too."

"Yeah, but didn't you say you stayed at the neighbors?"

"Yeah, but we were drinking the water there up until the day my dad made us stay with Mr. and Mrs. Dungcas. By then my mom was already infected, which means we should have been too."

"Oh, right," Missy mumbled, sinking lower in her seat as if embarrassed. "Never mind then."

"No, wait, it could still be that," Jacob chimed in, siding with her. "Maybe your mom was somewhere and she drank the water from someone else's well, Jason. That would make her infected and not anyone else in the house. You know? And why it was spreading elsewhere."

Jason didn't say anything for a moment. He just went back to tapping the steering wheel. I was starting to think it was a nervous or anxious habit, an obnoxious one at that. We all stared at him. I wanted to know now more than ever what he was thinking.

"Jason?" Jacob pressed, eyebrow raised, after about a minute passed.

His hands paused. "Alright, yes," he half-hissed, facing us. "It's a possibility, okay." He dropped his hand to the clutch, suddenly shifting into drive. "So nobody drink the water just to be safe. In the meantime, let's stop wasting daylight. You want to find your friend don't you?" And just like that, we were moving again.

"What's his problem?" Missy mumbled only loud enough for me to hear seconds later.

And as I stared at the back of Jason's seat, seeing just the top of his head, I realized I hadn't the slightest idea.

23

"Stop here." Jacob leaned forward in his seat. "This is about where I found the lighter."

Jason hit the brakes slowly, easing the truck to a smooth stop and shifted into park. His attitude had vanished some, but I think it was only because he was masking it for the most part. It didn't make me want to know any less. If anything, it made me want to know more. I just knew now wasn't the time.

I leaned over the front seat to glance out the windshield. We were parked diagonally on a walking trail. It was paved, narrow, and from what I saw from the back seat, completely sans Spencer.

Disappointment flooded through me. "So um, if he wasn't here, what was the plan again?" I mumbled, looking at nothing besides the surrounding campground, which I wasn't too fond of seeing at this point.

"Clues, duh," Missy said undiscouraged. She started pushing at the back of Jacob's seat. "Come on, let us out."

"Hold on, *Chica*, one sec," Jacob groaned, as Duke stepped over his lap, pressing his nose up against the glass, appearing as tentative as I and at the same time as restless as Missy. "I have to get *Cujo* off me."

Jason reached over, clicking the leash onto Duke's collar and then pulled him back gently to the middle of the seat. "Go ahead," he nodded toward the door. "I got him."

Double-checking first, Jacob slowly opened the door, stepping out. He folded down the passenger seat, so we could get out next. Missy crawled out, her yellow purse catching briefly on the seatbelt buckle. I unhooked it, following in her wake, stretching out my back once I was outside again. My legs were cramped from the lack of room and from way too much walking.

Jason stepped out last, easing Duke out with him, on the opposite side. We met him around the front end of the truck. It wasn't until now that I noticed the bloodstains mixed in with the bug guts and dents. I got an instant flash of the dead guy wedged between Jacob's truck and the other car in the parking lot. I quickly turned away, looking down the path, trying to keep my stomach from feeling nauseated. Sometimes the ability to remember things wasn't such a great thing. How Jason ever found the nerve to step into the truck and drive off in the first place was beyond me.

I could hear Duke panting calmly as Jason inched up beside me. Close enough I could feel his arm faintly touching my arm as he tightened his grip on Duke's leash. From the corner of my eye, I noticed his stance was less relaxed and more tense and rigid than normal. Only further proving to me something was seriously bugging him. I couldn't help but wonder if anyone else noticed or if I was the only one staring at him so thoroughly. *Obsessively, more like it.*

I purposely glanced forward again; I didn't need him to *know* I couldn't keep my eyes off him.

Seconds later, Jacob stepped in front of us, spreading his arms out wide. "So where are these clues?" He mocked, turning around to be more theatrical. "Because all I see right now is a big, fat piece of *nothing* and I personally think walking around aimlessly in this campground is just stupid, especially when we have a truck.”

“The clues wouldn’t be *here*,” Missy proclaimed sharply. “This is where you found the lighter. We have to search for clues *from* here. That’s how it works, smart ass. It’s not aimless walking. And I want to check out *that* area,” she urged, pointing toward where the path cut across a hill and curved, disappearing through a cluster of trees in the distance. “And the truck will *not* fit through there.”

He started shaking his head, the way somebody would if they heard something ridiculous. “Do you even have the slightest idea how to track somebody?” he asked, dubious. “Because I sure the hell don’t. Like how do you know if a footprint is his, or a piece of hair is his, or a piece of clothing is his?” He stared at her, his brown eyes locking on her face. “The chances of us actually finding something as significant as this lighter again is pretty slim, you realize that don’t you? It’s not like we are dogs. We can’t just sniff his scent and find him.”

“Ohmigod, that’s it.” I practically saw the light bulb go on above her head. “Duke.”

She rounded, facing Jason, ignoring Jacob. “Show Duke the lighter! We can find Spencer in no time!” A smile spread on her face. “Ohmigod! How come none of us thought of that before?!”

“It wouldn’t matter if we did,” Jason said, hesitantly. “Duke isn’t trained in tracking. Plus, scent wouldn’t absorb in a lighter, or at least not much. He’d need something more like a shirt or something, and we don’t have it.” He paused, apologizing with his eyes. “He can’t help us. I wish he could. But he can’t.”

Missy’s momentary enthusiasm burst, deflating quickly. “Oh.”

"I'm sorry, Mouth. Duke can do many cool tricks, but that just isn't one of them."

She shrugged, brushing it off. "Not Duke's fault."

Jason fidgeted slightly. "Well, if Jacob and Dee would rather stay in the truck, I'll go with y—"

"Hey, wait a minute," I blurted. It took a second or two to process what he was implying. "I'm not staying in the truck. I'm going wherever you guys go."

"Ditto," Jacob agreed surprisingly. They turned and stared at him, eyebrow raised. He sighed. "Look, we aren't doing that split up crap again. Regardless of our stupidity, we are smarter and safer in numbers. Everyone knows that. Plus—" His lips curved up as he looked at Missy. "Jason can't handle you and Duke alone, *you're* a handful."

"He does make a point there," Jason laughed.

Missy snorted. "Geez, I'm not that bad, am I?"

"That's debatable." Jacob smiled bigger and held out his right arm. "But come on let's go see if we can find our missing person."

She just stared at me, like he was whacked in the head or something. She didn't understand what he was implying because she didn't do that affection thing. I watched Jacob just shake his head, heard him mumble something incoherent, and then he walked over to her, placing his arm around her shoulder. When she tried to squirm away from him, he just squeezed her to him and turned her toward the path. "If you want to follow breadcrumbs, *Chica*, you have to actually walk."

And just like that, we started walking again: despite how bad my feet hurt, despite how tired I was, and despite the fact any second one of us could die. Because Jacob was right, we were safer in numbers and this was the wisest of our stupid choices.

Jacob only had his arm around Missy for a few minutes, then he released her, laughing. But because I was trailing a few steps behind them, I didn't catch whatever she said.

Jason was next to me, Duke on his left side, trotting beside him. He was not barking but his low whimpering was enough to keep me on edge. I didn't even keep the gun tucked away this time. Instead, I carried it in my right hand. My palm was sweating nervously. I continued to look around, really wishing we could have stayed in the truck. However, Missy was right. There was no way the truck would have fit between the trees up ahead. The closer we got the more narrow the path seemed to get.

And I hated that Jason wasn't talking to me, talking would have probably helped eased some of my anxiety. But he was obviously not in the mood, so I just had to appreciate the fact that at least he was walking beside me. I told myself whatever was his deal had nothing to do with me. At least I hope it didn't. I tried to rack my brain for a second to see if something I said or did could have provoked such a reaction in him. I came up with nothing.

We reached the trees faster than I thought we would and a quick glance back made the truck feel like it was miles away. I gulped, but I knew it was just my eyes playing tricks on me.

"Once we get through this patch of trees," Jacob said, snagging my attention back toward him and Missy and the path forward again, "we will be in the third camp area. Just reminding you ahead of time, it isn't pretty."

As if anything could surprise us anymore. I was going to have nightmares for the rest of my life already. What was one more flashback to add to them?

I carefully stepped over the broken branches on the narrow dirt path so I wouldn't twist my ankle or something, then stopped short, taking in the scene of the third campsite as soon as it came into view.

This camp area was smaller, and more secluded, but no less horrific. There were a total of three tents, all collapsed to the ground. Some bags were precariously placed around them, rummaged through with pieces of clothing thrown out. The fire pits on each lot had only cold ashes. The air though still held the scent of burnt wood. There were other unpleasant scents I didn't want to think about. Sadly, the bodies lying on the ground I couldn't ignore.

One guy was lying beside the fire, half his body gone. A bag of marshmallows had spilled out, little white puffs sticking to blood stained dirt. The guy beside him was dead, lying folded on the ground, a metal marshmallow stick impaled through his back. His black eyes were still open.

There was one car parked undamaged with the back door open. Footsteps trailed to it disappearing underneath. Not human foot prints. Paw prints of some wildlife. A small animal, raccoon perhaps. From what I could tell the car was empty. There was no sign of anyone. No sign of anything.

Duke started to bark, but Jason had corrected him with a gentle tug on his collar, silencing him as we started taking a few steps forward, cautiously heading into the lot. There was another car further away, reversed into one of the trees. Through the windshield I saw someone, but not clearly. I didn't care to see anymore. All I knew was it wasn't Spencer.

Averting my eyes, I glanced around my feet, making sure not to step on anything and kept walking.

"Okay, *Nancy Drew*," Jacob prompted, half serious, half sarcastic, "do you see anything *useful*?"

I glanced up in time to see Missy roll her eyes. She stepped ahead of us, surveying the area even more thoroughly. She peered into the first tent, the second. She turned her attention to the car with the door open, looking inside. Then all of a sudden, she peered over her shoulder with a smile and said, "Maybe. Come here."

My stomach fluttered with trepidation. *What could she have possibly found in the car to help us find Spencer?*

We came up beside her and peeked into the vehicle. The back seat was empty, except for a fast food wrapper on the floor. But on the front seat there was a purse, pulled to the edge of the leather cushion with contents emptied out of it onto the center console. And there jammed between the console and the side of the seat, I caught the glimpse of something small and black.

A cell phone.

I could have hugged Missy right there. We had a phone!

I didn't hesitate, I pushed her aside, reaching right in, grabbing the phone. I could call the cops, I could call my parents, call her parents…

I ducked back out of the car and immediately stared down at the screen, getting ready to start dialing. But the screen was black and no matter how many times I tried turning the phone on, it never changed. *Damn it!*

"It's useless," I grumbled tossing it onto the back seat in frustration and disappointment. "Battery's dead."

Missy surprised me by pushing *me* aside this time and picked up the phone, turning it over in her hand. Without a word she crawled further into the vehicle, leaning over the front seat, peering through the junk pile on the console and then stretched to open the glove compartment.

"No it's not," she urged seconds later, yanking something out of it. When she backed out of the car, she held up a phone charger to us. "All we have to do is find the keys."

Relief washed through me. *Okay. That could work.*

"I don't understand. What does that have to do with Spencer?" Jacob asked.

"Nothing," I mumbled, facing him. "But at least if we can charge that phone we can make some phone calls, like to the cops."

"Actually," Missy pressed, wiggling the charger in her hand. "I have a better idea."

Jason just glared at her, incredulous. "We have to call the cops, we aren't making any exceptions. This is way out of hand. The CDC needs to get here and fast before more people die."

"I'm not talking about the cops," she exhorted. "That's a given, I meant I have a better idea than using *that* phone." Raising my eyebrow, I watched as she handed Jacob the charger and then started digging in her yellow purse, retrieving her cell phone. "Look, I have the same exact cell so if we charge mine Spencer might be able to get a hold of us again. Or better yet, we could check to see if he left us any messages. Or anyone left us messages. It could help us with clues. Or at least help us know what's going on back at home."

"Hey, you know what, that's pretty freaking clever," Jacob proclaimed, impressed.

"Thanks," she grinned, obviously pleased with herself. "Now hopefully we find the keys."

"They got to be around here somewhere," he retorted. "Check to make sure they didn't fall under the seat or something, and I'll go check the bags."

She nodded, bringing her attention to Jason and me. "Why don't you two just check the ground and see if you spot them somewhere. Maybe one of these people accidentally dropped them."

"Okay." I took a step back, turning. "I'll go check behind the tents."

"Then I guess we'll go check by the other car," Jason mumbled, making a clicking noise with his tongue to get Duke to walk with him.

I hesitated just long enough to spare a few seconds to watch him over my shoulder. My mind was crammed with so many questions I was having trouble focusing on one issue at a time. But I had to concentrate on the most important, most prominent thing right now. *Keys...*

Sighing, I started toward the tents, passing Jacob who was just squatting down to rummage through the closest bag.

"Pick up the pace a little, *chica*," he urged, immediately tossing things on the ground. "I don't want to be out here too long."

Ignoring him I kept going. No faster. No slower. Don't get me wrong, I wanted to bounce too, but I was just too damn tired, tired of everything. Now that we were this close to another clue or better yet calling the cops, being able to call home, I felt myself giving in to exhaustion. Well, every part of me but my brain. That was still on overdrive. And each step I took, each second closer to the tents, I started thinking even more. Bugging out again really. For instance, what *if* we found the keys? Then what? What if the cops start asking us questions?

Like...how do we know that many people died? How do we know it can take up to six shots to kill them? Why is there blood on the front of Jacob's truck? What caused me to drive off the mountain and crash? Why was dirt covering a patch of blood by the crash site? Who's blood is it? Where's the body? Why didn't we report it? Why? Why? Why?

I almost started crying right there in panic. I did not want to go to jail and I knew I would. I would if they asked us those questions. We all would. And our lives would be ruined, ruined because our friend ran away from home, a damn friend who never said goodbye. Suddenly a vision of me sitting behind bars in a dirty orange jumpsuit, ratty hair, rocking back and forth on a small, uncomfortable cot flashed in my mind and my heart started pounding. *Ohmigod. Ohmigod. ohmigod.*

We can't call the cops. We can't. We can't. We can't. I struggled with keeping my cool, but I was dangerously close to spazing. And as I rounded the tents, I was so close to hyperventilating again, I wasn't paying attention. My foot caught on something and I tripped forward, falling face first toward the ground. Arms shooting out in front of me, I broke my fall the last millisecond before I ate the dirt. The gun slipped from my grasp. Making a face, I quickly picked up the pistol before Jason realized I dropped a loaded weapon *again* and stood up, brushing myself off.

Turning my head, I looked back to see what I stumbled over and cringed. An arm. I just tripped over a dead woman. I glanced over her full body, overwhelmed with a major case of the heebie jeebies and noted she was not missing any body parts. She had to be mid to upper twenties, strawberry blonde hair, no wounds except for some dried blood under her nose, dressed in jeans and gray tee shirt but no shoes. Besides the tiny hoop earrings in her ears, she had no other jewelry on and yet, something silver flashed from the top of her denim pocket. Hunching closer, I leaned down to see what it was. Keys. There were keys right smack in the dead girl's pocket. All I had to do was reach in and grab them. *Ugh. I can't catch a break.*

"I found keys," I shouted as I awkwardly leaned down to retrieve them. *Totally against my will by the way.*

I put my finger through the key chain loop and started tugging, careful not to touch her just to be safe. It was pretty easy actually. Then I heard something. Hardly a sound really, but it still sent a shiver down my spine anyway. I sent a wary sidelong glance toward my right and froze. Two black as coal eyes were staring at me, and I quickly realized that *sound* was the girl taking a hungered breath.

She wasn't dead.

Oh shit.

I jumped back fast, heart racing, just as two arms rose to grab me and I started shooting rapidly.

She kept trying to get up. I kept shooting her back down.

I heard everyone screaming for me, but most of their voices were lost in the echo of the gunshots.

Jacob was the first to bolt around the tent, just as the girl finally dropped back, falling limp and dead—for real this time—to the ground, blood oozing out of her chest and abdomen.

Jason appeared next, slightly winded. He had his gun drawn, aimed, ready to fire but no Duke. He must have given him to Missy to hold while he ran to protect me. Again. *My own personal Superman.*

"Are you all right?" he asked, his green-brown eyes locking on my face.

"Yeah," I nodded grimly. "She didn't get me." *Pretty freaking close though.*

He lowered his gun to the ground, observing her, kicking her body just to be certain she was actually a goner.

"Did you say you found the keys?" Jacob prompted, eyeing me with sympathy.

"Well I found keys," I replied, opening my left hand where the rigged edges of them dug into my palm and showed them. "But who knows if they are *the* keys."

"Well, they gotta work in one of these cars, right?" Jacob held out his hand. "Give me 'em, I'll go check."

So I did.

And that left me, Jason and the dead girl. Another body added to the *how-many-I-killed* list. Gulp. At this rate I was definitely getting the life sentence.

"Are you *sure* you are all right?" Jason never missed anything. It was so annoying.

"No, but I'll be fine soon," I looked down at the gun. "But maybe you should take this back." I held my hand out.

Shaking his head, he placed *his* gun in his waistband. "I have a feeling you might need it yet."

"Oh. That's exactly why I don't want it," I sighed.

He placed a hand on my shoulder. "I know but that doesn't keep you alive." Leaning forward, he kissed the side of my head comfortingly at the same moment we heard a car engine start.

24

Missy sat in the car, her purse plopped on the hood, holding her cell phone in her hand. The car exhaust reeked and the engine made a sound that made me wince but at least the battery was charging.

Jacob was leaning through the doorway crowding her space, but she didn't seem to mind. I was standing outside the back door with Jason, trying to listen to the voicemails Missy was about to play through the speakerphone over the engine noise. I knew the first one was going to be the message from her mom from the other night since she forgot to delete it, so I only listened half-heartedly. Duke sniffed the ground by my feet as I waited for the second message to play. Jason's arm was just barely touching mine.

I heard, "Message deleted. Next message," and tilted my ear closer to the door.

I recognized Spencer's voice immediately. It wasn't hard. He was yelling. "Hello—? Guys what happened? Where are you?" Static cut in and out of the call. For a moment we didn't hear anything. Suddenly Spencer started cursing. Followed by the same banging and screaming we heard this morning. My stomach twisted.

"Forget it!" Spencer shouted, frazzled a few seconds later. "Leave!" Static. "Do you hear me? *Leave!* I'm serious. I shouldn't have called you. Get out of this town! Fast! While you still can!" A loud bang blasted through the speaker. "Son of a—"

The call ended.

"Ohmigod," Missy gasped. "Ohmigod Spencer." Her eyes sought mine, worried. Jacob urged her to continue with the messages.

I fidgeted restlessly, leaning closer against Jacob. Jason was scooting closer to me. All our ears turned toward the phone, completely alert. There were still six more messages to hear.

The next two were Missy's mom repeatedly asking where she was. The messages were almost identical.

The third caught me off guard.

"Melissa, It's Mrs. Forrester." My mom. "If you are with Dee, *please* call us. Please. This isn't like you two. Your mom and I are worried sick." The distress was clear in her voice. My stomach knotted tighter. "Call us," she urged desperately before hanging up. I suddenly felt really homesick.

The fourth message was Missy's mom again. "Melissa! Where are you?! Is Dee with you?! Call me A.S.A.P! You are so grounded when you get home!"

Fifth. Mrs. Frink *again*.

"Okay, I'm really freaking out here. Where are you girls? Are you all right? If I don't hear from you by this evening, I'm calling the cops and filing a missing person's report. Is that what you want?" A pause and some sniffling. "Please don't do this to me. Please don't do what Spencer did to his parents. Just let me know you are okay. I can't deal with not knowing."

"Oh, mom," Missy sighed, as she deleted the message. I could almost hear the apology in her voice. And even my heart was breaking at the thought of our parents crying.

I expected the last call to be her mom again or my parents but to my surprise it was neither. It was Spencer.

"Guys," he pleaded desperately, in that same panicked, scared voice he had when he called us Thursday night to come get him. "If you are still here by any chance, if you haven't left, *help me!* I'm begging you. They are trying to kill me. I'm going to die." His voice got softer. "I don't want to die." He exhaled into the phone. "I should have never run away. I'm so sorry. I'm sorry for everything." A pause. Then unclear loud background noise and cursing. "*Damn it.* I shouldn't have —"

The line went dead, cutting off, leaving whatever he had to say unfinished, and us without any clue as to *where* the hell he was. And worse, we were out of messages.

Missy made an inaudible sound, clicked off her voicemail connection and dropped the phone on her lap, both irritated and upset.

Jacob cleared his throat. "That didn't really help us get any clues." His voice was half serious and half sarcastic, I know he was just trying to break the awkward vibe. His hand tapped the roof. "So now what?"

"Now the girls call their parents and we call the cops," Jason interjected, in that firm tone that leaves no room for objections. "We will deal with Spencer afterward. He's no longer the top priority." *Leave it to him to always take charge.*

Talking to my mom and dad was brutal. Lying to them was even rougher. But by the time I got off the phone they were reassured I was okay. I told them I was staying at a girl's house from school. I said I was calling from her number, and that I'd be home in time for class on Monday. Just like Jason told us to do, more or less. Surprisingly they hadn't called the cops but I was, as expected, grounded until graduation. Maybe even for life.

So was Missy.

We promised we'd call later when we knew more about my car. I hope that didn't come back to kick us in the butt too.

"Well that sucked," I groaned when I hung up the phone.

"Yeah. I lie to my mom all the time, but somehow this just felt wrong." *That's probably because there was a good chance we were going to die or end up arrested,* I thought as I looked at Melissa.

She was still sitting behind the steering wheel in the driver's seat, but she was currently checking her reflection in the rearview mirror, making a face as she tried to smooth down the frizzy strands.

A few moments later, she sank back against the seat frustrated. A beat of silence passed. "Well, I guess it's time to call the cops," she said grudgingly. She tried handing me the phone. I shook my head.

"It's your phone. You call."

"Whatever," she exhaled. She picked the phone back up reluctantly and started to dial.

I flinched. *Goodbye, college.*

She hesitated, pausing before dialing the last number and peered up at me. Her blue eyes sought mine.

"What?" I mumbled, standing there, looking in at her. The car door was against my back. I could feel Jacob breathing down my neck from the other side of it, as he leaned over it.

"We are going to jail, aren't we?" she asked, completely serious.

I know I usually try to make her feel better, but I wasn't about to sugarcoat this. This was real. "Yeah. Probably." I couldn't see how we wouldn't be.

She barely nodded in understanding. "We should have just told Spencer's parents when Spencer called, and let them handle this, huh?"

Finally, she was being rational. I shifted my weight to my other foot, restlessly. "Yeah. Probably," I repeated. "But it's too late now."

Her eyes shifted upward toward me one last time. "Sorry, Dee," she sighed. "I didn't know it would be like this." She glanced back down at the phone in her hand and went to hit the last digit.

"Hey, wait!" Jacob blurted, quickly nudging me out of the way, as he swung around the other side of the door. He reached toward her and placed his hand over hers, half covering the phone to stop her from calling. "I got an idea."

"We have to call the cops," Jason retaliated in exasperation, clearly implying there were no *ifs, ands or buts* about it.

"No. I know," he replied back, inches from Missy's face. He wasn't looking at Jason. "I just thought there's a better way." He nudged the phone out of her hand, making a point to unplug it from the charger. "Use the phone you found in this car to call instead. This way you can give a false name and they'll never be able to track you."

She stared at him incredulous. I think I had the same expression on my face too. "How do you figure? My prints are all over the phone and car."

"Yeah, so," he said, inching backward to give more space between them. "You weren't arrested before, right?"

"No, neither of us were."

"Then they won't be able to find a match," he replied confidently. "Your fingerprints have to be in the database for them to identify you. You have nothing to worry about."

"Seriously?!" A smile quickly spread across her face. "Oh, that's brilliant. Good thinking, Jacobo." She quickly repositioned herself in the seat so she could grab the other phone and start charging it. "Put my cell in my purse, will ya?" she prompted. Jacob did.

We waited a few minutes before turning the phone on, and with the charger still connected, Missy finally dialed 911. We leaned closely together again, listening thoroughly. I was more nervous than all of them, I think. I heard what Jacob said but I think I was too negative to believe it would be that simple. Nothing ever is.

"911, what's your emergency?"

"There's—" Missy began but her voice was drowned out by Duke's sudden spurt of barking. I jolted, turning my head to our left, having forgotten about Duke's bad ear.

His unexpected yank at the leash had Jason tumbling forward. I grabbed at his arm to catch him, steadying him, my heart immediately jumping to my throat.

Not one but two people were running straight for us from two different directions. And from how close they were, it was obvious how poor Duke's hearing was, and apparently ours too. Jason fumbled for his gun and started firing, clearly rattled. He was trying to back me and Duke up as he fired each shot.

I glanced over my shoulder when I heard Jacob start hollering. He was leaning back in the car, shouting to the phone. "Pine Star Campsite. Bring back up immediately. Get the CDC. There's been a contagious outbreak. We think it's bacteria in the water.

People are sick. People are mutating. We can't stop them. They are trying to kill us. Help!"

Then without hesitation he grabbed Missy's arm and yanked her out of the car, slamming the door. The car was still running, the phone was still on, but he didn't care. We had to hightail it out of there. More people were coming toward us now from another direction. It was like a feeding frenzy at a zoo. Only we were the food.

"Kill them," Jacob urged.

"I'm trying," Jason yelled. He shot again. It hit one guy in the side of the neck. The next went to the other guy's arm.

"Not shooting like that you won't."

"Shut up, Jacob." Jason struggled to hold on to Duke and fired a shot again. But this time it only *clicked.* My eyes darted to the trigger and I watched in horror as he tried it again. *Nothing.*

"Oh shit."

"What now?" Jacob called behind us.

"I'm out of bullets and my pack is in your truck!" He grabbed my arm and urged me along faster. "Dee! Give me your gun!"

I went to, but as I reached for it, I cringed. Becoming achingly aware of how many shots I used to kill that girl and what that meant for us.

I wanted to punch myself. My gun was useless.

"I only have *one* bullet left!" I replied in panic.

Jacob cursed in Spanish. We were starting to get cornered.

"Then run!" Jason prompted urgently.

"What?"

"Run!"

And we ran.

They chased us.

I didn't understand why all of a sudden they were coming after us. It's as if they heard us say we were calling the cops and they wanted to stop that from happening. But it's not like it mattered because it was happening. Six people *were* chasing us and there was nothing we could do about it. *Literally.* We had a pack full of extra bullets but that pack was still a good distance away in the truck.

My chest was on fire. I felt like my heart was going to explode. It was pounding so fast I was worried I was going to drop dead from a heart attack on top of everything else. I had to grab the gun because it kept slipping up out of my waistband as I ran. I wanted to use it so badly but I wasn't about to waste my last bullet. Because we all knew one damn bullet wasn't going to bring them down.

The wind whipped across my face, blowing my bangs into my eyes. I could hardly see where I was going as my legs pounded over the dirt, burning in agony. The back of my sneakers were rubbing up over my heels, splitting my blisters deeper. I was in pain. Head to toe. But being in pain meant I was alive. So I just pushed through it, because the alternative wasn't an option.

I was worrying mostly about Missy and Jason who were falling behind. Jason was still having a hard time controlling Duke; Missy was having a hard time running.

I glanced over my shoulder for the umpteenth time to check on them, horrified by how fast they were catching us when suddenly Jacob shouted something, grabbed my arm and spun me toward the left. "This way," he yelled.

I snapped my attention back, startled, to find to my horror three more people had come bolting out of the woods in the span of those few seconds and we had been running straight for them.

"Left!" I shouted to Missy and Jason immediately, my voice cracking and catching.

We changed course, running blindly. The truck was getting further away, the last thing I wanted, but we didn't have a choice.

"What…are…we…going…to do?" I gasped.

If we didn't think of something fast, we were all checkmate or at least I was. My energy was quickly depleting.

Jacob glanced at me, brown eyes wide with panic. "I don't know."

Duke's barking didn't cease. Behind us I heard his escalating angst. It was so loud I was certain it was drawing every person toward us.

But we kept running.

That is until Missy started screaming.

I halted, instantly spinning around, and saw her swinging her purse into a person's head.

"Missy!" I yelled at the top of my lungs, springing toward her without thinking.

There was no way Jason could help her. He was trapped up against a tree trying to hold Duke and defend himself and his dog with a thick branch that was slowly snapping into pieces each time he hit someone in the face. She was all alone, alone to defend herself. And we had just been running away from them. However, as I hurried forward it dawned on me that she wasn't screaming *for* help, she was screaming because she was helping save them. She was standing guard, swinging desperately, recklessly, taking out anyone that lunged for Duke.

There she was. My best friend. Risking her life for a dog.

And I realized instantly, that's what I was about to do too. Risk my life to save all of them. From the corner of my eye, I saw Jacob rushing past me. He was going to too.

And we weren't even thinking twice about it.

I sprinted closer, readying myself to use my gun to at least hit someone over the head, when Jacob suddenly jumped up, grabbing hold of a tree branch and swung his feet swiftly into two bodies, knocking them over.

Then he went all ninja-style and started karate-kicking them.

I joined Missy, helping her defend Duke. Mostly we just square danced with the bastards. It was a courageous moment. But it was suicide.

"Missy, *duck*!" I shouted as a guy turned, coming up behind her.

She dropped last second to the ground, leaving two pale arms slicing through open air. Making that agonized, hungry cry of frustration he bent for her and I automatically raised my gun, firing my last shot straight into his chest. He stumbled back, screeching, and Missy wasted no time, jumping up, kicking his leg out from under him.

"Give me your gun," she shouted as he went down and I tossed it to her without hesitation or question. She picked it up— the same girl who was completely anti-guns— and started beating the living daylights out of the man before he had a chance to sit up. I was so busy watching her I just barely dodged a girl with ruby red nail polish from biting my arm.

The smell of blood from the guy must have suddenly hit them, because they all started screaming and three of them—including the lady in red—pounced toward him, snapping and clawing at each other to get to him. And since Missy wasn't watching, I bolted to her, grabbed her shirt and pulled her away two seconds before they started tearing away his flesh.

She stood for a moment, startled. Then glanced down at the blood-tinged pistol in her hand before turning to me, a look of fear, anger and desperation darkened her eyes but I still saw the *thank you* amid it.

Though one was dead, three distracted, a couple injured…it didn't make a difference. There were still more. Still hungry. Still grabbing for us. We no longer needed help. We needed a miracle.

And I didn't see how that was happening before we died.

Then I saw it.

Like an answered prayer, a car speeding down the field toward us, driving right past Jacob's truck in the distance.

"Cops," I shouted in relief. The cops had come. We were saved. Except the closer the vehicle got I realized it wasn't a police car. It was a white pickup, driving recklessly across the grass. It was all over the place. Like there was a drunken driver behind the wheel.

All hope was lost.

We were doomed.

25

A bald-headed man lunged for me. I dove out of the way, hitting the ground, hard. Wincing, I scrambled back to my feet, but not fast enough. The guy grabbed me, squeezing his fingers into my arm, pulling me toward him. I screamed in reflex, struggling to break free, but I couldn't. And one desperate look around proved no one could help me either. This was it. The moment I've been running from. He leaned forward, his mouth opening, ready to bite me and I shut my eyes, cringing, thrashing about defenselessly.

Checkmate.

Or it should have been.

But suddenly *he* was screaming and his grip started slackening.

Flashing my eyes open in disbelief and relief, I yanked my arm away, taking a second to fully process what I was seeing.

Duke was latched onto his other arm, biting him ferociously, literally hanging in the air by his jaws. His leash hung to the ground.

Duke had saved me.

I almost cried.

I almost cried because I knew for a fact Jason had a tight grip on the leash this entire time which meant Jason let him go specifically to save me.

Oh, there was no way I was letting Duke die. No way in hell.

I sprung forward, grabbing the arm that just grabbed me so that the guy couldn't hurt Duke and held on. He jerked me around, but I continued to yank and pull with all my might. I could feel his elbow dislocating, his arm breaking within my straining hold.

From the corner of my eye, I saw Jason swing the branch forcefully, finally breaking it completely over another guy's head then start running for us. He leapt right onto the bald guy's back, instantly locking his arm around his throat, strangling him. As the body started to sag and drop, I let go, hurrying around their backs to coax Duke off the other arm.

Grabbing the leash and collar with two hands, I pulled and tugged screaming "Break," until Duke finally did. Then, clenching the fabric even tighter, I fought to hold him as he continued to bark and snap with bloody fangs, raring to attack him again, until the body fell limp.

The sudden roar of the pickup engine had me automatically turning my head but I barely spared it a glance as it sped past full speed. Until I heard the sound of breaks squeaking. Startled, I watched it whip around abruptly and come barreling back towards us from the side, taking out the three people surrounding Missy and Jacob without hesitation. Stopping twenty feet away, it swiftly reversed, running them over again, and drove forward one more time before hitting the brakes completely in front of us. *There was no way a drunk driver could have done that, that's for damn sure.*

Truck idling, a tinted window dropped down and a guy started hollering from the driver's seat. "Jump in the bed, hurry!"

And at the sound of his voice I froze, jaw dropping.

I knew that voice.

It was Spencer's.

I was certain of it. *Or almost certain.*

Standing on my tiptoes, I tried to peek through the window. "Is that—"

"I don't know," Jason urged, nudging me along quickly, taking the leash from me. "Don't care. Just move."

"But—"

"*Move!*"

Everything happened really fast after that, like really, really fast.

Jacob was already lowering the tailgate, helping Missy up. It was the first time I noticed she was limping pretty badly. Hopping up, he held out his hand to assist hoisting me up next. Once I was in, I spun around to help with Duke and that's when I saw the girl coming up behind Jason. I started yelling. Jason quickly told Duke to jump, supporting his hind legs as he did, then dove into the bed hollering, "Go!" though his feet still dangled off the end of the tailgate. Jacob hunched down, clasping his wrists to hold him, Missy grabbed Duke and I immediately started smacking the side of the truck screaming for *him* to drive.

The truck rocketed forward, jerking us. Jacob tumbled over, losing his balance, his grip breaking on Jason and I watched horrified as Jason started sliding backward, over the edge, his hands struggling to grab hold of something, anything. Jacob recovered quickly, springing to catch him, yanking him strongly toward us again as the girl chased us, reaching for him. Scissor-kicking his feet, Jason heeled her in the chin, whipping her head back. He was pulled up over the ledge before she was at him again but by then the distance between us and them, was lengthening.

Jason and Jacob fell backward onto the liner, trying to catch their breath. Jacob's head was by my feet, Jason's by Missy and

Duke. Their eyes were closed, evening sun beaming down on their flushed faces. The rise and fall of their chests slowly, slowly started to calm, and only then did the pounding of my heart finally soften. Realization began to sink in that we were *all* still alive. *After all that.*

No one said anything for a moment. There were a thousand words that could be said, but no reason to. It was over. We survived.

And as I sat there with my arm braced on the side of the truck bed, the cool wind stinging my face, blowing my hair out of control, I shifted my eyes to the back tinted window, wondering. *Was it really Spencer behind the wheel? Did Spencer really just save us?*

How was that for irony? We came here, dealt with all this, risked our lives for him, killed people, all so we could find him and rescue him and in the end *he* finds *us*, saving *our* lives.

It almost seemed impossible. I wouldn't put it past me to just be *hoping* it was him. My mind had a tendency to play tricks on me.

The unexpected sound of laughter had me furrowing my brow, looking down. Funny how laughter seemed so foreign a thing all of a sudden.

Jason was still lying there, on his back, but he was cracking up, covering his head with his arms as Duke continuously whimpered and pawed at him, trying to get his attention, wagging his tail excitedly in Missy's grasp.

Before I knew it I was laughing too. We all were. And I got to admit it felt good to laugh again.

"Okay boy… okay," Jason chuckled, rolling up into a seated position. "I get the point." Easing back against the side of the truck, he started petting him, a smile warming his face. "No worries buddy, I'm all right." He petted him behind the ears. "You're all right. Everyone is all right."

Turning his head, he glanced over at me, his eyes searching my face, clearly checking on me. Making sure I really *was* fine. And when our eyes met, I saw it—his relief, his gratitude and most prominent his feelings for me had deepened beyond attraction.

My stomach fluttered.

If Jacob wasn't lying between us right now, I probably would have crawled over to him, grabbed his face and kissed him senseless. Right there. In the back of a moving truck. In front of everyone. Because *damn*, if I wasn't falling hard for him too.

"Uh, guys," Missy suddenly said, breaking our moment. She was sitting in the corner of the bed, her purse on her lap. "I don't want to come off sounding ungrateful, but does anyone know where the hell we are going? Or like who is driving? Because we, uh,

just passed Jacob's truck." She pointed for emphasis.

"Oh, shit," Jacob blurted, hopping up immediately. "That's right."

"Huh?" Her blonde eye brows pulled forward in confusion as he walked up next to her.

"It's Spencer."

"What? Where?" Missy spazed, quickly turning, glancing around frantically.

"Try looking through the window," he laughed. "Yo, Spencer," he yelled, smacking the roof. "Stop! I need my truck!"

"Spencer?"

"Yeah, he's—" Suddenly the truck whipped around, making a sharp U-turn at full speed and Jacob went flying.

I lost my grip, tipping over onto the bed liner. By the grunts I heard and Duke's bark, Jacob and I weren't the only ones.

Missy was cursing. "Are you freaking kidding me? How the hell do you know it's Spencer?" She pushed at him. "And get off me!"

"Sorry," he grumbled, lifting himself up. When he fell he landed on top of her. "I saw him through the windshield."

"And you didn't *say* anything?" She shoved his legs and he barely caught himself before falling again.

I watched, keeping my mouth shut. If she was reacting that strongly, I wasn't telling her I already suspected it was him too.

Jacob started shouting. "When would you have liked me to say it, huh? When I was kicking someone in the gut, when I was helping you onto the truck, or when I was making sure Jason didn't fall off?"

She looked indignant. "What about when you were just lying there saying nothing? How about then?"

He hunched down so they were face level. "Listen *Chica*, why don't you—"

"Hold on!" I hollered, catching a glimpse of the truck from the corner of my eye. It was too close for it to be anything but an abrupt stop.

"What?" Jacob snapped, mid-sentence, turning his head toward me.

"Hold on!" I clasped the side of the truck tightly, just as Spencer rammed the brakes. The loud *thud* must have been Jacob. I managed to hold on this time, but my head still whiplashed back and forth.

"God damn it! Doesn't he know how to drive?" Jason hissed, his one arm was protectively around Duke, though he was half-knocked over.

"He doesn't have a license," I groaned, rubbing my neck, thankful the truck was stopped.

"Yeah…well driving like that isn't going to get him one."

Checking to make sure the coast was clear, Jason stood up, readjusting his grip on Duke's leash. "Come on," he urged, hopping to the ground. "Let's not test fate."

He didn't have to say it twice. I jumped up, wincing immediately at the ache in my legs. The side of my right thigh was scraped and already discolored from my fall, not to mention my blisters were bleeding through the back of my socks. Missy wasn't going to be the only one gimping.

Holding out his hand, Jason looked up at me from the ground, his green-brown eyes wishing away my pain. Offering a tight smile, I placed my hand in his and was about to step down when the truck door slammed, snagging my attention.

Spencer came hurrying toward us. "Holy crap! Holy crap! Missy! Dee! It's you! It's really you guys!"

Holy crap was right. I know I suspected he was driving. I know Jacob confirmed it, but seeing him standing there was still throwing me for a loop.

He looked awful. His shirt was ripped in several places. His hands were cut and wrapped with pieces of his sleeve. His shorts were dirt-stained. His knees were scabbed up, pieces of leaves stuck in his hair that was now chin-length, and his light eyes were bloodshot with dark circles around them. He also looked skinnier. I'm not sure if that was because he was taller or if he lost weight. Probably a combination of both.

Compared to him, Melissa and I looked like a million bucks. And that was saying a lot, considering we were banged up too.

"You're okay, right?" He pressed quickly, his voice rushed and anxious as he glanced back and forth between us. I could see the worry and panic embedded deep within his baby blues. He truly *was* concerned, and that right there was enough to convince me, despite the fact that he had run away, our friendship really meant something to him. *Still.*

"Are *you?*" Missy retorted, staring back at him. She was leaning her weight against Jacob, favoring her left leg, her purse hanging off her other shoulder. She sounded more uncomfortable seeing him than I felt. Surprising really, since it was her idea to keep looking for him, not mine. "I mean, you called *us* for help."

"Yeah," Jacob cut in, his voice angrier than normal. "Tell me dude, what were you thinking calling these *chicas* to come get you? You almost got them killed. Don't you have any sense at all?"

Spencer flinched. "Ah man, don't say that. I already feel guilty enough."

"*Hey.*" Jacob put his palms up. "I just speak the truth. And what you did is messed up. You owe them an apology."

Spencer's eyes flashed to Missy again and then back to Jacob. "I bugged out, all right. I wasn't thinking clearly. Dean came at us the other night and I panicked."

"You *split,*" Jacob said, shaking his head. "I would have taken you home, but instead we had to start a damn rescue mission for your ass."

Spencer started fidgeting, playing with some of the material around his left hand. "Fine. You want me to say sorry, then *sorry.* Okay?! I...am...sorry."

"It's not me you have to apologize to." Jacob was unconvinced. "And for the record, I wasn't just talking about calling them."

My eyes shifted back to Jacob. He was staring at Spencer with disapproval. I get Jacob was being *all brotherly* for us, but was it really necessary? *And was now really the time?* Spencer just saved our lives. We owed him some credit.

"All right, enough,." Jason interjected, adjusting his fingers around my hand again. "Play catch up and twenty questions later. Let's just get outta here." *Glad to see Jason was still making some sense.*

Spencer turned his head to us, his eyes looking at Jason first then trailing to me, brow creasing. "Wait, hold up. I don't get it. How do you guys even know each other?"

"That's a question." Jason helped ease me carefully off the tailgate while holding Duke's leash with his other hand. The fact Duke wasn't barking was a good thing. It meant not only were we *safe* for this particular second from *the others*, but that Spencer wasn't infected despite how he looked. *Thank God.*

I cringed slightly when my feet hit the ground again and watched as Jason reached his hand back up to help Missy down next.

"I got her," Jacob said, hopping down. "Handle Duke." He turned, looking up to face Missy with his wandering brown eyes. "Okay, don't start whining or do what you do, just scoot into my arms."

"Excuse me?" Her blue eyes narrowed.

Jacob sighed. "So you don't have to jump down. I'll support your weight and lower you down.'"

She grumbled something inaudible, but sat down, inching herself to the ledge anyway.

He placed his arms around her waist and lifted her off the tailgate, gently easing her to her feet before letting go. I didn't say anything, but I'm pretty sure his hands lingered longer than they should have.

Staring at Jacob for a moment, I realized he really did have a nice body, and strong arms. He had a pretty cute smirk, too, even with his busted, fat lip. And the way Missy's eyes fluttered up to look at his face, I think she was noticing it too.

Jason stepped past us and opened the truck's passenger door, taking out his backpack. Ordering Duke to *sit,* he started to unzip the first compartment while Jacob began walking toward the driver's seat.

Spencer took a step forward, appearing slightly awkward. "What can I do?"

"Get in my truck for starters," Jacob called, moving around the bumper.

"Okay," Spencer hesitated. "But can I do something first?"

"Take a piss later," Jacob urged, slapping the hood of the truck obnoxiously. "Let's go."

"That's not what—"

"Then what?" Jason asked, in exasperation, cutting him off. He impatiently peered over the pack at him, his hair sweaty across his forehead as he leaned against the side of the truck. "What do you want to do?"

Spencer cleared his throat. "Um, I just wanted to give them a hug."

Oh Spencer. I stopped mid-step, turning to face him, realizing suddenly that I've yet to say anything to him. No wonder he looked uncomfortable. We hadn't exactly shown him a happy reunion. And yet, there he was still wishing to hug us *hello.*

"You never have to ask," I said, forcing a smile. I started to hobble toward him. He took two giant steps forward and met me half way, pausing right in front of me. *He definitely got taller.*

"It's been awhile, huh?" he uttered, a strained smile on *his* face.

"Yeah." I stared up at him, really processing the fact it was him and he was all right. I didn't know if I wanted to cry, jump for joy or punch him. I did neither. Instead I threw my arms around his neck in a huge hug. He instantly hugged me back. And it wasn't a crap hug either. It was a Spencer hug. *My favorite.*

"God I missed you," I mumbled. And I meant it, every word. He didn't have to say anything back, his hug said it all.

Seconds later, Missy startled us by tossing her arms around the both of us. "Damn it, I hate hugs," she complained, but she didn't let go. Even my best friend can make an exception when it matters.

And there we were, the three of us, *finally* back together again. Could it really be that simple?

"Hey *Brady bunch*, we don't have all day," Jacob shouted, breaking us up. He was standing on the doorframe of his truck, looking out over the roof at us. "Come on."

"God, he *definitely* is more annoying than *Hallmark*," Missy groaned, hopping back a step.

"Hallmark?" Spencer looked confused.

"Jason," she retorted, as she adjusted her purse strap.

"Why—"

"Long story," I laughed, chiming in.

I turned to Jason, still smiling. He was leaning against the truck, watching us. His expression blank but his eyes open windows to his soul. I could see it all. His frustration, his exhaustion, his impatience, his emotions…I wonder if he knew I could.

I patted Spencer on the shoulder and started walking to the truck. "Let's go. The boys aren't in the mood for loitering." *Couldn't really blame them there.*

As I started to step into the truck, Jason reached his hand out in front of me, stopping me. "Here," he prompted, holding something.

I looked down. It was food. *Of course it was.* Smile remaining, I took it and climbed inside, over the backseat.

Missy scrambled over the seat next, but just as she slid closer to me to make room for Spencer, Duke started barking in warning outside.

Spinning in the seat, I instantly glanced out the back window, eyes scanning frantically, heart picking up. I didn't see anyone yet, but Duke heard them, and that's all we needed to know.

"Time's up!" Jacob hopped inside, slamming the door. "Hurry up!" He jammed the key into the ignition, starting the engine immediately.

Jason pretty much pushed Spencer inside.

"Dude, I'm *not* going to fit back there," he said, peering over the headrest. *It was probably true.*

Jason cursed. "Fine, get in the front seat."

Spencer started backing out the door. "I'll just follow in the other truck."

"No," Jason commanded. "We aren't splitting up. Just get in."

Reluctantly, Spencer crawled back in, scooting over to make room for Jason. Though I didn't see how the four of them, Duke included, would fit in the front either.

After a few unsuccessful attempts, Jason finally coaxed Duke inside. His barking hadn't eased up. In fact it got louder.

"Hold him," he urged, forcing Spencer to take hold of Duke's collar. But instead of jumping in, Jason was stepping back.

I started to panic, realizing Jason wasn't planning to sit next to Spencer. "*What* are you doing?"

"Making room," he proclaimed, shutting the door.

My eyes rounded as he rushed past the side window, quickly tossing his backpack into the bed of the truck, then himself. He landed on his side with a grunt and a *thud*. It was so loud I even heard it over Duke's barking.

"Are you okay?" I shouted out the back window I had crawled through earlier today.

"I'm fine," he called, giving a small finger wave. "Tell Jacob to go."

Over the bed of the truck I finally saw the person emerging from the wooded area kitty-corner to us and I screeched. It wasn't a guy. It wasn't a girl. It was a boy, *the boy*—the same one from before. The younger brother of the boy I killed.

"Oh shit, it's that kid—" Missy began, stopping immediately to glance at me and see my reaction.

"What kid?" Jacob said, peering over his shoulder.

"Never mind, just go. Jason's fine."

Duke was barking even louder.

"What? I can't hear you."

"Go!" Missy and I yelled in unison.

"Oh." Jacob didn't hesitate. He threw the shifter into drive and took off. I watched nervously through the glass as Jason and his pack slid across the bed. It was nowhere as horrible as Spencer's driving.

Once the acceleration leveled out to a steady speed, Jason righted himself and scooted back toward the cab, back to us. I was still spun in my seat, feeling on edge, heart racing, watching him. I knew he was safe, *we were all safe*, but I couldn't settle my heart for anything. The boy was nowhere actually *near* us when we took off. We left in plenty of time, but I was still freaking out for Jason.

"Move over," Jason told Missy, coming right up to the window.

Without a remark, she shoved her purse into the corner and slid across the seat. I inched closer to the other side, trying to give him some room. Relief washing through me that he was going to squeeze in with us after all. *Though I wasn't exactly sure how.*

He started leaning through the window and Duke stopped barking, so I turned my head to avoid being accidentally kicked or elbowed in the face. Only his hand clasped my chin, stopping me. Startled, I glanced back at him with intentions of asking him *what,* and I was met instantly with a kiss.

A quick, passionate, *suck the air right out of my lungs*, kiss.

Talk about a total mind spin.

He pulled away, halfway hanging through the window, a cocky grin spreading on his face. "See, I'm fine," he said, his green-brown eyes locking with mine. "So stop worrying." Then he started creeping back out through the opening—*damn he never had intentions of sitting with us*—and added, "Oh and make sure you eat something. Don't want you passing out."

I wanted to say, *you sure?* With a kiss like that, I'm surprised I didn't!

Someone cleared their throat and I became embarrassingly aware that everyone was staring at us.

Red-faced and smiling, I did the only thing I could think of. I lifted the plastic bag off my lap and held it out to them. "Trail mix anyone?"

Duke snatched the bag and we all started laughing.

26

Obviously we saved the trail mix, but it didn't last long. The four of us finished it off in a matter of minutes. Jason sat up against the back of the bed, eating his own snack, but was listening to our conversations through the open window, every once in a while chiming in.

He even put the straw of his pack through the window opening to let Missy and I drink some water. It was hot and disgusting, but hey at least it was water.

"So did we decide?" Jacob asked, looking in the rearview mirror, his hands on the steering wheel. "The turn is coming up." We were finally out of the campsite.

"Uh," Missy glanced at me. "Your call, Dee."

I peeked back at Jason, the outside breeze slightly hitting me in the face. His head was turned, his green-brown eyes looking at me, wondering too. *So it was my choice, huh?* I brushed a few strands of hair behind my ears, really considering. *Do we go home now or stay the night, leave first thing in the morning?*

A glance out of the window proved night was upon us. The sun setting in the distance was almost lost behind the mountain range and the sky was slowly turning to indigo. This was possibly the longest day of my entire life and you know I was kind of too tired to drive three hours' home. Plus, we were already out this way, and I already lied to my parents.

"We'll leave first thing tomorrow morning," I said, glancing back at everyone. "I think we all could use a little *R & R*."

A smile formed on Jason's freckly face. *Hopefully I didn't just make the most idiotic mistake of my life. Then again, if I die I won't remember it.*

"Okay, then back to my pad it is," Jacob prompted, relief clear in his voice. "We can wash up and crash there."

Jason leaned his arms and head through the window opening. "Actually, I have a better idea."

"Oh God," Missy groaned. "*Please* not Buck and Kyle's place again."

"Damn, you know *them* too." Spencer half-spun in his seat. Duke was panting loudly next to him, his snout pointed toward Jason.

"That tends to happen in small towns," Missy grumbled, sinking back against the cushion, a pouty expression on her face.

"And you *stayed* with them?" Spencer's tone was incredulous.

Missy nodded. "Not our finest hours."

"How crude *were* they?" Jacob cut in, his curious brown eyes reflecting in the mirror again.

"They were tolerable," Jason replied, skeptically. "I handled it."

I pushed back Jason's shirt sleeve and started fiddling with the bracelet on my wrist that he made me. *Oh, he handled it all right. By staying up all night, that is.* I shifted my eyes back to his profile, staring at his scruffy cheeks and under eye circles. "So, what's your suggestion then?"

He lowered his chin to his arms. "Well I was thinking that we stop at Jacob's place so Spencer can get his things together. Then, we should all crash at my place. Well, my neighbor's place. That way, I can check on the twins, we can have a hot meal, and hot showers. We already know the well water is safe there, and we'll be closer to your car in the morning. Plus, once the cops come, they might block this whole area off, and we won't be able to leave," he sighed.

Silence spread throughout the truck for a moment. We were all remembering exactly what we wanted to forget—the scenes in Pine Star Campsite that would be branded in our mind forever.

"Okay," Jacob finally said, turning the truck onto the street toward his house. "Your house it is." He shifted the truck into second gear, slowing the truck speed. "Perhaps I should pack some of my own belongings, a trip to *mi madre*'s sounds pretty good right now."

"Didn't you say your mom lives in Spain?" Missy asked, her blue eyes peering at the back of his head.

"Exactly." He didn't have to make his point any clearer. We got it.

We talked briefly after that, limiting our use of words. The distance between Jacob's house and the turn in the road wasn't long, so we were pulling into his junk-filled driveway in no time.

Jason, Duke, Missy and I stayed in the truck while Spencer and Jacob ran inside. Since Duke had such a reaction last time to the *infected* blood stains on the floor, Jason didn't want to let him out of the truck. And since Missy and I were both gimping, we thought it best to just stay put too. We'd only hold them up.

I was sitting in the seat listening to Jason and Missy talk about Duke, who had jumped over the seat and was now sitting in the back seat between us, when it hit me. "Oh crap," I mumbled, remembering. "We still have to return the quads."

"Ugh, crap, that's right." Missy's hand paused in the midst of petting Duke.

Jason rubbed at his exhausted eyes. "Don't worry about it. I'll go with Kyle and Buck tomorrow and get them."

"You sure?" I felt bad.

"Yeah, your car is close to their trailer anyway."

"But you and the twins *have to* get out of here," I urged, thinking about him staying behind. "Tomorrow it could be even worse."

"Maybe I'll take one of the quads to town then," he said, fake smirk on his face. "Will make the trip quicker."

Trip? Then it hit me. *Ohmigod that's right, the truck battery.*

"No," I replied, firmly. "We'll take you."

"What?"

I thought about how he gave up his plans to help us find Spencer. How he was risking everything for us. And I wouldn't just drive away and leave him without returning the favor. We'll just risk our lives a little longer, and pray we make it out alive. I didn't know where Jacob was going once he got his truck working, but I'll be damned if I let him handle zombies alone. "Once Jacob tows my car back on the road, I'll drive you to town to get the battery and take you back."

"That's completely ridiculous. Once you get out of this town, you keep going and you don't turn around. Do you understand?"

"Well, we will *after* we make sure you and the twins can get out too. We are all in this together, remember?"

His green-brown eyes locked on my face and I could not clearly identify the look in his hazel tones. I stared stubbornly back.

"*Mouth*, tell her she's being reckless," he said, eyes still focused on me but speaking to Missy. "Tell her to listen to me."

Peering past his head and Duke's, I could see Missy sitting there, listening but not answering.

"Mouth," he repeated, turning his face to her, his tone more forceful. "*Tell* her."

"I can't," she mumbled, staring at him.

"Why?" he sighed, in frustration.

"Because I agree with her."

Jason didn't say much after that. I could tell he wanted to argue some more, but he could see it would be useless. I wasn't changing my mind. Jacob and Spencer came back into the truck within the half hour, both carrying bags. Spencer had changed. At least he looked a bit more *himself*. He was now wearing a pair of jeans and a skater hoodie.   When he walked out of the house, he had the school backpack that I remembered slung over his left shoulder and a duffel bag in his right hand. I could see the relief in his eyes that he was leaving, but also his trepidation about heading home.

Jacob only looked eager. He was hauling a large green cargo bag. He had changed only his shirt. Instead of his sweat-stained, see-through white t-shirt he was now wearing a red one. But he wasn't wearing his hat. His hair wasn't by any means combed or clean, but it looked as if he tried to finger-comb it at least.

They had tossed their stuff into the bed with Jason and then climbed back inside the truck with us. Neither commented on the silence. Jacob just turned the key in the ignition, put the shifter into reverse, and we were on our way again.

We had been heading down the road for ten minutes probably, when Spencer unexpectedly started talking, breaking up the uncomfortable quiet.

."I left because I was getting expelled," he regretfully admitted. "Or arrested. I'm not really sure which."

I stared at him, my jaw dropping in shock. I wasn't expecting him to just come out and say something to us. I thought we were going to have to hound him for an answer. And I definitely wasn't expecting him to say *that* when he finally *did* answer.

"What? *Why?*" Missy prompted, instantly sitting taller in her seat, her attention focused on him. Her tone revealed she was as dumbfounded as I felt. Her expression was as startled as mine must have been. Spencer was not a *bad* kid. He was an average-grade student and for the most part stayed out of trouble. So why the hell would something so extreme happen to him? *Or almost?*

I noticed even Jacob and Jason were listening attentively, waiting for his answer.

"Do you remember Tim Rugby from my woodshop class last year?" He was staring down at his hands in his lap.
I thought for a moment. "Is that the kid with the glasses and bowl-cut hairstyle?"

"No," Missy interjected, "That's Tim Reece and he's in our grade." She paused for a second, remembering. "Rugby wasn't that kid who got arrested for possession of marijuana was he? That had to do community service all summer?"

As soon as she said that, my gut twisted. *I didn't like where this was going.*

"Yeah." Spencer was hesitant.

Missy immediately narrowed her eyes, glaring at him disapprovingly. "What does he have to do with this, Spencer? Were you doing drugs?"

"No," he quickly responded. "No. But, I *did* have drugs in my locker."

"Rewind a sec, bro," Jacob cut in, trying to concentrate on the road and Spencer at the same time. "If you weren't doing drugs what were they doing in your locker?"

He glanced over at him for a second before looking back down at his hands. "Well Tim never stopped smoking apparently and somehow the topic of it came up between a few of us guys after school one day. I told them I never tried it. The next week, he gave me a small bag of it. Told me it was for my birthday. I didn't know what to do with it, so I left it in my locker."

"If you didn't want it, why didn't you just flush it? Or toss it?" Jason asked then.

He didn't answer.

"Ah…" Jacob said, nodding absently. "Because you were *tempted* to try it."

"Considered it, yeah," Spencer agreed. "Never got the chance though."

Missy shook her head. "I don't know what to say to that."

"Not looking for a lecture, okay. Just figured you probably wanted to know why I'm out here." He peered back at us, his blue eyes apologizing. "And that's why."

I continued to look at him, trying to fully comprehend everything. "I just can't believe you left your Mom and Dad without a word. I mean, that was really messed up. They are so worried about you."

"Yeah," Missy cut in. "And *I* can't believe you left *us*. Dude, we did like everything together. I don't get it."

"I know. I bailed. I always do when I freak out." He turned his head toward the window, glancing out. "I probably made it worse than it would have been, huh?"

"Well," Jacob replied, "The cops would have probably drug tested you and you would have been clean, and since you don't have any previous offenses, I doubt it would have been too terrible. You're a minor after all."

Spencer laughed dryly. "I was more scared of what my parents would do. If I got busted with drugs, trust me my ass was on the curb anyway."

"But what you did to your parents," I began again. "Was not okay."

"Well after a while I just *couldn't* come back. Like what would I say? It was just easier if I stayed out here."

"But you didn't even call *us,*" Missy stretched in emphasis again. "We aren't your parents. We would have kept your secret. Hell, we probably would have even come visit you. We looked for you every freaking day."

"I've missed you, too. Thought of calling you, but I didn't want to put you two in the position of knowing where I was and not being able to say anything. *Dee*, I know you. You hate seeing people hurt. My parents would have been hounding you and you would have been a wreck. And *Melissa,* you hate lying. If you knew where I was you would have kicked my ass until I agreed to come back."

"I believe that," Jacob mumbled jokingly, earning a glare from Missy he couldn't see. "What I don't get though is why you called them and not someone else when Dean attacked us."

"Because at that point, I didn't care anymore. I just wanted to go home and I knew they'd come." He hesitated, rethinking that. "Or I was hoping they would."

"Do you really not care anymore?" Missy retorted, skeptical. "About going home?"

"After what I've seen and what I've done these past couple days, heading back home is the least of my problems," Spencer sighed.

I wanted to ask him what he'd done, but then thought better of it. Even *I* didn't want to talk about what *I'd* done.

"Okay, I got a question," Jason chimed in again. "Explain the truck and how you knew where to find us?"

"I *wasn't* looking for you guys. When I called them and told them not to come for me but to leave, I knew the only way I could get out of this town was to steal a car. So I just tried opening every vehicle I saw in the campsites until I could get one started. Then when I was driving, I happened to pass Jacob's truck parked in the middle of the campground and thought maybe Jacob was looking for me or was in trouble, so I started driving back and forth until I found him. Just by luck, *all of you* were with him."

"Well thank God, you stole a truck," Jacob said, turning the steering wheel to the right. We were now heading down a smaller, more secluded road. "Saved our butts."

"Yeah, well, speaking of stealing cars," Missy said, "Why didn't we just steal the damn car that I was charging the phone in? We wouldn't have needed our butts saved."

"Simple," Jason replied, reaching his arm through the window opening to pet Duke again. "We are trying to keep our involvement in all this under wraps, remember? That would have defeated the purpose." He looked past Duke, peering toward the windshield. "Now Jacob, remember it's the first turn up ahead, not the second. Everyone always misses it."

"'Kay thanks." Jacob downshifted again.

"I still think we should have taken the car," Missy grumbled, purposely pushing a moot point.

"If we took that car," Jason responded, his tone disbelieving. "We'd still be looking for Spencer."

27

When we pulled into the driveway, I couldn't take my eyes off the lot next to Jason's neighbor's house. The entire area was just one empty, burnt field. There was some grass sprouting up, but hardly any sign of *life*. It was mostly just the yellow-brown straw-like remains of once living grass. I couldn't believe a house used to be there because everything was pretty much *gone*. There was still left over debris at the end of the now useless driveway. Some burnt wood, a charred refrigerator and a blackened bed, melted clear to the springs. It was sad to see.

As I climbed out of the truck, I stepped off to the side and continued staring, trying to imagine what Jason's home used to look like, trying to picture a family that still had both parents living there. Trying to picture something *good*, not the sadness I saw.

A chill worked its way down my spine, and I crossed my arms. I couldn't even imagine how hard it must be for him and the twins to wake up every day and see the remains of what once was their life. To be constantly reminded of where they used to live, of parents that should still be alive if it weren't for this horrible illness.

The sound of Spencer's voice behind me suddenly aggravated me. There was a kid who still had both parents, a nice home in New Jersey, and he willingly left it. I couldn't help but wonder if Jason thought the same way. *How could he not?*

A gentle hand touched the lower half of my back. Jason's. "Come on," he softly said, guiding me away. "There's nothing there left to see. My home is this way now."

And as he led me across the stone pathway to the front porch of his neighbor's house, my heart ached for him. Though he was touching me, he was not looking at me. His eyes were drawn toward the door. Duke was already on the porch, tail wagging, pawing at the glass, barking excitedly. He obviously was happy to be back. Jason, not so much.

By the time we reached the steps, the door opened and a thin middle-aged woman peered out, almost immediately getting knocked over by Duke, who darted inside. She caught herself on the door frame.

"Jason," she proclaimed, surprised. "We weren't expecting you yet." Her chestnut brown eyes shifted to me, widening slightly. "Friends?"

There was so much question, confusion and worry in her voice.

"I know," Jason sighed. "Sorry, long story. Do you mind if they crash just for the night? We'll be out by sunrise."

I didn't have to be right next to her to see how uncomfortable she was with that.

"I would never do anything to harm you guys, trust me," he urged, his voice understanding and reassuring at the same time.

She nodded, a tight smile forming on her pale face. "Of course, come on in. Brandon and Frankie are in the back room, playing video games."

All of a sudden, I heard screaming from inside the house. "Jason! Jason! You're home!"

"Well, *were* in the back room," she chuckled, moving out of the way as a young girl burst through the doorway, leaping into

Jason's arms enthusiastically. Jason caught her, squeezing her into a bear hug before letting her down.

"Hey, I've got to go check on dinner," his neighbor announced. "I'll catch up with you inside."

Jason looked over his sister's head, smiling. "Okay, Meg, we'll be right in. Thank you."

She nodded and started to walk away, closing the door. *So her name was Meg.* She was a pretty woman of Asian-decent, with straight, chin-length dark hair, but I could tell she was stressed out. *And not just from our arrival.*

Jason peered back down at his sister, giving her another quick hug. "It's good to see you too, twerp."

She surprised me by punching him in the gut. "Don't go off without me again. You left me with Brandon."

"I'm sure you managed just fine," he said.

"Hmph! Whatever," she grumbled sulkily. "By the way, you need a shower, you smell!"

Jason laughed, and retaliated by reaching his hand out and messing up her long, auburn hair.

"Hey," she whined, punching him again. This time he caught her arm, trapping her against his side, spinning her to look my way.

"Dee, this is Frankie, my crazy and wild kid sister. Please excuse her rudeness."

Frankie's eyes widened as if she just realized I was standing there. "Sorry," she mumbled, her cheeks blushing. And in that second, I saw exactly how much alike her and Jason's eyes were. But Jason was right, besides their eyes there really was no other comparison. For starters her skin was darker and she didn't have any freckles.

"Hey, no problem," I teased, siding with her. "I've wanted to punch him all day too." Frankie's lips split into a grin.

"Real nice," Jason mumbled. "I'll remember that." He looked past me to where Missy, Spencer and Jacob were standing. "Hey mouth," he called. "Why don't you shut up for two seconds so we can go inside?"

She spun around, glaring at him. "Hallmark, why don't you just—" But the moment she saw Frankie standing there, she stopped whatever she was about to say.

"That's what I thought," he said, smiling. "This is my kid sister," he exclaimed, his arm still wrapped around her shoulder. "So do me a favor and watch that mouth of yours while you are here. I'd like to keep her as innocent as I can."

Frankie squirmed loose from his grip, pushing away from him. "Shut up, I'm not a little kid anymore. How many times do I have to tell you that?"

Jason's lips remained curved in amusement. "You'll always be my kid sister though."

She groaned and started walking to the door. "Well at least you are better than Brandon."

We followed Jason and Frankie into the house, down a hallway into a TV room. The first thing I noticed was the way the house smelled. It reminded me of home, of all those times I came into the house, smelled dinner cooking in the oven and felt my stomach instantly growling in response. I was suddenly so homesick I couldn't take it. I missed my mom and my dad. I missed my room. I even missed our little Jack Russell and our gold fish in the living room.

This house was cozy, warm and inviting. The moment I stepped through the doorway, it was like we were stepping into a normal life. As if it was just any *normal* day. The place was clean. More importantly, inside here I felt safe. And now I could understand why Jason wasn't so worried about his brother and sister while we were out on the roads and in the woods. Because here, inside these walls, life was continuing as if nothing bad was happening out there. I instantly understood why Meg seemed so stressed now, because she was the one working so hard to keep that *normalcy* for all of them. She was fighting to hold it together, the way Jason acted. Because if either of them gave up, what would the twins have left?

Nothing.

And neither Meg nor Jason wanted Brandon and Frankie to see how bad it truly was. Losing their parents and their home was hard enough for them to comprehend.

"So like how do you know my brother?" Frankie said, sitting down on the coffee table in front of the television.

There was a gun shooting then a loud explosion as the character on the television screen blew up and died. The words *game over* appeared behind her back instantly.

"Damn it, Frankie. You just killed me." A boy jumped up, pushing her out of the way, his hand clasping a video game controller. *That must be Brandon.*

Frankie shrugged, not even sparing him a glance, not leaving the coffee table either—just sitting on the edge instead. She continued to look toward Melissa and me, waiting for our response.

"Well, we sort of just met," I replied, feeling silly saying that considering we were sleeping over.

"Oh so you're not from around here?" Her hazel eyes rounded. "Where are you from? Why are you here? Who are you visiting?"

"Well aren't you just Ms. Chatty," Jason said, motioning for all of us to take a seat and relax. "Why don't you save all your questions for after dinner? Everyone is pretty beat."

"Yeah, and get off the coffee table, you're *still* blocking some of the screen," Brandon interjected.

She snorted, and stood up. "Whatever, I'm going to my room then. Nice meeting you," she mumbled as she walked past us, back down the hall.

Jacob laughed, dropped his bag on the floor and sank down on the couch cushion next to Jason's brother.

"Guys, this is Brandon if you haven't guessed," Jacob introduced, stretching his arm out across the top of the couch, leaning back in comfort. It was obvious Jacob had been to the house before. He had no awkwardness about being here.

"Hi," Brandon replied, not even looking at us. His eyes were already glued on the television again. He was leaned over, his fingers moving quickly over the controller buttons, shooting monsters.

"Excuse his rudeness, too." Jason sighed, half-serious. "Apparently both my siblings forgot what manners were while I was gone."

"Hey," Brandon countered, his eyes remaining glued to the TV. "I said *hi*... what else did you want me to do?"

Jacob started shaking his head. "You know; I worry about him. When I was his age, if two hot chicks walked in the room, video games were the last thing on my mind. That's for sure."

Brandon exhaled in frustration and hit pause on the screen, turning to us finally.

"*Hello*," he grumbled, over-exaggeratingly. "Better?"

Jason rolled his eyes. "I'm going to go take our bags into the bedroom and then go wash up," he informed us, ignoring his brother. "If any of you need to use the bathroom, there's a half-bath in the hall. First door to the right." He leaned down and picked up Jacob's cargo bag. His own backpack was slung on his other shoulder.

"I'll carry my own stuff," Spencer said, tightening his grip on his duffel. "Just show me where to go."

Jason nodded. "'Kay, this way then." He started past me, pausing. "I'll bring you two some clean clothes to change into. Then you can take a shower or whatever."

"Thanks," I said, grateful.

"Mmmhmm." He left, leaving Melissa and I alone with Jacob and Brandon.

We both used the bathroom and then sat down, relaxing on the couch. Brandon had immediately gone back to playing games, with Jacob joining him. Meg came out telling us it was time for dinner, and life *was* normal again.

A full stomach had me rejuvenated and energized, making me feel like a completely different person. And that first step into the shower seriously felt like a little piece of heaven. But that content, wonderful sense of *normalcy* disappeared as fast as the shampoo rinsed from my hair, vanishing down the drain. The longer I stood in the stream of hot water, the more bone-chilling memories of the past two days came back to me. Suddenly I was shaking, dropping to my knees, crying. It was the hardest I ever cried in my life, and I couldn't stop. I was crying because of everything I did, everything I still had to do, the fact I almost died, *and* the fact that after all of that I was still *alive*.

Sighing heavily, with trembling fingers I gripped the safety rail and staggered to my feet. I tried to scrub away the pain, the fear and the unwashable grime of filthy memories. Filth coated my skin and was caked under my fingernails, but the more I scrubbed, the harder the tears fell from my eyes. I was so grateful the bathroom fan and the sound of running water drowned out my sobs because I was seriously— without a doubt— a wreck. *I hadn't even realized I was this bad.*

But I was.

I truly completely was.

And I wasn't sure I was ever going to be the same.

I stayed in the shower until the water started turning cold and the tears had stopped. I shut off the faucets and tiptoed out, still shivering—this time though mostly from the temperature change. Drying off, I took a deep, calming breath and held the towel to my face a little longer than normal. Slowly, I started to dress into Jason's over-sized sweats, seeking comfort from the clean, worn cotton. I rolled the waistband a couple times to make the pants fit.

Then, taking the brush Missy left on the sink for me, I combed my wet strands of hair and used my other hand to smear away a streak of steam off the mirror. My reflection showed a completely different person than I felt. The girl in the glass looked like a *regular* teenage girl. I was not *that* girl anymore.

Well, with the exception of one thing.

Jason.

Despite everything, even just the thought of him had my stomach reacting in butterflies, and my heart pitter-pattering. But even that was bitter-sweet, because what was going to happen after I dropped him off at his truck tomorrow with the battery? I was going to drive away, and he was going to follow suit, except he was going in a different direction than me.

Falling for a guy like Jason would only break my heart, but falling for a guy has been and will always be against a girl's control. I can't help liking him. No matter how much I try not to.

But really, I shouldn't even be concerned with what happens *after* tomorrow. There's still a chance I might not survive it.

Tossing my towel into the laundry basket, I walked out of the bathroom, to get on with the possible last hours of my life.

"Here," I said, handing Missy her brush back. "Thanks."

She nodded, taking it from me and placed it on the nightstand. She was unrolling a sleeping bag on the floor in Frankie's room. Meg's husband, Germaine, had taken a couple out of the attic for us to sleep on, after dinner. He was a quiet guy, a lot more reserved. But he was nice. He worked from home, locked up in his office most of the time from what Jason said. He had graying black hair, wore thin-framed circular glasses and dressed a little too dressy for someone who worked in his own home, in my opinion. *Maybe it helped him with his own normalcy.*

"What's everyone doing?" I asked, leaning up against the wall. "Where are they?"

"Spencer said he was beat and was going to bed. I think Jacob, Frankie and Brandon are still playing games." She plopped down on the blue material, crossing her legs.

"And Jason?"

"Last I saw he was talking to Meg and Germaine, but they just walked down the hall to their room." She looked at me knowingly. "He's okay, Dee. He's around somewhere."

"I just want to talk to him."

"Okay, well I think I'm just going to ice my ankle a little more and then try to sleep. Don't stay up too late. We leave at sunrise."

"I won't. I'll be back shortly." *Sleep was the last thing from my mind though.*

Duke trotted past me in the hallway and I followed him, figuring he'd lead me to Jason. But he only led me to the water bowl. I petted him anyway, then kept going. My feet felt so much better without the back of my sneakers rubbing against my blisters and I was hardly gimping now as I walked barefoot across the hardwood floor.

Peering into the TV room I saw that Jason wasn't in there either. And that Jacob actually had his head back, sleeping, while Frankie and Brandon played some game. The clock on the wall proved it really wasn't that late. It was only ten-thirty.

Frankie turned her head and saw me standing there. "Hey!"

"Hi."

"You want to play?"

I smiled at her. "No thanks. I was actually looking for your brother."

"Oh, he's out on the porch probably."

"The porch?" My brow scrunched in confusion.

"Yeah, he goes out there a lot."

"Oh, okay. Thanks."

She nodded, shifting her attention back to the game because Brandon was getting impatient.

Turning around, I headed back down the hallway, passing Duke again. The front door was closed, but I noticed it wasn't locked. Peeking out the window beside it, I saw him. Jason. He was sitting on the top step, hunched over, face in the palms of his hands. And by the slight shaking of his shoulders, I could tell he was crying.

I almost didn't want to go out there.

Almost.

Slowly opening the door, I stepped out onto the cold concrete. Jason instantly jolted, jumping up, swiping his hand under his eyes.

"It's okay, it's just me," I said quickly.

Still he spun around, trying to act as if he *wasn't* just crying. The porch light however, showed his bloodshot eyes clearly, and there was no mistaking it. For his sake though, I pretended not to notice.

"What are you doing out here?" I asked, crossing my arms over my chest. The night wind bit at my exposed skin hungrily.

"I just needed some air," he replied, turning his head, his eyes gazing out into the shadows surrounding the house. His voice was coarse and half-caught in his throat. Even further proof he was clearly upset.

An ache started in my chest again as I continued to look at him, he looked like he was carrying the weight of the world on his shoulders. "Maybe you should come inside. It's cold out and it's dangerous out here."

He nodded in acknowledgment. "I'll be in soon. I'm not staying out here long."

I got the cue he wanted me to leave. I wasn't dumb. But, I took a few steps forward anyway and sat down beside him. "Then I'll sit with you."

"No you don't have—"

"I want to," I said, cutting him off, his eyes staring at me in disbelief. "And if you decide you want to talk about it, I'm right here. And if you don't, that's cool too. At least you won't be alone."

He pulled his eyes away from my face, peering down at his hands. For a moment he didn't say anything then suddenly he reached out, putting his arm around my shoulder, drawing me toward his side. "Well there's no point for you to freeze while you sit here," he said. "I can at least keep you warm."

And there it went again, that little pitter-patter of my heart I couldn't control.

I had absolutely no idea how long we sat there. All I know was the entire time I sat with my head on Jason's shoulder, snuggled up against him. I had given up wondering if he was ever going to say anything and was just trying to enjoy sitting out there in the quiet of the night with him. But though it felt amazing to be in his arms, in the back of my mind I was still worrying about who was out there in the shadows—if there was anyone— and if I blinked or pulled my eyes away, would that be when they attacked?

And the worst part was I think Jason was too busy wrapped up in his own mind to even notice to our vulnerability.

I almost considered going back in—my bare feet were freezing—but just as I was about to pull away from his embrace, Jason started talking.

"I hate it here," he uttered, quietly. "No matter how hard Meg and Germaine try to make us feel welcome, I don't feel it. Not really. I feel like an impostor." He paused, looking in the direction of where his house used to be. I followed his gaze. "I hate waking up *next door* to where I should be waking up. I hate being reminded every single day that my house is gone, that my parents are gone. I hate having to raise my brother and sister when I still have my own growing up to do."

"I hate all of it, but I was coping. I *was*, Dee. I was getting on with my life. I was fixing my truck, I was going to take the money that my parents had saved, and I was going to get the twins out of this town."

My stomach knotted. "Until we came and screwed that up," I mumbled, beginning to feel incredibly awful all over again.

"No," he said, squeezing me in reassurance. "You didn't screw anything up. Stop. I'm still getting out of here."

"But you got so mad this afternoon. You must be pissed at us. There's no way you can't be. We messed up all your plans. We risked your life."

"I wasn't mad at any of *you*," he sighed, the tone of his voice instantly shutting me up, suppressing my guilt. "It's just, it's just if we are right, and this illness isn't spreading through physical contact then that that means my father, well, he killed himself for nothing." Jason grew very quiet. I didn't have to look at him to know he was trying *not* to cry again. I said nothing, waiting.

"And how do I cope with that, Dee? I *was* better, but now I feel like I just lost my parents all over again."

The ache in my chest spread. I wanted to cry too. *For him.* I tried to think of something to say, something inspirational or sympathetic—something that would make him feel better. I thought really hard. "Your mom bit your father, right?" *Not exactly inspirational, but I think I had a point.*

Jason's hand loosened on my shoulder, slightly. "Yeah, she did." I could tell he didn't want to talk about this right now.

But it began to occur to me. "Well, maybe it *wasn't* for nothing then. Your father, I mean."

"Huh?" Jason dropped his arm away.

I half-spun toward him, my knees brushing into his leg. "I was just thinking, this illness might not be spreading through touch, but your mom *bit* your dad. I'm not a doctor, but I do know a lot of illnesses are spread through salvia or blood contact. It's probably a completely different outcome if contact is made *through* the skin, not *on* the skin. So your dad probably would have gotten sick regardless."

Jason stared at me for a long moment. Then, exhaling, he pulled me back into his arms. I knew instantly I said something right.

"Thank you," he mumbled, his lips brushing the top of my head. This time he was hugging me against his chest. I could hear his heart beating through his shirt.

"I didn't say anything I don't believe. And besides no matter what, your father didn't die for nothing. He died thinking he was saving your life and that is *something*. That shows how much he loved you. He gave his life to protect you and the twins. There is no greater selfless act. Always remember that. "

I could hear the change in the rhythm of his heart so I quickly wrapped my arms around his waist to comfort him. He squeezed me even tighter, holding on to me as he struggled with his emotions. I could feel each rise and fall of his chest as he breathed and was relieved to hear his heartbeat slowing. Steadying.

He smelled of soap and aftershave, even hours later. And I still couldn't get over how much younger he looked without his scruff—he had shaved in the shower—but he still looked *good*, just younger now. Seeing him in sweatpants and an undershirt didn't help either. Somehow it made him look more like a high school boy right out of gym class instead of the nineteen-year-old he was.

Either way, he still had an effect on me.

"You know what, Dee Forrester?" Jason murmured above my head, about two minutes later.

I was twirling circles on his back with my finger, my face still pressed against his heart. "What Jason?"

"My Mom and Dad would have liked you."

A smile formed on my lips at the kind remark. "Well, if they were anything like you and the twins, I would have liked them too," I responded.

There was a beat of silence as Jason ran his fingers through my hair.

"Dee?" I heard his heartbeat changing.

"Yeah?"

His hand paused in my still-damp strands. "I just want you to know I think you're pretty great."

My smile spread. *And I couldn't help but think he was too.*

We were still sitting there moments later when something caught my eye. I glanced out into the shadows of the night, my stomach instantly knotting. "Is that—"

Jason immediately jumped up, pulling me with him. "Yeah." *It was them.* He started pushing me toward the door. "Inside. Hurry." And just like that the peace and quiet of our night was over.

I stumbled forward. He caught me.

Reaching out, I grasped for the doorknob, fumbling to turn it. Jason grumbled behind me anxiously, rushing me. *If he wasn't so up my back, I probably could get the damn thing open.*

Finally, I yanked the door open. Jason immediately grabbed it, holding it, shoving me gently inside. I had one foot through the doorway when someone yelled.

"Wait!"

I froze, startled. *They can talk?*

"Please!" The voice urged again. He was definitely male and he was out of breath.

I turned, spinning right into Jason's chest. He still tried to push me inside.

I braced myself onto the doorframe, holding myself there. "Maybe he needs help—"

"Not our problem," Jason said, nudging me forward again. I still held my ground, trying to look past him, but he kept blocking me and he wasn't looking behind him either. Jason only had his eyes locked on me. "Please, Dee, just get inside." He was practically begging me. I could hear the worry in his voice, as if he didn't want to lose me too.

I dropped my hand and turned back around, moving inside. Jason stepped in after me. Just as he was shutting the door, we heard his name.

"Jason!" The guy hollered again, this time a lot closer.

Jason paused, looking over his shoulder. I still couldn't see, but I saw Jason's body tense up. That couldn't be good.

I heard *whoever* it was come running forward, breathing hard, feet pounding heavy on the pathway. "Dude! Seriously help! I don't know what to do." His breathing was so loud he must have been at the end of the steps.

Jason made an inaudible sound, slowly pushed me further into the house, then he stepped back outside, shutting the door between us, locking me in. I darted to the glass, peering out. And just as Jason moved, I saw *him.*

It was Kyle. And he was hunched over, hands on knees, pleading for Jason to help him.

28

I tried to get back on the porch, but Jason wouldn't let me out. He stayed there, leaning up against the door.

"Kyle? What's wrong? What happened?" Even through the glass I could hear the confusion, hesitation and worry in Jason's voice.

Kyle peered up at him, sweat dripping from his brow. And I could tell he was drunk again. *Maybe even a little high.*

"It's Buck," he exhaled, panicked. "He's sick. I don't know what to do."

Jason rubbed his temples, like he didn't have the patience for this conversation. "He's probably just drunk, Kyle. He'll sleep it off."

Kyle started shaking his head. "No it's worse than that".

"Then maybe it's alcohol poisoning."

"No. No. He's *sick*," Kyle urged, desperate, his eyes round and dilated. "Like he's turning into one of them zombie things."

"*What?*" Jason dropped his hands immediately, stepping forward, his entire persona changing. "Are you sure? What happened? Were you attacked?"

Kyle dropped to the porch step, exhausted. "I don't know what happened. I thought he was just hung over this morning, but he wasn't. He was actually sick. And he's just been getting worse."

I used this moment to quietly step back onto the porch, creeping to the side. Jason acknowledged me for a brief second when the door shut, but the message in his eyes was clear. *Either get back inside or do not come closer.* I nodded, staying put, right up against the brick, exactly under the porch light, listening.

"How bad is he?" Jason asked, fidgeting. "And how much well water did he drink? And when did he drink it?"

"Well water? What the hell are you talking about?" Kyle stared at him, confused.

Jason looked down at him. "We think people are getting sick from bacteria in the water. If we know how much he drank and when, we might be able to figure out how fast it's spreading and how much time we have."

"I don't know," Kyle replied. "I have no clue what he drank besides a twelve-pack of cheap-ass beer."

Jason exhaled in frustration, like he was dealing with a toddler. "Well, how bad is he? What are his symptoms?"

"He's sick, bro. Like *sick*. I can't even put it into words. You should know, your mom had it. You've seen what it does to people."

My eyes quickly flashed toward Jason at the mention of his mother, but he wasn't reacting to it, at least not visually.

"And what about you, how are *you* feeling?" He cautioned, concerned and weary.

"Besides drunk and slightly winded, I feel fine. But I'm bugging out, dude. Buck's the only family I got left. I can't lose him."

"I understand completely."

"I know you do." Kyle persisted, anxious and confused, "But this is worse. He's scaring the shit out of me, dude. Not just because he's sick, but because he's talking all crazy."

"Talking crazy?" Now Jason and I were the confused ones.

I stood there, crossing my arms. *Was that one of the symptoms, mental psychosis?*

Kyle jumped up, swaying slightly. "He said he's gonna blow up the entire town before he becomes one of them. He told me to leave town tonight because tomorrow morning he's going out in a blaze of glory. He told me to find you and warn you guys to retreat so he doesn't accidently kill you too." He straightened out, pulling up his sagging alcohol-stained jeans. "I love my cousin, and he's great, but we know damn well that lunatic is crazy enough to do this and he's got all the ammo he needs."

I stared bug-eyed at Kyle. *What the—? "Blaze of glory?" What is wrong with those two rednecks?*

Jason started pacing, cursing.

"What do I do, Jason?" Kyle spazed. "Like seriously, *what*? Tell me."

"Well there's only one thing we can do," Jason said, spinning toward him. "We have to get to the trailer and get Buck to a hospital, get him help right—"

Kyle started shaking his head again. "No, no we don't have insurance, dude. And they'll find traces of drugs in his blood. He can't go there."

I couldn't believe him. "If he doesn't go, he'll die," I prompted, chiming in. *For someone who cared so much about his cousin.*

"He has a record, Dee. He's been busted before. He won't risk it."

"If he's as bad as some of these people are getting," Jason urged, "he won't really have the consciousness to argue with us."

"Yeah, but dude, he will never, ever forgive us."

Jason just stared at him. "I'll risk it."

"I'm begging you," Kyle replied, placing his palms together. "Find a different solution."

"I'm not a doctor," Jason snapped back. "I can't cure this. If I could I would have cured my mom."

"*Please*," Kyle pleaded again desperately. "Just help him without involving the hospital."

Jason raked a hand down his face, clearly frustrated. "Fine, but we don't have much time. We got to contain him. Stop him from destroying this town no matter how bad it's getting out there. These are people. They are ill. Not zombies. There *has* to be a cure."

"Well what is it then?" Kyle proclaimed.

"I don't know," Jason exhaled, "but I have to start asking questions, it's the only way to get answers." He turned around to face me. "Dee, I'm—"

"If you think for a second you are leaving without us, you have another thing coming to you," I blurted, stubbornly.

A strained smile hit his face. "Actually I was just going to say, I'm going to grab the keys, write a note to Meg and Germaine then start the truck. I was going to tell you to go wake everyone up, tell them we have to go and to grab my pack for me out of my room before you come back out."

Oh. I bit my lip. "Alright, yeah." I shifted my feet over, placing my hand back on the door handle. "Wait, what do I say to Brandon and Frankie if they ask where we are going?"

Jason just stood there. "That I'll be back tomorrow evening and to stay put." *Somehow I didn't see that going smoothly.* "But Dee?"

I peered over my shoulder. "Yeah?"

"Try not to wake them if they're asleep. It's just easier."

I nodded. *That's better.* "And Duke? What about him?"

Jason looked at the door. "Try not to let him out when you open it."

Huh? My eyes turned to the glass. Sure enough Duke was right behind it, breath fogging it up. "How long has he been there?" I asked, startled. I never heard him.

Jason shrugged. "A few minutes. He's just watching us."

"I'm surprised he isn't barking."

"Why? There's no reason. Nothing's going on." He stepped up to me. "Okay Kyle we will be right back, promise." I couldn't help, but notice how Jason *didn't* offer Kyle to come inside and wait. If I had to take three quick guesses *why*, it would be because Kyle was drunk, this wasn't *Jason's* house and Jason probably thought Kyle was infected too. Then again, Jason just always assumed everyone was sick until proven otherwise.

Carefully opening the door, I squeezed in past Duke and hurried down the hall into Frankie's room, relieved to see her already asleep in her bed.

Tiptoeing inside, grateful for the night light on the wall, I crept up to Missy.

"Psst."

She rolled over and looked at me. "What?"

I could tell she wasn't sleeping, just staring at the window, restless. A melted bag of ice was lying on the floor next to her sleeping bag.

"We've got to go," I whispered.

"What?" She sat up instantly.

"Shh!" I pointed dramatically to Jason's sister.

She made a face and lowered her voice. "What's going on? It isn't sunrise yet."

I crouched down next to her. "Kyle's outside. Buck's *sick* and he's planning on blowing the whole town up, including himself, tomorrow morning."

Her eyes widened. "What the f—"

I quickly covered her mouth with my hand, silencing her. Missy was so loud Frankie started moving around in the bed, mumbling in her sleep. We both stared at her, waiting to see if she awoke, both saying nothing. After about thirty seconds, I dropped my hand from her mouth. Once I was certain all was clear, I helped Missy out of the sleeping bag and onto her feet.

"I have to get dressed," she urged, looking down at the baggy extra-large t-shirt she was wearing.

"Okay," I mumbled, taking a step. "I'm going to go wake up Spencer and get Jason's pack. When you're dressed, wake up Jacob, I think he's still on the couch."

She nodded, pushing her long hair off her face and I rushed quietly out of the room to Jason's room.

Stepping foot inside wasn't as awkward as I thought it would be though, but that probably had to do with the fact the room didn't feel like a guy's room. It just felt like a very small, tidy guest room in someone's home. There were no posters on the wall, no dirty clothes slung on the floor, no stacks of disorganized, teetering CDs or DVDs. There was no television, computer, or phone. The clean clothes in the closet were the only sign that Jason even slept in there. That and the fact his backpack was leaning up against the wall and Spencer was passed out on the floor. It made me suddenly wonder exactly how many nights Jason actually slept in this house. An earlier comment made at Kyle and Buck's trailer—about how many times a week he goes there—made me think Jason spent more time staying at friends' houses than with the twins here. At least Frankie's room looked girly and *lived* in.

Though Spencer was the only one in this room, I still had to be quiet because Brandon's room was right across from it. Luckily the door was shut, and I could hear his snoring coming from the other side, so I wasn't *too* worried.

Thinking this would be easy, I walked up to Spencer and shook his shoulders gently.

Spencer didn't move.

I tried again.

Still nothing.

Again.

Nothing.

Exhaling in frustration, I knelt down beside him and shook him harder. I *was* trying to wake him, but apparently waking Spencer was like trying to wake a hibernating bear.

"Spencer," I said, struggling to keep my voice down. "Wake up!"

I waited, still shaking him, but Spencer just wasn't responding.

If it wasn't for the slight snuffing sound coming from him, I'd probably be freaking out right now. Instead I was just getting impatient. We didn't have time for this.

"Okay Spencer, you leave me no choice," I grumbled, shaking my head. I couldn't believe I was about to resort to something so childish.

Taking his arm, I pinched his skin, twisting it until Spencer jumped awake.

"*Ow*…what?"

I let go. A bruise was already starting. "We are leaving," I replied, standing back up, heading for Jason's backpack. "So get up!"

The truck ride was absolutely miserable. The six of us were crammed *inside* Jacob's pickup and we were all exhausted, irritable and anxious. Spencer and Kyle were squeezed into the back seat, stuffed back there like sardines in a tin can. Jacob was driving, his eyes half-shut, constantly yawning. Missy was in the middle, restless and agitated, and I was sitting on Jason's lap in the passenger seat. The seatbelt was snapped around the both of us, plus his arms were wrapped around me too, but I was still holding onto the *"oh shit"* handle because I felt like any second I was going to go through the windshield.

Jacob had the high beams on, but it hardly made a difference. Between the unnerving length of darkness and the fact the windows kept fogging over, I could hardly see a thing. Jacob couldn't apparently either—though I think some of his grogginess was contributing to that— because he kept slamming on the brakes, having to make sharp, quick turns when the road suddenly curved in front of us. He even drove accidentally into a cornfield on one swerve, taking out two sections of stalks before finding pavement again. Oh yes, I was definitely holding onto that *"oh shit"* handle, because I was being knocked around like one of those little metal balls in a pinball machine. *Not fun.*

Jacob hit another pothole and started apologizing immediately. "Sorry, Dee," he urged for the umpteenth time, "I swear I'm not doing it on purpose." His eyes were a little more opened now, more focused. Thanks to the dim overhead light Jacob insisted stayed on, I could see everyone pretty clearly.

"I know," I mumbled, readjusting my sweaty grip on the handle. I tried holding some of my weight off Jason's legs, but it wasn't easy since I was being jostled around. "How much longer though?" My knees were killing me. They were touching the dashboard, banging into it every time Jacob hit a bump. *Like I needed more bruises.*

"A few more minutes, promise."

I nodded, staring out the window. I hated the fact I was still dressed in Jason's sweats but I just didn't have time to change into my clothes, which were washed and nicely folded, sitting on Missy's lap right now. Thankfully Meg was kind enough to wash our things for us and I couldn't wait to get to the trailer so I could slip back into my shorts that fit. If I was going to have to make a run for it sometime in the near future I wanted to make sure my pants were staying up. Missy—lucky her—was already back in her jeans.

Jason kept insisting I relax and sit comfortably against him, but I just kept shaking my head. We were almost there, no point now.

"Know what I find funny," Jacob said, without humor. He kept his eyes focused on the road, both hands on the steering wheel, his expression serious. "That we've spent all day running from sick people, and now we are rushing to go to one in the middle of the night."

"He's not one of them, *yet,*" Jason retaliated, in kind of a sigh, "and we are trying to save him. That's why. If he can give us details before he gets worse, maybe we can pinpoint where the well is that's causing this and find a cure."

"It has to be in the campsite," Spencer yawned, cutting in. Though he was finally awake, he didn't *look* awake. The bags under his eyes were even worse.

"No, it can't be there," Kyle countered, still half-buzzed. In such a confined space, I could actually smell the alcohol sweating off him, though I wouldn't be surprised if that was his natural scent. "Buck never goes to the campsite, no reason too. It has to be somewhere else."

"I don't know, dude," Spencer urged. "That campsite is like the worst area ever. You obviously haven't seen it."

Kyle stared at him with blood-shot blue eyes. "No, I haven't, but I'm telling you Buck *doesn't* go there."

"And I'm telling you—" Spencer began, but Missy quickly interjected, shutting them both up.

"Maybe you are both right, all right?" She shifted in her seat, to peer back at them. "Maybe there's more than one well? Maybe that's why it's spreading so fast."

"I don't see how that could be," Jacob refuted, putting in his two cents too. "The same bacteria aren't just going to grow in some wells and not others."

She turned her face toward him, giving him a defiant look no doubt. "Well it could—"

He started shaking his head, not letting her finish. "Nah, doubtful."

She sank back against the seat, grumbling. "Well damn it, there has to be some common denominator. Do you have any suggestions then?"

"Nada," he replied, remaining focused on the road.

Dee? Jason?" She urged. "Anything?"

I wasn't sure what to think. Shrugging, I looked at Jason, waiting to see what he had to suggest.

"We just have to wait and ask Buck," he prompted, catching my eye. "That's the only way to know for certain. Let's hope he's coherent."

"Is he really *that* bad?" Missy asked, shocked.

"He's bad," Kyle agreed, clearly upset.

"But he was so normal last night." She meant healthy, not sane. "I don't get it."

"Yeah, me either." Jason turned slightly to glance over the seat. "You didn't notice anything odd about Buck prior to today, did you Kyle? Like any sick symptoms? Something resembling the flu?"

"No dude, he's been fine. You've seen him."

Jason exhaled, his grip tensing around me. "I know, but I just don't understand. It doesn't make sense." I could tell this was frustrating him. "Going by what I know, there's at least two or three days before you start getting really bad, but you usually have visible symptoms. Nosebleeds, vomiting, severe headaches, exhaustion…" He stared at Kyle again. "None of that? Are you sure?" As if the first time he answered him wasn't good enough.

"Not that I saw anyway."

I considered everything they were saying and considered Buck. I tried picturing him last night, sitting around the couch drinking beer. He was laughing, talking, getting drunk. Probably a little high, but most definitely he was *not* sick. He seemed well enough. So what could be the reason he got so sick so fast over night? I thought pretty hard, taking in his horrible *habits*. The booze, the drugs, and what that does to a person. "Maybe he has a weaker immune system?" I suggested, peering at all of them. "That could affect him faster, right?"

The way the silence spread suddenly, I could tell I made a valid suggestion. Naturally I was expecting someone to comment on or rebut my opinion, but I wasn't expecting what Jason said next. I mean sure, it was obvious, but I just hadn't thought of it.

"I hope you're wrong," he mumbled, his tone taut. "Because if that's the case then we have even less time to save Buck and I'm still not sure if we even can."

29

As soon as Jacob threw the truck into park, we wasted no time jumping out into the cold, onyx night, hurrying toward the trailer. Jason trailed behind us, gun drawn just in case, especially since we were so close to the woods. I was on edge and paranoid, hoping these next few seconds wouldn't be my last. I had a grip on my waistband, holding up the sweats, wishing my borrowed gun wasn't sitting bullet-less in Missy's purse. As I ran, my eyes dashed around frantically, searching for *them* and hoping I saw no one.

I exhaled in relief as I leapt safely into the trailer, but my heart was still pounding. Jason almost ran right into me as he bolted through the doorway too.

"Where is he?" Jason asked, sparing no seconds, as he slammed the door closed behind him, locking it to be safe.

Kyle, who was stuck in the corner of the small front room with the couch, pointed over our heads, down the hall toward the bedrooms. Being we were all squeezed in that tiny area, I was starting to feel a little claustrophobic and hot, on top of everything else. Missy's elbow was annoyingly jammed in my side.

Jason scooted us out of his way, rushing forward to Buck's room, tucking the gun into his waistband as he went. I was the first to follow him, grateful for a little breathing room. *Though not so much for breathing...*

The trailer might have looked the same—maybe a few beer cans less on the counter, but it smelled funky. Like vomit. It was a moment like this that I was glad we left Duke at Meg and Germaine's because he'd have been barking his head off right about now. That smell was coming from the end of the hallway.

The door to the bedroom was cracked open and Jason lightly pushed at it, proceeding slowly inward. "Buck?" He called, stepping fully into the room, leaving me standing in the hallway, staring in. My eyes immediately went to the bed.

Buck was laying on it, curled up, in a fetal position, groaning. Blood tinted his nostrils, his chin, and stained the collar of his t-shirt. He was sweating profusely, but shivering. The covers were kicked off the edge and his perspiration soaked through the sheets. The window beside the mattress was open, the cold wind rattling the blinds against the glass, and even from where I was, I felt the chill hitting my skin. Instantly wrapping my arms around my chest, I walked into the room, to the side, so the others could come in too.

"Oh, man," Kyle exclaimed, slipping inside next. "He looks even worse."

Even worse?

I continued to stare at Buck, cringing. I didn't think he could look any worse really. He was so pale he already looked corpse-like.

Even though I had the pre-warning—that Buck was sick— I still don't think I was expecting *this.*

Missy actually gasped when she saw him.

"Buck?" Jason pressed, stepping away from us, up to the bed. "Are you well enough to talk? We need information."

Buck opened his eyes. Admittedly it was weird seeing him without his glasses on, but I noticed right away the changes in his irises. They weren't black but they were definitely darkening.

"What are you doing here?" he grumbled, embracing his stomach. "Get away from me."

Jason squatted down beside the edge of the mattress. "No. I'm here to help."

"You can't," he moaned.

"Actually I might be able to." I did not miss the lack of confidence in Jason's voice. "But I have to ask you some things."

"What things?" Buck coughed and his nose instantly started bleeding again. "Ugh." Groaning, he reached for the already blood-stained rag beside him.

"This might sound odd," Jason began, sounding hesitant. "But I need to know the last time you drank well water and where? Your answer might help us pinpoint the source and hopefully find a cure."

Buck scooted himself up some, to sit against the headboard, holding the material to his face. His eyes squinted shut against the light and, what looked to me like pain. Like when you have a killer headache pain. "Come on, dude," he grunted, "You know I only drink bottled water." A few awkward seconds passed as we all processed that. "Don't you?"

Jason stood back up, his stance rigid. "Do now." It was like I watching a balloon deflating before me. All hope was disappearing fast. "Just curious," he said, shoving his hands into his sweat pant pockets. "How long have you been drinking bottled water?"

Buck opened his eyes again, staring at Jason over the dirty rag. "Since I was about fifteen. I like the taste better."

Jacob made an inaudible sound and leaned up against the bedroom wall. "Well that pretty much screws up the whole well theory we had, huh?" He looked as exasperated as we all probably felt at that moment, but he didn't have to vocalize something we already knew.

"Yeah," Jason mumbled, peering back over his shoulder at us, but staring directly at Kyle. "You couldn't have mentioned this *before?*"

"Dude, I wasn't thinking clearly. I'm sorry. I forgot." He started pacing, shaking his head. "Damn it, how could I forget that?"

"Maybe because you're always wasted," Missy mumbled beneath her breath, but luckily he didn't seem to hear her.

Kyle paused, spinning around, as if it just occurred to him. "Wait? What's that mean? We can't help him?"

Jason didn't have to say anything. His eyes said it all. Suddenly Kyle freaked, catching on moments after everyone else. "No. No. No." He rushed toward Buck's bed, right up beside Jason. "We *have* to do something. There has to be something. This can't be it." There was so much desperation in his voice and yet I couldn't help but notice how he wouldn't touch his cousin's bed or his cousin. It was as if he was completely terrified of him. *Didn't he know you can't contact the illness through physical contact?*

"Let it be, man. It's over," Buck interjected sounding oddly okay about it, which startled me completely. Had Buck really accepted his own death so easily? Or was this just an act? Or worse, did the idea of going out in a 'blaze of glory' really excite him that much? *I really hope it wasn't the latter.*

"No," Kyle replied. "It's not. Stop talking like that. I won't let that happen. We will figure something else out." He turned his face to Jason. "You came up with one theory, can't you think of something else?"

Jason started rubbing his temples again like he had on the front porch. "Really it was Mouth's theory, not mine."

"Dude, I'm *begging* you," he pleaded then turned to face all of us. "I'm begging *all* of you."

"I told you," Jason exhaled in frustration. "We aren't doctors… he needs a doctor. That's the only way to help him."

"No," Buck and Kyle said in unison. "No doctors."

"Buck," Jacob said, kicking off the wall. "You're *dying,* don't be a moron."

"I can end this," he said, dropping the rag to the mattress again. The nosebleed had stopped. "All I have to do is blow up the town or shoot *them* before I turn. Then you won't have to worry about cures or anything. I can be a town hero."

"You'd be the town whack job," Missy proclaimed, shaking her head. "What is the matter with you, *seriously?* Have you lost your mind already?"

"Yeah, man, stop talking like that," Kyle urged. "I told you that before. You *aren't* doing that. We are going to save you."

"And I told *you*," he retorted, making a face of discomfort. "You can't save me. You have to just accept it."

"I won't."

"Well you're not going to have a choice. Ask Jason, he knows."

"I don't want to ask Jason. *I know* his mom died!" he shouted. "That's why I went to him for help. And we *are* going to help you! So just stop! Stop saying you're going to die. Just freaking stop!" He started striding toward the doorway, pushing Spencer hastily out of the way. "Move! I need a freaking cig now!"

Dumbfounded, Spencer caught his balance on the dresser before falling. And it occurred to me, he's been pretty much sleeping standing up this whole time. Unbelievable.

"What?" Spencer's eyes were round and dazed.

"If you'd stop sleeping so damn much, you'd know," Missy snorted.

"I'm sorry. I'm tired," he complained. "I haven't slept in a couple days."

"Then go lay down on the damn couch!" Jason snapped, before turning toward the bed again. "We don't have time for this shit. It's your own fault your even here." And there it was—the breaking point for Jason. He was finally losing it in front of everyone, not just me. It wasn't right. Jason didn't deserve this. Kyle was putting too much pressure on him. It was obvious. He was already emotional about his parents. I imagine seeing Buck dying the same way was giving him painful flashbacks too. How could it not?

My heart continued to ache for him. I couldn't just stand there and watch him have a mental breakdown or take on the responsibility of saving Buck's life himself. I had to do something. I had to at least help, though I wasn't sure exactly how. It's not like they teach you how to cure a "zombie" outbreak in high school. *Though that would have been a lot more useful than algebra right now.*

I stepped forward, placing my hand comfortingly on Jason's arm. "Okay look…" I said, contemplating quickly. "We can already cross off a lot of things we know *didn't* cause this illness. So it wasn't from well water, okay, but something in this town *is* causing it. Perhaps if you tell us what you've been doing this past week Buck maybe that might shorten the list?"

"I still think it has something to do with the campsite," Spencer chimed in, snagging our attention.

"Oh, you're still up? I thought you were tired," Jason retorted sharply.

Spencer rolled his eyes. "Just ask him if he was at the campsite."

I turned my face to Buck, humoring Spencer, though I was certain I already knew the answer. "Were you at the campsite at all this week?"

He shook his head. "Nope. Don't ever go there."

"Well at least Kyle remembered something legit," Jacob said sarcastically. "Sorry amigo, I guess you're wrong."

"Whatever," Spencer mumbled crossing his arms over his chest and leaning back against the dresser. "It wouldn't be the first time."

Now *I* was rolling my eyes. *Okay, moving on.* "All right, this is going to sound even more obvious, but I am just throwing it out there. By any chance did you get bit or scratched by any one this week that was obviously infected?"

"No," Buck grimaced, holding his stomach again. "I would have shot them if they got that close."

That much I figured. I considered some more options. Where else could he have gone? "What about public bathrooms?" *They are always loaded with germs.* "Maybe you picked it up from there?"

Again he shook his head. "Haven't used one in a long time."

"Did you share a drink with anyone recently?" I countered. *My mom is always saying not to share drinks with people that's how you get sick, so maybe...*

"Just Kyle," he groaned, squeezing his stomach tighter and slinking down against the mattress again, curling his knees toward his chest.

Never mind.

"Well I don't know exactly what drugs you do," Missy added, "but if you used a dirty needle—"

"No, I never shoot up," he said, cutting her off.

Okay. What else was there?

"Got with any chicks lately?" Spencer prompted. "Maybe you got something from them?"

"Nah, girls don't come around here much."

That wasn't surprising.

"Okay so if there was no human blood contact, saliva exchange or sexual relations, wouldn't that pretty much rule out humans?" Jacob suggested, shrugging. "Just a theory."

"You're right," Jason agreed. "That would be the logical assumption."

"So what else is there?"

"Well, it could be anything. Maybe something he ate?" He looked at Buck. "When was the last time you went hunting?"

Buck was starting to shiver more and it took him a few seconds longer to respond. "With you before you left."

"It wasn't an animal then," Jason sighed. "We all ate the same thing." I didn't have to turn around to know Missy was making a face. "But it still may have been from that day though. Thinking back did anything bite you? A snake? A spider? A tick?" *I thought we already ruled those out at the store?*

"No," Buck said again.

"What about rashes?" Jason pressed. "Did you have any rashes? Touch any poisonous plants? Touch stagnant mud, maybe?"

It was like Jason was now just grasping at straws. "What about cuts? Maybe you got cut on a thorn bush and rubbed up against something—"

Buck started shaking his head. "Nothing happened that day, dude."

Jason exhaled and continued rubbing his temples. "And what about the days since then? You haven't done anything out of the norm?"

One look from Buck showed the same response.

"What about yesterday or today? Nothing odd happened to you at all? Are you sure?" He dropped his hands back to his sides. "Try new weed, maybe?"

"Same shit, man," Buck grunted through clenched teeth. "Give it a rest. It's useless. I told you."

"I can't," Jason grumbled. "It doesn't make any sense, none of this makes sense. I saw you yesterday. You *were* fine. Now today you're like *this*? What the hell happened in the last twenty-four hours?"

Staring at Jason, it instantly dawned on me. *We* happened in the last twenty-four hours. Staying overnight in their trailer was out of the norm—well maybe not for Jason, but definitely for Missy and I—what if *we* brought something in. "We did," I said out loud, so they could know what I was thinking. "We stayed here last night. What if we brought something in from outside with us?"

"Ohmigod," Missy suddenly gasped.

"What?" I said, facing her, immediately defending us. "I'm not saying it's *our* fault he's sick. I'm just saying maybe we accidentally brought in a germ or something. We *were* carrying that dead guy." Now that I thought about it more, it made perfect sense.

But Jason was not buying it. "No, we didn't touch that guy. We used the gloves and blanket to avoid that. We were extra careful."

Things can still happen. "Maybe we got blood on us anyhow or on the bottoms of our shoes, you never know."

"No, no that's not what I was thinking," Missy prompted, shaking her head. "I didn't think you meant it was *our* fault, Dee. I just had an insane thought."

"Is it relevant to this?" Jason asked her, skeptically.

"Yes, you ass," she said, narrowing her eyes at him. "What she said just made me think of something. But it's just too crazy. I gotta be wrong. Though for the record, I don't think it was from carrying the dead guy either. Blood cells and viruses die pretty quickly once exposed to oxygen. And even so, you'd have to have an open wound or physically touch it. Buck wasn't touching our feet or crawling around on the ground last night so chances are, it's not that."

"Okay," I agreed, realizing I was wrong. *So what was it?* I still had a gut feeling that this had something to do with us coming here last night.

"When you say your idea is crazy?" Jacob wondered out loud. "How crazy we talking?" He was staring at Missy. "Because I don't know about you, but this whole thing is pretty freaking crazy, so it just might be right up its alley?

"It's insane," she insisted. "Trust me. I don't even understand how it could be. It doesn't make sense. Just forget about it. It's not it."

"Tell us what it was anyway," Jason urged. "Right now we need anything."

She looked uncomfortable. "It's just what Dee said about bringing in something from outside with us... well, last night

Buck made a point to tell me to shut the door before more mosquitos got in. I mean we were wearing bug spray so they didn't bother us, but I remember he did get bit. And for a second I just thought maybe…."

"Mosquitos?" Jason mumbled, furrowing his brow.

She started fiddling with her purse strap, looking embarrassed. "I know it was just stupid."

"No," he said, shaking his head, as if he was truly considering it. "No it's not."

"What?" Her fingers paused, startled. "Yes it is. It doesn't make any sense at all."

"Yes it does," he urged, his voice filling with confidence. "I'm serious. Think about it. Mosquitos are known to carry diseases. They can transfer all kinds of viruses. But not every mosquito is a carrier." He started pacing, placing his palms behind his head. "Holy shit. Mouth, you're brilliant. That's it. It makes complete sense."

"Huh? No it doesn't."

"Actually it would," Jacob agreed, his expression mirroring Jason's. "That would explain why there is more of an outbreak at the campsite than in town because there's ponds there and mosquitos need water to survive. Especially stagnant water. It's like the perfect breeding ground for them."

"So my assumption about the campsite was pretty much right?" Spencer said, sounding pleased but also a bit freaked out.

"Yeah, kind of was," Jacob replied. "And really mosquitos can fly anywhere in a short mile radius. So you could be *anywhere*. Jason, your mom could have gotten bit in your yard or going to the store. Dean could have gotten it coming to my house, Buck, *here*. And bite marks go away pretty quickly for most people so they might not even realize or most people wouldn't even think anything of it because they are so common. But all it takes is one mosquito to feed off an infected host and then bite someone else and the virus is spread."

"But if that's the case," I said, agreeing but not agreeing. "Why haven't we heard of this before? Mosquitos have been around forever. The news constantly talks about all the viruses you can catch, but never mentions this one?"

"Maybe there's never been an outbreak like this before. If the original host is from this area, there wouldn't be other cases. Perhaps it all started with a sick animal. This virus stage is a lot like the rabies virus, but more aggressive. So maybe a mosquito bit a rabid animal here and then transferred the disease to a person, but when mixed with other DNA, the virus mutated and changed. Or it could be an animal with distemper not rabies. I mean that stuff is common around here. Either way, the first outbreak is happening now."

I felt my stomach knotting up. "If this is *real,* it's not good. There are shots for rabies and stuff, but you have to get to a hospital to get them. We *can't* get a cure for Buck. There is no quick antidote. Just the rabies virus is a serious thing in people and takes a series of shots to cure. And we don't even know if that *is* what caused this, but if it is and it's some mutated, aggressive form of it, Buck needs that vaccination *now* and probably blood transfusions and a whole bunch of antibiotics."

"Yeah," Missy agreed. "And how the hell do you take out an entire mosquito population? Like how do you cure this outbreak?"

"By blowing up the town," Buck persisted, grimacing in pain. He was shaking and sweating profusely. "We all know I'm going to die. Let me be useful."

"She just said you can get help," Missy snapped at him. "Stop being a baby and go to the hospital. Actually, I don't know why we are even listening to you. We should have dragged you there already."

"She's right," Jason agreed. "You're not thinking clearly, dude. I know you don't want to die. You're just trying to compensate your fear by thinking you can save the day. But if you blow up this town, you're killing people who aren't infected too and that makes you a murderer. And shooting down sick people like you won't stop this virus from spreading either. It might lessen the numbers, but won't stop it." He paused, peering down at Buck with a serious expression. "If you really want to be a hero, you'll go to the hospital so that they can do tests and find out exactly what's going on inside you. Maybe with your help they can make up a new vaccination to save people in the future, including your life."

"That won't stop the mosquitos," Buck grumbled.

"No, it won't, but now that we have a pretty good guess at what is causing this virus, we can let authorities know. There are pest control companies all over this state, they can spray and do whatever they have to, to kill them. We might have to temporarily evacuate, but then people can come home to *their homes* where they belong. All this can be fixed with your help."

"I don't know, dude. They're gonna bust me for drugs and I don't have insurance."

"I'd take my chances if I were you," Jacob prompted. "Just saying. My truck is parked right outside."

"Outside?" Jason suddenly said, his eyes widening. "Oh shit. Kyle."

And just like that, I remembered—we all remembered—Kyle went out for a smoke and never came back.

Jason immediately started running for the front door.

30

Jason threw open the door, bolted out and instantly tumbled forward, flipping over Kyle who was sitting practically in the doorway. I heard the loud *thump* of the two of them hitting the ground, before I actually saw them both on the dirt.

"What the hell, bro," Kyle said, standing up, dusting off his clothes.

Jason clenched his jaw and stood up too, mirroring his actions. "Sorry. I didn't expect you to be right there."

"I said I needed a cig. Where did you think I was?"

I glanced down at their feet. The ground was littered with cigarette butts. *Apparently he needed more than one, like the whole pack.*

"Yeah, well, you just been gone awhile," Jason explained, awkwardly.

Missy took that second to come up and lean around me, shouting outside. "Yo idiots, get inside before you're either bitten or attacked."

Kyle turned toward her, eyebrow raised. "What's the difference?"

"None really," she replied in a surly manner. "You'll die either way."

I exhaled, shaking my head at her and started pushing her away. "Come on Miss, enough."

"What? I'm just being honest. In which case, do we have any more bug spray? I'd kinda like to put more on now."

"That's an excellent idea," Jacob said, walking toward us from the bedroom. "Especially since it looks like were leaving. Buck just said *yes*."

It took a bit a time after that to fill Kyle in with everything and how we theorized it was mosquitos, but after that I swear it was like seeing a whole new person. He was so relieved and optimistic even though Buck was getting worse by the minute. I'm not really sure how I could tell, he didn't look much different, but I just could and I was starting to worry about how much time he really had *left*.

We stood outside the bedroom letting Buck rest, as we came up with our next plans of action. I was grateful to be back in my shorts again, but I was cold now, and kept trying to inch up closer to Jason without being too obvious or obnoxious. A couple times he did put his arm around me, but I don't know if it's because he caught on or just wanted to.

By the time the final plan was set, my arms and legs were glistening with bug spray—oh yeah, I smelled great—and I was preparing myself mentally for *goodbye*.

The plan sounded simple enough. The boys were driving us to my car, where they would fix the tire and tow it back onto the road so Missy, Spencer and I could leave. And that was it, at least for the three of us. As for the boys, they had another adventure left. Once they were done with my car, Jacob was driving into the next town to drop Buck and Kyle off at the hospital. Then, at first light, they were going to drive Jason to the car shop for his truck battery. After that Jacob was taking Jason back to Meg and Germaine's before taking off. Jason and the twins were leaving down soon after.

Oh it sounded like the perfect ending to this horrible situation—you know everyone gets away safe and Buck lives—but for some reason it made me more apprehensive than happy. Don't get me wrong, I wanted that ending, but I wasn't naïve enough to think it would actually happen. I realize I'm one of the most negative people in the world, but nine times out of ten nothing ever goes exactly as planned.

I wouldn't be there this time to help any of them either.

I wouldn't even know *what* was going on because I'd be on my way home. Somehow it didn't feel right, but at the same time I had to think about *my* life, *my* future. I've already risked it enough. I wasn't staying.

"These are the only two we have," Kyle said, snapping me out of my thoughts. I watched him place two battery-operated lanterns on the counter. "They should be bright enough, but if not we have a few flashlights too."

That was one of the first complications of the *plan*. It was still pitch black out and the boys were going to have to do all of this exhausted, with very little lighting, with the pressure of mosquitos flying around and infected people on the prowl. We couldn't be standing still on that mountain for long. We had to be quick about it. And I didn't even know how that was going to be possible.

"We'll take as much as we can," Jason replied. "The more light the better."

"Okay." Kyle opened a drawer beside the sink and started taking out flashlights. "What about weapons?"

"I think less is best," Jason answered, sounding unsure. "Though not exactly safer, I know. It's just heaven forbid we get pulled over, we don't want to be in a truck full of loaded guns."

Kyle slowly nodded in agreement as he placed another flashlight on the countertop, his hand hesitating on a handle. "What about knives?"

"Your call, amigo," Jacob chimed in, grabbing the two lanterns. "I don't really care. I just want to get the show on the road."

"Yeah, the sooner the better," Jason insisted holding his hand out for one of the lights. Jacob handed it to him. "I think we are just waiting on Spencer, right?" His green-brown eyes sought mine.

"Yeah," I said, trying to swallow down the knot in my throat. "He's still in the bathroom."

"Okay check on him, make sure he didn't fall asleep on the floor. I'm going to go start the truck then help them get Buck outside."

"Alright."

"Wait," Missy prompted as Jason started to step away.

 He peered over his shoulder, impatiently. "Yeah?"

"How we all fitting in there?"

He half-shrugged. "Same way we did before except now you are sitting on someone's lap too, I guess."

"Great," she mumbled, less than thrilled. "Okay. I'll go check on sleeping beauty. She turned around, hollering. "Yo, Spencer what did you do, fall in?" She went up to the bathroom door and started pounding on it.

"Shut up," he replied, his voice muffled but loud. "I'll be right out."

"You okay?" I called, furrowing my brow, as I stepped up beside Missy. I didn't like how he sounded.

"Yeah." I heard the bathroom sink shut off then moments later the door handle started to turn. Spencer appeared shortly after drying off his face. "Sorry I got bug spray in my eye, it was kind of burning." He tossed the towel into the sink, stepping out into the hall.

"Can you see how many fingers I'm holding up?" Missy said, giving him the middle finger.

He started to laugh. "With you, it's always the same number." He peered over my head, his eyes visibly blood shot. "We ready to go?"

I heard the truck starting outside. "Yeah sounds like it."

"Okay," he said, placing his arm on our shoulders. "Then let's go home."

Walking down the mountain in the dark on Friday night seemed a lot faster than this drive to the mountain to get my car now. Once again I was squeezed in the truck, in the passenger seat, sitting on Jason's lap, befriending the *"oh shit"* handle, feeling even more claustrophobic than earlier. This time Spencer was next to us too, with Missy sitting on *his* lap and neither of them seemed too comfortable with it either, but there was no way she'd be sitting on anyone else's lap, that's for sure. Buck was directly behind Jacob, his head on a pillow, his eyes shut, sleeping or trying to at least. He had taken up wheezing every time he took a breath now which worried me more, but at least he was still breathing. Though I was starting to wonder what would happen if he suddenly turned into one of *them* while we were all still in this vehicle.

The thought freaked me out immensely. Shuddering slightly, I tried thinking of something else, anything else, which wasn't too easy actually since the other things on my mind weren't too comforting either. The fact that no one was talking didn't help, but at least I wasn't surrounded by awkward silence again. In fact, there wasn't silence at all. This time the radio was playing quietly through the speakers and Jacob was even humming along. *Making me curious, was I truly the only worried one?*

A quick side-glance to Missy proved maybe not. She was to the left of me, anxiously chipping the rest of her nail polish off her fingernails. But, that could have meant anything or nothing at all. It *was* an annoying habit of hers.

The clock on the dashboard caught my attention, showing the time in bold, red numbers. I couldn't believe it was already three-forty-eight in the morning and that I've been almost up for twenty-four hours straight. No wonder I was exhausted. At this point, I was going to need one of those extra-large, double espresso, highly sugared, flavored coffees just to make it home.

Otherwise, with my luck, I'd fall asleep behind the wheel and crash again.

Mentally groaning, I glanced out the windshield, into the dim-lit shadows, trying to see if I could even see enough *to* drive home—night driving was not my forte—and instantly, my eyes caught on an obscured shape in the middle of the road.

"What the hell is—" I never finished. Suddenly Jacob was slamming on the brakes, his headlights fully illuminating the hunched-over figure, and I was flying forward. Jason's arms immediately tightened around my waist. I half-collided with the dashboard before being yanked backward by my grip on the handle and Jason's grip on me. Missy barely missed smacking her forehead on the windshield. Luckily Jacob had shot his arm out reflexively in front of her and Spencer had actually been awake enough to hold her too. By the *thud* I heard behind me, I am guessing Kyle and Buck crashed hard into the seat though.

But there wasn't time to worry about that. Heart-racing, I watched horrified at the sight in front of us. A person was squatting down, holding an arm to his mouth eating, his coal black eyes glistening in the light. A limp body lay at his feet, covered in blood and shredded clothing, one arm and one leg already missing.

"*Mierda*," Jacob cursed, his voice completely startled. "That's Dean."

"I don't care who it is!" Missy snapped. "Either drive around him or run him over, but don't just sit here." *It was obvious she was pretty pissed about the sudden stop and almost hitting her head, but she was scared too.*

Jacob's hand hesitated on the shifter, looking conflicted. "But he's a friend, maybe we can help him?"

"He doesn't even know you anymore. He doesn't even know himself," Jason sighed in exasperation, leaning around me. "Look at him, dude. You want to save a friend, stop wasting time and get Buck to the hospital and get these three out of this town."

"But he's…screw it," he quickly grumbled, shaking his head. "You're right. Sorry, guys." He threw the truck into drive, hitting the gas pedal. "And sorry, Dean, but I'm doing you a favor, really."

Then, just like that, he ran him over. The last thing I saw before I felt Dean's body *thump* and *crunch* under the tires was Dean's vacant cold stare and somebody's half-eaten arm dropping from his grasp.

"I think I'm going to puke again," I mumbled, as the last tire rolled over the flattened bodies.

Jason immediately lowered the passenger window, letting fresh air inside. "Only a little longer and we're at your car. Can you hold it together?" Jason asked, completely sympathetic. *Could I? I wasn't so sure.*

"I hope so," was all I said. I didn't dare look back and I was thankful it was too dark to see anything even if I did.

And from my peripheral vision, I could tell Jacob was thinking the same thing. I honestly couldn't believe he ran him over, but I guess in the long run it was better because Dean would have just went after someone else and he was eventually going to drop dead from the illness anyway. *Though I still don't know if that made it right.*

"How can you even tell where we are?" Missy asked a few minutes later as Jacob slowly and carefully started driving up the mountain side. "It all looks the same and it's so damn dark, how we going to find the car?"

"It shouldn't be hard actually," Jason answered, sounding confident. "You girls crashed near the top of the mountain. I figured once we hit the highest point in the road, I'll jump out and check the area with a flashlight. Once I spot the car, I can direct Jacob where to go from there."

"Oh." Missy looked over at him, furrowing her brow. "Isn't that a little dangerous though? I mean, considering *them*. It's not like Duke is with you this time."

"I'll look with him," I quickly blurted, not sure if I had thought that completely through or not but I couldn't just leave him alone out there. Missy was right. "Two sets of eyes are better than one anyway," I pointed out because I knew Jason was just going to argue against it.

"Then let me go with him," Spencer suggested, surprisingly. "You and Miss already risked your lives enough."

"Yeah that's not happening," I muttered. *I haven't come this far, dealt with all this, for him to die now.* "You don't even know how to use a gun. I do. I'll be fine."

"And *I'll* be fine," Jason interjected, "by myself. Seriously guys, I appreciate it but this isn't my first rodeo."

"Honestly I think you all should just get out," Jacob said, chiming in. "You're gonna have to once we find the car anyway, so this way we might even find it faster."

"Really Jacob?" Jason uttered in disbelief. "You think that's the best idea?"

Shrugging, he kept his eyes focused on the road, trying to stay in between the lines. My pulse was heightened at the thought of falling over the edge again. "I don't know what I think anymore," he mumbled, achingly honest. "Five minutes ago I never thought I'd run my friend over, but yet, I did. So maybe you should ignore whatever I have to say. I'm obviously whacked in the head."

"Dude, at this point I think we all are," Missy suggested in agreement. "In fact I'd be seriously concerned if you *weren't.*"

I couldn't agree more.

Moments later, Jacob reached the highest point of the road and hit the brakes lightly, easing slowly into a stop this time.

"Look," he said, anxiously tightening and untightening his grip on the steering wheel. "Personally I wish none of you had to go out there, but whether it's one of you or all of you, just please be careful. Okay?"

"It's going to be all of us," Jason grumbled, obviously displeased. "Because I know if I go, Dee will just be stubborn and follow me. Then Spencer and Missy will follow her and we'll all be out there anyway." He paused, peering up at me, his expression clearly upset with me. "Am I wrong?"

I shook my head. Sometimes I wonder where my common sense goes but it never stops me from being an idiot.

"Very well, let's get on with it." He opened the passenger door, and I hopped out, instantly taking a flashlight from him and turning it on. I silently hoped we found my car fast.

***

Okay, I was bugging out. Like a lot. I couldn't help it. It was pretty freaking dark. I don't even remember it being this dark or this scary when we were walking this mountain Friday night. Maybe that had a lot to do with the fact we had Duke, and Jason and Missy were holding my hands. I don't know. But one thing for certain was I really wish that dog was with us now. Bum ear and all.

I know I could have avoided all this by staying in the truck and a part of me wanted to run back to it now, but I wasn't going to. Not unless I was being chased down by a swarm of mosquitos. I just had to toughen up and remind myself I could handle mostly anything; I mean I had a gun in my hand after all. Jason had insisted I take his while he braved it with Kyle's knife and for once I didn't argue. Because if it came down to it, I knew I had better chances of living with it than without it.

As for Missy, she was grasping onto Spencer's arm, holding a lantern, begging me not to walk too far from her. Of course I did though. Not that I wanted to, but we weren't going to find my car faster if we all stuck together like a bunch of scared kittens. We could have done that in the truck. No, I *had* to venture out but I never walked too far where I lost the flash of their lantern sparkling in the night like some jumpy, mutated firefly. As long as I saw that, I knew they were still okay and that was just going to have to be good enough.

Jason was out of eyesight though and I hated that, but I couldn't do anything about it. Besides pray. *Repeatedly.*

Taking my flashlight, I shone the light onto the ground, careful not to fall as I stepped through some pretty tall weeds on my way further down the mountain. I distinctly remember it was a bit of a drop off the edge, so if I was going to find my car it was going to be somewhere down there, in the congestion of the trees.

If only I could see further than the length of the light beam.

Above me somewhere was the high-pitch squeaking of bats and the flapping of countless wings. It made me feel the size of an ant, and as vulnerable as a chipmunk below a hawk. I had to remind myself constantly to ignore *those* sounds and inched forward. I had to listen for the other, critically important sounds only— footsteps, labored breathing or insect buzzing—but it wasn't easy.

With each wave of my flashlight, my attention scanned around anxiously, and my feet stumbled to keep up. If I didn't find anything soon, I was turning around. Chances were I was probably searching in the wrong area anyway. But while I was down this far I might as well check it out thoroughly. I was hoping I would just hear somebody scream, "They found it," so I could get the hell away from these trees.

Palms sweating, I continued to grasp the gun in my right hand, finger lingering above the trigger just in case. I didn't want to *have to* fire the gun, but I wanted to be ready if I was forced to.

Stepping cautiously around a tree, I shone the light brightly out in front of me, making sure the coast was clear before I started peering at the bark, looking for any signs from our crash. When I didn't see anything, I went to the next tree and the next, always checking for the same thing. I was also making sure to watch for any tire marks in the ground as I walked.

Something finally caught my eye. It wasn't my car, but up ahead there was something small lying on the ground.

Furrowing my brow, I stepped toward it, approaching it the way one might approach a ticking box. It wasn't ticking though and it wasn't a box. It did have a dark, boxy shape though.

"What the—" As I got closer I saw it was broken into a couple pieces actually. I hesitated, contemplating picking it all up to see what it was when I suddenly heard shouting. *My car*. Missy and Spencer had found my car. *Thank God.*

Instantly forgetting about whatever was in front of me, I started hurrying toward them, hollering to them to let them know I was on my way. I was feeling momentarily elated, trudging through the thick weeds, thinking everything might actually work out for once. Then something touched my leg, quickly wrapping around my ankle.

I screamed.

Loudly.

31

"Help me," a raspy voice begged, his bloody fingers clinging desperately and painfully to my foot. I couldn't break free. *"Please."*

I shone the flashlight directly in his face, my right hand instantly aiming the gun at his head. He was on his stomach. His one arm outstretched, grasping me, his other bent in front of him, burrowed slightly in the ground, as if he just army crawled to catch me.

Smeared dirt and dried blood covered his cheeks. Labored breathing parted his lips. Agony and light reflected in his eyes, his slate gray eyes.

My index finger quivered on the trigger, torn. I had no clue if that was his natural eye color or not.

Someone was yelling for me, checking on me, but I did not look up. I did not respond. I know I should have considering I just screamed loud enough to make a few birds fly off the trees above me but I just couldn't. My heart was pounding. I was nauseated, freaking out at the way his bloody grip was on my skin. *What if he was infected? What if he bit me?*

My eyes stayed pinned on him, whoever he was, assessing him, watching him. I tried to kick him off me, but he was not letting go. However, he was not fighting me either or making any further movements toward me. He was just lying there, reaching out to me, begging me for help, but I had no idea why. Grass and shadows concealed most of his body and I was afraid to shift the beam of light away from his face. As if that somehow was preventing him from doing anything.

Gulping in panic, I adjusted my grip on the gun, and said to him, what everyone's been saying to each other lately in this town. "Who are you? What's your name?" Finally, completely understanding *why* everyone demanded the answer the way they did and why they even asked it. Because they were scared out of their minds just like I was scared out of mine.

He stared back at me, grimacing. He wasn't too many years older than me, maybe six tops. He still had a baby face, freshly shaven from what I could tell, and his hair was dark, cut super short. "Wesson," he answered, struggling to respond. "Brien Wesson." He finally let go of my leg, lowering his hand to the ground. "I'm a trooper."

I almost dropped the gun. "Did you just say you're a cop?" *I was pointing a gun at a cop. An injured cop. Oh shit.*

"Yeah," he grunted, his face distorting in pain as he tried scooting up onto his side.

I tensed, unsure what to do. He looked like he was in *a lot* of pain and I wanted to help but I was also afraid too. He could still be infected regardless if he was a cop.

"You're hurt," I prompted, though obvious. "If you're a cop, where's your partner? Or your back up for that matter? Why aren't they helping you?" A sudden flash of Dean eating that arm in the middle of the road crossed my mind. On second thought maybe I didn't want to know.

Brien made an inaudible sound as he sat further up, a cross between a groan and a curse. "My radio broke, and I can't get to my car to call for help. I can't walk."

The radio. That's what that boxy, broken thing was earlier. *Of course.* But how the hell did *that* break? There had to be a pretty bad scuffle. "Why can't you walk?" I cringed, instantly worrying, expecting the worst. Like his legs were bitten off. Taking the flashlight, I quickly shifted the light away from his face, scanning it over the rest of him. I heard Missy and Spencer's hollering getting closer but I still didn't answer. I know. I'm a terrible friend.

"It's my leg," I heard him say, through gritted teeth again, as he tried shimmying further up into a seated position.

Though I hadn't noticed before, mostly because I was staring at his face and freaking completely out, I could now see he *was* in uniform. So he definitely was a cop. His uniform was just coated with layers of dirt and blood.

His belt was missing however. There was no gun, no handcuffs, no pepper spray or even a nightstick wrapped around his waist. There was nothing. *Had he lost all of it?*

I almost asked, but then the light hit his right leg and I couldn't. Instantly I was gagging, fighting to keep from upchucking everywhere. *Ohmigod. Ohmigod it had to hurt.* I had to turn my head. I couldn't bear looking at it. *How was he not screaming? How wasn't he passed out?*

His legs weren't bitten off, but his shin bone *was* sticking out of his skin, his flesh split open. There was dried blood and fresh blood oozing out. The belt that I assumed was missing was actually tied around his leg, stopping the blood flow as best as he could. The lower half of his leg was turned sideways, bent in an awkward angle, looking gelatinous.

No wonder he grabbed me so desperately for help. He *needed* help. He was suffering to death.

And I couldn't just stand there knowing it. I had two options: shoot him to put him out of his misery or get him to the hospital. Knowing he could still be infected, I started *finally* yelling to the others anyway. Point blank there was no way I was killing a cop.

Missy and Spencer were there in less than two minutes, slightly out of breath, eyes wide. "Goddamnit Dee!" Missy cursed, as she shone the lantern toward me and realized I was still in one piece. "What the hell? *Don't* do that shit to me ever again. Why didn't you answer? You scared me half to death."

She was still clutching to Spencer's arm. Spencer was staring at me, relief washing over his pale face. I instantly felt bad.

"Sorry guys," I mumbled, shining my flashlight back on Brien. "I'm okay, but he needs help. I can't do it alone."

They jolted as if just realizing he was even there. "Who the hell is that?" Missy barked, immediately tensing, as her eyes scanned over him. "Why the hell do we—*ohmyfreakinggod*!" She quickly spun around, gagging too.

Even Spencer was making sounds.

"This is State Trooper Brien Wesson," I said. "We can't just leave him like this. Where's Jason?" I glanced around.

"I don't know," she answered hesitantly, still recovering from the shock of the trooper's leg. "We haven't seen him. He hasn't come back."

"What?" Suddenly I felt like I was slammed against a wall, my breath catching.

"I'm sure he's fine, Dee," she urged quickly, too quickly, her voice giving away her doubt. "You know Jason. If anyone can handle this shit, it's him."

"Right," I mumbled, trying to agree. But deep down I knew he wasn't fine. He couldn't be. If Jason heard me scream like *that* and I hadn't answered yet, he would be here. He would be racing up to me, trying to save me. My gut twisted, my heart pounding achingly in my chest. He was either hurt or dead, and it was my fault because I had his gun.

"One thing at a time," Spencer regretfully said, as he hunched down to hoist Brien up with his permission. "Let's get him to the truck and then we can search for Jason. Okay?" Spencer looked at me, and in one single look, promised me we wouldn't leave until we found him.

I nodded, but it did not make me feel better.

Spencer struggled under Brien's weight, and I knew someone had to help him.

"Here hold this," I prompted, handing Jason's gun to Missy.

"But—"

I paused in the act of scooting my head under Brien's other arm. "Someone's gotta have our backs," I said, my brown eyes glaring at her. "You wanna trade?"

She made a face. I knew that would work. Missy didn't want her friends putting their arms around her, let alone a stranger with blood-stained hands who might be infected with a contagious deadly disease.

"Fine," she grumbled, though I could tell she wasn't pleased at all, and entirely freaked out by it. I got that she hated guns, especially loaded ones, but seriously now wasn't the time for it.

I was impatient. I just wanted to get to the truck and go find Jason now. If he was still alive, I needed to help *him*, not anyone else. Otherwise I should be on my way home, getting the hell out of this town, worrying only about *my* life. Of course I never could be *that* person. I always want to help everyone else.

Stupid. I was just plain stupid.

We were making our way slowly, getting closer each step. We could see the truck, the headlights shining bright like a beacon of hope. The weight of the cop's arm dug into my shoulder, pulling my neck forward, making it difficult for me to walk. I flashed my eyes back and forth between the ground and the truck, calculating the distance, wincing against the pain starting to radiate throughout my body. All my muscles were cramping back up, reminding me that I was still sore from head to toe. Of course whatever I was feeling was *nothing* in comparison to Trooper Wesson, who was beginning to teeter on the fine line of consciousness. And I had to keep reminding myself that when I wanted to start whining.

A nerve-wrecking thought kept hounding me though whenever I saw his head bob forward or felt his body starting to sag more heavily into us. What if Brien wasn't on the verge of passing out, but on the brink of turning into one of *them*?

Right now, like this, so close to him, we were shark bait.

I tried to hurry but picking up the pace was almost impossible.

Out of nowhere Missy started, suddenly spinning around, shining the lantern in our eyes. "What was *that*?" Her voice was a couple octaves higher than normal.

We instantly stopped and I shone my flashlight in my right hand up at her. "What was what?"

We waited a beat. I *wanted* to tell her she was just being paranoid, that I didn't hear anything, but the thing was now I did. I heard the *snapping* and *crunching* sound of feet running over pinecones and broken twigs toward us. My immediate thought was Jason.

But when Missy started screaming, that hope was instantly replaced with fear.

Right away I knew it was *them* and we were about to be ambushed.

"*Shoot them,*" Spencer shouted to Missy, who was the only one with a weapon. Missy fumbled nervously with the gun, almost dropping it. "*Come on.*"

"I'm trying, damn it!" She yelled, quickly clasping the handle firmly. She lifted her arm, aimed and fired. The gun kicked back. I forgot to mention that type of gun had a slight kick to it. I didn't have time to scream *Duck.* Yes, she was ahead of us on the mountain, higher up the slanted ledge, which meant anyone that knew how to shoot would have had a perfect, clear view above our heads to hit them with no danger to us, but Missy didn't know how to shoot. And I realized that too late.

Trooper Wesson instantly cried out, body jolting as the bullet hit him in the chest. Spencer stumbled from the movement, falling down, cursing. Brien fell with him, the weight pulling me down next like a domino effect. The cop howled even louder as his leg hit the ground.

Missy kept shooting. The second bullet ricocheted off my flashlight that rolled away from me. The third whizzed over my head, making me sprawl frantically across the ground as to not get shot too.

"Shoot higher," I screamed to Missy, with the side of my mouth against the dirt. Another shot went off, this one hitting one of them. I scurried forward, to get to her.

She fired another shot. I had no clue where it went. I was just determined to get to her before she wasted all the bullets. Her hands were shaking terribly on the gun. "Wait!" I yelled before she shot again then jumped up, quickly taking the gun from her. I saw how close the two of *them* were and I knew it was useless. I couldn't shoot both at the same time.

I tried anyway.

As Missy held the lantern, I shot unwaveringly, hitting the guy Missy already hit right in the gut. The next shot, I aimed at the girl's head but she moved so fast that I ended up hitting her shoulder. I cursed and fired again, lodging a bullet right into her side. She slowed down, and I took that second to shift the pistol back to the guy, firing a killing shot into his chest.

Without wasting a beat, I fired back at the girl. *I could do this after all.* The trigger clicked. No shot fired. *No!* I pulled again, frantic, but it was useless. The chamber was empty.

I screamed at Spencer and Brien in a panic, unsure what else to do. I had messed up. I was no better than Missy. I wasted two shots and now they were going to die. The girl lunged at them, mouth open.

Trooper Wesson suddenly moved and an unexpected shot fired.

I gaped, jumping in shock. A bullet blasted right under her chin, up through her head, and out, killing her instantly.

As she fell, Missy and I ran forward, down the mountain side, the lantern light bouncing wildly from Melissa's grasp.

Brien was lying on the ground, his firearm in his hand. *So he had his gun on him after all, in his waist band.* Spencer was lying next to him, scooting up, wide-eyed.

"Last bullet," he wheezed, his face grimacing in pain. He was so pale. "I was saving that for me." Then just like that his fingers let go of the gun and his eye lids started closing.

"Brien!" I urged, dropping to my knees, gasping at the fresh blood that was oozing through his shirt. He was wearing a vest, but Missy must have hit him right above it.

His lids fluttered, but did not open. Missy was flipping out, crying. "I didn't mean to kill him. *Ohmigod.* I killed an innocent person. I killed a cop."

"He's not dead," I snapped, checking his pulse on his neck just to be certain. "But if we don't get him out of here, he *is* going to die." I looked up, saw the headlights on the road and just started shouting for help, hoping someone would hear me. *"Jacob! Kyle! Anyone!"*

The truck was close, but not close enough. Hollering was pointless. "Okay, they can't hear us. We are just going to have to carry him." I picked up his gun, tucking it into my shorts.

"Or we can leave him," Spencer said uncertainly. But then he shook his head. "No. I can't. He just saved my life."

Yeah. He probably just saved all our lives.

Spencer stood there for a moment, staring down at him. "I'll carry him," he offered. "Just help me get him in my arms."

"Okay," I prompted. "I'll try to stop the bleeding then." At this rate, his blood was already on me. If I started getting sick, I'd just go to the hospital too. Though I didn't have any open wounds on my hands, so I should be fine, *plus* I was starting to realize Brien didn't have the typical symptoms. Sure he kept fading in and out of consciousness but a person's body can only tolerate so much pain. And with that horrific break, it was no wonder.

Spencer and I walked *very* slowly, side-step by side-step up the mountain side. He was directly across from me, his arms grasping Brien carefully but definitely struggling. I was leaning forward, my hands pressed tightly against his shirt, trying to stop as much bleeding as I could. It was working but it wasn't working great.

Missy was ahead of us by a couple feet, leading the way, saying nothing, no doubt feeling extremely terrible for shooting him. She carried both the flashlight and lantern in her hands, waving them back and forth absently. I could have said something, and maybe should have to make her feel better, but I was more concerned with keeping Brien alive. And I wanted to get to the truck fast, I had two guns in my waistband—I had picked up Jason's too—and neither one had bullets, which meant if someone attacked us we were screwed.

I sighed with relief when my feet hit pavement again. We were almost there. The truck was only twenty yards away at the most. *Thank God.* Spencer paused, catching his breath, readjusting his grip and I leaned with his movements, careful not to remove the pressure from Brien's wound.

Once he was ready, we started back up, shouting toward the others again to let them know we were coming, that we needed help. That's why we must not have heard the footsteps.

Suddenly someone was *right* next to us.

Missy screamed, spun, and started flailing her arm with the flashlight. She didn't stop screaming. She just hit and hit and hit. Spencer and I froze, startled. There was grunts, groans, and *whacking* sounds. The lantern bounced wildly in her other hand. All I saw was a pair of sneakers and the bottom hem of sweatpants.

My eyes bulged, realization kicking in.

It was Jason.

She was beating up Jason.

Instantly I was yelling.

32

"Ohmigod!" Missy gasped, horrified, immediately dropping the flashlight and backing away. It hit the ground and rolled. "I am *so* sorry. Are you okay?" She lifted her right hand, shining the lantern directly onto Jason who had sunk to the ground, grumbling. "I didn't know it was you. I swear!"

"Geez Miss, first you shoot a cop now you beat up Jason. What's next, you going to stab me?" Spencer was completely stunned, but clearly being sarcastic. Though I knew Missy wouldn't take it that way.

"I'm not trying to hurt all the wrong people," she insisted, getting hysterical again. "Honest."

"You didn't know," I mumbled to her, giving Jason an once-over to check for any visible injuries. I didn't see any besides the bruises forming on his arms. "You could have said something," I pressed, a slight edge to my voice. I was happy to see him, but my heart was beating wildly with worry. "You can't just sneak up on people, not out here anyway."

"I did say something," he groaned, not looking up. "I guess no one heard me." He shook his head, rubbing his shoulder.

I took a breath, exhaled. "I *thought* you were dead..."

He finally peered up at me, his face half-masked by shadows. "It was a close call, but I'm okay. Really." He motioned to Brien as he lifted himself back up, taking the attention off him. "That the cop?"

"Yeah."

"Is *he* still alive?"

I sighed, glancing down at my bloody hands. "Barely. Missy shot him right above the vest."

"Great… this just keeps getting better and better, doesn't it?" His tone was mocking. "Remind me, Mouth, never to piss you off again."

Missy went to say something back—no doubt another apology—but Jacob took that moment to call out to us, running up to us, lantern grasped tightly in his hand. He was slightly out of breath.

"Sorry I got here as fast as I could. What happened? Who's hurt?" He saw all of us, his brow creasing. "Wait, if you're all here, who's that?" He shone the light at Brien.

"And why are we hel—"

The light hit his leg.

"Ah Mierda! No importa lo tengo…."

Jacob turned around immediately, directing the lantern back toward the truck. "I got the car hooked up, but I still got to tow it out. If it works, I can get him and Buck to the hospital before sunrise. Otherwise, I can have the chains unhooked in five minutes and I can take them now?"

"What's that mean?" Spencer pressed. "We would *all* be going to the hospital then?"

"No," I answered, staring at the headlights with uncertainty. "It means we can either stick to our plan, or he'll leave us here and come back for us."

Call me selfish, but I for sure didn't want to stay here any longer regardless if two lives were at stake.

"Yeah, that's not happening," Jason countered, as if reading my mind. "It's not safe to wait around here. We'll stick with the original plan, we just have to hurry and do our best to keep them alive. Let's go."

I hated that I was happy about that, but nevertheless I was. I just wanted to go home.

Jacob wasted no time hopping inside the truck—which wasn't actually on the road after all, but on the mountain side—and starting the engine. It *hummed* loudly and we stepped away from it, lowering Brien to the ground. I hunched with him, keeping my palm pressed hard against his tacky, wet shirt and my eyes forward. Within seconds, the large treaded tires started to spin, kicking up dirt. The chains rattled, *clinked*, stretched. Slowly, my car started to shimmy to the left, then to the right but it wasn't actually moving anywhere.

Jason started shouting for Jacob to give the truck more gas.

The chains pulled tighter, tighter, tighter...*too tight*. Now Jason was yelling for him to stop, back up and try again. This went on and on for what felt like *forever*. And the longer I sat there, the more I began to think we were doing the wrong thing, especially since Kyle kept bugging out, pleading with us to just go. Apparently Buck was doing *that* bad.

After the sixth failed attempt, Jason ran up to the driver's window and uttered something quick to Jacob, who was leaning his head out the window. It was still dark so I couldn't really see them clearly, but I saw their movements.

Almost instantly, he backed away, running past us. "Help me push her car," he barked to the guys. "Let's help Jacob out."

That seemed to work. The car finally started moving forward, the chains no longer to the point of snapping. As it slowly got pulled up the mountain, I noticed something dragging behind it.

My bumper. Or part of it anyway. *Great, how was I driving home like that?*

The tire was flatter than a deflated basketball, and I remembered we still had to change that too. I wasn't sure Brien and Kyle had enough time left for *that*.

"He's going to die, isn't he?" Missy said glancing down at me and him, biting her nails.

I didn't answer.

"I know. You don't have to say it." Sighing, she sank down beside us. "You think he came here to find us? To save us?"

I peered over at her. I hadn't really thought of that. "If he did, he succeeded."

She stared ahead, making a face. "I wonder how long he's been searching; how long it took them to find our location." She paused. "You think he fell or *they* did that to his leg?"

I didn't have to think about that one. "It was them. If he only had one bullet left in his gun, then he had to use it. I'm guessing he was fighting off a few at one time. He wasn't bitten though so they must have just been pulling at it the wrong way." I didn't want to dwell on how painful that must have been.

Missy said nothing for a few seconds. "Yeah, I hate to say this, but I kind of hope he dies soon if he's going to die. I don't want him to suffer. I don't want to know it's because of me he's suffering more." She dropped her hands to her lap. "I can live with what I done to the others, but he wasn't trying to kill me."

"Miss, it was an accident. You didn't mean to shoot him," I replied, making a mental note of how much his breath has already diminished. She might get her wish after all.

"But I still did, that doesn't change the fact." She took a breath, exhaled. "I'm regretting ever answering Spencer's call."

My eyes shifted once again toward the guys and my car. "You won't once we are back home and safe, trust me."

Jason started shouting to Jacob, this time to letting him know my car was successfully on the road again.

Missy stood up, brushing dirt off her jeans. "I hope you're right," she mumbled, sounding doubtful as Spencer jogged over to us.

I sighed, suddenly unsure and anxious. *I hope I was right too.*

"Your car doesn't look too pretty," Spencer said as way of greeting. He bent down to pick up Brien again.

"We don't need it to look pretty. We need it to run," I prompted, mirroring Spencer's movements so I wouldn't allay pressure. I motioned for Missy to take the lantern that was sitting on the ground. She did.

"And the bumper?" Spencer pressed, slightly winded as we started uphill. "What we doing about that?"

"We will have to tie it up or something, obviously." I was watching my steps, careful not to fall. *Why hadn't we just stayed on the road in the first place? Why did we walk back down the mountain too when Jacob jogged to his truck?*

"With what?" he laughed, his tone sarcastic. "You got a bunch of string in your car that I don't know about?"

"I uh—" I thought about it, grimacing. "No. I don—" Suddenly the lantern light flashed on us, highlighting my arm, as Missy turned around. "Actually yeah!" A smile instantly hit my face. *I had the bracelet!* My shirt sleeve was pushed up to my elbow, my forearm exposed and there, dangling from my wrist was the bracelet Jason made me. *Didn't he say there was five feet of cord in that thing, cord that could apparently hold my body weight*? Problem solved.

I explained how to Spencer and Missy as we stepped back onto the road.

Jason heard his name and looked up from helping Jacob release the chains. "What's up? It will just be a few more minutes."

"Oh nothing, I was just explaining these bracelets to Spencer."

"Oh. Okay." He shifted his focus back to his task, moving his hands quickly. "Once everything's unhooked here, I'll start changing the tire. It shouldn't be too long after that."

"Spencer," Missy said, fidgeting beside us. "Don't you know how to change a tire? Didn't you change your mom's that one time?"

He peered over at her. "Yeah? Your point?"

"My point is I think they should go and we should stay and change the tire ourselves."   Jacob and Jason both paused, chain in hand.

"Say what, *chica*?" Jacob muttered.

"I just think you guys should go and get them out of here. We don't *need* your help for the tire, so there's no point to make them suffer more, you know? If there's a chance, still any chance at all to save them, you should take it."

Jason looked over at Jacob. "I can stay with them, dude. I'll make sure they get off safely. You can come back for—"

I immediately started shaking my head. "No! Not happening, Jason. You aren't staying around here." My gut twisted. I hated having to say it because I didn't want to say goodbye to him, but I wanted him to be safe too. He had the twins to take care of after all. "We are sticking to the original plan, you said it yourself."

He looked dubious. "Yeah the original plan involved—"

"Involved someone changing the tire," I proclaimed. "And someone will still be changing the tire. It just won't be you."

"I still don't—"

Kyle started pleading again, begging them.

"Okay, fine," he said, not pleased at all. But I knew it was only because he was concerned about us. If Jason had his way, we'd have all been safe and sound already. "Go put Trooper Wesson in the front seat. Kyle, I'm going to need you to keep pressure on that wound until we are done."

"Alright, *wait,* what?" He sounded horrified, finally catching on.

"You want to save Buck or not?" Jacob urged. "You have to help us out here. You won't get sick. I promise."

Reluctantly Kyle agreed, walking over to us, replacing my palm with his. I stepped away shaking out my arms, cringing at the blood dripping off my hands. *I could really use a shower again.*

The exhaust hit my nose repeatedly as the truck idled and I took another side step away from the bulk of it. The cold breeze began to hit me again, now that I wasn't focused on something and goose bumps spread down my skin. I don't think it had to do with just the wind though.

A glance up at the sky proved not as much timed passed as I thought. Stars still shimmered across the onyx sky.

Missy grabbed her purse out of the truck and came up beside me, offering me tissues and water. "I saw this rolling around on the floor of Jacob's truck before, figure you can wash up with it."

"Thanks," I mumbled, pouring the lukewarm liquid over my hands. Red turned to pink to clear. I dried off with the tissues, which kind of sucked because a bunch of tiny, fuzzy pieces stuck to my hands then. But it was better than the blood. Anything was better than the blood.

With the little water I had left, I even wiped down my ankle from where Brien grabbed me. Then I just swiped my hands across my shorts to avoid the tissue fuzz balls.

It wasn't more than three minutes before the boys finished. Jacob wrapped up the last of the chains and tossed them back into the tool box mounted in the bed of the truck.

I began to wonder how often he was towing vehicles that he even had chains in the first place. But after driving in this town, and seeing how easily it was to drive *off* the roads in this town, and how bumpy the roads were, I finally understood why my car was an abnormality around here. People needed four-wheel drive in this neck of the woods, not some beat up, drives-like-hell-in-the-snow-and-rain car like mine. Don't get me wrong, I loved my car, but I loved it in the cozy little town I lived in, where the roads were straight and smooth. And I didn't have to worry about driving off mountains.

Jacob hopped off the bed of the truck, his feet hitting the pavement. "So you are sure you know what you're doing?" He urged, speaking directly to Spencer.

He was standing off to the side, rubbing his arms that were no doubt cramping up. "Yeah, I can handle it."

"Okay. Well, I guess this is good bye then."

Spencer dropped his hand. Holding it out, he walked over to Jacob. "I just want to say thanks, for everything."

Jacob clapped his hand into his then pulled Spencer into a hug. "Anytime. You became family, kid. Take care. Stay out of trouble."

Spencer patted his back. "Ditto."

And so, the farewells began. One after another.

Jacob hugged me tightly, kissing my cheek with his still slightly swollen lip. Kyle yelled goodbye from the truck. And Jason, he just stared at me.

I paused, my heart picking up in my chest and stared back at him, my mind racing all over the place.

I didn't want to go.

Yet I wanted to go.

Part of me wanted to go with him.

The other part wanted him to come with me.

Why did Jason have to be so great? Surely if he was a jerk, I'd be able to head home eagerly without even the slightest temptation of peering back in the rearview mirror.

But Jason wasn't a jerk. He was the nicest damn guy I ever met. *Hell with it, I wasn't just letting him go without my number at least.* If he wanted to find me, he could. I'd leave that up to him.

"One second," I said, jogging away from him. I ran up to Missy who was talking to Jacob.

"Excuse me," I mumbled, unzipping her purse without even asking. I dug through it until I felt a pen. I held it up to her, "Thanks," then hurried back to Jason, who hadn't moved at all.

"I've decided I'm not saying goodbye. I don't want to. I don't know what tomorrow will bring, but I think we've all been through too much to just forget about each other." I grabbed his hand, showing him the pen. "I'm going to give you my number. Call me sometime. And if you're ever looking for a nice, *safe* town to live in, stop by and visit. I'll show you around."

I made sure I made the writing as legible as possible without hurting him. And I made sure I wrote on the outside of his hand, not his palm, so it wouldn't sweat off.

"Dee…," he finally said, making me glance up from his hand. But it was kind of dark and I was afraid I didn't write it right, so I quickly peered back down to double check. "Dee," he repeated, his tone incredulous. Suddenly his other hand was lifting my chin back up so I was staring at him. "Look at me."

"I *am* looking."

His lips curved. Even in the dim lighting I saw that. "I want you to know I was never planning on saying good bye. I mean obviously if you weren't interested I would, but I wouldn't be happy about it. From that first moment I saw you, I've been kind of hooked. You know that. And when we kissed, I knew you felt the same. Only an idiot would say goodbye right now." His finger brushed softly across my lip. "I'm not stupid. I know a good thing when I find it."

And before I even had a chance to respond, he kissed me. No passionate hot kiss. No *this is the last kiss we will ever have kiss*. Or a peck that just said *we will always be friends*. This kiss was a sweet, tender, body-warming kiss that made promises, promises that spoke of unmade memories, happy tomorrows, and the start of something great. In the middle of a town full of dark, scary things that terrified me, haunted me, and chased me. This kiss was like the light at the end of the tunnel, giving me instant hope.

I was finally able to leave this town without looking back in the rear-view mirror in fear I was leaving something behind because I wasn't, we weren't saying goodbye.

We were just saying *we'll figure it out later*.

As he pulled his lips away, he pulled me into his chest, hugging me tightly for a brief moment then he let me go.

I quickly took that second to double check my phone number again, and he chuckled, kissing my head as I did.

When I looked up, I saw Jacob grab Missy and kiss her. My jaw dropped. I'm not really sure why, I kind of saw it coming, but still I could not wait to tease Missy about it.

I kind of expected her to slap him, but she never did.

I got another quick kiss from Jason. Then he was gone.

33

"Hurry up, damn it," Missy urged Spencer. She kept looking over her shoulder nervously, the lantern light shaking slightly in her trembling hand.

"I'm almost done, relax," Spencer said, tightening the last of two bolts. The spare tire was in place; we were almost ready to go.

But between tying up the bumper with the cord and changing the flat, it had to be forty minutes already. Way too long. That restored hope I had was already gone and now I was as anxious as Melissa. I think Spencer was too—though he wasn't saying it—because he kept fumbling with the tire iron. Of course that could just be because he was so extremely tired and his arms hurt from carrying Brien.

Each sound, loud or minuscule, made me jump. I was super aware of the fact we were still in danger, that any moment someone could come after us again. I had the keys already in the ignition just to be prepared for a quick getaway. *That is if we could even get inside the car...* I fidgeted at the thought. We didn't have any weapons. *Ugh... come on Spencer. Hurry up!*

Spencer stood up about three minutes later, holding the jack and tire iron. "'Kay that should about do it. Just got to put everything away now."

Missy blew out a breath, shifting her weight from her left foot to her right beside me. "Okay *good*, I want to get out of here. I am really starting to--" A *whirring-whopping* sound suddenly distracted her, distracted all of us, and we glanced up at the sky. "Freak out. Is that a helicopter?"

A red light flashed in the near distance and what appeared to be a bluish white spotlight.

"Looks like it," Spencer commented, his tone curious.

"You think it's looking for us?" Missy pressed, her voice changing. "Or Trooper Wesson?"

"Who knows," I replied, keeping my eyes drawn upward. "Maybe none of us."

The *whop...whop...whop* grew closer, louder.

It clearly wasn't slowing down.

"I bet it's going to the campsite," Spencer prompted. "I bet that's where most the troopers and paramedics are and why no one was out here looking for Brien."

I thought about that. They'd need a lot more than cops and paramedics there if that was the case. As soon as the helicopter passed overhead, the spotlight skimming over the treetops, I turned toward the car, slightly disappointed. "Alright let's just finish up here. Enough wasting time."

"Good idea," Spencer agreed. "And on the way home can we stop for food? Because I'm starving."

"Men always think about their stomachs no matter where they are, don't they?" Missy said rhetorically.

Spencer started walking toward the trunk. "They do when they haven't eaten in hours." I heard him drop the tire jack and iron into the car. "So what do you say, Dee, can we stop for food? Please."

I wasn't hungry by any means, but if we stopped at a rest stop I *could* pee and get that coffee I wanted.

I opened the driver's door. "Alright, fine. A half hour isn't really going to make a difference anyway."

"Well out here it could," Missy grumbled.

"Hence why we aren't staying any longer," I retaliated. "Come on, get in."

"Don't have to tell me twice," she said, gimping toward the passenger door. "I'm ready whenever you are."

I've been ready since the moment I drove off the mountain.

I sank down in the driver's seat, starting up the engine. Missy crawled in the passenger side, plopping her purse on her lap and shutting off the lantern.

Spencer jumped in last, slamming the door. "Well, didn't think I'd say this so soon, but I'm finally heading home."

As I started up the engine and drove out into the middle of the road, all I could think was *finally.*

Finally *we* were heading home.

We stopped about ninety minutes into the drive, pulling into an older rest stop area. The parking lot was partially occupied, but those occupants were sleeping off hours of driving in big rigs that were taking up a big chunk of the parking spaces.

Inside the building, it smelled of fried foods, floor cleaner, and coffee. I immediately headed to the ladies' room. I wanted to wash up even more, just in case I still had blood on me. The last thing I needed was someone to spot me with blood on my clothes. I could only imagine what type of questions that would provoke.

Afterwards, I rushed to the coffee counter, only to remember I still had no money the moment I stood in line. *Son of—*

To my relief, my best friend spotted me again. She really was wonderful, right? I ordered my drink, then the two of us sat down in orange plastic chairs to the right, waiting on Spencer.

He came up to us carrying a tray with some really greasy-looking breakfast sandwich, a hash brown, a plate of rubbery pancakes, a blueberry muffin and large orange juice. Humored, I stared at the plate. *Teenage boys and their bottomless stomachs.*

He took a few large bites of food, and then started talking through his mouthful. "So what do you guys think my parents are gonna do? Should I like try to call them first? Or at least ring the doorbell?"

"Uh, yeah," Missy said, incredulous. She was drinking an ice tea and placed the bottle down on the Formica table. "You can't just walk into your house! Your parents would think you're a robber or something."

He chewed his food obnoxiously. "Yeah, you're probably right. Guess I will ring the doorbell." He took a bite out of the hash brown hungrily. "My mom is definitely going to cry. Not so sure what Dad will do, probably still kick my ass."

"They are just going to be happy," I mumbled, considering him as he sat there eating. I waited a bit. "So Spencer, what's your plan now that you're coming back? What are you doing about your education?"

He gulped down his mouthful. "Not sure. Guess that depends on what the school says, if I still have to do some community service or go to jail. Otherwise there's always getting my GED." he took another swig of the juice. "Knowing mom, she will lock me in my bedroom, making me homeschooled because she's afraid I'll run off again."

"Are you?" Missy countered, narrowing her eyes at him. "Leaving again, that is?"

Even I looked at him, skeptical.

"No, guys," he answered, picking up his fork and stabbing a pancake. His blue eyes peered over at us. "I promise."

"Good, because if you were—"

Suddenly a girl at the coffee counter turned up the radio station, hushing one of her co-workers. "Damn it! Will you just shut up a sec?! I'm trying to hear this." Shocked, Missy stopped talking and we all turned in our seats.

Static flickered in and out. The girl with the auburn curls kept playing with the antenna until the station came in clearer on the dated device.

"…all roads in and out of town are being shut down to public. Officials say residents are not permitted to leave their homes until further investigation occurs. Death toll at Pine Star campsite keeps rising, but names of victims have not been released. It has been verified though that among the deceased and injured are the state troopers that first responded to the 911 call. An inside source states the call was from a panicked young male claiming there had been a contagious outbreak. That bacterium in the water was making people ill and mutating them, causing people to turn on each other.

Authorities have instructed residents of the town and surrounding areas not to panic. They are testing the water now and confining people for their safety, but are asking residents to prepare for emergency evacuation just in case it is necessary."

"Holy shit," Missy mumbled beneath her breath. "That was Jacob's call."

Spencer had the fork paused in front of his open mouth, shocked.

"You know," I whispered, indiscreetly pushing back my chair to stand up. "I think it's time we get out of here." I suddenly felt like every eye was on us, though when I looked around the place was pretty much empty. The girls behind the coffee counter were still listening to the radio, ignoring us.

Spencer shoved like four more forkfuls of pancakes in his mouth, grabbed the rest of his orange juice and his muffin, and stood up. He followed a couple steps behind us, still chewing.

As we were walking out the glass doors a couple walked in talking about what was just on the radio. My stomach knotted up just hearing about it again. Sure, the three of us got away it seems just in time, but if all roads were being shut down to public that means Jason and Jacob couldn't get back to Meg and Germaine's. Which meant Frankie and Brandon were stuck in their house and were going to be kept from Jason for who knows how long. Jason was going to be freaking out and I prayed he wouldn't do anything rash to try and get to them.

Deep down, I knew it was our fault—had he never helped us they wouldn't be stuck there—and guilt ate at me. Plus, honestly, I feared what the government was going to do to the twins. What type of tests they'd run on them, procedures, and so forth before verifying they were not ill?

At this point there wasn't much I could do to help them, besides go home and wait it out. And pray Buck stayed alive long enough for them to find a cure.

This time on the way home, none of us talked. We just listened to the radio station broadcast new updates every fifteen minutes.

***

The days that followed were a hard adjustment for me. Just as I expected it would, jumping back into my normal routine proved challenging. For starters I couldn't fall asleep without the light switch left on otherwise I was jumping at every pipe creaking in the walls or every sound outside my window. Then when I slept—if I slept—I dreamed of awful memories, images of all the people I saw dead or dying, waking too often crying or my heart racing.

It was all over the news, so there was no escaping it either. Authorities had confirmed it was not contaminated water, but had yet to say it was mosquitos, making me wonder if Jason and Jacob ever got the chance to tell anyone. Maybe they were locked up somewhere in the hospital, quarantined, unable to get out.

Possible, since I still haven't heard from him.

The names of the victims were starting to be released. I watched every day for Buck and Trooper Wesson's name, but so far I haven't seen it. Or anyone's name I know for that matter.

My mom asked me constantly when I was home if I was *all right*, and though I told her I was, I knew I wasn't.

I was exhausted, jumpy, anxious, and worried. I could tell Missy was the same, but we tried not to really talk about it. It's not something we really wanted to remember. We didn't know how Spencer was doing or what he was up to because since we dropped him off at home we hadn't heard from him either. That was understandable though. He had a lot of catching up to do with his family and his own crap to settle. I wasn't worried about that.

And though I knew I had to be there, sitting in school seemed completely ridiculous. I couldn't concentrate on anything but the one thing I *wanted* to stop thinking about. My history teacher called on me—*twice*—and embarrassingly I had no idea what she said. There was a pop quiz on Wednesday in my science class and I completely missed answering five questions. *Five! How does one even do that?* And to top it off, in gym class I zoned out on the tennis courts and got a nice attention-getting ball welt on my forehead.

In the hallway, students buzzed past me, no more interesting than a swarm of flies and just as obnoxious. In fact, the first time someone bumped into me on Monday, I almost beat the living crap out of him on reflex. That's when I realized right away school definitely wasn't the right place for someone suffering with a mild case of post-traumatic stress disorder.

It only got worse from there.

Luckily by the weekend, things slowly started to get better though.

At least we saw Spencer again.

And at least, surprisingly, I wasn't grounded anymore.

34

Two weeks passed in a blur, but were not as bad as that first week. I was slowly coming to accept everything I'd been through, and I was trying to move on. Though I still zoned out here and there in class, I wasn't completely screwing up on tests anymore. I became obsessed with studying actually. Perhaps that's why I was feeling a little better, because I wasn't really giving my mind a chance to wander off. I was forcing it to absorb something else.

Spencer decided to just get his GED. The school said they'd take him back, but he would obviously have to repeat a grade and he didn't want to do that. He said he didn't care either way because he just wanted to be a carpenter when he graduated, like his father. And thanks to his dad speaking with the police station and the fact that he was a juvenile, Spencer wasn't getting arrested, but he was getting a lot of community service. I mean *a lot*. I had a feeling his dad had something to do with that, like that was his father's way of punishing him for everything. Sucks for Spencer, but hey, he kind of deserved it.

By the start of the third week, it was all progressing. The news was finally reporting that it was mosquitos and appropriate actions were being taken to eliminate the issue. Residents of the town had already been evacuated from their homes and placed in a shelter, where they were all being tested for the virus. Medications and vaccines were proving most successful in curing those infected. No further deaths have been reported.

A list of symptoms flashed across the screen constantly as a reminder for anyone that might have been around the area recently with instructions to please report to a hospital immediately if experiencing such symptoms. Again, listeners were told not to panic if you lived outside the county. For they were claiming these infected mosquitos were localized only to a ten-mile radius, and that the original hosts were believed to be an ill coyote pack recently found dead on the outskirts of town.

I was thankful things were progressing well, but there was still no news from Jason.

The next month and a half flew by just as fast. I was getting close to graduating high school, at last. Not only did I have my normal homework, but now Missy and I had final exams to start preparing for and senior projects to complete too. Oddly, I was grateful for them, which probably made me the only senior in the entire school who was. I concluded I was definitely whacked in the head. The weather was beautiful, the sun was shining, but Missy and I continued to sprawl out across my bedroom floor working on essays. Not that she wasn't begging me constantly to take a break and do something *fun*. A part of me *did* want to, but I was afraid to stop. I was afraid if I stopped, all the horrifying things would come back to me.

After four straight days of studying in my room, Missy finally snapped. "Okay. That's it. No more. No more reading. No more writing. I can't take it anymore. My brain hurts."

I sighed, dropping my pen onto my notebook. "Fine. What do you want to do?"

"I don't care. *Anything* but this."

I glanced at the clock. We were already studying for three hours. "Okay, you hungry?"

She sat up, brushing her blonde hair back behind her shoulders. "I could go for some French fries."

Me too. "Alright, how about we head to the diner for a bit then?" I lifted myself to my feet. "We can swing by Spencer's house on the way."

"That sounds awesome," she replied, following me out of my bedroom eagerly, relief in her voice. "And, Dee?"

"Yeah?"

"Don't forget your purse this time."

I found out that night that I missed *hanging out* and I was actually laughing a lot. It was even more therapeutic than excessive studying. So I started slowing down with the work and started spending more time with them, quickly beginning to feel like a normal teenager again. At night, I was even sleeping, a massive improvement even if I still needed to sleep with the light on. And even though I already knew this, I realized just how grateful I was to have Missy and Spencer in my life. *So very, very grateful.* The more we hung out, the less we watched the news. Pretty much once they reported residents were being allowed back into their homes, that the mosquitos were taken care of, we stopped watching. I had all but given up on Jason.

I was sitting in eighth period study hall thirteen days later, when my cell phone started ringing. I was so startled I quickly grabbed it, hitting "ignore call" without looking at the number. I apologized profusely to my teacher, but she just gave me a warning and that "*look.*" Making a face, I shoved my phone back into my book bag and went back to reading.

It wasn't until the bell rang and I was sitting down in my next class that I got a chance to see who called. I didn't recognize the number. Immediately I thought of Jason, but if it was Jason, wouldn't he have left a message?

There were no voicemails.

Disappointed, I put the phone away again and took out my math book.

On the way to senior parking, my phone was ringing again, this time a different number. I answered it hesitantly. I wasn't in the mood for telemarketers.

"Hello…?"

"Bad time?" a male's voice said, and instantly my heart started racing.

"Jason?" I gasped, stopping mid-step. "Ohmigod, hi! How are you?"

"Good. Sorry it's taken me so long to get in touch with you, but I've been kind of detained."

"No, no, don't worry about it." I felt a weight start to lift off my shoulders and a smile spread across my face. "And the twins? Are they okay?"

"Yeah, they are fine. They are chilling in the truck with Duke."

"Oh. Where are you?"

"On our way to Jersey."

"What?" My voice squeaked. "You are? Really? Where?"

"I don't know," he chuckled, no doubt from the sudden excitement in my voice. "That's why I'm calling."

"Huh?" My brow creased.

"Well I vaguely remember you telling me if I ever wanted a nice *safe* town to live in, to come visit you and you'd show me around, except you never told me where you lived. So I kind of have no clue where I'm headed."

The smile spread wider. "You are coming to see me?"

"That depends," he said. "Did you still want me too?"

"That was a dumb question. Of course I do." I saw Missy walking across the grass field and I waved enthusiastically to her, motioning for her to hurry up. "But Jason, what then? Where do you plan to stay in the meantime?"

"The first available pet friendly motel I can find. That is until I decide what my next plan of action is. Right now however, I really just want to see you."

The way he said it made my heart speed up even more. I suddenly felt super giddy. I sputtered my address to him quickly, instructing him to call me right away if he got lost. Then I hung up and jogged the rest of the way to Missy, the largest, most pathetic smile on my face.

I couldn't believe it. I couldn't believe in three hours I was seeing Jason again.

35

I was sitting on the front porch, my leg tucked under me, my attention turned toward Jason, listening.

It was so great to see him, and not just because I had a thing for him. I was just so happy to see him and the twins alive, well and smiling. I had forgotten how great his smile was and how green his hazel eyes could be. But sitting here now, staring at him, I was drawn to both all over again.

"…Then we were held in this quarantined room for like four weeks. I don't know what we were thinking, expecting we could just walk out of the hospital after we dropped them off. I mean for starters we were carrying a state trooper who was shot and had a leg snapped in half. I'm surprised they didn't just arrest us on the spot."

"Were you arrested?" Missy asked. She was sitting to the right of me on the top step.

"No. When more troopers started coming in injured they realized it wasn't us. That's when the mayhem really started and they took Buck's condition seriously and confined us immediately."

"And all this time you couldn't get in touch with the twins?" I asked, feeling sympathetic. What it must have been like for him, Jacob and Kyle stuck in a tiny hospital room unable to get released, but desperately wanting to.

"No," he said, briefly looking over at them as they played catch on the front lawn with Duke and Spencer. They were laughing and having a good time. "But once I found out the entire town was pretty much on lockdown; I wasn't too worried. I knew as long as they stayed with Meg and Germaine they'd be okay. I just worried about them worrying about me."

"What about testing?" I asked. "I've been so worried about what types of things the twins and you would have to endure. I was having all these horrible thoughts of government testing and probing?"

He started chuckling, turning his eyes back to me. "They didn't do anything but a couple routine exams on us actually. They asked us if we were experiencing any of the symptoms, checked our eyes, did some memory tests, and took blood samples."

"Really?" Missy sounded incredulous. "That's all?"

"Yeah, well, they didn't really need to do a lot of testing on us because they had Buck. They just checked us for similar symptoms." He made a face. "Of course they always wore hazard suits and masks around us which sucked, made me start feeling like I was infected too."

"But Buck *is* still alive?" I pressed. "Right? That's what you said."

He nodded. "Yeah, he is finally out of ICU."

"And Trooper Wesson?" Missy asked hesitantly. "Did he make it? Or was he infected?"

"He was still in serious condition, last I checked." He glanced over at her. "Sorry don't know anything else, but doctors did confirm he was not carrying the virus."

A flash of relief coursed through me. Sure I have been feeling perfectly healthy, but it's still good to hear Trooper Wesson wasn't sick too. It was one less stress on my mind.

She shrugged, starting to pick at her purple nail polish. "You think they are going to be looking for who shot him?

"Right now," Jason replied softly, though no one else was home yet, "that's probably the last thing on their mind. They've gotta make sure all those medications and stuff keep working and he lives first."

"Medications?" She furrowed her brow. "For what? The virus?"

"No. So he doesn't lose his leg."

"Oh."

"Yeah," he mumbled, "it wasn't looking too good for him."

Spencer jogged over to us then, sweating, slight smile on his face, his hair pushed across his forehead. He had gotten it cut shorter recently, really bringing out his light blue eyes. "Man, it's hot out here."

He plopped down on the steps, wiping his brow on his sleeve. Though it was partly cloudy out today, it was eighty degrees and kind of humid.

"Yeah," Jason agreed, looking down at his watch. "Speaking of which, I should really get going and get Duke out of this heat. Plus I'm gonna have to find dinner for the twins."

I pouted slightly. "Are you coming back?" His green-brown eyes shifted to me. "I mean not today, but sometime?"

He smiled. "I'll call you tomorrow when you get out school."

Jason didn't have an actual cell phone plan, but sometime since we last saw him he did purchase a prepaid phone. It made me happy. At least he had a way to communicate with us. With me.

He stood up and called out to the twins, to let them know they were leaving. I was already looking forward to tomorrow.

As he turned his head back to us, Missy looked up at him. "Just curious. What's Jacob doing once he gets back from visiting his mom in Spain?" I couldn't miss the hint of something *more* in her voice. Like maybe she actually missed him. I never did tease her yet about that kiss.

Jason smirked, as if he picked up on that too, and leaned back against the porch railing, crossing his arms. "He said he'd give me a ring and let me know. I guess that all depends on what he's coming home to. He did tell me to tell you, if I saw you, that if you ever decided to admit you want him, to give him a buzz."

"Ohmigod," she blurted, her cheeks flushing red. "That conceited, self-centered, annoying—"

"Relax, Mouth," Jason laughed, dropping his hands and pushing off the railing. "I was only messing with you. Jacob didn't say that. Last I checked his house phone wasn't even working." He shot a glance at Spencer to verify that.

"Yeah, that broke a while ago," Spencer said, chuckling. "Why are you getting so worked up, Miss? Because you *do* want him?" His voice was teasing.

Since he was right next to her, she punched him in the shoulder. "Shut up, you ass."

He laughed louder. In fact, I did too. And as Jason and the twins left with Duke, Spencer and I continued to bust her chops about that kiss.

Hey, that's what friends do.

36

We were all in the backyard, chilling out under the umbrella of the patio furniture. It had been a couple weeks since Jason and the twins first came to visit. They were still here, still renting a room in the motel about fifteen minutes from my home. He hadn't decided what he was doing yet in terms of finding a permanent location, but he was looking for a job somewhere close by. Right now, he was just using some of the money he had from his parents' death and keeping it simple. The twins didn't care where they lived. They said they liked it here, and the motel had a television so they were still able to play video games. For them, that's all that mattered.

The twins were sitting on lounge chairs to the left of us, playing their hand held devices. This time the game was about some alien invasion. They were oblivious to any of us.

Duke was lying next to Jason's feet, sprayed down with the hose for the second time this afternoon. He whimpered on and off, panting against the cement. It was so humid out.

Jason's hand kept brushing up against mine, his fingers lightly touching my skin every so often as if letting me know he was still next to me, still thinking of me, even if the conversation wasn't directed at me.

Spencer was telling us about his community service that morning, being all animated, though he looked pretty tired. It seems waking up early every morning and working out in the sun half the day was wearing him out.

I listened, half-heartedly, my mind drifting, thinking of graduation in one week and what was going to happen after, when the sound of the back door opening and my mom's voice had me turning my head.

"Dee?" she said, a weary look on her face. She was holding the cordless phone in her hand.

"What's up, Mom?" I asked, instantly worrying. *Did something happen to Dad?*

"There is a State Trooper Brien Wesson on the phone for you?"

At the sound of his name, I jolted and everyone instantly shut up. I could hear the question and concern in my mother's voice and understood it now. Like why was a cop calling me? How did he have this number—which by the way I was wondering—and what did I do?

I jumped up out of my seat, walking to her nervously, thinking about how Melissa shot him in the chest and that he was able to tell my mom where I was that weekend. If she found out, oh God, I could only imagine how fast she would start spazing. Not just because I lied to her, but because I was *there*, in the town with the *sickness*.

As I reached out to take the phone, she cuffed her hand over it and whispered sternly, "Care to tell me what all this is about?"

Not really. "Later?" I mumbled. She shook her head, clearly upset with me, handed me the phone and walked away.

I gulped down the knot in my throat, brought the phone to my ear and turned around to face the others. "Hello?" Staring at them somehow made me more confident.

"Dee? Hi. This is Trooper Brien Wesson. I know this might be a little unorthodox, but I just wanted to say thank you to you and your friends for saving my life."

Woah. Not what I was expecting. I exhaled, relieved. "Oh, you didn't need to thank us." *Maybe he forgot we shot him? Could we be that lucky?* "You're doing better, I trust." *Didn't Jason say two weeks ago he was still in serious condition? Amazing what doctors can do.*

"Well, I'm still hospitalized," he said. "I'm going to be here for a long time, I think." I didn't miss the frustration in his voice. "But each day is an improvement."

I didn't dare ask him if he got to keep his leg. That was probably a really touchy subject. "I'm happy to hear that, but sorry you're going to be stuck there."

"Eh, it's okay. I'll bounce back."

A moment of awkward silence passed. I didn't really know what else to say to him, besides asking him the questions racing through my mind. Without meaning too, I blurted, "How did you get this number, by the way?"

He chuckled then, creating a little static. "I'm a trooper. It's really not difficult. All I needed was your license plate number, which I had written down when I spotted your car."

"Oh." I suddenly got really nervous. "Um, should I be expecting any more police to come knocking on my door or something?"

He chuckled again. "Don't worry, the only thing you should expect to be doing is dealing with your insurance company about the condition of your car. You don't have to worry about any cops."

"But what—" I quickly bit my tongue, realizing I was about to say something about shooting him.

"Anyway, I won't hold you up. I just wanted to personally thank you. My Chief was going to call you, but I wanted to be the one to say it."

"Again, you didn't need to thank me. I am just happy I was able to help you."

"Honestly," he said, his voice changing. "I'm truly surprised you did with everything happening out there. I can't say I would have done the same." He sounded angry about that.

"You're a cop," I mumbled. "I bet you would have."

I heard him exhale into the phone. "Maybe. Well Dee, stay out of trouble and take care of yourself."

"Okay."

"Oh and Dee, could you do me a favor and extend a message to your friend, the girl with the blonde hair?"

My heart immediately skipped. "Uh?" I glanced at Melissa across the table. "She's actually right here, if you'd like to speak to her."

Missy's eyes widened. *I don't know why I told him that.* When he said he wanted to, I motioned for her to take the phone. She got up slowly and dragged her feet toward me, her eyes questioning me. I shrugged and handed the cordless to her. I had no clue what he was going to say. I didn't get a vibe he was going to arrest me. Of course, *I* didn't shoot him.

Leaning around my chair, I grabbed my glass of lemonade off the tabletop, then spun back around, keeping my eyes focused on my best friend.

She spoke into the phone quietly, looking down at the ground, fussing with a strand of her hair anxiously.

I couldn't hear what Trooper Wesson was saying, which drove me crazy, but I tried catching on by listening to her.

It was useless. She was talking too softly.

Jason bent forward in his chair, inching up to me, asking me what Brien said to me and if I was all right. I gave a quick, whispered response. Missy was already hanging up. *That was fast.*

"So? What happened?" I said, stepping away from the back of my chair. I was stirring my lemonade with my straw. "What did he say?"

She peered up at me, looking humiliated. A crease etched between her eyebrows. "Pretty much he just said if I have some free time I should really consider taking shooting lessons." Her face flushed.

My hand paused on the straw. "That's all? Seriously?"

Her blue eyes bugged. "Ohmigod are you kidding me? That was the most embarrassing thing I ever experienced."

"Yeah, so you aren't getting arrested, right? That's the most *important* thing."

She lowered her arm to her side, still holding the phone. "He told me not to worry, said everything will be fine. He's taking care of it, whatever that means."

Duke started whimpering again and Jason reached down, patting his side gently. "I'm assuming that means everything will be fine," Jason mocked, face tilted up to Missy, his hazel eyes blazing green against his sage-toned shirt. "That's just my suggestion." His smirk showed he was purposely being sarcastic.

She rolled her eyes, ignoring him. "So you think your mom is going to bombard you with a million questions tonight now?"

I groaned, already dreading it. "She's still hammering me about what *really* happened to my car. She knows I'm lying, but since I won't tell her, she's making me pay for all the damages. Once we graduate, I have to get a job. And now that she knows cops are calling me, I'm screwed. I might as well kiss my summer goodbye. I'm never going to be able to tell her the truth."

See everything can't always be fine.

"It was nice seeing you while I could, Jason," I mumbled, pouting.

"I have to get a job to remember," he replied, bemused. "We'll figure something out. I'm not going anywhere."

I stared down at the melting ice cubes in my drink. "What if I am grounded for life though?"

He just laughed, continuing to pat Duke and shushing him. "Then I'll be waiting for a long time."

I shook my head, but my lips twitched. *I liked that answer.*

"Uh, guys," Spencer said then, and I instantly remembered he was trying to tell us something before Trooper Wesson called, something about his community service.

"I know," I exhaled, stirring the lemonade again, feeling the condensation on my palm. "Sorry, you were saying?" I gave Missy a look, like humor him, and spun around, trying *not* to think about later. I didn't want to bring myself down yet.

"No," he said, the sound of his voice immediately snagging my full attention. "That's not what—" My eyes shot across the table top to him. "Oh *fuck.*"

I froze, the glass of lemonade sliding from my hand, shattering around my feet.

Duke started whimpering louder.

I didn't look down.

I just stared forward.

Not moving.

Not even breathing.

Spencer stared back at me, *at us*, his blue eyes terrified. His hand was cupped in front of his face. Blood was gushing from his nose.

And in that very second, I became achingly aware of everything. It all made sense now. Duke wasn't crying because he was hot. Spencer wasn't looking tired because he was working too hard. Spencer was *sick*.

He had the virus. After all this time.

That meant eliminating the mosquitoes in Pennsylvania hadn't solved the problem.

We were wrong. The police were wrong. Everyone was wrong.

Suddenly, I didn't care about being grounded. Turning, I sprinted toward the back door, screaming, "Mom!"

About the Author

Having developed a love for reading, writing, and drawing at a very young age, Natalie has often been described as being "creative and artistic." Spending most of her free time caught up in the make-believe world, whether it was something she read or something she wrote, because she enjoyed the adventure and mostly the happily-ever-after endings. To this day, she still loves the happily-ever after endings.

When she isn't curled up on a couch reading, writing a poem, short-story or these days a new young adult novel, or getting her hands covered with paint and oil pastels, she can be found running, taking pictures of nature, watching her favorite movies like Grumpy Old Men, Turner and Hooch and Sweet Home Alabama, or simply just spending quality time with her husband and their five dogs.

Though currently residing in New Jersey, Natalie makes frequent trips back to her hometown in Pennsylvania.

www.ingramcontent.com/pod-product-compliance
Lightning Source LLC
Chambersburg PA
CBHW051005180726
48291CB00006B/1982